PRAISE FOR KELLY HARMS

The Good Luck Girls of Shipwreck Lane

"A perfect recipe of clever, quirky, poignant, and fun makes this a delightful debut."

—*Kirkus Reviews*

"Set in small-town Maine, this first novel is a story of rebuilding, recovery, and renewal. Harms has created two incredibly likable heroines, allowing the strengths of one woman to bolster the weaknesses of the other. While the central conflict of the story appears to be resolved fairly early, a succession of plot twists keeps the reader intrigued and invested. In the manner of Mary Kay Andrews and Jennifer Weiner, Harms's novel is emotionally tender, touching, and witty. Great for book clubs."

—*Booklist*

"Spunky leading ladies that you can take to the beach."

—*Fitness* magazine

"The story is funny and heartbreaking throughout."

—Melissa Amster, Chick Lit Central

"Another perfect summer diversion is *The Good Luck Girls of Shipwreck Lane*. Kelly Harms writes with love about a trio of women desperate for a change and smart enough to recognize it may not be exactly what they planned. Delicious."

—Angela Matano, *Campus Circle*

T0026829

"The friction between the Janines, along with a few romantic foibles and a lot of delicious meals, results in a sweetly funny and unpredictable story that's ultimately about making a home where you find it."

—Madison, *Cap Times*

"Kelly Harms's debut is a delicious concoction of reality and fairy tale—the ideal summer book! You'll feel lucky for having read it. And after meeting her, I guarantee you will want a great-aunt Midge of your very own."

—*New York Times* bestselling author Sarah Addison Allen

"Warmhearted and funny, *The Good Luck Girls of Shipwreck Lane* pulls you in with quirky yet relatable characters, intriguing relationships, and the promise of second chances. Harms's debut is as refreshingly delightful as a bowl of her character Janey's chilled pea soup with mint on a hot summer day."

—Meg Donohue, bestselling author of *How to Eat a Cupcake: A Novel*

"Funny, original, and delightfully quirky, Kelly Harms's *The Good Luck Girls of Shipwreck Lane* shows us that sometimes, all we need to make it through one of life's rough patches is a change of scenery and a home-cooked meal."

—Molly Shapiro, author of *Point, Click, Love: A Novel*

"The characters are so well drawn that they practically leap from the page, charming dysfunction and all! A poignant, hilarious debut that's filled with heart, soul, insight, and laugh-out-loud moments. It'll make you rethink the meaning of what makes a family—and if you're anything like me, it'll make you want to pick up and move to 1516 Shipwreck Lane immediately! I'm such a fan of this utterly charming novel."

—Kristin Harmel, author of *Italian for Beginners* and *The Sweetness of Forgetting*

"Clever and memorable and original."
—Samantha Wilde, author of *I'll Have What She's Having*

"Janey and Nean each have a common name and uncommon hard luck, and when they suddenly have in common a sweepstakes house, their lives begin to change in ways neither of them could have imagined. Their quirky wit will win you over, even as they fumble through their crazy new life. *The Good Luck Girls of Shipwreck Lane* is alive with warmth and wit; I enjoyed it right through to the satisfying end."
—Kristina Riggle, author of *Real Life & Liars*, *The Life You've Imagined*, *Things We Didn't Say*, and *Keepsake*

"Kelly Harms's *The Good Luck Girls of Shipwreck Lane* is a delightful book bursting with good humor, fast action, and delicious food. Aunt Midge is a pure joy, and I loved Wimmer's surprising, spirited, and generous slant on what it takes to make a family."
—Nancy Thayer, *New York Times* bestselling author of *Summer Breeze*

The Matchmakers of Minnow Bay

"Kelly Harms writes with such tender insight about change, saying goodbye to her beloved yet troubled city life, and hurtling into the delicious unknown. Her characters sparkle; I loved Lily and wished I could have coffee with her in the enchanted town of Minnow Bay."
—Luanne Rice, *New York Times* bestselling author

"The temperature in Minnow Bay, Wisconsin, may be cold, but its people are anything but. Kelly Harms has created a world so real and so inviting that you absolutely will not want to leave. *The Matchmakers of Minnow Bay* proves that a little small-town meddling never hurt anyone and that, sometimes, it takes a village to fall in love. Kelly Harms has done it again!"

—Kristy Woodson Harvey, author of *Dear Carolina* and *Lies and Other Acts of Love*

"*The Matchmakers of Minnow Bay* is a glorious read, full of heart and humor. Lily is the kind of character you'll root for to the end, and the delightful residents of Minnow Bay will keep you chuckling with each turn of the page. Kelly Harms is a talented author with a knack for writing a story you'll want to read again and again."

—Darien Gee/Mia King

"In *The Matchmakers of Minnow Bay*, Kelly Harms weaves together a small town and big dreams into a delightful and heartfelt tapestry of friendship, love, and getting what you deserve in the way you least expect. I was hooked from page one, then laughed out loud and teared up while reading—exactly what I want from romantic women's fiction. Kelly Harms is the real deal."

—Amy Nathan

"In *The Matchmakers of Minnow Bay*, Lily Stewart is Shopaholic's Becky Bloomwood meets Capote's Holly Golightly. This charming tale is filled to the brim with eccentric characters, uproarious predicaments, and a charming (if not chilly!) setting. Kelly Harms has created the most lovable character in Lily, a starving artist with a penchant for disaster and a completely unbreakable spirit. One for the beach chair!"

—Kate Moretti, *New York Times* bestselling author of *The Vanishing Year*

"Filled with witty dialogue and an unforgettable cast of characters, *The Matchmakers of Minnow Bay* is a complete charmer. I rooted for Lily from the first page and didn't want to leave the magical town of Minnow Bay. Kelly Harms delivers another heartwarming novel that lifts the spirit."

—Anita Hughes

"*The Matchmakers of Minnow Bay* is the perfect feel-good read. An irresistible premise, a charming—though forgetful—heroine, an emotionally involving love story, lovely writing . . . it all adds up to cozy hours in a fictional place you'll wish you could visit. Don't miss this delightful novel!"

—Susan Wiggs

"Sometimes you read a book that hits all the right notes: funny, charismatic, romantic, and empowering. *The Matchmakers of Minnow Bay* is that book. Kelly Harms's enchanting writing lured me into the quiet yet complicated world of Minnow Bay, and I never wanted to leave. I loved it in every way!"

—Amy E. Reichert

"Delightful, and sure to captivate readers and gain new fans for author Kelly Harms. With sparkling dialogue and a winning heroine who finds her big-girl panties amid the disaster zone her life has become and heads in a new direction, finding love along the way, it had me turning the pages into the night."

—Eileen Goudge

"I loved this book! Fresh and devastatingly funny, *The Matchmakers of Minnow Bay* is romantic comedy at its very best. The talented Kelly Harms is one to watch."

—Colleen Oakley, author of *Before I Go*

"*The Matchmakers of Minnow Bay* thoroughly entertains as it explores friendship, flings, and finally finding yourself. Harms tells the story in a funny, fresh voice ideal for this charming coming-into-her-age novel."

—Christie Ridgway, *USA Today* bestselling author of the Beach House No. 9 and Cabin Fever series

The
Overdue
LIFE OF
AMY BYLER

OTHER BOOKS BY KELLY HARMS

The
Overdue
LIFE OF
AMY BYLER

KELLY HARMS

LAKE UNION
PUBLISHING

Text copyright © 2019 by Kelly Harms
All rights reserved.

No part of this book may be reproduced, or stored in a retrieval system, or transmitted in any form or by any means, electronic, mechanical, photocopying, recording, or otherwise, without express written permission of the publisher.

Published by Lake Union Publishing, Seattle
www.apub.com

Amazon, the Amazon logo, and Lake Union Publishing are trademarks of Amazon.com, Inc., or its affiliates.

ISBN-13: 9781542042963 (hardcover)
ISBN-10: 1542042968 (hardcover)

ISBN-13: 9781542040570 (paperback)
ISBN-10: 1542040574 (paperback)

Cover design by David Drummond

Printed in the United States of America

First edition

This one goes out to single mothers everywhere.

Dear Mom,

So here's the thing. And I know you're going to make some weird big deal out of it because you're a mom and a nerd and you can't help yourself. You're going to, like, make it into a Facebook meme and then needlepoint it onto a pillow because you're crazy. But whatever, here it is: you were right.

Not right about reading. Mom, reading is . . . something I do because I love you and because I want to get into college. The books you gave me were 90 percent less boring than the books I've read for school. But they were still boring. Did you know half of these books you picked have been made into movies? The reason is because movies are better and people who are reading books are always thinking, "God, this would be so much better if it were just not a book."

Ok. Anyway. You were right about Dad.

I didn't want you to be so right. I wanted you to be happy, for sure. But not right about this one thing. I wanted things to be so much more black and white, because honestly, it's just easier to make sense of things that way. What happened to our family was much easier to understand when it was all because Dad was a terrible person. But he's not a terrible person, now that I've gotten to know him. He's just really, really complicated. Even after all this time, after the last three months, if you asked me how our family got to this point, I wouldn't even know where to begin. I'd be all like, "Uh . . . you tell me?"

And the thing about being in this hospital, Mom, is that I do know EXACTLY how I got here. I know the stupid decisions that I made, one by one, until I was in this beeping room with all this stuff stuck into my arms and up my nose. And I would not do things the same again if I had it to do over.

That's regret, right? That's what you were hoping to spare me and Joe when Dad first showed up this spring and you asked us to give him a chance. Regret. But here I am, drowning in regret, and maybe I'm not ever going to get a chance to make it right. So guess what. I know how Dad feels now. And I don't want anyone else to have to feel this way.

So whatever you decide about him, Mom, then, ok. It's your decision. I won't be a brat about it. I want what I want. Joe wants his own thing. But for once in your nerd mom life, what we want most of all is for you to make a choice that will make you happy.

And if this is that, well then. I guess. Go for it.

Love,

Your favorite daughter (Cori)

CHAPTER ONE

Three months earlier

There are a lot of people you don't expect to run into in small-town Pennsylvania. And a few you do. I run into my best friend, Lena, almost every day—she teaches in the same school that I do, so when we don't go out of our way to see each other, we're seeing each other anyway, in the halls, the teachers' lounge, the parking lot, scraping frost off our cars as late as April.

And my daughter's best friend, Trinity. God, a day without Trinity would be a thing to behold. Trinity at school, Trinity at my house, Trinity's car parked outside my daughter's swimming lesson waiting for her to be done so they can go wander around downtown and look at boys.

And my dental hygienist. I see her every Saturday at the farmers' market, where she sells handmade soaps and candles with the other church ladies. If I don't swing by their booth and say hello, she writes me a little note and puts it in the mail, and since she's extremely cheap, I know exactly how much trouble that gives her. *Dear Amy*, it will read. *I'm worried about you. Please let me know you and the kids are ok. In God's Love, Miriam.*

Then there are the people you don't expect to see. Jamie from *Outlander*. Despite looking, and hard, I see him exactly never. Not at the market, not at school, not at my son's Odyssey of the Mind competitions.

Or Oprah. I would love to run into Oprah. I think she'd be fun to talk books with.

Or my husband.

Except there he is. My husband of eighteen years. Last seen three years ago, when my daughter was twelve and my son eight, and he packed up one roll-aboard carry-on-size suitcase with shirts I'd ironed and ties I'd picked out and a change of suits and some running clothes and his shaving kit and his six different kinds of antianxiety medication and went on a business trip to Hong Kong. And never came back.

He's back.

That's definitely him, standing over there by the Band-Aids at our local drugstore. He is looking at me. He is forcing a smile. I know in an instant, in a painful, *I have dreaded this moment for years* instant, why he is here.

It was only a matter of time.

He wants his life back.

———

Like any self-actualized, successful, capable adult woman would do in this situation, I duck behind the Q-tips.

It's a pointless move. John is standing maybe ten feet away from me, and he definitely saw me. He just gave me a sheepish smile I would know anywhere. It comes with a little shoulder shrug. It is the "Sorry I forgot to pick up milk on the way home but here I am exhausted after a long day and now it's too late to send me back out so can't the kids just have dry cereal tomorrow morning?" smile. My students have a similar version. The "Can I have an A for effort?" smile.

But the problem is John did not forget to pick up the milk on the way home. He forgot to come home, full stop. He forgot to come home, raise his kids, pay his bills, and be faithful to his wife for the last three years, and it really, really seems like there should be a different facial expression for that. I would prefer it if he were wearing the facial expression you'd make if your ex-wife were about to hit you about the head and shoulders with a blunt instrument, for example.

From my crouching position at the endcap of the first aid aisle, I look around for blunt instruments.

All I see are fluorescent-pink Hula-Hoops. It would be hard to beat a man senseless with a plastic Hula-Hoop covered in sparkles, and yet for a long and rather pleasant moment, I consider trying.

"Amy?" John asks. "Is that you?"

He knows it's me. I know it's him. I would know him anywhere. For almost a year after he left, I kept thinking I saw him in other cars when I was driving around town, and my heart would seize up, and then it would collapse in on itself when I got a second look, and I would feel immeasurably tired from each of these tiny false alarms. One time, only a few weeks after he left us, I thought I saw a John-shaped man in the back of a car with a ride-sharing label on it turning onto our street, and I got this absolutely certain feeling, the feeling of just *knowing*, and my blood began to race through my veins, and I felt like, I don't know, like I had been trapped in a canyon without food or water, and now someone was coming with a rope ladder to save me. I pulled over and waited for the car to pull into our driveway. But it didn't. It passed right by while I sat there staring at it in my rearview, watching it drive past without slowing. I took it so hard I couldn't see to drive for twenty minutes.

This is not that. This is not a drill. He is back, and I would rather die of thirst than take any rope he has to offer me now.

"John," I say, pretending, pointlessly, to have only just seen him. I come around the corner into the aisle where he stands. There are ice packs and packages of gauze and tubes of Neosporin. Everything we would need to fix him up after I pulverized him with novelty children's toys and jumbo bottles of vitamin D.

"I can't believe you're here," he says, and I stare at him, dumbfounded. He can't believe I'm here? In the town where we lived together for almost two decades? Where our children said their first words and took their first steps and are currently waiting for me to get home with—I look in my basket, having completely forgotten what the hell I came here for—microwave popcorn, tampons, and Clearasil? "I mean, I was expecting to have to come to the house to talk to you, and I was worried how you'd take it, and how to catch you in private before seeing the kids, but this is better, right? Because I'm not invading your space?"

I continue to stare at him. I want to scream. I want to cry. I want to be the kind of person who can claw another person in the face with her fingernails. But I am not that kind of person, and we are in a drugstore, so I just stare.

"Amy?" he asks. "Amy, are you ok?"

"Go away," I hear myself tell him. "I don't know why you're here, but we don't need you. Go away. Now." I set down my basket, which has suddenly become painfully heavy, and make a little shooing motion, as if he is a bird who landed too close to me at the park.

"I'm sorry," he says. "I'm so sorry, but I'm not leaving."

It hits me in an instant: They sell walking canes here. I could do real damage with a walking cane, especially the ones with tripod feet at the bottom for added balance.

"Amy?" he asks again. Am I smiling? Maybe even grinning? Is this the day I finally well and truly crack up? I feel like I'm going to start to laugh, and I have no idea why. "Do you need to sit down?" John asks.

And then he does something so unacceptable, so beyond the pale, that I almost, *almost* decide to hell with the onlookers, to hell with the gossips, I am going to have to just scream at the top of my lungs to make him stop.

He reaches out to take my arm.

I whip it away. "Oh no," I say, and all at once my wits come rushing back, and fantasies about physical assault and screaming and hiding all fall away, and at last, at long last, I am in the reality of this moment. I inhale. "I have no idea what you are doing here right now, John, but it has been three years since you showed your face, since you lived with me and my children and shared my bed and shared our table and shared our life every day, day in and day out. Three years. More than a thousand days. And you cannot come back here and shop in my drugstore and buy Band-Aids from my Band-Aid selection and try to take me by the arm like I'm some kind of invalid. Not after all those days and nights and mortgage payments and electricity bills and trips to the goddamned dentist. You cannot. You can not."

John looks shamed. His sheepish smile has been replaced by a pain as deep and wide as my own. I see at once that he, too, has been in a canyon. And he thinks that I am the one with the rope.

He shakes his head as he speaks, and what he says are all the things I dreamed of him saying to me years ago when he first left us and my whole world fell apart. Only now they sound like a high, painful ringing in my ears.

"You're right," he says. "I've done something terrible, and I'm so, so sorry. But I'm not here to hurt you again. I'm here to fix things."

"I don't know how you could ever do that," I tell him honestly.

"It's not your job to figure that out," he tells me, and the words are so disarming I am rendered speechless. "It's mine. And that's why I've come here. I want to be the man I should have been before, be a real father to our kids. I want to try to be the kind of father they deserve." He picks up my basket off the ground. "I want to make things right."

—

"He wants what now?"

My daughter, Corinne; my son, Joseph; and my best friend, Lena, are sitting in my—in our—house, a good-looking Foursquare within a short walk to the Country Day School where I work. Like most good-looking things, my house is high maintenance. My house makes it so I never, ever have any extra money. If my house starts to notice I've been squirreling away a hundred dollars here or there to try to get my kids to a national park for a week, the house breaks something. I think it has abandonment issues.

When John lived here, it was not a huge problem. He was terribly handy, happy to putter away in the house and fix what needed fixing and watch YouTube videos about how to do it all day long. When he broke down and called a contractor, his very solid paycheck as in-house counsel for a large food producer covered the bill.

The house was a project from the start, of course, a hundred years old when we moved in and not getting any younger. But oh, it was all fixable, one thing at a time. The wiring was brought up to code, the rot was pulled out of the walls, the basement was resealed, the wood siding was replaced in an architecturally dignified way. One thing at a time, no rush. Having grown up in Amish country without access to a Home Depot, John was incredibly competent at fixing just about anything with his own two hands.

Except, I guess, himself. To fix what was wrong in his life, he took a two-pronged approach: Step one, keep all his emotions a secret so that none of us knew anything was wrong. Step two, run away from his wife and family.

"He wants . . ." I fish around. I'll be damned if I'm going to let my kids believe their dad is an asshole now, after protecting his reputation—protecting their memories—for three long, lonely years. "He wants to spend time with you guys. He loves the hell out of you and always has. He hasn't been here for you, and he regrets it."

Cori makes a teenage mouth noise that has, since the time of cavemen, meant, "Bullshit, you don't know anything / I'm inventing feelings right now / Get out of my way, old lady." Sort of the sound you'd get if you tickled her while she sneezed. Thanks to two long and difficult labors, if I make that kind of snort-laugh sound, a little pee leaks out.

"Let's hear what he has to say," I say. "Let's have a little family meeting and hear what he has to say." And then, as though the very thought doesn't make my stomach churn, I tell them what he told me in front of the Band-Aids, when I finally was calm enough to really listen. "Summer break is coming up, and he's interested in spending the first week with you."

"What?" asks Cori. "No. Absolutely not. Pass."

That is exactly what I thought at first when he asked me. Absolutely not.

"I know how you feel, I think," I say, then realize my mistake.

"You have *no idea* how I feel. Your dad didn't abandon you the week you turned twelve."

"That's true." Lord, am I patient with this girl. "But my husband did leave me with two wonderful kids and a wonderful, expensive house and no job or money, and I can use that situation to empathize with you."

She rolls her eyes. "But it's not you he wants to take back."

And there it is—the secret superpower of teenage girls. She didn't mean to, but her words cut to the heart all the same. Did I think he was coming back here for me? In that first instant when I heard him calling my name? When he tried to hug me when it was time to leave? When he looked at me with something like longing?

How could I not?

I set my chin. "I think the best move is to discuss this without extra drama. There will be no kidnapping. We will make this decision together, the four of us."

"I already decided. No."

Like mother, like daughter. Those were the very words I said to John when he first asked for a week with the kids. A week, to make up for being gone for three years. No. Not good enough.

"Let's have that family meeting before deciding," I say, faking some kind of disinterest. "I'd love to see what you can learn from him and the experience of facing someone who has caused you hardship."

"Thing the first," says my studious son. "He cannot come to a family meeting. Family meetings are for family only."

Cori nods dramatically and crosses her arms. "Family only!" she echoes. I have to laugh. When the kids were little and I was in over my head from their nonstop bickering with each other, I'd sometimes say menacingly, "Don't forget your father is coming home in two hours," and they would immediately fall into line, suddenly the best of friends. Even now the mere thought of John's appearance renders them a united front.

"Thing the second," Joe goes on. "I have nothing to learn from my dad. Unless you want me to learn how to have a nervous breakdown and go to Hong Kong and use stupid younger women to rebuild my self-esteem at the expense of my existing family."

I set my jaw. Should I be annoyed or grateful that Joe's therapist is so good that he can put voice to all these feelings at the tender age of twelve?

"May I?" starts Lena. We all nod. Lena is part of the family in some weird way, or she's become so in the last three years. Would I have survived John's leaving without my best friend stepping up, helping with the kids, wrangling me a job, cooking my meals, holding my hand while I sobbed? I can't imagine so.

Lena's voice projects. "I think if we are going to rule against your father, to speak in his legal language, we need to think about what we would have to prove in court to cut off ties from him forever. According to my extensive study of *The Good Wife*, we would need to prove he did real and irreparable damage to you guys by leaving."

Cori, an unabashed fan of all legal dramas, pays attention. Joe, a fan of logic but rather disinterested in TV in general and dramas in specific, waits patiently.

"Did he do real, tangible damage to you guys?" asks Lena. "I would argue, not really. Because your mom is so awesome. She went from staying home with kids to working as a school librarian in basically thirty seconds so you guys could stay at your fancy private school without missing so much as a day of class. She got the house refinanced in the blink of an eye so she had more money to buy you guys Eggos and LEGOs and . . . uh . . . Speedos, even without your dad paying child support. In terms of quality of life, you guys haven't suffered at all from your dad moving out."

I look at her. The thought is kind, but what's really made plain by this speech is that I have suffered plenty. I am a poster child for low-grade chronic suffering. If an ad agency wanted to make suffering into a thirty-second spot, they would make a time-lapse video of me in my three colors of elastic-waistband teacher pants shoveling eight inches of snow at five a.m. so my kids can get to their early-bird activities on time, then teaching 250 overprivileged kids how to not use computers for porn for ten hours, and then collapsing in front of *Outlander* too tired to even find, much less turn on, my vibrator at the end of the day.

It would be kind of a dismal video.

But Lena's not done. "Now, on the not-so-tangible front, we could prove emotional pain and suffering, right? Because it had to hurt when he left. But is it irreparable? That's the question he wants answered now. He wants to know, Can he make up for lost time?"

"Who cares what he wants to know?" interjects Cori. "What about what we want?"

"Ok," says Lena. "What about what you want? Can forgiving him and enjoying time with him now actually make you feel better than holding a grudge against him for the rest of your lives? In other words, is punishing him what's truly best for you?"

Corinne groans audibly. "Lena. You make it sound so unreasonable to hate him forever."

"It is unreasonable to hate *anyone* forever," I say, mostly to myself. "Lena is right, as usual."

She shrugs and gives me a smug smirk. "What can I say?"

"I am not happy with your dad," I tell my children. "In fact, if I'm being totally honest, he hurt me quite a lot when he left." And if I'm being even more totally honest, he gave me quite a wallop to the heart today when I first saw him again too.

"Duh," says Cori.

"But as appealing as punishing him may sound at first, I have to remember what I want most in this life. I want your happiness more than anything. Well," I add upon further thought, "that's not true. I want you both graduating from college without criminal records more than anything. After that I want your happiness. I think time with your dad—and trying to forgive his past mistakes—can lead to more happiness, not less."

Do I believe this? Do I believe that strongly in forgiveness? So much so that I could ever forgive John? Move past what he did, take him back into my life like the whole thing never happened?

Probably not. But don't I want that belief for my kids?

"Now, you guys know that your dad didn't leave us for no reason, even if that's how it felt at the time. He left us because he truly believed we'd be better off without him. He left because he was so sad and upset he thought he was bad for you guys, and he thought leaving would fix that so he could one day come back and make things right." I try not to wince. No matter how much he swore to me it wasn't personal, how can it not be when the man you love says he has to get far away from you to ever hope to be happy again? "And you know that he's never stopped thinking of you. Those ridiculous cards . . . ," I remind them, referring to John's habit of sending inappropriately large checks with the cards he sends for the kids' birthdays, for holidays, even one year for Labor Day. "They show that even when he hasn't done exactly the *right* thing, he's tried to do *something*."

Joe makes his thinking face. Lena and Cori and I stare at him. Whatever he says next will probably go for the whole family. That's the kind of kid Joe is. Reasonable. Elbow deep in reasonableness. I am a little bit martyr, and Cori is a little bit drama queen, and John was always a little bit selfish. Joe is the good sides of all those coins—generous, intuitive, striving—and then on top of all of this, he is very, very smart. I don't understand him, but I love him all the more for it.

"Aunt Lena," he asks, and I know a philosophical question is coming, because Lena, before becoming a teacher at Country Day, was a nun. "Do you think forgiveness is a skill learned through practice, like playing chess, or a talent given to you at birth, like singing in tune?"

"Yes," says Lena, in her way. "Some people have to practice forgiveness and will never be naturals. They'll either do the work and get awesome at it but always have to think it over—or never do the work and die with a sack of hurts the size of an elephant. I know, because I'm in danger of being one of those people whenever I stop paying attention."

Then she nods at me. "Some people, like your mother, forgive so naturally they don't notice it happening. They'll get hurt twice as often because they are so quick to forgive but feel it half as much because of their ability to let things go."

I twist my lips. I'm not sure I agree, but I appreciate Lena making me seem cooler than I am to my kids.

Cori sighs. "I'm still pissed about Trinity buying the same color lipstick as me. That was supposed to be my trademark," she says. I bite my tongue so I don't say anything bad about Trinity, who is not my favorite of all of Cori's friends. "What Dad did is way worse than that. I want to be mad at him for, like, another two years. Can I do that?"

"Of course you can," I say. "I think you'll miss out, but ok. What about you, Joe?"

"I'm doing whatever Cori is doing," he says in his clever, even-handed way. "If she doesn't want to spend time with him, not even a week, then we won't spend time with him. Not even a week."

13

Lena smiles and leans back. She knows exactly what just happened here, even before I do.

Cori sighs mightily. "*Fine.* Jerk." She directs this at Joe. "A week. I'm fine with a week."

Joe smiles a little, but he doesn't think we see. Lena and I exchange our own look that we don't think they see.

"A week at the beginning of summer," I say. "Just a week. It sounds like it will be great for everyone. And if it's not, I won't be far away," I promise. "I'll be there to pick up the pieces."

Little do I know in that moment that it will be me in pieces before this coming adventure is over.

CHAPTER TWO

Dear Mom,

I realize that you won't even see this so-called reading journal until the end of the summer. Nevertheless, I would like to lodge a series of formal complaints.

1. School isn't even out, so why am I already supposed to be starting a summer reading project?

2. Why should I have to do a summer reading project when the whole entire point of summer is: Not Reading?

3. Do other kids whose parents are Not Librarians have to do things like this? I mean, really? Ask yourself. Do dentists' kids have to do a special three-times-a-day flossing regimen all summer long? What about the children of people in the army? Do they have to, like, go to the shooting range every day?

By the way: I would rather floss and shoot guns in a heartbeat.

4. A word about book selection: This book, The Curious Incident of the Dog in the Night-Time. *Here are some things I can relate to in reading a book about an autistic boy who lives in England and has a rat: ZERO THINGS, MOM.*

I see in future assignments I will be reading about people who lived a hundred years ago, fought the Nazis, live in the actual future, and are from a totally imaginary kingdom based on a Disney movie.

Mom. Have you never heard of John Green or Stephenie Meyer? Would a little Hunger Games action kill me? Is the whole point here for me to be made to suffer as punishment for being born into a family of book-worshipping Einsteins?

It doesn't seem fair. Because, um, it's not fair.

I hope in the afterlife you are made to spend an entire summer at the pool with Trinity.

Love,

Your dumbest daughter, Cori

—

A week. At the beginning of summer. It doesn't really hit me until the next day at school. A whole week. No kids. No work. No nothing.

I am standing in the library when I overhear a student telling her friend about her summer choir-camp plans. I look at the calendar and see that summer is not a thing that is abstract, like commercial space travel or bikini waxing, but is in fact a real thing that is really going to happen in three weeks. In three weeks my husband—well, my former husband—is taking my kids. They will not be with me, the expert parent, the one who knows the story behind why Joe doesn't eat clam chowder and how to keep chlorine from turning Cori's hair green. When John left, they were still young kids. Now they are something much more dangerous. Will he know how to ride herd on teenagers? Will he be able to tell them no, or will he just cave to every desire? The last time they were with John, they were both a foot shorter, or so it seems, and so much more trusting. Will he hurt them again? Will they let him get close? Will they even feel safe?

For the third time this week, I duck into the teachers' lounge during my prep period and call John.

"Hello, Amy," he says flatly. His voice isn't annoyed. It's unsurprised.

"What do you do if Joe gets a beesting?" I demand into the phone, instead of saying hello.

There's a momentary pause. "This is a trick question. Joe isn't allergic to bees," he replies.

I frown. For better or worse, I wanted him to get it wrong. "It would still hurt," I say, sounding as petulant as I feel.

"Ok," John says. "Then I'd apply baking soda poultice. Then ice."

I nod to myself. "Yeah . . . ," I say, trying to think of something that would truly stump him. Cori's Social Security number? But I don't actually think I know that. So many damn sevens.

"It's going to be ok, Amy. I'm ready for whatever they throw at me."

"They're mad at you," I say. *I'm mad at you*, I think. "They might give you hell."

"Yes," says John. "I hid behind that for a while. But I created this wall between us, and I'm the only one who can fix it."

I shake my head. "It might not be fixable," I tell him.

"It's my job to try. And who knows," he says. "It might be good for everybody."

The bell rings. My stomach churns. I mutter a quick goodbye and rush to my next period, where I immediately break out in a flop sweat. Which is really saying something, considering the institutional air-conditioning we have at school, designed, I suspect, to prevent any excess leakage of pheromones by freezing the teenagers solid. After I greet the kids and get them started on their workstations, I do what I think all librarians do when any anxiety sets in: I make a list.

Here are some of the things that are going to happen while my kids are in the care of their irresponsible, untrustworthy father:

- They are going to take up smoking, drinking, and sex in quick succession.
- Cori is going to get pregnant, and Joe is going to get herpes.

- John is going to get all three of them matching tattoos. Of what, I have no idea.
- Neck tattoos.
- He will lose the kids in one of those scary old broken-down carnivals from the movie *Big*, and they will be forced to sleep in cardboard boxes with stray cats and used heroin needles until I retrieve them.

And as likely as all that is, there's the worst possibility of all: They will be fine, and I will not be fine.

Though Lena—who, I should note, has zero kids—tells me it's a "wonderful opportunity," I'm not interested in being away from my kids for anywhere near this long. I don't want to tour Europe for a week by train, even if I could scrape up the money to do so. I don't want to spend the time finding my inner watercolorist or potter. Like every mother in America, I'm tired. I could sleep for a couple of those days straight. But then after that, what? Three days bingeing on HGTV? Take-out pizza and Target wine cubes? A long, leisurely wander through Costco with no list?

I try to imagine my house empty of children. My calendar empty of places to be. I feel some nauseating cocktail of relief and loneliness. I think of the three-day weekend last year when my parents picked up the kids and took them to do the museums and monuments in Washington, DC. Day one: streaming *Gilmore Girls*, doing about twenty loads of laundry, cleaning every surface of my home, building an IKEA bookcase, listening to five hours of librarian podcasts, and knitting a baby hat. Day two: crying in front of the refrigerator. Day three: "surprising" them a day early at the aquarium in Baltimore. Not one of the proudest episodes of my life.

I'm behind on some of my shows, I think. *Maybe I could paint the kitchen.*

I look over the students using my media lab. It's my planning period, and they are all doing their own thing on their iPads. Probably nonstop texting plus a little background research for the School-Wide Seasonal, a massive Country Day project designed to keep the kids just a smidgen engaged in the long, muddy slog from spring break to summer. The students sophomore through senior "declare" a major and spend the first half hour of every day pursuing it, from writing up a fake schedule of classes they'd take based on college course guides, to researching a "thesis" project in their subject, to doing work-study programs in the community. If someone wants to do an SWS major in premed, they have to figure out how to finance med school, how to get all their prerequisites taken without overloading on hours for any semesters, which labs they'll need, what their books will cost, and which academic groups to join. Then they do a minithesis—ten pages at least—learn about med school entrance exams, and finally, in the last week before summer, shadow a professional in the field well enough to get a good recommendation. Grades are based on that recommendation, their educational plan, their financial plan, and their thesis. And the faculty who grade them are those who aren't burdened with the grading of normal finals. A.k.a.: me. Me, the counselors, special-subject teachers, coaches, even the nurse. It's all hands on deck.

The kids in my room are doing some approximation of that work, and I will be grading some of them. I want them all to get As as a point of pride. So I slowly, dramatically move up to my whiteboard, where a countdown of days left before the project is due waits. An anxious silence falls as I erase the *15* and write in *14*. Fourteen days left before SWS finals are due. Then I meaningfully write under the countdown:

Educational Plan?

Financial Plan?

Thesis?

Recommendation?

Saying nothing, letting the list of burdens and the days left in the year speak for themselves, I keep one eye peeled on their screens as I pull out my own tablet and message Lena.

Amy:

I'm living with you while my kids are gone.

Lena:

No.

Amy:

No, really. I am.

Lena:

No.

Amy:

It'll be fun. I'll make dinner for us and we can have a Daniel Craig film festival.

Lena:

We do that every Sat. anyway.

Amy:

Why buck tradition?

Lena:

You need to get a life.

Amy:

Aren't nuns supposed to be sweet?

Lena:

I'm not sure where you heard that.

Ok. So then I won't spend the week with Lena. I'll go visit my parents in Florida. I'll spend the week in the blazing-hot Tampa sun contemplating how exactly a person can be switched at birth and yet still look exactly like her mother and father. Who do not watch anything but Fox News, with the volume turned to just above Jackhammer and just below Permanent Brain Damage.

There's got to be something I am supposed to be doing during this week alone. Beyond laundry. Something meaningful. I haven't had a week off from everything since before the kids were born. Surely I'm full of longings and desires that have been unfulfilled over these last fifteen years. Or short of that, responsibilities. Things to do that I've been deferring. Continuing education, maybe?

Aha! Continuing education! Now I'm onto something. Country Day faculty are expected to get a lot of continuing ed credits every year. I can get some hours and learn some new software or review a new curricula set for a week, and then I'll be back home ready to police Cori's cell phone usage and make Joe go outside once a day for the rest of the summer.

I open up the American Library Educators Association page for conferences and continuing ed. It's bookmarked, in my librarian way, under two labels—Green: Professional, and Blue: Books. I wish, not for the first time, that the two categories would combine on the screen and form aqua.

The calendar on the website loads slowly. Maybe there will be something in Scranton, a short daily drive back and forth. Or better still, online. I can stay home, eat soup, and study in my pajamas. Please let there be something online I haven't taken already . . .

New York, NY
June 1–4
Hosted by Columbia University

The School Library of the Future: Learn how new resources are being implemented in the most forward-thinking schools, private and public, throughout the nation. Study new ways to bring the future into your curriculum and keep the best parts of the past relevant. What will be your students' "normal" in ten years? A multiscreen tablet? A projection watch? A folding phone? The future is in New York this June!
10 CEU—*PRESENTERS STILL NEEDED*

Huh. New York.

Yes! New York. Close enough to race home if John does something wrong. Far enough to count as an actual vacation. And I haven't been in New York since . . . since I met John. I used to love New York. My college roommate Talia and I used to come down on the train every chance we got, staying on sofas and in dodgy hotels and once, when we were out dancing until four, on the twin velvet chaises in the lobby of the St. Regis, thanks to a white lie told to the swing shift desk clerk.

Oh, the things we did in New York. I never told John about most of our adventures, much less shared that kind of juice with my kids. As such, I haven't thought about the city much for the last fifteen years. Since John and I pulled the goalie and got pregnant with Corinne. Since I started craving the settled life and the big house with the pretty kitchen I have now. Of course, I didn't crave the disappearing husband and the lack of child support payments for three years, but this life was all I wanted, more or less.

Except there was a time when it wasn't.

A loud, rowdy, fun time. Many, many years ago. When I was someone else.

I open the messages on my tablet again. I haven't texted Talia since . . . maybe a year after John left? Just after that last promotion she got at the magazine? Either way, it's been too long. Embarrassingly long.

But I know that she'll understand—that the minute we are in the same room together again, it will be like not a day has gone by. It's always been like that between Talia and me. All at once I want to see her again, see what life is like without kids and husbands and a wardrobe acquired almost entirely at Target while there anyway for toothpaste and panty liners. I type:

> Hey girl. Coming to NYC
> 1st wk of June. Coffee or
> a drink?

There's no response. Then three dots. Then nothing. I get a little nervous. Will she be mad at me for not being in touch? Does she even have my number anymore? So I add:

> It's Amy.
> Amy Byler.

Then the three dots again. Ok. She saw the message . . .

Talia:
Amy . . .
AMY!

That seems like a good sign.

Talia:
AMY BYLER WHERE THE HELL HAVE YOU BEEN?

I start to type back an apology. I've been busy. Life has been kind of hectic. I let her fall off my radar—

Talia:
You're staying with me.

I delete what I wrote and type:

Amy:
Really?!?!??! Are you sure you have room?

Talia:
Can't talk. In meeting. Call when on way.

I stare at my tablet in happy surprise. Well. Now I won't have to bunk with some strange librarian from Idaho at the conference and spend $200 a night for the privilege. I can use my per diem, should Country Day offer me one, for actual food. Or . . . *drinks*.

Amy:
Ok that sounds amazing. Thank you! I will call you.

Talia:
Leave me alone I'm working

Amy:
Sorry. Just excited

She doesn't respond, no dots, no emoji, nothing. Conversation complete. I put down my tablet. I'm positively shaking with excitement. Could it be this easy? Could life be this aligned for once? A short trip to the big city to hang with fellow book nerds and reconnect with a footloose and fancy-free old friend, and all within my budget? While my kids are looked after by their once-absent dad? Is this a real thing or some kind of weird trap set up by the universe?

My tablet blinks at me. I bring it back to life and look at the new message. It's Talia. A map link. I click it, and it takes me to a block in an unbearably hip neighborhood in Brooklyn. This is where she lives. The map is studded with location flags. Bars. Restaurants I've heard about in magazines. Shopping. An artisanal organ meats store. Good god. Talia is so *cool*.

The tablet blinks again, and I click back to the message app. Talia, in her succinct way, doubling down on her cool in four little words:

this party is on

—

Fate or no fate, I am still me, so I still insist that John come over and have a family dinner with us to prep for the week after school's out. And since I am still me, there is an agenda.

Agenda for "Family Meeting," Tuesday, May 9, 5:30–?

No minutes from previous meeting

Plan for first week of summer:

Discuss Sample Daily Schedule, weekly obligations

Behavioral expectations: Joe

Behavioral expectations: Cori

Parenting expectations: John

Ground rules

Daily communication plans

Tutorial: using the EpiPen in case of accidental peanut ingestion

Tabled issues:

Why did John leave Amy?

Why is John back now all of a sudden?

Does John still love Amy?

When will Amy ever have sex again?

Needless to say, I do not plan to share my agenda with the meeting participants.

John is fifteen minutes early, and I am not exactly emotionally prepared for this, but here he is, standing at the door, looking at me expectantly. I take a moment to look at him. He is still so handsome, so square and broad and sure. In a rush it all comes back. Dad jokes at family dinners. Pokémon hunts in the neighborhood. Toddler touch football, where Cori squealed in joy whenever he would pretend Joe was the ball. John's impeccable Daffy Duck impression.

"Where are the kids?" he asks. Not in his Daffy voice.

"Home in a half hour or so," I tell him. "Cori is finishing up her thesis, and Joe is at debate. Cori's going to work at school until he's done and walk him home."

"I thought the kids would be here," he tells me.

"Yeah," I say, unapologetic. "They're busy kids."

"Of course," he says. Then, "I kind of left work early. I was eager to see them."

"It's a very sudden-onset eagerness," I say.

He says nothing but looks stung. I try to swallow my anger, but seeing him here, in this house again, makes me feel hot and red, like a star right before it goes supernova. "Would you help me out?" I manage to ask him in a normalish voice. "The dining table is serving as makeshift study carrels right now. I need it to go back to being a dining table."

On days when they don't have after-school stuff, the kids come home and do homework on opposite sides of our six-seater dining table. Because Cori is too good at turning algebra drudgery into the fine art of distracting her brother, we constructed this little divider between them from two back-to-back paperboard science fair presentations. On top of the *Are Potatoes Electrical Conductors?* side, Joe made a vision board of good grades he's received in the past, colleges he'd like to attend, and careers he's interested in learning more about. Reminder: this poor child is twelve.

In place of the *Measuring the Heat of Colors* side, Cori put up pictures of the guy from *Arrow* and Benedict Cumberbatch. We just call him the Batch.

I do not entirely mind that from the kitchen, where I tend to be at this time of day, I can only see Cori's side.

John looks all this over with eyebrows raised. "I'm really hoping this side is Cori's," he tells me, gesturing to a shirtless Stephen Amell. And though there have been signs that Joe suffers from a crush on a slightly older girl named Macy Feathers who usually beats him at chess, I let myself erupt a bit at John's narrow-mindedness.

"Oh? Worried I might have let your son go gay?" Then, archly, "Would you walk out on him if he were?"

He colors, as he should. "Sorry. You're right. I don't care either way. It was just me being awkward and nervous."

"You should be awkward and nervous," I tell him. "You did a terrible thing, and we"—I gesture at the study carrels, as though the Batch is one of the family—"are the people you did it to."

John sighs. We made it to better terms after a while, but that first couple of months after he left us, I called his voice mail on a pretty regular basis to tell him what a sleaze he was, to compare him unfavorably to a segmented earthworm, or to try out words heard previously only on HBO original series. So my anger won't be totally new to him.

"I see you've been frozen in time for three years," he replies.

"I have not," I say indignantly. Defensively. "I have been frozen in place, maybe. I have been working and taking care of two kids and sacrificing everything I need or want so that they can go to a good school and eat good food and have a good home. I have learned how to live on a teacher's salary alone and how to fix a toilet without calling a plumber and how to make an Elizabethan costume out of rickrack and Goodwill clothes. I have learned how to survive on coffee and office naps and the sale flavors of Lean Cuisine. Busy busy busy!" I snap. I sound kind of manic. "Hardly frozen in time," I add more quietly. But by now I know I'm protesting too much.

John looks equally guilty and annoyed. This expression—which seems to suggest that he feels terrible enough already, and I should not be feeding the fire—has always made me feel contrite. "What can I do, then?" he says wearily. "I've said I'm sorry a dozen times."

I have no useful answer. "Go back in time and don't leave us high and dry and vanish to Hong Kong, maybe. Have you thought about that?" *Or go back even further*, I think. *Two years before that. And this time, when the chips are down, come through for me.*

He sighs wearily. He is always the injured party in the end, and today will be no different.

"I'm here now, Amy. Can we make it a tiny bit less painful before the kids come home?"

I don't respond to that. "Clear the table, please."

He clears. I cook. In five minutes we've become some reasonable facsimile of a couple, a very tense couple, getting dinner on the table, coming together as a family. It all feels so familiar to me, and at the same time so sad. These moments are, after all, part of what I lost when I lost John. This is what I've spent three years convincing myself I didn't need.

I'm roughly chopping basil and garlic for pesto. A big salad is waiting to be dressed with red wine vinaigrette. This is not haute cuisine, but neither is it our usual Monday fare of veggie fried rice with pot stickers out of the bag. From the corner of my eye I see that he's setting the table, having no trouble finding what he needs from the buffet. Everything is right where he left it. Even me.

Why am I trying to impress John with real cooking? I wonder silently. *What is that about?*

As the pasta water simmers and the pesto whirs in the Ninja, I start to remember the things I should be talking about with John before the kids get here. Limits for the kids during their week with their dad. Rules. Parameters. "John," I call into the dining room. "Maybe this is a good time to talk about parameters?"

But John isn't in the dining room anymore. He isn't anywhere that I can see. I turn off the blender and wander into the front of the house. He's sitting on the old gray canvas sofa, head in his hands. Next to him is a photo book the kids made for me last Christmas called "Stop Calling Us Tweens," and it is filled with a year's worth of snapshots of the kids doing their various things. Diving, public speaking, Halloween, making our Sunday breakfast burritos in silly toques.

I freeze. In all our years of marriage, I saw John cry maybe three or four times. He was raised in a household that highly valued male/female dichotomy, after all. He told me once he'd never seen his own father cry. John cried when both kids were born, and he cried on the phone from Hong Kong when he told me he was never coming back. That call . . . we were both crying so hard none of our words made any sense; none even sounded much like words. "I'm sorry," he said over and over and over again. "I'm sorry. I have to do this. I'm dying."

And in that weird way the brain sort of frosts over in crisis and picks out the thing that it can handle, my brain picked out John saying, "I'm dying," and I thought, for just a second, *Oh. Well, in that case. If he's dying, then this is ok. He's not leaving me. He's dying. Thank god. For a second I thought he was leaving me.*

And then of course the brain defrosts just enough to let a reasonable thought peek out. *He's not actually dying. That asshole.* "You're dying? Living with me is killing you?" I remember asking. And he said, "What?" about three times because I was sniveling too much. And that he couldn't somehow understand me through the choking sobs made me angrier, and then I just tumbled down past angry into hurt and said over and over again, "You're a horrible person. This is a horrible thing. You are doing a horrible, horrible thing," in a pointless chant. At some point he disconnected, but I kept the chant up for months, saying it to all my friends who would listen, to my parents, to his parents, to everyone except for two people: Cori and Joe.

I take a deep, deep breath and sit down next to him on the sofa. "John," I say gently, putting one hand on his back. It's an old movement born of muscle memory rather than intention, and yet when I touch him, I wish I hadn't. "This is not unsalvageable." I am talking about his relationship with the children. But at my own words, unbidden, the image of my wedding ring, upstairs, in the farthest corner of my jewelry box, pops into my head. I never did get rid of it. Told myself I might need the money for a rainy day. Never mind it was pouring at the time.

He looks up at me. "It's been years. A fourth of Joe's life."

I nod. And because of the way pain shifts time, weighs it down to an exhausted plod, it feels like it's been half of mine. "But they're not predisposed to hate you. They have animosity, and probably a lot of really hard questions for you. But they also are going to want—desperately want—you to be able to make this ok." I am speaking for the kids, of course. I'm not speaking for myself. I don't think.

He shakes his head, defeated. Always out of ideas. Always so quick to give up. I feel my anger bubble back.

"Don't be lazy, John. If you don't intend to work for this, to invest in this, don't stay another second. I won't let you stay another second," I say. "Not if your endgame is disappointing them again." Or me.

He shakes his head. "Of course it's not. I'm just . . . I'm daunted."

"I'm sure you are. I'm daunted too. But the thing is those two kids are way smarter than either of us. They'll see right through it if we're faking this. If you want to see them for a week and then be gone another three years, they'll pick up on it. They'll torture you to see if it makes you falter. They'll push you away just to be sure you're committed. So don't waste any of our time if you're not."

"Oh, I'm committed. I want this more than anything," he says. "I am not trying to scare you, but I want something real with these kids. I'm a VP now, and I can work remotely all summer. It's a short flight away to the Chicago office if something comes up. I'm not needed back in Hong Kong until September, and in the years following this promotion, I'll have more and more freedom and autonomy. A week with the kids could be just the beginning . . . I mean, if you were open to it."

I blanch, taken by surprise. Every mama-bear cell of my body starts vibrating with fear. Does he intend to ask for custody? Is he trying to steal my kids?

"Ok, back it up there," he says, seeing the panic on my face. "You just asked me if I'm in it for the long haul. I am telling you I am. Stop mentally hiring lawyers and writing the script for the Lifetime movie."

I take a deep breath, then nod. He's right, of course. How can someone I've been without for years still know me better than anyone else in the entire world? And how can the right answer feel so terrifying?

"They live with me," I say, mostly for my own reassurance.

John nods. "They live with you. You're their mother. I just want to . . . be their father a little better."

I raise my eyebrows.

"I just want to be their father at all," John amends.

"Then I will help you," I say, though it all feels so terribly unfair. Helping him repair what he did to the kids. Even though he did it to me too. "But I'm not helping you, exactly," I clarify. "I'm helping them."

And that sneaky, hopeful, idiotic part of my heart whispers to herself, when she thinks I'm not paying attention, *And maybe helping myself too.*

CHAPTER THREE

Dear Mom,

Ok, I can already guess what you would say: I'm not supposed to spend the entire journal entry complaining about the books. Noted. I'm supposed to write about my innermost feelings about what I read that week, and I'm supposed to write it this way, by hand, in a big fancy notebook, so I can learn how people lived in the olden days when cars couldn't fly and dinosaurs roamed the earth.

But see? See how weird it is to write a joke and not have anyone write LOL back to you? Texting is so much more natural. It's a conversation. You know when you're understood. And when you're not. This, this handwriting all by yourself, is unnatural. There's no response to journaling. It's like shouting into the oblivion. Will you even read this? When? Are you laughing? Are you skimming? Do you have anything to say to me?

I love you, Mom, I really do. But I don't think you understand at all what it's like to be a . . . what, a young adult? A new person. That's what I am. I have been a person for fifteen years, which is time to understand the world but not time to get all creaky and jaded. And before you creak (see) to me about wisdom and experience, let me tell you, I know you and Dad went to Paris for your honeymoon, but what other experiences have you had exactly since then? What do you even DO for fun? All I ever see you do is work and hassle me and Joe.

Which, like, ok. I can see just from writing that last sentence that your life isn't probably all about having fun right now, and that's not exactly your choice. It was Dad's choice. I think it's his fault you do nothing but work and buy groceries. If he had stayed, you'd have gone back to Paris, I'll bet.

If he had stayed, would we all have gone to Paris?

So this is all to say that after careful consideration I have decided NOT to read The Curious Incident of the Dog in the Night-Time, *which is probably "Very Important" but definitely not "Very Interesting." And instead I am going to read* Five Days in Paris *by Danielle Steel, which, let me tell you, is already off to a very exciting start. There's a senator, and his wife falls in love with this other rich guy. You know how it goes.*

Wow. You cannot argue with me, because this is a journal, not a text.

Wow.

Ok, I'm sold.

Love,

Your illiterate daughter, Cori

———

The moment the school bell rings the next day, I positively prance into Lena's office.

"Lena!" I hiss. "Lena. Quit doing whatever you're doing and come get coffee with me."

"Can't," she says, bent over her computer screen. "Huge sale on RealSteal." Lena, the former nun, the teacher of values and ethics, the spiritual leader for not just me but my kids, too, is also a consignment-sale junkie. "I need this handbag."

I pull up a chair next to her desk and peer into the computer. "You know, the first step is admitting you have a problem."

"I always wonder about that. The first step is *believing* you have a problem, right? Then admitting it? If you admit it before you believe it, will that do any good?"

"You have a problem," I clarify. "Believe it."

"I have a passion," she corrects. "Look at this." She angles the screen toward me. It's a pretty bag, all right. It is nothing like Lena's style, though. Longchamp. Conservative. Staid. Almost painfully classic. "In ten minutes they're going to drop the price ten percent. I have to hit refresh right when they do so no one else gets it."

"I feel like your time is worth paying ten percent more," I say, just to hear her argue.

"And I feel like the first ten minutes after school gets out are worth zero dollars. If we go anywhere outside these walls, there will be students. Students in the coffee shops, students in the parking lot, students in the parks and gelato stores and probably even Batteries Plus, because there is literally no place they will not go at three fifteen except back into the classroom. You wanna talk to me? Close the door and get comfy while I hit refresh, because this is the only place in the entire county where none of our students will overhear."

I shrug. To Lena's credit, she does actually have a pretty comfy chair, a curb find of a slipper chair she reupholstered herself with a loud floral print and a staple gun. She believes people tell you more when they're sitting in a soft chair. Perhaps for that very same reason, she herself sits in a standard-issue "teacher chair" from Office Depot.

"John came over last night," I say the second my butt hits the soft seat.

For the first time since I came into her room, Lena looks up from the computer. "Oho," she says, eyebrows raised, bemused look on her face.

"He cried," I tell her.

"Seems appropriate," she replies, returning her gaze to the screen. "What else did he do?"

"Complimented my cooking. And my parenting. And the kids' grades. And their table manners. There was a lot of sucking up. It was kind of exhausting, really."

"Exhausting or highly satisfying?"

Lena knows me so well. "Both, I guess."

"And the kids?" she asks.

"I was watching them like a hawk. Last night and this morning. Looking for any sign of stress or upset. They seem . . . fine. Finer than me, really."

"Kids can be incredibly resilient," Lena says.

"I know; that's what I told myself too. But after he left, there was a long time when they were incredibly fragile." I think of the way Joe and Cori eyed John when they first walked in the door last night. They were a tough crowd, at least at first. John led off with apologies, but he's apologized to them before.

I flop back in Lena's confession chair. "Three years, Lena. How does someone apologize for three years in the life of a child?"

Lena thinks on this. "One doesn't. One just proves he can do better. Does John have a plan for that?"

I pause. A lot of planning got done last night, but not all of it sounded good to me. "Let me tell you about this stunt he pulled."

She clicks her mouse, watches the screen, and then leans back in her chair. "Go ahead."

"So the first half hour or so is insanely stiff. Joe and Cori are staring at John like he's an alien invader, and I'm staring at the kids like they're my glass menagerie, and John is looking like he is ready to break into a tap dance number, he's trying so hard. Cori keeps threatening to go to Trinity's house, and Joe is literally shrinking into his chair like he's hoping to blend into the wood grain. I'm about five minutes away from pulling the plug on the whole thing. And then John reaches into his pocket and pulls out a tiny bottle of lavender oil."

"Lavender oil?" asks Lena.

"Monster spray," I say. "Joe and his phobia of closet monsters—do you remember? When he was four or five, John and Cori made a fake 'Monster Repellant' label and glued it onto a lavender oil diffuser with Mod Podge and convinced Joe that a whiff of the stuff would kill any monsters on the spot. That exact same bottle from all those years ago—that's what he was carrying with him last night. John handed it to Cori and said they could use it on him at any time if they really, truly wanted him to go away, and he would go. He told them he loved them more than he loved life, and he wanted to be here, but if his presence hurt them, all they needed to do was say the word."

"Oh, wow," says Lena.

"I know," I say. "And it changed everything. Cori looked at the bottle, opened it, and took a whiff, and the smell filled the air. It was the first time I had smelled that since Joe was little, and you know how scents work." Lena nods. "Everything just all came back. Running through the house spraying lavender water on the tiniest dark corners and under all the furniture. Laughing and swearing we could see the monsters wither and crumble into dust—'There goes one now! You just missed it!' And then ending up in a pile of giggles on Joe's bed complaining about how long it would take us to clean up all those invisible monster corpses."

"You were a take-no-prisoners sort of family," Lena says with a soft smile.

I nod. "And then Cori put the bottle next to Joe. And he put his hand on it, and for a second, he pointed it at John. And we all held our breath. And then he put the bottle down by the side of his plate and said, 'Mom, I'm starving. Is there any food?' And that was it."

"Wow. That's pretty amazing."

I think about this. Yes, it is pretty amazing, if you disregard the slurry of confused and betrayed feelings about John that clouds my own view. But setting aside my own feelings—and isn't that kind of the heart of this job I call motherhood?—my kids being able to reunite, however cautiously, with their dad after three years apart is indeed pretty amazing.

"So that was the stunt you mentioned?" asks Lena.

I snap out of my reverie at that reminder. "Oh, no. Nope, that comes next. We're passing the pesto and eating the pasta, and the mood keeps getting easier and easier. And I swear to you John is watching my wineglass like a hawk. Ready to top it off at any moment. As if I'd be fool enough to get tipsy around him. Anyway, everyone is just warming up to each other, and it's going annoyingly well. The kids are so much like him, you know, in so many ways."

"Are they?" Lena asks. She and John were socially friendly, but never terribly close.

I nod. "Joe has the same thoughtful expressions. And the same instinct to flee any danger, disappear from any tension in a puff of smoke, rather than fight it out. They're both like . . ."

"The wizard, not the werewolf?" Lena says.

"Yeah. The wizard, not the werewolf," I agree. "Cori is . . . just a straight-up half woman / half tiger."

"A weretiger," Lena supplies.

"That's not a thing," I tell her.

She just ignores me. "And how is she like John?"

"The sense of humor. I guess even with him in Hong Kong they still watch all the same shows. There were a lot of Jimmy Fallon references at the table. Like, I'm pretty sure Jimmy himself was there with us and then left, and no one noticed. And they even listen to a few of the same bands. It was kind of like a first date in some ways. 'Oh, you like so-and-so? I *love* so-and-so! I saw them play live when they came over. They played "Skunky McGee"!' 'Wow, they never play "Skunky McGee"!'"

"What is 'Skunky McGee' now?" interrupts Lena.

"My attempt at thinking of a name of a hip band song," I tell her.

"You are bad at that," she says and hits refresh.

"Yeah," I willingly admit. "You know you're uncool when you can't even make up something that sounds like it might be cool."

"Cool is not your area."

"No kidding. The thing is the more they broke the ice, the more they got all excited about the agenda for their week together. And then the conversation turned from all the awesome things they're going to do for the week to what awesome things I'm going to do while I'm kidless. And for a while I didn't say anything, but then finally I admitted that I might take a trip to New York, and all hell broke loose."

"You might take a trip to New York?" interjects Lena, almost a shout. "That's really, really great!"

I shift my eyes sideward. "I might," I say. Though by now I have already applied to speak at the library conference. To get Country Day to pay for the registration, I have to do at least one presentation, so on a wild hair I decided to float the latest reading-engagement idea I've been trying this spring. It was surprisingly fun to flesh out a conference proposal, put fingers to keyboard, and hit send. "There's a library conference at Columbia," I tell her. "I thought it might be worthwhile. Plus I'll get my continuing ed hours done early."

Lena frowns and loses interest. "I was hoping you were going to New York to party and have sex with strange men."

"Oh, yeah, that sounds just like me," I say sarcastically. "Maybe I'll get a tattoo while I'm there."

"The infinity symbol on your lower back?" she asks.

"One twenty dot one twenty-five," I banter back.

Lena looks at me questioningly.

"The Dewey Decimal classification for infinity," I supply. "Not that we use that anymore. It turns out one twenty dot one twenty-five was not actually infinite."

"That's deep," says Lena. "Oh! I got it!"

"Got what?" I ask, still thinking about the larger 120 category in Dewey. It's epistemology. Knowledge about knowledge. One of my favorites.

"The bag. Look!" She tilts the screen again. Next to the window of the consignment site, there's the Longchamp website. Same bag, a full $1,000 more.

"Holy crap! What in god's name are you going to do with an eleven-hundred-dollar bag?" I ask.

"Sell it on eBay," she tells me simply. "For five hundred more than I paid for it."

"You've got to be kidding me. People will pay that much for a used purse?"

Lena shrugs. "They have the last few times I've done this. Maybe they turn around and sell it for nine hundred dollars. Who knows?"

"I take everything back," I tell her. "That was ten minutes well spent."

She nods with a smile. "See?"

"What exactly are you going to do with that extra five hundred bucks in your pocket?" I ask her. I've never known Lena to have a ton of extra money, which I previously put down to a teacher's salary and a handbag habit.

"I'm buying a mic stand and a new cordless microphone."

I look at her, confused.

"For the DAYS camp. Talent show night." Domestic Abuse Youth Services. Lena's volunteer passion.

"Oh, Lena," I say. "I love you."

"I'm buying myself this too," she says, clicking over to a cute canvas slouch bag with some gentle wear on consignment for thirty-five dollars.

"Now that looks more like you," I say.

"You can borrow it anytime you want," she says. "Maybe take it to New York."

"If I go to New York."

"Please go to New York," says Lena. "Please consider having just a little bit of fun while you're there."

"That's what John said, after a fashion. Right in front of the kids. Like it's not his fault my life isn't cartwheels and champagne fountains."

"He said you should have a little bit of fun? What's so bad about that?"

"He tried to give me his credit card," I say, spitting out the words.

Lena pushes away from her desk and looks up at me in surprise. "What now?"

"He wants to treat me while he's with the kids. That's what he said. It made me want to barf."

"A man wants to care lovingly for your kids and give you a blank check to spend while he does so? And that makes you want to . . . barf?" Lena asks.

I roll my eyes at her. "I can take care of myself. I don't want to be bought off."

"I suppose you could look at this that way."

"I'm not taking his money, Lena. It's dirty money. When John ran for it, he left me really hard up. We were used to his level of income, I was staying home with the kids, and I hadn't put my MLS degree to use at all in, what, twelve years? If this job hadn't come up when it did, if faculty didn't get reduced tuition . . . my kids' lives would have been turned upside down. It was an awful time. I mean, to leave a librarian stranded on her own with two kids—it's not cool."

"No. It's not. You did an amazing job hitting the ground running. Letting John give you a week's spending money wouldn't undo that."

I tighten my jaw and shake my head. "It feels like it would."

"So you told him no?"

"I did. I told him thanks but no thanks. Then the kids started in on me, saying I should take the credit card."

"I bet they did! They're on your side. Just like I am."

I refuse to hear this. "They just like spending other people's money. Cori was talking about New York restaurants she's seen on Bravo shows. Joe was going on about the glories of the Natural History Museum. And the Transit Museum. And the Tenement Museum? Oh, that boy. God save me if he wastes all his greatness on a history degree."

Lena laughs. "You don't want Joe to get a history degree now?"

"I want him to get a degree in 'Joe being happy for the rest of his life,'" I tell her. "Short of that, I guess prelaw."

"I actually think those two majors are diametrically opposed. But then what do I know? I teach ethics."

I laugh at her and shake my head. "I know it's not my future to choose, but it is so, so hard not to see what you think would make your kids happy and just . . . sort of herd them in that direction. Joe is so good in his heart. I'm afraid he'll do a job that is not well valued in our society, like social work or public school teaching, and his little spirit will get broken."

"I hear you. I can only imagine how it feels to let your kids make their own mistakes," says Lena, gently reminding me that in both my mothering and teaching jobs, that skill is probably the single most important tool we have. But it's hard—looking ahead, seeing their mistakes coming, and then, unless they are in actual mortal danger, holding their hands as they make them anyway.

"Point taken. I think the thing about Joe that makes it so tricky is that he always makes such good decisions. I don't have any practice letting him screw up on his own."

Lena smiles at me. "Then he'll make a good decision on careers when the time comes. A good decision for *himself*. In the moment he's in."

I nod and then spot myself an excellent segue. "And not taking John's credit card is the right decision for me, in the moment I'm in. But the kids acted like I was being the biggest party pooper, and John insisted—I mean, he went on and on and on, until I finally agreed I'd take his card for emergencies and 'incidentals' as they came up. So now I'm the proud owner of my ex-husband's American Express number. And here's the worst thing. Are you ready for it?"

Lena nods. "Lay it on me."

"I say to him, right there at dinner, trying to defend my position, I say, 'Well, there's no point in my even taking it because my using a card with a man's name on it is going to raise some serious eyebrows, isn't it?' And do you know what he says? He says, 'I already had the company issue me one with your name. Should be here in two days.' And I say, 'What? They'll give you a credit card with your ex-wife's name on it?' And he says, right in front of the kids, 'Well, you're not really my ex-wife, are you?'"

Lena starts and spins in her chair. "What now?"

"That's what they said too!"

"You're still married to John? I thought you filed years ago."

"I definitely filed. Isn't there such a thing as a common-law divorce?"

"There is *not* such a thing as a common-law divorce," says Lena with conviction. "As you well know. Don't play dumb with me."

I shrug. "He was in Hong Kong. Lawyers are expensive. Working through a divorce seemed too painful at first, and then just entirely unnecessary as time went on."

"Um, unnecessary how? Wouldn't you have gotten court-ordered child support?"

I sigh. "He should have paid without a judge telling him to," I say. "I shouldn't have had to demand it. He should have been here, taking care of his children without a court order."

Lena's eyebrows hit the ceiling. "So you martyred yourself rather than stand up to John."

"I stood on my own two feet," I correct. "And it probably came out for the better anyway. Most of our assets were—are—in the house, and he signed the deed over to me without a word. And . . ." I'm hesitant to tell Lena the next part, hesitant to voice my selfishness even to myself.

"Yes?"

"I got the kids." I don't admit how afraid I was to press the divorce through, on the off chance he might ask for some custody. The legal starting place is fifty-fifty split placement, and I'd have a hard road to get full time with the kids if he wanted his share. As heartbroken as I was when he left, I wasn't ready to contemplate missing every other week of my kids' lives on top of that pain.

"You're still married," Lena says, shaking her head in wonder.

"I'm still married," I agree. "To John."

"After three years apart."

"I don't know what to tell you. It was on my list of things to do."

"That must be quite a list."

I try to explain another way. "Getting unmarried was more of a picky detail in a chaotic time when those details had to be ignored so I could survive. It was like how I stopped scheduling haircuts for a year. And then one day things calmed down enough for me to notice that I needed a haircut, and I got one. No big deal."

"So now you notice you need a divorce," Lena supplies. "And you go get one, and it's no big deal?"

I blink. I haven't taken the analogy that far yet. "I guess so," I say.

But I don't guess that at all. Deep down, I have no intention of getting a divorce, I suddenly realize. I don't think now is the time to upset the applecart.

But I cannot tell Lena that. Honestly, I don't even want to think about it too much myself.

"John may be an asshole," I say needlessly, "but he's a reasonable one. A divorce will simply be a matter of putting pen to paper. Just like the haircut. No big deal."

And then I pretend not to notice Lena's unquestionably skeptical expression.

———

A week later I'm in my bedroom packing. With a full week to go before I leave, it's almost laughable to be packing right now. But Cori is going to be crazy busy for the next five days before the end of school, and I will, too, with the presentations and theses to read and just the nonstop rushing around of finals, grades, transcripts. And for once Trinity isn't here. So if I want my fifteen-year-old daughter's approval of every stitch of clothing I'm taking to New York, I have to get it now. And I do. She is the sartorial authority around here.

The bedroom is spacious, and Cori's sort of draped on the uphol-stered bench at the foot of the bed, using her foot to poke the pile of my shoes near her, trying to unearth something that doesn't offend her. She has, at least once a day since she was eight, sprawled on this bench to tell me the secrets of her heart or the dramas of her friends. Not for the first time I thank my lucky stars that, against all odds, we never had to move after John left.

We had a great mortgage and loads of equity, and I suppose that's down to him—he insisted we put nearly a third down on this house to keep the monthly bill low and get it paid off faster. John was always really funny about debt. When he left, I refinanced from fif-teen years to thirty and didn't feel even remotely upset about it—and that dropped my monthly payment yet lower, making it cheaper to stay in our lovely big house full of memories than to rent anywhere nearby.

And it is a lovely house. The kids have their own rooms, plenty of closet space, which has gone from holding LEGO sets and dress-up outfits to being packed with comic books (Joe) and mall sweaters (Cori). My daughter owns every mall sweater ever sold. Some in mul-tiple colors. If I take her to the mall, I can be sure she is coming back with a sweater. She brandishes them with double clearance tags and her frequent-shopper discounts and tells me they were $6.88 or some other ridiculous price, but I cringe at the way she accumulates them, wears them once, and leaves them in a puddle on the floor for the rest of their days.

Still, she always looks so nice, not just from youth but also from some kind of eye for color and shape that skipped my generation. Anything I bring home from the store has to go by her before I cut the tags off, and many times she just looks at the clothes still in the bag and then raises her eyebrows skyward and says something like, "It's kind of exhausting to love someone who will never learn," or "Are you buying ugly clothes to make a point?"

I have just such a shopping bag today. I went to Target with a one-hundred-dollar budget—basically an extravagant no-limits shopping spree in clearance-rack dollars—and bought a stack of shirts and pants from the middle part of the store—not the totally dowdy "work" collections I usually beeline for just before the maternity clothes and the dressing rooms, but not the juniors madness of the front third of the store either. In my bag there are shirts in "trend" colors with vaguely low-cut necks, flowing blousy things with lace and embroidery, and even a just-above-the-knee skirt, though truth be told, I'm not entirely clear on how to wear skirts. Do they go with boots and tights in late May? I don't think I can do bare legs, can I? Is there some sort of publicly agreed-upon age limit for bare legs?

I also brought home two pairs of dark jeans with two very different cuts, even knowing at least one of them is heinously wrong and confident Cori will tell me which. That I have become pants blind—a common condition of aging, where you can no longer say with any authority which of your pants are cut fashionably and which are mom jeans—is proof of my complete inability to shop without help.

I take them all out while Cori watches me keenly and lay them out on the bed. "I was thinking," I tell her cautiously, "that these tops would match these pants, and these other ones would match the skirt, and then I won't need to take much luggage."

"Shoes?" is all she says.

"Oh yes. I am planning to wear them, absolutely."

She sighs. "Look. In New York City, with a schedule of conferences, meetings, dinners, and dates, shoes should make up approximately half of your baggage weight."

I blink at her. "Is this some kind of scientific finding? Can you direct me to the abstract for my own review? And who said anything about dates?"

"Mom. Stop being weird. You're going on dates."

I start to tell her I'm not but stop myself. A date might be kind of nice, actually, though I have no idea where any datees would come from. "Is any of this . . . date appropriate?"

She looks down at the clothes with scrutiny. "Well . . . maybe . . ." She pulls the lowest-cut top from the jeans side of the bed to the skirt side of the bed and drapes it with a long jangly necklace. Then she rolls up the skirt at the waist twice, making it significantly shorter, and puts it down with the top. Then she waves the "wait a second" finger at me and disappears into her room. When she comes back seconds later, she is holding a pair of shoes I'm pretty sure I would not have approved had I known she had them. She puts them at the bottom of the outfit and says, "Date clothes. Not a fancy date, but you're not really that fancy anyway."

I look at the conservative size-large mom clothes she's somehow turned into a hooker costume. "Cori, I'm not wearing that."

"Well, it doesn't matter, does it? Because no one said anything about dates." She waggles her eyebrows at me.

Just for a moment I indulge myself in the idea of meeting someone in New York. "These are really pretty shoes," I say, picking up one slingback and marveling at the luck of having a stylish daughter who wears the same shoe size as me. The toe is a black-and-gold geometric print—just a bit eighties, very "me" thirty years ago. The slingback strap loops all the way around the ankle, too, and is black leather.

There is a tiny gold buckle. They are at once feminine and authoritative, understated and sexy. They are the most aspirational shoes I have ever seen. I want to be the kind of person who wears these shoes.

"May I really borrow these?" I ask.

"Of course, Mom. Not like I'm wearing them around Dad anyway. If he's any kind of dad at all, he shouldn't allow it. They're weirdly sexy for how low the heel is, right?"

"You're right. You're not allowed to wear these."

Cori just laughs at me. "They were practically free anyway," she tells me, launching into the story of how she had a fifteen-dollars-off card and there was a 40 percent off sale at Macy's and so on and so forth. I tune out for a few moments, tilting my head and considering what it would feel like to wear a short skirt, slingbacks, and a slinky top around Manhattan in early spring. It would, I decide, feel incredible.

"I'll buy them from you," I tell her right in the middle of her story. "Or buy you another pair that are less . . . adult."

Cori beams. "Deal! Here." She hands me her smartphone, where she's already pulled up a pair of ridiculous teal lace-up gladiators marked down below twenty dollars. "These are the replacement pair," she says to me.

I look at them for a moment. They are flats. Flats.

"These are flats," I say aloud. "So then . . . it's going to be Brian?"

Cori sighs deeply and lets her head tip to the side. "Brian. He's very short."

"But cute," I say. "Are you taller than him?"

"We're the same. Do you think he has a short-man complex?"

"He's still growing, Cori. Besides, that's a thing people invented to justify judging men by their height."

"But what about Napoleon?" she asks me.

"Power-hungry madmen come in all shapes and sizes," I tell her. "Rather than worry about Brian's measurements, let's figure out if he's good enough for you."

More sighing from my teenager. "I don't know how to tell," she says.

"Slowly," I say. "With your shirt on."

Cori raises an eyebrow at me.

"Ok, pants."

"I can do that," she says, and every single bone in my body sings with motherly joy. "What am I looking for when I try to figure out if someone is good enough for me?" she asks.

"Well, what do you like most about the people you like? Include yourself," I instruct.

She thinks for a moment. "I like people who are pretty kind deep down. And also who tell the truth. I like people who show up when they say they're going to. Oh, and people who don't think they're better than everyone else."

I nod. "That's a terrific list of things to watch for in Brian. I see all of those things in you, so you deserve all that and more."

Cori chews her lip and works her jaw.

"What?" I ask her.

"Sometimes I act like I'm better than everyone else. You know, boys like it when you have confidence."

I smile. "Maybe it's not an act. After all, I think you're the best girl I've ever known."

"You're my mom. You have to think that."

I shake my head at her. "Not true. But anyway. You are wonderful. But there's plenty of wonderful to go around, so keep that in mind if you find yourself walking around with your nose in the air."

"I will if you will," she says.

"Will do what?" I ask her back.

"Not be a snob. You're not too good for the entire male gender."

"What? Who on earth said I was?"

"Well, why else wouldn't you go on a single date once in three years?"

I blink at her blindly. What can I say? Because I was convinced John left me because I was unlovable? Because I am a forty-year-old mom-shaped librarian, and not the porn kind with glasses and long hair in a bun but the regular kind with clogs and pants blindness? Because every man I meet in my daily life is a parent of one of my students or a teacher of one of my kids? Because somehow after all this time I am still married to my ex-husband?

"Mom? Are you there?" Cori is waving her hands in front of my face. "Ground control to Major Mom."

"Sorry, I spaced. I was thinking about . . ." My eyes dart around the room and land on the clock. "I was thinking about your brother. I'm supposed to bring oranges tonight. Do we have any oranges? I'd better get to Wegmans before pickup. Do you want anything?"

It's as easy as that. My daughter loves the Wegmans sushi counter. "*Sushi*!" she cries jubilantly, and all talk of dating is forgotten.

"Ok, sushi it is," I reply. "I'll be back in an hour and a half. Will you bag up whichever clothes are awful and match outfits for the rest while I'm gone?"

"Duh, Mom," she replies. "What do you want me to do with the other hour and twenty-nine minutes?"

I cock my head at her. "How about you write a college-admissions essay on the fine art of shoe packing for airline luggage weight restrictions?"

"I'll get right on it," she says sarcastically.

"Or text with Brian," I add as I'm halfway out the door so she can't feign disinterest. "Just a thought!"

———

When it is finally time for me to go, I feel like I am the child and my kids are sending me off to summer camp. John, Lena, and my neighbor Jackie, who has offered to watch over my house and be a backup plan for the kids if they need it, are all there for the big goodbye, and I have the distinct sensation of being shoehorned out the door. Before I know it, I am being reassured that all is well and I'll get lots of video calls and Jackie will look after the yard and mail and Lena will look after anything else. John looks so . . . capable as we all say goodbye. He brought extensive pics of the condo he's rented, which looks immaculate and well equipped, and he even is driving a rented Volvo. I can't help but think, *This is ok; they've got this*, even as my mom brain screams, *NO! WHAT ARE YOU DOING? DO NOT LEAVE YOUR CHILDREN!*

The sensation is so powerful that I actually make the cabbie turn around and drive me back by the house, pretending to have forgotten something. But when we reapproach, I see that the kids are sitting on either side of John on the front step, looking down at something. The book of hiking trails he brought over is open in his lap, overleaf unfolded wide to a map. His posture is relaxed and easy, leaned back, with each hand propping him up on either side behind the kids' backs. Cori's and Joe's heads are tilted in toward him, and they are laughing.

What did Cori tell me this morning? "Your work is done here, Mom." I laugh at the very thought. My work will never be done here. But for today, it's time for me to go. I tell the driver never mind, and we turn around, head back to the station. And I feel something happening to my shoulders that hasn't happened in five years—or maybe longer.

They're relaxing.

I feel the unfamiliar weight of my shoulders sliding down and the pleasant sensation of tension unwinding from my neck and the base of my head. *How long have I been holding my shoulders up by my ears?* I wonder. *And why was I doing that?*

I immediately think of the Christmas I caved and brought home a gaming system for my kids. The use policy on it is pretty stringent even now, and the first rule was I play every game they play. No *Call of Duty 17* coming in under the radar at my house. Joe wanted to play a driving-simulation game that required a little steering wheel attachment to the controller. He saved up and saved up and got the controller and the game, and then he came home with it knowing full well he would have to immediately hand it over to me.

I took it, we opened it, and Joe gave me the gist of the game: steer, don't crash, try to collect floating coin things, use turbo points. It looked almost exactly like the driving games I played at my guy friends' houses when I was in high school, except for better graphics and a very impressive soundtrack. I thought it would be no problem. But once I was playing, I was terrible. I couldn't steer and work the turbo at the same time, and I kept crashing into various obstacles like I was drunk. Finally Joe grabbed me by the shoulders from the rightward lean I was in as I tried to steer the car out of a puddle and said, "Mom, steer with the controller, not your body."

Now, as I sit on the hard wooden bench waiting for the New York express train, I realize I have been driving my life with my body. Trying somehow to carry my worries and sorrows and insecurities on my shoulders, as though I could wad up all the hurt and fear I've felt since John moved out, stuff it in a backpack, and hike through life with it. Every time I have fretted over Joe's social life or lain awake listening like a hawk for Cori to make curfew or looked at my income and our bills and tried to figure out who won't get paid, I have put that in the backpack and carried it around on my shoulders. They ache, and I haven't even noticed until right this minute.

Consciously, I take a huge breath. I bring my mind to those poor muscles and sinews and vessels and think, *Melt*. I think of my kids safe with their father, overseen by Jackie, who is overseen by Lena, and think again, *Melt*. I think of my waiting guest room in Talia's swank apartment and the classes I'll get to take at Columbia and the lunches at bistros with big, gorgeous, fresh salads and crisp white wines I'll linger over, and I just feel it happen for the first time in as long as I can remember: I melt.

And it feels so good.

And then my train comes, and the entire adventure begins.

CHAPTER FOUR

Dear Mom,

You're in New York! Having a life! Mom, I am so freaking proud of you. You are, like, a marvel and an inspiration to us all. I am totally being sarcastic, in case that's not clear. But really, I am proud that you finally took a vacation, even if it's not really a vacation and you're actually doing library stuff nonstop and the only way we got you to do it was to sacrifice our own week, which, let's be clear: Dad is not our first choice right now. But here we are, and Dad is, like, Mr. Happy Cheerleader, and he is going to give us anything we ask for out of guilt, and I will have failed myself and my country if I don't get out of this with a new car. At least. Joe is angling for Space Camp, did you know that? I am so proud of him. I didn't know he had it in him. And all you get is a stupid week in New York probably staying at, like, the Super 8 in Yonkers and reading books in bed all night.

You should have brought me with you. I'd show you how this whole vacation thing is done. We'd be at the spa—not the $12 nail salon but the spa that, like, rock stars go to. We'd get you a makeover and then go out to Balthazar and then go see Hamilton. *We would eat that pizza you fold in half, and we'd go to the art museums, and you'd let me drink white wine.*

Here is what I'm doing instead: the same thing I'd be doing pretty much if you were here. SOMEONE gave Dad a copy of Coach's summer rules, so I'm on curfew, and he is serving salad with every meal. Also, when we first walked into his apartment, there was Diet Coke freaking everywhere, and I was so pumped. Then, while I was literally in the bathroom doing my hair, the Diet Coke just vanished. Did you, like, text Dad and tell him no Diet Coke? How can you hate Diet Coke, Mom? Diet Coke is the foundation of America. Why do you hate this country so much?

Dad said I can have Diet Coke once a day before noon but only after practice, and he said I have to have a shot of wheatgrass juice to go with it. And I said, "Where is this wheatgrass juice coming from, the Bucks County Municipal Pool concession stand? Is it right next to the Slurpee machine?" And do you know what he said back? He said, "Your team doesn't have a juicer?" No kidding, Mom. (I was going to say "No shit." But I'm moving into my summer vocab for lifeguarding, so, no kidding.) I was like, to Dad, "Hey, Dum-Dum, on what planet does a community day school have a juicing machine for team sports?" And he got out this link to Harvard Business Review, *which is something he reads, like, on the regular, and showed me a story about a juice-bar company that revolutionized the efficacy of NFL double-day practices, and then he went on his Amazon app, and—no shit— he bought a wheatgrass juicer for the team.*

He is from another planet, Mom. Planet Rich Guy. But look, it's not all bad because now my team gets a juicer, and I got a subscription to Harvard Business Review, *and I am pretty sure I used the words* revolutionized the efficacy *appropriately in that sentence up there, so it's win-win-win! Dad buys our love, I get a vocabulary, team gets a juicer. Except I guess you are the loser. I have to remind you of that, according to every teen movie I have ever watched.*

But if it makes you feel any better, it's almost like you're here every time you text me and tell me to get reading on my next book. And not in a good way. Untwist your thong: I will get on with it. I'm just letting the love story of the senator's wife and her rich married boyfriend wash over me.

Next, according to you, I'm supposed to read The Book Thief. *I read the first chapter, and let me tell you, it sounds GRIM. Pro tip, Mom: It's not summer reading if the narrator is actual Death Incarnate. Like, if you open any magazine ever and look at their Summer Beach Reads Roundup and see a book starring Death, just let me know. Until that day, I am reading* Twilight *again because if I am going to be goth, then it should be sexy goth at least.*

What? At least I'm reading.

Love,

Your vitamin-rich daughter, Cori

—

New York is exactly as I left it—and entirely different. Grand Central is the same grimy/glossy crossbreed that it should be. The oyster place is going nowhere. The hubbub is as loud, the goings-on are as ongoing. But the clothes are different. The stores are unfamiliar. The sense of having been here before and yet being utterly lost is pervasive.

I march through the echoey corridors and try not to look confused searching for the right subway stairs. Then I get my carry-on suitcase stuck in the turnstiles and give up on coolness. Hello, New York! Get ready to chew up and spit out another willing bumpkin.

Last week when I gave her the high sign about my arrival, Talia told me her apartment is a zillion miles from Columbia and tried to talk me into skipping the conference and just using my time to "lie about the apartment looking wan and drinking wine." I couldn't look wan if I were on a hunger strike, so I stuck to my plan, believing there are worse things than an hour on the train each way. I can read. It will be peaceful.

But it's rush hour, and I wedge myself on the local because the first two express trains are too full to fit my suitcase, much less my body, and there is nothing peaceful about what happens next. We are packed in so tightly that I do not need to hold a handrail to stand upright, but the helpful spinner wheels on my suitcase that are so nice when rushing through an airport—something I never do, by the way—become deadly on the train. At every stop—and there are about four hundred stops— the bag demonstrates the "thing in motion tends to remain in motion" principle and rolls into the person next to me, banging them against the shins. I attempt to hold the suitcase back but am being pressed forward by the postworkout gym rat behind me, who is carrying a duffel on his shoulder and letting it hit me in the kidneys every time he shifts an inch. And so we go. My suitcase bruises shins, the duffel of rocks bruises me, and just out of reach, eight middle-aged men in suits sit comfortably on the benches that line the car, legs spread open like they are on their own personal Barcaloungers, papers folded into precise fourths, phones clenched in right hands for dear life. It's a funny little thing, the miracle of getting a subway seat, and I am starting to feel bitter that I do not have one when a woman with a pregnant belly the size of a small neutron star gets on the train, and the humanity parts. She is sweaty and wide and no kind of fertility goddess, but first one, now two, then three men leap to their feet in something resembling a panic. "Ma'am," each shouts. "D'ya wanna sit down?" She does, and one of the men who wasn't lucky enough to actually give up his seat to her puts his phone away and carries her enormous Bed Bath & Beyond bag on his lap for the rest of the ride.

Oh, how it warms my heart, this whole little play that runs a thousand times a day. New York. The city that never sits.

When we get to Brooklyn Heights, I pop out of the train like a champagne cork the moment the doors open. I walk the wrong direction on several slanted, crisscrossing streets, falter a bit, and then become the woman getting turn-by-turn directions from her phone while walking. Luckily, it is New York, and nothing here is noteworthy. Certainly not me.

Finally I find Talia's building. It is not what I expected. Based on Facebook updates, her monthly editor's letter, and my memories, Talia is very glitzy. This building is not glitzy. It's redbrick, no edifice, very institutional. It's not a divided brownstone with cute wrought iron gates or a shiny glass tower with a bank of elevators zooming to the stratosphere. It looks to be about ten stories high and utilitarian in design, and the lobby is not exactly inviting me in.

Even so, I grab the handle and pull.

The door is locked.

I tilt my head. Pull again. No, this door is definitely locked. I put my hands around my face and try to see inside. Another bank of doors, then a small lobby with a desk. A concierge desk, one would think. A desk of a person who would, ostensibly, see me struggling with luggage and a locked door and get over here and let me in.

There is no one at the desk. There is no one in the lobby, period. There is no indication whatsoever that anyone has ever been in the lobby or that this apartment building is in fact an apartment building and not an abandoned shirt factory. Are there even mailboxes? I don't see any in the vestibule. What kind of no-doorman building doesn't have mailboxes in the vestibule?

Also, why did I assume this was a doorman building? Why did I figure Talia had amazing digs? Did she even answer me those weeks ago when I asked her if she had room for me? I look back at our texts. She did not answer. But it seemed like a yes to me at the time. What if she lives in a studio and expects me to crash out on the couch? Well, then I guess I will crash on the couch, I realize with some kind of gloomy disappointment. I was imagining at least a bed to myself.

Ah well, I'm a grown woman, and a week on a couch four feet from the kitchen is kind of a bummer at this stage in my life, but a far smaller bummer than a thousand-dollar hotel bill. And besides, Talia is so fun. Wherever she lives, it will be fun. Think of the zillions of trendy, twee spots I passed on the way to her apartment, after all. An artisan candy-bar shop that sells homemade Snickers and crème de menthes. A patisserie prominently displaying a wedding cake made entirely of lemony-yellow macarons. A bar designed to look like an ancient dive with a high shine on it that gives its youth away. A chalkboard sign outside, intricately hand-lettered with vintage flair, reads, FAR OR NEAR, WE DRINK BLATZ BEER. And next to it, the ubiquitous cotton-sportswear store boasting thong leotards and inexpensive American-made T-shirts cut for the bodies of five-foot-eight toddlers.

I do not need a bed proper to enjoy a week in Brooklyn among the young and beautiful. We are going to have an amazing time. I text Talia.

how do i get into your apt?

There is no immediate reply. Oh well. I guess I will go have a cup of sustainably sourced, frog-safe, hand-roasted, burr-ground pour-over coffee while I wait for further instructions. It's a good thing I only packed one very small suitcase.

Two cups of $7.50 coffee later, I have not heard from Talia. I also haven't heard from the many other people I texted to pass the time. Nothing from the kids, which makes sense because they should be at Cori's diving meet right now. A thumbs-up and the swimmer emoji from John, who is doing "same." Nothing from Lena, who has plenty of good reasons not to be sitting by the phone waiting to entertain her lonely, temporarily homeless friend. My neighbor Jackie writes back when I say, "How's it going there?" But all she says is "All's fine. Hope you're having fun!" so I do not take that as an invitation to chat.

I have my e-reader, and I've started and stopped a few different new YA titles, always looking for those unputdownable reads that I think will appeal to my trickier readers, and I've checked the address Talia sent me a few hundred times, and the weather, and the conference information page, and anything else I could think of to pass the time. Now it's getting on in the day, and there's supposed to be a cocktail meet and greet up at the conference in two hours. Knowing it could take a full hour just to get there, I am starting to feel nervous.

I text Talia again, sending her back the address she sent me and writing,

Do I have the right address? I'm sorry I didn't think to figure out the key situation. I guess I assumed you had a doorman?

Then I wait five minutes and call her. No answer. I leave the calmest possible voice mail and then say, out loud, "Ok. This is bad."

And this being New York, no one bats an eye.

I collect my things and go back to the building. There is still no doorman, no mailboxes, no buzzers, no way in.

I wait ten minutes. No one so much as walks down this side of the street, much less opens the door.

I look harder for a buzzer, planning to start disturbing the neighbors. There is no buzzer. In what universe is there an apartment building with no doorman but also no buzzer? This cannot be the right place. I triple-check the numbers on the door against the numbers Talia sent me. This is the correct address. Could a person get her own address wrong? Could she have given me the wrong street name?

Who would do that, though?

For the tenth time now I scroll back to our minimal planning. She said to text before I came; I texted. She wrote back telling me to go straight to the apartment and that she'd "tell the people downstairs to watch for" me. I assumed that meant there would be a doorman. What other people downstairs could there be? Maybe a landlord or super? But there's no basement apartment where such a person would be accessible, and no way to the back of the building that I can see either. Just a locked side door with no window that I presume is for trash removal.

Totally stumped, I step to the other side of the street and look up at the building. This is a big, amazing city. People work all kinds of hours. Someone must be home right now.

But the windows are all dark, reflecting the city back to me, and on this fine, sunny day, there is no way of knowing who is home. Or if anyone lives here at all. Or what the hell is going on.

I call Talia again. This voice mail is a little more panicky. When I hang up, I realize it is time for me to give up on this building and move on to plan B.

But what on earth is my plan B?

—

There was one moment after John left, not a long one but a real one, when I thought I was going to die.

It was money that did it. Money, a broken tooth, and bed-wetting.

Joe was eight years old. He was a late bloomer in everything, so different from Cori, who, after spending a day at her grandmother's farm and playing with older kids from a neighboring farm with no indoor plumbing, asked them why they went into the tiny house with the moon shape cut into the door. They explained—quite clearly, I suppose—that tinkling in your diaper was for babies, and from that day on she peed in a little potty I had to put outside and rig a tarp around. I'm not sure what we would have done if it had been winter. A few weeks of that, and she came in, climbed up on the real toilet, pooped, and demanded a cookie, and that was toilet training.

Joe, not so much. For Joe I tried all culturally approved methods, including letting him toddle around the house naked from the waist down, which resulted in pee in all rooms of the house *except* for the bathroom. I had some decent success with bribing him with toy trains, but at night he used a pull-up diaper for a year longer than many moms might have tolerated. My mom, especially, was horrified by this, and I remember crying from the disapproval after every visit. Even after all that tolerance, though, when he was finally in "big-boy underpants" and completely housebroken by day, if he got sick, had a nightmare, or drank too much before bed, he'd wake up wet until he was almost five.

Then, three years later, his dad disappeared, and Joe took it out on his mattress pad.

I was already tired. Cori was so mad all the time. She called me names, said I was ugly and that was why her dad left, said she was ugly and that was why her dad left, said she hoped he would die. After any little normal frustration of life, like a lost shoe or a hard test, she'd rail and rail, and then after twenty minutes she'd let me put my arms around her, and she'd cry and cry. Joe had started sneaking into my bed, coming in silently around four a.m., tossing and turning and kicking me after he was out cold again, leaving me to choose between his twin bunk or the couch until the sun came up. We were out of money, but I refused to consider selling the house and was paying old bills out of the modest salary I got from Country Day and then putting new bills on one of three low-rate introductory cards I'd taken out the minute I'd realized I could. I hadn't figured out how to be a working single mother yet. I was disorganized and grieving and wouldn't surrender to the situation, too wedded to the idea that this all was temporary, that it was only a matter of time before John appeared back in our lives.

So we were surviving, but only just.

Then I got a cold. It was just a run-of-the-mill cold, but it was enough to destroy our precious balance. I couldn't get myself to cook after a long day, so we ordered pizza, so we ran up more bills, so we maxed out a card. I was stoned on DayQuil all day and got reprimanded at work, and Cori caught me crying in the car. Then I caught her shoplifting a lipstick. Then Joe started wetting his bed. That added a half hour of awake time to my night, changing sheets and getting him back to bed, and hours of worry to my day. Then while he and I were visiting the child psychologist I couldn't afford to deal with the bedwetting, Cori fell off some friend's longboard and broke one of her front teeth in half. The goddamned moron mother of the friend called 911, of all things, instead of just calling me. It was a chipped tooth in a cul-de-sac ten minutes from the dentist's office, but now I was paying for an ambulance.

Thankfully I was able to meet them at the ER before she was fully checked in. I turned her around, looked her over for other damage, took a pamphlet on concussion, and marched her right out of there before anyone took my credit card. The tooth was repaired, the child psychologist was reassuring, and the ER bills had been narrowly averted. The crisis was over. And yet, around two a.m. that night, I had a panic attack that felt like nothing I had ever experienced before.

In that moment, I knew I would die. Knew with certainty. Knew if I took one more step ahead in this hard life I had tumbled into, I would collapse. I had to stop everything. I sat up in my bed, wheezing, and the room began to go black. I was in a tunnel of light. The air stopped coming in. I was breathing, but air wasn't reaching my lungs. I tried sniffing in through my nose and felt light. I thought, *I am dying*, but I didn't feel afraid of that. It was another day like this one that scared me so. Another day like this was just not something I could survive. In the minute, the hour, however long this attack lasted, I made all the plans I could possibly make to escape my situation. My house would sell for enough. My mother would come and watch over the kids until John came back. Maybe I would be brave enough to kill myself for the life insurance—oh, that awful panic that made that seem like the best plan—or maybe I would just run away, as far as I could get, and be alone for the rest of my days and never feel true joy again.

In that moment, those were my only two choices. I believed that. I thank God I was so sleep deprived that night, because the only thing that won out over that deathly panic in the end was exhaustion, as well as confusion over which pills to take and whether I had enough to do the job.

The next morning, early, I called Lena. I didn't tell her everything—but then, I didn't have to. I said only, "It's too much. I can't."

She didn't say, "You can."

Better still, she didn't say, "But you have to."

She said, "I'll be there in ten minutes." She was. She put me to bed with half a Benadryl and told me to sleep as much as I possibly could. I was barking orders about the kids, and then she pulled up the covers and said firmly, "*Enough*." I was so tired I fell asleep the moment she turned out the light.

And so when the choices were sleep or die, I slept. I woke up two days later. The kids were told I had gotten really tired. They were told they had a new set of chores befitting their new status as equal members of a three-person household rather than two kids and two adults. Using one of those teacher-size note boards, Lena made a list of all the work needing done in a regular household and then asked Joe and Cori to put a tick next to everything they could possibly do. The first two were "earn money" and "drive." The kids quickly figured out that since they couldn't do those two highly vital tasks, they had better take on a lot of other things. They needed to be asked, and they always waited until two hours before allowance time, but they did their fair share from then on out. Lena used a lying-around pay stub to sign me up for Supplemental Nutrition Assistance—food stamps—and gave me a stern lecture about pride. The state started sending me almost $350 to pay for groceries each month. I caught up on my bills, rented out my garage to someone who wanted winter storage for his boat, canceled our streaming services, sold my stuff, got my shit together, threw a fit until our insurer paid for Joe's therapy, and solved each problem in its turn until the crisis was over. And when it was, I told myself I'd never be as dependent on any one person again as I had been on John.

And I never will be.

So I'd better think of somewhere to sleep in New York City.

———

Plan B, it turns out, is to forget how to get back to the subway.

Once again I am juggling luggage and listening to turn-by-turn directions just to retrace my steps for six blocks. When I arrive at the station and am able at last to put away my phone and get myself together, I find myself sort of disappointed in this kinder, gentler New York where no one robbed the slow-moving target I made of myself. Then I wait for the train . . . ten, then fifteen, then twenty minutes before another packed Manhattan-bound train pulls up to the platform. Just as it does, I realize that I am on the wrong platform—worse, the wrong station—to get up to Columbia. And when I finally do straggle into the conference, I will be the dope wheeling my suitcase and wearing stretch pants. I cannot think of how I could possibly get into my cocktail attire between here and there. Even buying a cup of coffee in a Starbucks won't get me the kind of bathroom where I could safely, say, take my shoes off without acquiring several diseases and maybe some cockroaches too.

I could look up the location of Talia's offices and try her there, but there's no indication that she'd be there (or is even still alive), and since the magazine she works for is part of an international multimedia conglomerate in midtown Manhattan, there's no chance of me getting past the front lobby alone.

But then I think of the old St. Regis maneuvers Talia and I used to pull. Do I still have what it takes to pull a fast one on a hotel clerk?

I guess there's just one way to find out.

The only time John and I came to New York together, we stayed the night at a lovely three-star boutique hotel on the Upper West Side. Right on the way to Columbia. It had a gorgeous French bistro with the prettiest, cleanest, sunniest dining room I had ever eaten in, with glass doors in lieu of walls that folded open in the warm afternoons so that tables spilled out onto the sidewalks and the glasses of white wine glinted in the sun.

The rooms were a small fortune per night—maybe double the nicest hotel I'd stayed in previously, and there's no way I can swing that cost as a single mother. But I don't need to actually buy a room to attempt a trick I learned from Talia in college.

I spend the whole train ride to the Upper West Side working up the guts to try it and simultaneously trying to make myself look like the sort of person who would succeed. After I switch trains twice I get a seat and dig around in my luggage for lipstick, mascara, and a very expensive gold necklace John bought me when I had Cori. I mess around with my outfit a bit and finally, feeling wildly self-conscious, change into Cori's black slingbacks, stuffing my Dansko clogs into my bag and jamming it shut. Finally I switch my black nylon travel bag out for my ace in the hole—a real, honest-to-god Céline handbag Lena gave me to use for this trip. It's beautiful, rich black leather, lambskin lining, gold chain, and iconic sprawling folded sides, with the stamped logo front and center for good measure. If I succeed, it will be because of this bag.

At Seventy-Ninth Street I come up to the street. It is still bright and sunny, though a little less light reaches through all the tall buildings and dense streets than it did in Brooklyn Heights. I put on my Target sunglasses, hope they don't look quite as Targety as they probably do, and feel around the two blocks for the hotel, hoping it is right where I left it all those years ago.

There it is. The bistro is still there, too, with no sign of change. The doors are open, and a few early diners are at the sidewalk tables, enjoying the early evening glow. There's a pleasant buzz about the place. Lots of people are going in and out of the hotel doors. That's exactly as I want it. So here we go.

I take in a deep breath and try to channel Jamie Lee Curtis in *A Fish Called Wanda*. The Platonic ideal of a con woman. I push open the door and quickly size things up.

Ok, good, one person at the desk, a line to check in. This is going to be easier than I thought. I get in the line as if to wait, but I have no intention of reaching the front of the line. I check my watch—which I'm actually not wearing. I sigh loudly and look around. I spot a bell-man who is already looking at me. I take my opening.

"Desculpe," I say. "Necesito un favor?"

He replies in a quick tongue I can barely follow. Apparently I fooled him into treating me like a fluent speaker. That'll teach me.

I smile meekly. "I'm waiting to check in, but the line is long, and I'm supposed to meet my husband for drinks in five minutes. Can I just stow my luggage with you and check in later?"

"Of course, ma'am," he replies in English. "What is your last name?"

Knowing there's a tiny chance he might try to connect it to a room number, I say, "Actually, if there's a bathroom I might use first, I'll freshen up quickly and then give you my bag. Could you point the way?"

The helpful fellow does just that. I rush to the ladies', which of course is beautiful and clean and has all kinds of lovely toiletries. There I turn myself into the most presentable version of me I can be without a shower and dash out. I am wearing a skirt now, and a pretty cap-sleeved rayon blouse that wouldn't wrinkle in an avalanche, and a little light-weight wool blazer. I feel like a person. A librarian person, but still. A person. I am so, so glad I shaved my legs this morning.

Five minutes later I come back out, find the helpful fellow, give him my bag, and act very rushed. It's easy, because I am in fact very rushed at this point. I tip him ten bucks, and when he asks again for my name, I just holler, "Just write *Sondra* on it! Gracias!" and rush out the door before he can push the issue. I say Sondra because Sondra is the most elegant name in the world, and anyone named Sondra should be staying in a beautiful hotel like this whenever she travels anywhere. And then I burst out into the sunshine again and mentally give myself a high five and say to the city, "See, New York? I can still handle you. I can still handle you just fine."

CHAPTER FIVE

Dear Mom,

I have a question for you when you do read this: Were you and Dad ever really happy? I look back and I don't remember you guys being especially happy or sad. Now Dad seems incredibly happy, but I'm not sure if it's forced happiness to make us think we're all having tons of fun together or if he's just a happy person or what. And I'm wondering, Was he like that when we were all together? Did you guys, like, dance around the kitchen while you were cooking together or hold hands at the park while Joe and I played or stuff like that? Sorry, I know those are both scenes from movies, but I don't have a ton of real-life married love experience to go on. Trinity's mom is getting another divorce, did I tell you that? Whenever I think my dad is an asshole, I just have to look over at her house and think, "Could be worse." Sorry, Trinity, but Hashtag Truth.

So I guess I'm asking, Did Dad make you happy? Does being in love make you happy? Were you two ever in love? Super easy questions.

Brian makes me sort of happy. He's, like, not that tall, as I've mentioned, but he's still very cute, and he compliments me a lot. I like that. Other than that, I'm not so sure about the whole thing. He texts me more than even you do. His texts are moronic. Like, "Sup." And then a poop emoji. I don't really want to encourage that. So I don't write back, and then ten minutes later I get "U mad?" and another poop emoji.

It's almost enough to make me lecture him about the lost art of letter writing, but then I don't, because I am not an almost forty-year-old librarian. Unlike some people.

When I started hanging out with Brian, he seemed interesting. He had a lot of smart things to say about school and our futures. Like, I was talking about colleges—which ones had scholarships and good loans. He said we had to shape our dreams around the world as it would be, not as it was. Which at first, huh? And then he talked about how his dad went to school for being a newspaper reporter and he took out a ton of college loans and then when he graduated there weren't any more newspapers left and now he hates his life, and how the most important thing is we don't mortgage our futures to the past.

So that's interesting, right? Like, you love your job, as you never stop telling us, but will there even be any libraries by the time I graduate from college? We talked for hours about other dying jobs, like writer or cab driver or mail carrier or store owner. We talked about a future where we just read social media posts in self-driving cars, and when we need something, we print it out on our 3-D printers.

So right, that's Brian. A few weeks of kind of cool futurist theorizing and then, the second I agree to go out with him, poop emojis. Today I tried to get him into another one of his interesting conversations, and the whole time he was trying to make out, and then he said, like, "Forget the future. We have to live in the now!" and I was like, get off me.

But what can I do, Mom? You go into summer with a boyfriend, you are stuck with him until September, unless you want to be the third wheel for the rest of the entire summer. And I know that sounds heartless, but I had high hopes for Brian, and I don't want to stay home every night while everyone else is coupled up. Trinity is madly in love with Dane, so we can forget about seeing anything besides the back of her head until that wears off. I guess if they break up, I'll have a single friend and I won't have to worry about being a social pariah, but if they don't, it's so nice to have a plus-one, and when we're together, we do have fun, even if his texts are a drag. Plus, Brian is a good kisser.

Added benefit: Dad is going to absolutely hate him.

Love,

Your heartless daughter, Cori

—

The great hall of Columbia's main library is a crush. The American Library Educators Association has many smaller events all over the country, but this is one of the big ones—popular because of the fun destination, well attended because of grants for rural and urban teachers alike to stay on top of media trends. It attracts everyone from young MLS candidates to grizzled vets who are already collecting their pensions but just can't quit the lifestyle. I fall squarely in the middle—decent credentials and a plum job at a spendy school, but no academic chops like the herd of PhDs who get invited personally.

This evening's event is sponsored by a publisher of early-reader material, so there are familiar recurring-character cardboard cutouts all over the room. Many grade school teachers are posing next to Flat Stanley, setting down their plastic cups of wine first so they can post the resulting pictures in their offices. For elementary school librarians, a picture of yourself with Flat Stanley is about as close as you can get to full-on street cred.

There are passed trays of food, and I position myself near the door the caterers first come through and try to eat my weight in tiny quiches so I can have a glass of wine without toppling over. While I snarf, I review the program that was tucked into the gift tote the publisher's PR youth handed me when I registered. All the while, I constantly check my phone. Nothing from Talia. I am starting to imagine scenarios where she was hit by a cab on the way to work. I know this is a ridiculous worry—Talia is famously scattered and disorganized and probably just put her phone down somewhere and hasn't noticed it's missing yet—but I still find myself trying to figure out what the hell I should do if I don't hear from her by the time the event ends in a few hours. Call hospitals? Check with her mom back in Ohio? I don't have the first idea of where I would start tracking her down.

It is while I am juggling my phone, my conference brochure, and two—yep, two—crab tartlets that a woman comes up to me and tells me loudly, "You're doing it wrong."

I look up and drop the brochure and then the phone. The tartlets, obviously, I save at all costs.

The woman is a tall, imposing character with the face of a Disney villainess. Her nose comes to a sharp point that actually threatens me. "Am I in your way?" I ask, because I have no idea what else to say, and I'm kind of spooked.

She laughs, and her eyes soften as she picks up my phone for me. "Here, you eat those—I'll hold this."

Obediently, I stuff a tart in my mouth and free up a hand to take back my phone.

"You're supposed to guzzle the free wine first, before it runs out, and *then* gobble up the tiny food," the stranger says, gesturing with her head to her own glass of red. "And you're not supposed to look at that stupid brochure. It doesn't have the important information in it."

I tilt my head at her. "What is the important information?"

"The most important information is how few of the boring conference courses you can go to and still get your continuing ed credits. Like, for example, there are two guest speakers at this party, so even though there is free booze and food, it counts just as much as it would to go to two sessions early tomorrow morning, where they only serve weak coffee and bananas."

I frown. I am teaching an early session here tomorrow morning. "Oh, I see," I say. "That explains why it's so crowded."

"Don't tell me you came for the speakers," she says, her voice warm and teasing at once.

"Well, I missed dinner due to some logistical snafus . . . so I'd have to say I came for the crab tartlets," I say. "But after I get some more food in my stomach, I will be most interested in the speakers, yes."

"You're the model citizen," she says. "Or you just need some wine. I'm Kathryn. From Chicago Public Schools, and I don't know another living soul here, but largely these attendees look about as fun as a rainy day in Cleveland. Have you ever seen so many embroidered polos? White or red?"

"Red, please," I say. "Nice to meet you. I'm Amy. Byler. From Pennsylvania."

"Be right back, Amy Byler."

While Kathryn fetches me a glass of wine, I check my phone one last time. I send a text and a Facebook message to Talia and call it out of my hands for the rest of the night. If I don't hear from her by the end of the evening, I'll . . . what? I guess I'll find a Days Inn. Even the swankiest city in the nation must have a Days Inn. It will probably cost me a month's grocery budget, but what else can I do? Maybe I can try for reimbursement from school when I get home.

I am just putting the useless phone away when Kathryn returns. "Kids?" she asks me as I take the generous glass of wine she brought back.

"I teach in a K–12 private school," I begin. "But I do adolescents—"

"No, I mean do you have kids," she interrupts.

"Oh." I nod. "Yes. Two kids, both in the upper school. One girl, one boy. The girl does—"

"I have two children in diapers," Kathryn interrupts again. "One year old and almost three. Both boys. Both hellions. I haven't been out of my house without at least one of them clinging to some part of my body since the first one was conceived. Until today. Let me tell you, I have had more complete thoughts in the last three hours than I had in the previous three years. Do you know how many people's butts I've wiped at this conference so far?"

"Uh—"

"Zero butts. And I will wipe zero butts for the next three days. Well, I will be responsible for my own butt. Unless there is a bidet in the hotel room! How great would that be?"

"Uh—"

"Still, one butt is a third as many butts as I usually have to wipe, so this is the greatest weekend of my life."

"I remember those days," I tell her wistfully.

"Tell me it gets easier," she says. "You did this. You haven't driven your car off a cliff yet."

I nod. "It gets so, so much easier," I tell her. "My teenagers are totally potty trained, for one."

She laughs.

"And you will come to get to know their personalities and really like them," I go on. "That takes a little while, but it happens. Then things get progressively less intense. They start dressing themselves and entertaining themselves and feeding themselves, and then one day they are in driver's ed scaring you out of your wits." *And abandoning you to hang out with your common-law ex-husband*, I add silently.

"That is very good to hear," she says.

"You're in the thick of it," I say.

"Right now, my idiot husband is in the thick of it," she says. "I told him, you put these babies inside me; now you are going to keep them alive all by yourself while I drink myself silly and dine out on world cuisine and sleep in until nine a.m. every day and watch *Golden Girls* repeats on the hotel cable."

I smile. "That is an excellent plan."

"Thank you. Why are you here?"

"What do you mean?" I ask.

"Are you running away from your kids too?"

"Oh. No. Well . . . no. I mean . . . no, definitely not. If anything, they're running away from me," I finally finish.

"What do you mean?"

"Well . . ." I take a swig of wine and try to decide how much to tell this vivacious, friendly, but definitely evil-looking woman. "My ex-husband has been out of the country for a while, and he came back to spend a week with them. So I had nothing else to do."

"Oh my god. You are the luckiest woman in the world."

I laugh. "I can see why you'd say that."

"So you'll be spending an entire week in New York with no kids? That's like . . . my wildest dream. You're living the dream. Where are you staying?"

I inhale. "I'm not . . . entirely sure . . . ," I start. "I am definitely staying with a friend from college after the conference is over. But tonight I haven't been able to reach her. So I think I need to find a hotel."

"You don't have a hotel reservation?"

I shrug, acting like I'm not shot through with panic over this myself. "It's New York. Lots of hotel rooms."

"Lots of tourists too."

I force a confident smile. "Something will pan out."

"Hotels here are so expensive."

I take a drink of my wine. I'm starting to feel pretty freaked out. Does tonight end with me cowering on a park bench until dawn?

"What time is the first speaker tonight?" I ask my frightening new friend.

She looks at a pretty gold watch that dangles on her bony wrist. "Thirty more minutes until the first one. It's that author who wrote the first twenty Dum-Dum Doofus Dorkface books. Groan."

I can't help but agree. Tonight is the night the publisher gets to trot out the jewels in their literary crown, but this particular jewel is more akin to a thorn in the side of every early-literacy instructor. "She gets a lot of kids interested in reading," I say charitably.

"Hmph," says Kathryn. "Reading about farts."

I cough on my wine. "And boogers," I add, when I have my breath back. "Who else is tonight, again?" I ask, because somehow despite staring at that stupid program five minutes ago, I cannot keep the many keynotes that this conference offers straight.

"It's last year's Library Educator of the Year. The hot one," she adds gleefully.

"I didn't realize there were hot library educators," I admit.

"You mean besides the two of us?" Kathryn laughs gaily. "Yes, this is that super hot guy from the inner city who *Dangerous Mind*ed all the kids into reading Shakespeare in 4K or something."

I nod because this is vaguely familiar. "It wasn't Shakespeare. It was Bradbury, and they were sixth graders, but they were reading above grade level by the end of one semester. So it's pretty astonishing."

She nods. "Plus he's super hot. You'll see. Oh! Are you single? It sounded like you were single. I wonder if Hot Educator of the Year is single. How do we find out?"

"Maybe they'll say when they introduce him. 'Our Hot Educator of the Year studied at Caltech, specializes in ELL coaching, and loves long walks on the beach.'"

"Heh!" says Kathryn. "Perfect. Then we just have to do your star charts, and we're set."

"Kathryn," I say slowly. "Would you mind saving a seat for me for the Dum-Dum lady? I am starting to have flop sweats over my hotel situation."

She smiles obligingly. "I wouldn't mind one bit. You're my only friend here, after all," she says teasingly, and I have to laugh that a woman who looks so much like the bitch boss from a rom-com is so delightfully chummy.

"One friend is all you need if she's standing close enough to the crab tarts," I say. "I'm going to make some phone calls and find you before the keynotes start. Hopefully it won't take long to get myself a bed for the night."

"If you strike out, there's always the Hot Educator of the Year," she says with a wave. "I'm sure he'd be happy to share."

———

I call the Upper Manhattan Days Inn. I call three other nearby places with similarly low star ratings. These places are all booked. It is Friday, after all, and they are very sorry, but did I realize a library convention was in town?

I start calling affordable-sounding places in Lower Manhattan, and they, too, are booked. A bloggers' convention. A nursing convention. A convention for conventioneers. It's the first weekend of summer in the most fantastic city in the world, and all the people on budgets in the entire United States—nay, the world—are in town right now, and they made reservations. There are no hotel rooms in my price range.

I check to see if I can still get an online deal, but no luck—the sites don't let you book day-of rooms after six p.m. I look at the train schedule to see if I can get back home tonight. Nope, last train leaves in four minutes. I text Talia again. All illusion of being cool and all hope of not being a pest are gone, so I just send a message that reads, "SOS HOMELESS," and stare at the screen for two minutes, waiting for three dots that show she might respond to my message. There are no three dots. I call the offices of her magazine. I slowly type her last name into the directory and then go straight into her voice mail.

Finally, desperate, I call the Hotel la Provençe. After all, my luggage has been enjoying their hospitality for hours now. Maybe I can live like the other half, just for one night. I can always get a part-time job to pay it off later. Maybe it's time I learned to be a fry cook.

"Hello," I say, sounding as stilted as I feel, when a human answers and thanks me for calling the Hotel la Provençe. "I'm wondering if you have any rooms free for tonight?"

"Oh yes, I'm sure we can find you something," says the friendly feminine human. "Two doubles or a king?"

"I . . . well." I don't care, as I can't afford either, so I say, "What rates are available?"

"Rates, ma'am?" says the voice. "No special rates at the moment, I'm afraid. Well, there might be a fill rate. Could you please hold?"

I hold. I try to imagine numbers she might say. If she says less than $150, I will just do it, because I need to sleep somewhere. But what if she says more? Then I guess I will just do it, still, but it will hurt.

She comes back on the line. "Wonderful news, ma'am," she says. "We do have a king room available, and it's at our lowest available rate, which is thirty percent less than our regular rate. Would you like me to book it?"

"Um," I say. "How much?"

I hear typing. "Before taxes and fees . . . oh! It only comes to two hundred and seventy dollars per night."

My brain statics out, and I audibly moan. If I have to stay there for all three days of the conference, I will be out eight hundred bucks on hotel bills I wasn't expecting to pay. That is many, many pizza nights with my kids, many trips to Wegmans, a whole week of sleepaway camp per child. I do *not* want to spend it on a stupid hotel room in stupid New York. I will only be in the hotel for a few hours, and most of them asleep. This situation makes me so mad.

"I'll take it," I say.

"Very good. And when would you like to check out?" she asks politely, as though I haven't just groaned into the phone like a sexual predator.

"Tomorrow, thanks," I say.

"Ok, one night, then, and what credit card would you like to use for the reservation?"

Then it hits me. Credit card. John's credit card. Which he gave me for emergencies. "This is an emergency," I think out loud.

"Sorry, ma'am, did you say an emergency? Do you need me to call someone?"

"No, no, sorry, I just . . . hang on and let me get my card."

I read her John's credit card number, she tells me the total, and I flinch again and then try to make myself laugh. This is what the card was for, right? For emergencies. John told me to use it. I bet he didn't think I'd put $300 on it, but so what? Screw that guy. He owes me way, way more than that in emotional damages.

Still . . . will he be angry? Will I have to apologize when I get back home, or worse, pay him back?

But I can't know the answers to any of those questions, so I read out the card information and pray for the best. Just before I hang up I tell her to put the reservation under the name *Sondra Sawyer* because that way it will match my luggage and also because that is the most elegant name in the world, as mentioned.

After all, Amy Byler does not stay in the Hotel la Provençe. But Sondra Sawyer does, using her ex-husband's American Express. And she might even order room service.

—

What I wake up to the next morning is not real life. It is Sondra Sawyer life. I am lying in a sumptuous king bed with beautiful pressed cotton linens, down pillows, and a coverlet that smells faintly of lavender. Next to me on the marble-topped nightstand is a bottle of Perrier, and in a matter of minutes someone will be knocking on my door with a hot breakfast—oh, and they're here now! I grab a hotel-provided robe, noting with great pleasure the way it perfectly matches the hotel-provided slippers and hotel-provided sleep mask, and throw it over my worn T-shirt and jammie pants and open the door.

I feel like a princess in a fairy tale. Yesterday I was scrubbing mildew out of a teenage girl's swim cap. Today a smiling young man has brought me breakfast, and he's setting it up now on my bed. There's a carafe—an entire carafe!—of coffee, and pastries and freshly squeezed juice and artisanal bacon and perfectly poached eggs over asparagus, and I think I have died and gone to heaven. Within moments I am alone again with this feast, and I simply cannot believe my good fortune. I settle back into bed, pull the tray of food close, and then, in an act that would earn either of my kids a lecture, I turn on the TV and eat to the soothing nonsense of a network morning show.

I do not know which I find more delicious—the food, the hotel room, or just knowing that I do not have to rush. I linger over every bite, reminding my body how to chew, how to taste, how to breathe and eat in turn. I pour tiny cups of coffee, add just the perfect amount of cream, and drink them one by one, while they are hot. I have no one to drive anywhere, no missing items to find, no breakfasts to make and then be criticized for; I am not party to a confusing conversation about something a child promised to bring to school in twenty minutes but did not yet procure. I do not have to brush my teeth while peeing, because I have time to do each task separately, and no one is waiting for me to finish in the bathroom. This is sweet, sweet paradise. The only task I must accomplish in the next three hours is to get myself back to Columbia to teach my presentation. "E-reader Anthologies for the Next Generation of Passionate Readers" is what I called it. Not very snappy, and if Kathryn was right last night, I'll have a nice, manageably small crowd, put forth my little concept, and then spend the rest of the day in other people's presentations, learning how to be better at a job I love. For lunch, maybe Thai food? Eaten alone, with a book. My god! Sweet peace! Why didn't I do this years ago?

Because of my kids, of course. But why then did I ever have kids?

Laughing at myself, I grab my phone and text a picture of my still-not-empty coffee cup to Cori and Joe. "Breakfast in bed! Your mom could get used to this . . ."

"Don't get any ideas," pops back Cori right away. Good. It is seven a.m., and she is awake. There is consistency happening.

I text John.

How is it going?

He writes back right away too: "Same as it was last night at ten p.m. Cori's leaving in ten for chlorine breakfast"—this is what her summer swim coach calls the crack-of-dawn practices they have in the outdoor community pool during the summer—"and Joe and I are going to watch her swim and then have actual breakfast."

"With fruit," I text back.

"Aye aye, Cap. Do lime Jolly Ranchers count as fruit? :P"

I send back the thumbs-down emoji because I know I'm being annoying and I don't think he needs to remind me that I'm being annoying. Being annoying is a huge part of a parent's job description, and he would know that if he had been around once or twice in the last few years. He responds by calling me.

"Sorry for the snark," he says when I pick up. "Keep sending the tips—I need them!"

There. That's better. I soften back into the bed.

"Are you guys having fun?" I ask him.

"So much fun. Last night we each picked one of our own favorite movies and did a marathon, talking through what we loved. Joe can really put away the popcorn. It was a good icebreaker. I already feel like I have a better grasp on who they are. Miles to go, of course."

I feel a twinge of jealousy, then look back at my breakfast spread and my beautiful hotel room. *Sweet peace*, I remind myself. No dishes, no rushing, no chlorine breakfast.

"What did the kids pick?" I ask, privately making my own guess. Joe picked *Empire Strikes Back*—his favorite of all the *Star Wars* movies. And Cori, disgusting brute that she is, picked . . . *Wedding Crashers*? *Anchorman*? maybe *Bridesmaids*?

"Joe picked *Raiders of the Lost Ark*. I was kind of surprised. It's weird to think of him as a little innocent kid and then see him cheering when

Nazi faces melt off. I mean, that is a great part of the movie. But it's so grown up. Just another reminder that I have a lot of catching up to do."

Huh. Ok, I was pretty close there. Stephen Spielberg instead of George Lucas, but same star, same vintage, same genre. "What did Cori pick?" I ask.

"Do you even have to guess? *The Notebook*. My god. I guess it has to happen to every teenage girl at some point."

"*The Notebook*?" I repeat dumbly. When she and I watched that together, we made fun of it nonstop. Why is Ryan Gosling so against shirts? Can't all this be fixed with a couple of reasonable conversations? Why don't they just go inside and kiss where it's dry?

The romance we both love is *Notting Hill*. "I'm just a girl . . . standing in front of a boy . . ." Mother-daughter swoonfest. Or so I thought.

"She sort of clutched her heart and teared up at the end. I don't get it."

I catch myself, not wanting to admit this is total news to me. "What about you?" I ask. Maybe to be polite. Maybe because I want to know.

"Oh, that's easy. *MILFs Take Manhattan*. It's a classic—have you seen it?"

"Please be joking."

"I'm joking. I didn't do my actual favorite, since it's extremely R, and you and I hadn't discussed it first. I did *Fletch*. Funny and dumb and old enough that there's no way they'd seen it already."

"*Fletch*. Good call. What was your actual favorite . . . no, wait, I know, don't I?"

"It's been years. You might have forgotten."

"*No Country for Old Men*," I announce.

"Yep. A movie about manhood. Sometimes I think I didn't watch it enough before I left you guys."

I drop my fork. Am I annoyed or pleased to hear him show contrition? Either way, it makes me incredibly uncomfortable. "I'm trying to enjoy my breakfast here."

"Sorry. The point is we are all doing great. Keep enjoying yourself, and stop worrying about the kids so much."

"Yep. Because I'm going to be the first mother in the history of the *entire universe* who stops worrying about her kids when she's told to."

"Fair enough. Worry your heart out. But we're good."

I nod. "Yeah," I say miserably, "it sounds like you are."

After we say goodbye, I look down at my breakfast and feel ten times less smug about it. It's just breakfast. I could fix it for myself any day of the week, and it would probably cost ten times less. I have a nice bedroom at home too. I could take a nice breakfast up to my nice bedroom in my nice house while my nice kids are still sleeping if I want to eat in bed so badly.

Of course, then I would be the one washing the dishes. And washing my sheets to get the bacon grease off of them.

Still. Then my kids would be with me, not off with a man who feels in many ways like both my long-lost best friend and a total stranger.

The John I married never ever showed regret for anything he did. It just wasn't in his coding. I saw it as confidence at first, but like in all long-term partnerships, what first drove me wild came to drive me nuts. I learned that small setbacks—a career dip, a few nights of bad sleep—felt personal to him and were anyone's fault but his. I found that under the veneer of self-assuredness was a small but dangerous current of entitlement. I discovered that when life got well and truly hard—and it did get hard, almost unbearably hard, about two years before he left—John had no idea how to cope. He certainly didn't know how to ask for help or say he was sorry.

Post–Hong Kong John has done nothing but.

Which makes me wonder—is he a new man, with his contrition and his sudden interest in parenting and his "in case of emergencies" credit card? Oh shit, the credit card! I forgot to warn him about the exorbitant cost of my housing in New York. And I still haven't heard from Talia, so there's no end in sight. My god, what if I don't hear from her for the entire week? Is that a possibility? What then? Do I just go home with my tail between my legs and admit I don't have a week's vacation in me?

My phone rings just as I'm falling down the rabbit hole of rumination, and I flail for it excitedly. Maybe it's Talia.

Or it's the kids.

Or it's John saying the kids are missing.

I look at the screen. It's an 888 number. Cripes, I had too much coffee. I tap the answer button and listen for what I expect will be a robocall from my pharmacy or something.

"Heh-low," says a relaxed, sexy robot-lady voice. "This is the fraud-prevention department for your"—pause—"American Express ProGold family card. Please hold for a representative."

Oh. Of course. Using a new card in a new city for an expensive hotel. Guess I have to verify it's really me.

A woman comes on the line, her voice low and friendly. She introduces herself as Marlene and asks to verify the last four digits of my Social Security number and "secret code word," which I guess is *presto* because that is what John always picks. And then she tells me that my account has been flagged because of suspicious activity.

"Oh," I say cheerily. "Nothing suspicious here. I'm staying in New York for the week."

Marlene cuts me off. "Actually, ma'am, the charges are coming from multiple locations. So I'm going to review them with you, and if the charge is legitimate, say ok."

"Ok," I say, slightly confused. I'm thinking this call would be better suited to John, who must be using the card in Pennsylvania, but maybe it's just a matter of going through the motions. "Go ahead."

"The first charge is for a Hotel la Provençe, Seventy-Ninth Street, New York, New York? The charge says king deluxe accommodation, $292.40. Charged at 6:45 p.m. yesterday, eastern time."

"Yes, that's right."

"And then the next charge was at 10:44 p.m. eastern. The charge says Sphinx Hair Removal Salon, 2, 2 Wellington Street, Central Hong Kong, in the amount of $92.65?"

"Uhhhh . . ." Huh? John was definitely not getting waxed in Hong Kong yesterday. I'm pretty sure my kids would have mentioned it.

"And then the one after that is the Hotel la Provençe again, hospitality, $26.00 charged at 7:02 this morning."

"Ok, that one is definitely legitimate. I'm not so sure about the other. Let me think of what it could be . . ."

"And here is the last charge: Adorables Gifts dot com. Women's fashion, $482.96. It's an online store, but the ordering address came from a Hong Kong IP number, according to our fraud-prevention department. Was this charge made by a cardholder on your account?"

"No, no, definitely not. Well, wait. Hang on," I say and try to puzzle this out. John definitely is in PA with my kids. I'm in New York. Did John order something online from Hong Kong? Since my laptop is in reach, I grab it and type in AdorablesGifts.com. Up comes the most elaborate, exotic lingerie I've ever seen in sizes I will never be. It is the pictures of the gorgeous young models that make the penny drop.

"Marlene?" I ask cautiously. "Do you know how many cards have been issued to this account?"

"Yes, ma'am," she says. "Two cards. One in your husband's name and one in yours."

My heart sinks.

"Do you have the shipping address for the flagged charge?"

"Yes, ma'am. It's going to a Ms. Marika Shew."

"Then, I guess . . ." I think about telling her that the charges are fake. That the card should be canceled and Marika Shew should be hoisted on her own expensively waxed petard. But instead I say, "I'm sorry for the confusion. The charges are all legitimate." I sigh. "Is there a way to put a note on the account that we'll be using our cards in different locations for a little while?" I ask her.

"Of course, ma'am. It's simply protocol that we flag an account if it's being used in a new location, like New York, while still being used in the previous location, where it's been in service for a few years. Now that we've checked it out, you won't be bothered by us again."

"Thank you, Marlene," I say as nicely as possible, because it is not Marlene's fault John is still keeping his . . . well, she must be thirty-three by now . . . his thirty-three-year-old bit on the side waxed and laced up just waiting for his return.

I sink back into the bed and wrinkle up my face, trying not to cry. Marika Shew is the woman John took up with after me. I must have online stalked her for an entire year straight before Lena found out what I was up to and got me to stop. All I know about her is that she works at his company and lives in Hong Kong and her social media use is exclusively related to French bulldogs and Yorkshire terriers.

Somehow I had come to the conclusion that their relationship was long dead. But why? Why did I assume that they were broken up? Maybe because I thought that was why John came home.

Maybe I thought he wanted me back.

Of course I thought that. What an idiot I've been.

Look at me. I'm as far as a human woman can get from professionally waxed and decked out in high-end lingerie. I'm soft and mom shaped, in an old T-shirt, eating carbs in bed with a novel and CBS on TV in the background. In no universe would a man leave his gorgeous mistress for this. No, he's just getting a week of parenting out of the way before he goes right back to business as usual.

And to think I felt guilty for taking his credit card! While he has been buying Marika $500 worth of black teddies and marabou slippers this whole time!

I punch my pillow, throw off my covers, and stalk to the shower. Breakfast in bed is officially ruined. I'm going to take an angry shower and get angry dressed and storm up to Columbia and *try* to focus on my very important presentation even though I am full of fury over my duplicitous ex-husband—who isn't even my ex-husband—and then I'm going to—

The phone rings again. My traitorous heart lifts. It must be John calling to explain. Maybe he broke up with Marika but didn't have the heart to take away her credit card? Or maybe she stole a card from him when he left? Or maybe . . .

It's Talia.

"You're alive," I say angrily. Anger is spilling out all over; I have to think Talia deserves a smattering of it.

"Barely. And then I see your messages, and oh em gee, I nearly started crying. I'm so sorry," she starts. "I can't believe you were homeless last night. You found a hotel—tell me you found a hotel?"

"I found a hotel. And then I put it on my ex's credit card. And then I just got a call from the credit card company verifying five hundred dollars' worth of waxing and lingerie purchased by someone in Hong Kong. Someone thirty-three and size two, and oh my *god*, that bleeping bleephole!"

Talia has the good sense to remain quiet for a moment.

"He has my kids right now. That bleephole has my kids."

"Um," Talia gently interrupts. "You have John's credit card?"

I take a beat. "I do."

"I mean. You see the opportunity for revenge here, right?"

Anger is quickly replaced by shock. "I could never do that."

"No. Of course not. You're a good, kind, thoughtful, and honorable person."

"Well," I say, because I'm not feeling any of those things right now. "Thank you?"

"I am less of those things," she says. "Keep that in mind in case you have the urge to 'accidentally leave the card lying around' in my apartment."

In spite of my mood, I laugh. "I absolutely will. And honestly, I'm in a gorgeous hotel on the Upper West Side, and I just finished up breakfast in bed on his dime," I tell her. "So I guess things aren't all bad.

Maybe tonight, instead of checking out, I'll buy an in-room movie and not even watch it."

"You wicked woman."

"Yeah, I'm not doing that. Can I come stay with you tonight?"

"Um . . . no. Because I can't get back into my apartment until Sunday night. Apparently there was a little murder."

"What now?"

"See, I have kind of a good excuse for screwing you over last night."

"I am beginning to understand that! What happened?"

"It's a long story. Key point is that the murder itself did not happen to anyone I know, and it did not happen in my apartment."

"Thank goodness for that," I say, feeling very much like a small-town bumpkin.

"But my phone was in the apartment at the time of the . . . slaying? I forgot it at home and was out all day on location, and then I couldn't get any of the dummies to let me in to retrieve it until this morning. I guess there was, like, forensic evidence in the hallways? I was like, 'Who do I have to kill to get my phone back?' And let me tell you, that one dropped like a stone with all those super serious beat cops."

I laugh again, more of the rage trickling away. "So how long do you have to stay away, and where are you staying?"

"Oh, you know. There's a guy."

"Really? A serious guy?"

Talia just answers by laughing. "Let's just say that I'll be glad when I can get back home on Sunday."

"Does this mean I can still stay with you after the conference?"

"Yes. I swear on a stack of my own magazines that you can count on me for housing from Sunday on. How long are you staying? Two months?"

I laugh. "Try a week. I do have children, remember?"

"And they do have a father, remember?" she quips back. "Oops— art direction starts now. Ciao!"

"Bye?" I say, but the phone gives its three bloop-bloop-bloop hang-up tones while I say it. Which is fine because my brain has pretty much short-circuited in the last twenty minutes, and I have no idea what I was even going to do next.

Oh shit! The presentation! I look at the clock and see I have thirty minutes to get showered, dressed up, and to Columbia. It's going to take a small miracle to get there on time. A miracle, or a cab.

Luckily I have plenty of room on this credit card for cab fare.

CHAPTER SIX

Dear Mom,

Dad gave me three hundred bucks.

In cash. He told me to use it to buy clothes and go on dates with Brian. Mom. He is the worst.

I'm using the money.

Is that cool with you? I will buy a book, too, just to be sure.

Love,

Your money-grubbing daughter, Cori

—

Cabs are wonderful things because they give you time to do your makeup in transit. I don't wear much—why bother? I look like a mom no matter what I do—so it's just lipstick, moisturizer, and mascara, and I feel truly gussied up. I've got my presentation on my laptop, and it's a good one. One I'm pretty invested in, actually. It addresses a problem that I noticed cropping up when I started with a class that had a higher-than-usual number of what educators like to call "reluctant readers." Not every student—not even every bright student—comes to books like a thirsty camel to an oasis. And generally speaking, English teachers and librarians have no personal experience with reluctance toward reading. If we weren't voracious readers, we would be teaching social studies or even, you know, doing a job that pays well. So typically there's this sort of unintentional downgrading of students who don't gobble up every reading assignment thrown their way.

I know because I got caught with my pants down on this very issue. With, of all people, my own daughter.

Cori was never supposed to be my student. That was kind of a big deal to me. I'm a librarian, not a classroom teacher, so it seemed utterly reasonable that even at our very small private school, I should not be personally responsible for grading my own offspring at any point. But the reading curriculum in Cori's seventh-grade English class—a curriculum I personally had designed for the school—was kicking her butt. Every night, the homework was reading a chapter and journaling about it. And every night she would whine, procrastinate, wheedle, and do everything but read her chapter. I couldn't figure it out. The book—*Lord of the Flies*—wasn't hard reading. In fact, Cori was in the lowest reading group for her age, so it was the easiest choice available without dropping back a grade. The subject matter was relatable to a seventh grader. It was a classic that every kid read, and in fact, lots and lots of my students really connected to it.

I asked Cori what was up with this behavior, and she said the words that drive ice into the hearts of librarians around the world: "Sorry, Mom, but I just hate reading."

It was a dark day.

The next morning I felt like the gauntlet had been thrown. It was the day of the week that I had Open Books—a study hall when several kids who had tested into the lowest-level reading groups came in and diligently slaved away at, for example, *Romeo and Juliet*, knowing full well that their friends in the next room over were breezing through *Hamlet*. It was through their eyes that I saw our dilemma: there was stigma to low reading levels, despite our euphemisms, and no other way of challenging many different students at the same time than to assign leveled reading. I started pulling titles from our New Releases shelf and combing through them. They were generally way too easy to be considered scholarly. No one, not even the Romeo readers, would be making any literary progress on half these books. But they might enjoy them. They might even become engaged with them. Was that nothing?

The Hamlet readers—they would probably only be challenged by a fourth of them. The Othellos would be almost bored if the content weren't so fun and juicy. And what made them juicy? They all had such wonderfully youthful themes. Search for identity. Science fiction and speculation. Social justice. Rebellion.

In fact, those were the exact themes I had been trying to stress in my choice of the school's reading canon.

But thinking of Cori, I realized somewhere I had gone wrong.

I stewed over it for weeks. During that time, Cori made it through *Lord of the Flies* (rebellion, speculation) and started wading through *The Good Earth* (identity, social justice). She took absolutely no joy in any of this reading. She began to internalize her position at the bottom of the lowest-level reading group and to describe herself as a bad reader. Her for-fun reading—weepy YA romances, generally—started to taper off. This was the end, I suddenly realized. This was my last chance.

And then in a burst of inspiration it came to me, fully formed and all at once. I had figured out how to make the leveled reading groups virtually invisible to the students—by making them group themselves by choice.

And I had the perfect guinea pig: my very own daughter.

———

I click onto the next PowerPoint slide. It's a picture of Cori gazing into the screen of a small dedicated black-and-white e-reader. I've just told a lecture hall full—ok, not full, but pretty close for nine a.m.—of library science people how I came to the idea of something I've come to call the Flexthology. Everyone is listening. Clutching their coffees from the hospitality table for dear life, but still, listening.

"So at this point I thought of the themes that were most meaningful to my students, picked the most popular four, and chose four books for each theme. One is below grade level, two are at grade level, and one exceeds grade level. Now, if you want to do this in your classroom, you want your spread to be the same as the spread of your actual students. So if fifty percent aren't reading at or near grade level, then maybe pick two below or two above or whatever makes sense for your class." I look at the large clock in front of me. It's taking me so long to describe this thing. I only have half an hour left to show my results and take questions. I know I'm supposed to hate public speaking, according to all librarian clichés, but once I get going it's hard for me to stop.

"Right. So you've got your sixteen-book selection right there, all loaded up on the class e-readers ready to go. Perfect, right? And then from there you present the e-readers to your students and assign the first chapter or fifteen pages or whatever is most reasonable for your readers from each of the books within your given theme. And at that point, that's all that's unlocked on the e-readers you distribute, so even if they *want* to read on, they simply cannot until you go forward. Each student selects his or her favorite work and is grouped with the other readers who chose the same work, and then they study that book for the rest of the unit. And boom, just like that, reading-group levels become invisible. Students are reading at the interest and ability level that best suits them, and they are invested since they chose the book—and maybe even the theme—themselves."

A hand shoots into the air. "Excuse me," a man says before I can call on him, and for a moment I have to remember that these are adults, not children, and I cannot therefore tell him to wait for his turn. "But why wouldn't students just all gravitate toward the easiest book?"

I shrug. "I don't know exactly what the mechanics are, but they haven't done that at my school. Here, this next slide"—I click over to a spiderweb graph Joe had to help me make—"shows the way the student choices were distributed over four Flexthology units I ran last year. As you can see, the reading levels were pretty evenly distributed among the three choices. In unit two, only three students out of twenty-nine chose the higher-level titles, but then, in unit two, the state-testing results for that class report only ten percent of classmates reading above grade level. So self-selected reading levels, at least in this small sample, worked."

The interrupter looks satisfied. My next slide is a list of titles for the four units. "This shows which titles I chose and the number of students who chose each as compared to standardized-testing results for the class. This illustrates the second benefit of the Flexthology. Not only do we get kids invested in their own reading choices and teach them how to pick books for the rest of their lives, but we also get data on what works for kids as generations change."

The next person with a question raises his hand and waits. I look at him, a square-jawed fortysomething man with Asian features and brown skin. I believe this is someone Kathryn would call a potential "Hot Librarian of the Year."

"Do you have a question or comment?" I ask him.

"I do," he says. "I was loving this idea, but when you listed the titles you chose, my heart sank. Maybe they're fine for a private school in farm country. But I teach in New York. My readers are generally the perfect storm of reluctant and underserved. We're talking three levels below grade sometimes, and with a social distrust of academics. You've got a list of dead white guys a mile long writing about repressed feelings and politics. My kids won't give two shits. Pardon my French."

The class laughs, and I blush. I feel, suddenly, incredibly white and incredibly daft. Then I remind myself I had the same concern and was faced with the stark reality.

"Now, here's the major downside of the Flexthology system," I say. "Since it's just a wild hair from a private school librarian in farm country"—my questioner gives me a polite nod at my reference to his dig—"and not, say, funded by a million-dollar NEA grant, I had to choose only from books in the public domain—books with no copyright that are free to download. It's not a ton to go on. My students are largely wealthy—and yes, they have e-readers from the school—but even so, there is no way I can afford to purchase sixteen new e-books for thirty readers every two months and then just dump half the books unread. Expensewise, private or public, almost all of us have budgets for only one active copyright at a time for each student—that's if we're lucky. And it's the same book year in and year out. That hardly allows for any variety or growth.

"But that said," I add as an afterthought, "it wouldn't be so hard to put any book into this format, if you could afford it."

The hot librarian tilts his head. "So you're guessing this system can work with any books, but you need a huge budget to include anything relevant to a diverse student body," he concludes.

"Or a medium budget and a very forgiving publisher," I say woefully.

"Bummer," he says.

"But maybe still worth a try?" I say.

"Maybe," he says reluctantly.

The rest of the class goes on. I get lots of very enthusiastic questions and come away feeling generally like the Flexthology idea could work in oodles and oodles of classrooms. But the concerns Hot Librarian presented linger on as I receive one-on-one questions from the shy contingent after the presentation is over. This being a librarians' conference, there is a large shy contingent.

And then there he is again. The hot librarian. Standing a head taller than me and waiting patiently for his turn. I feel nervous and fairly sure that whatever question he might have for me next will be the one that breaks me. But instead he says, "Hi, I'm Daniel."

"Hi. I'm Amy," I say.

"I know," he says, and I blush.

"I'd like to buy you a cup of coffee," he tells me.

Now I really blush.

"Real coffee," he says, dismissing the tureen of institutional dishwater on the hospitality table. "Maybe something sweet too."

I can't think of what to say, so I half smile awkwardly.

"Are you doing anything right now?"

"Uh . . ." Am I? What was next? Oh, right, a roundup of new nonfiction for young readers. Behind us, the panelists are already taking their places. Soon the hot librarian and I will be standing in the middle of the next presentation.

"I . . . ," I start to say.

"I'm also free at two p.m. today, if that works better," he supplies.

"I think . . ."

"We'd probably better get out of the way here," he says, and he touches my arm.

I freeze up like an old desktop that's been asked to run too many programs at once. He's touching me. When was the last time a man touched me like this? I am standing in front of a room that is filling up with people again. Did he like my presentation after all? What am I wearing?

"Let's do two," I finally manage. "At the coffee cart outside?"

"Perfect," says Daniel the hot librarian. "We can take the coffee to that little square and sun ourselves like lizards. Enjoy the panel," he says and leaves me standing there, confused and shy and stammering. I guess I am a true librarian after all.

———

Six months after John left, after the broken tooth that nearly killed me, and after I learned the annoying truth of the old maxim—that which doesn't make you kill yourself will probably make you tough as an old grizzly and twice as mean—I found out about Marika.

It was Facebook, of course. Marika "liked" a photo of John's and Joe's school pictures side by side that I had posted almost a year earlier, and I thought, *Who the hell is this person?* It soon became clear from her photo stream that she was dating my absent husband and had been for at least a couple of months. From there, it was easy to extrapolate that she was prettier and younger than me, that she had no kids, and that she made John feel like god's gift to womankind—something I certainly had not been able to do anymore.

This was my very first "fuck him" moment. Forgive my French if you can; that is simply the only way I can describe how I felt when I looked at a filtered photo of a lissome thirty-year-old in a bikini gazing at my chubby, pasty, hairy husband like he was Sexy Jesus Incarnate. Fuck that guy.

And just like that, I reached the anger stage of my abandonment. It was wonderful. I sent a scathing message to John in which I criticized the quality of his erection. I told John's mother the truth about what he had done to us, instead of feeding her a "He needed to find himself and focus on his work" line one more time. After one particularly large glass of wine, I PMed Marika and told her that there was no reason to worry that John would ditch her when her breasts fell from nursing, just because he had done it to me.

Hell had no fury.

And as if it would somehow punish John from a distance, I went on a date with a man who had long been interested in me and pursued me, quite shamelessly, even when John had been around.

The guy in question was Terry Brans, this borderline-sleazy friend of John's from college who sold real estate and had gotten us our house in a very successful negotiation. His "game," such as it was, was to occasionally call and schedule a visit to "reassess the market value" of our house and to "guide our improvement decisions" but mostly just to have dinner and drink our wine. Every single time, he'd make some of those "How'd a nice girl like you end up with a loser like John" comments, and every single time, we'd laugh politely until John got genuinely mad roughly ten minutes into dessert. Terry would apologize and pour John another glass of wine, and then we'd all simmer down. And every single time, utterly unabashed, Terry would clear the plates and insist on doing the dishes, knowing full well that I couldn't sit there and let him do all the cleaning up by himself, and knowing also that John could.

So it would be me and Terry in the kitchen. Terry would talk about his recent big sales, joke about the personalities that clashed in the purchase of four-thousand-square-foot manses, complain that he was running out of reasonable ways to spend his money, wish aloud he was the kind of guy "insecure enough to spend a hundred grand on a car," and talk about how much he regretted buying his boat. It was a one-man pissing contest, and I was supposed to be impressed. Which I never was, but oh, how I was flattered that someone took an interest enough to make such a fool of himself.

After a week of fuming over Marika, I called Terry and told him I could really use some advice about the best updates to make in our house for maximum return on investment. I remember thinking, after I said it, *Is it our house anymore?* but of course, I didn't tell Terry what was going on. Even if I hadn't been embarrassed, I wouldn't have wanted the pressure.

He came over two nights later when the kids went to a high school basketball game. I wore something cute but approachable—a jade-green cotton jersey dress from Kohl's that hadn't yet been washed enough times to lose its springy, flattering shape. I cooked something. Probably pasta. I remember when I opened the door, he said, "Mmm, something smells wonderful," and then leaned in to smell my neck, and I said, "Cool it, Pepé Le Pew," and he laughed hard.

It occurs to me now, much later, that Terry's ability to laugh at himself and be rejected repeatedly and still keep flirting was exactly why asking him to come over seemed like such a good plan. I thought I wouldn't have to give him a thing—no encouragement, no physicality, not even a low-cut shirt—to receive the ego boost I so desperately craved and spite John in the same night.

But I was wrong.

"Where's John?" he immediately asked, the moment he had finished telling me how much better my front door would look painted bright orange.

I told him, "John and I are . . . separated. We're working on some problems." Like the problem that John wanted to pretend our life and our two kids had never happened.

Terry's face shifted quickly. "What?"

I only shrugged. I didn't want to say the same lame lie twice in a row.

"Did that loser hurt you?" Terry asked sharply.

"The loser you've been friends with for twenty years?" I asked. Terry only arched an eyebrow. "No," I answered feebly. "We're just at a crossroads."

Terry frowned. "I'm very sorry to hear it," he said. Then he sighed laboriously. "I guess that explains why you called."

I blushed pink. I had been hoping my tiny come-on would go unnoticed. But he only said, "So are you planning to sell, then? I have the perfect buyer for you. Actually, three perfect buyers. One of the families, though, you would really love—"

"No," I said, shaking my head. "I am going to try to keep the house for now. I just . . ." I thought about saying I wanted to spend some time with him. Or wanted to try an evening with a man not my husband. Or wanted to have sex with him and then have him tell John out of spite. "I just wanted to talk the house over with you, figure out what my options were, figure out what it was worth."

Terry nodded. "Smart. Smart. I assume since you're an at-home mother, you'll keep the house in a divorce?"

I thought about this. Seeing as John was in love with a woman in Hong Kong, the chance of a battle over PA real estate seemed low. "I assume so," I said.

"In that case, I need to go take a look at your powder room. Last time I think I remember mentioning how inexpensive it is to gussy up a powder room? I have the perfect handyman to refer. He could throw up some nice wallpaper in there, maybe do a floating vanity? Easy equity; buyers love it."

Terry disappeared down the hall. I almost fell over from relief the minute he left the room. Spitefulness or no, I didn't want this man here in the house alone with me. I had wanted to feel adored, but only by my husband. I didn't want to be intimate with anyone but John, and I couldn't imagine ever feeling any other way. As angry as I was, I still loved John, a feeling so real and so inexplicable it was like an itch on an amputated limb. I got through dinner with Terry that night, which was easy, since now that I was available he seemed to have zero interest in flirting, and then I vowed that that would be my last attempt at dating until at least one of my kids was in college.

But now I seem to have made a date. And I am not dreading it at all. In fact, it is quite the opposite.

—

It is 1:50 p.m. in New York City.

I have talked to my children twice today already. Given a fairly successful presentation to a large audience. Had a calamari salad and a glass of white wine for lunch. Walked through several shops without buying anything. Gotten six continuing ed hours. Seriously considered a quickie manicure and then came to my senses.

It is while I am circling the coffee cart waiting for my, well, my date and pretending to look like I am going somewhere that I run into Kathryn, of last night's wine reception. She is looking a little softer today—maybe from a good night's sleep, or maybe because I now know she doesn't bite—but her manner remains as refreshingly sharp and familiar.

"Aha!" she says upon seeing me. "At last, the woman of the hour!"

"Hmm?" I ask.

"We need to talk about the Flexthology. I can't stop thinking about it," she tells me. "I love it."

"You were at my presentation?" I ask. I don't remember seeing her.

"I was not. I told you how I was planning to sleep through this entire conference, didn't I? Remember, two kids in diapers? Mommy's big weekend off?"

I nod. "I remember. So how do you—"

She cuts me off. "My lunch table were all talking about it. They thought it had a lot of promise. I got a copy of the handout and chewed the whole thing over. I'm afraid it might be dead in the water."

My face falls. "Oh. Well, I suppose—"

"But damned if I don't want to do it in my own classroom."

"Um . . ." I'm not sure where I fit in for this conversation.

"Did you ever think about begging?" she asks me. This time I know not to answer and just wait calmly. It is the right call. "On a small scale. I'm thinking I set aside the e-readers and just try to beg for funding for the variety of books. I know the e-reader is one of the best aspects of it, but I'm never going to get two grand for twenty devices I send home with kids and just hope they bring back. They keep talking about getting our students some tablets, but *talking* is the key word. Speaking of which, guess what! My one-year-old met all his milestones! While I was gone, too; can you believe that bullshit? I leave those kids with my husband for three days—that's all!—and the minute I turn my back, he's all, 'Cognitive delay? What cognitive delay?'" Kathryn assumes a baby voice: "'Matter can neither be created nor destroyed . . .'"

I shake my head. "The e-readers are important. It's what makes the reading-level choices invisible."

"But they'll talk to each other anyway, right?"

"If they want to, after they choose," I say. "But they won't have the obvious book covers, and they won't be looking around the room seeing what the cool kids or the smart kids pick when they make their own choices. They won't have the gendered nonsense that covers bring or preconceived notions about the subjects. They'll just pick the book they want to read based on the actual story. I mean, if it works."

Kathryn sighs. "I can't see the funding," she says heavily. "I could find money for the e-readers *or* the book copyrights, but not both."

I nod. "And I've realized the books I picked for my school aren't representative enough of a diverse student body."

Kathryn breathes deeply. "Not dead in the water. But not swimming either. Let's look for some good public domain diversity." She pulls out her phone and starts tapping away. "What have you got so far?"

"Not much. I've got a few women authors, and something from Du Bois," I tell her.

"Right, I saw that," she says. "Maybe a travelogue?"

I shrug. She nods. "You're right, kind of a lame solution. What else?"

I start racking my brain for age-appropriate and diverse reading material that might be in the public domain. "*Twelve Years a Slave*?"

Kathryn frowns. "It's a challenging book, though, if I remember right. AP level."

"Oh!" I announce. "*My Bondage and My Freedom*!"

"Never read! Would it work on reading level?"

"I think so! Let me download it," I say. "It's been years."

It is while I am updating my Gutenberg app that Daniel approaches us.

"*My Bondage and My Freedom*!" I blurt to him.

"Hello to you too," he says. "What an enthusiastic greeting. Confusing, but enthusiastic."

I exhale and smile at myself. And him. He is awfully good looking. "The Frederick Douglass autobiography. For the Flexthology. It's in the public domain." His eyes are very pretty. My stomach starts to hurt.

"Ah," he says approvingly. "Good thinking. I had some ideas about this too."

"Excellent," says Kathryn, who I had momentarily forgotten to be alive. "Would you like to be on our planning committee? We have a lot of room on this committee at the moment."

I laugh. Then worry that my laugh sounds forced. *Get it together, Amy.* "Daniel, this is Kathryn. She's from Chicago Public Schools."

Daniel smiles and extends a hand. "You're a long way from home," he says warmly. He doesn't look nervous or awkward. I need to just calm down.

"I'm hiding from my children," she tells him conspiratorially. "I'm not changing any diapers."

Daniel nods. "Understood. I will be sure not to ask." He gives her a wink. Seriously, he could be the Hot Librarian of the Year.

"And on that note," Kathryn says, after sending a meaningful look to me and then tilting her head toward Daniel, "I am en route to my hotel right now to get a nap. Second one of the day. So I must bid you goodbye."

"Carpe somnum!" calls Daniel. "Seize the naps!" It is such a dorky thing to say that I start to feel more at ease. I feel even better when, as Kathryn disappears from view, he holds up a notebook where he's made notes about my presentation. "Shall we?" he asks. "I've got some books to run by you."

I nod, relieved at the thought that we might spend this meeting talking books. Books I can do. If this were some kind of date . . . that would be upsetting. "We shall."

"Great. Before we start shouting more titles at each other, though, perhaps we should get some libations. Is this a coffee date or a drinks date?" he asks, and all my progress calming down is immediately erased.

"It's not a date," I say, too loudly.

"Right," says Daniel quickly, looking down. "Of course. Sorry."

I'm about to apologize, too, just out of habit, when I take a beat. Daniel thought this might be a date. This very handsome and bookish guy asked me out on a date. I'm single, mostly. This is a good thing. This is not a bad thing. What am I doing?

"I mean, is it a date?" I ask. "It could be a date."

He just laughs. "How about it's coffee."

"Yes!" I agree manically. "Let's get some coffee."

"Maybe decaf?" he says with a smile.

We get in line at the cart. Daniel, though he seems awfully fit from where I'm standing, orders two pastries and a black-and-white cookie with his coffee. I order a decaf with milk, because he's right—any more caffeine might give me a stroke at this point. He tucks his paper bag of pastries under his arm and walks me west, to a pretty green space by the river that I didn't know existed. Of course, that's true of 90 percent of New York. As we walk, we chat over the titles in my e-reader and in his. He reads widely, but I detect a leaning toward speculative fiction.

"Oh yes," he admits freely when I ask him about it. "My daughter got me started on the young-adult postapocalyptic stuff, and then it was like sliding down a hill."

"A slippery slope," I say with a smile. "You have a daughter?"

"I do. She'll be a senior this year. Let's grab this bench and have a scone."

We sit down on a surprisingly clean bench facing out over the Hudson, with a foot of space between us. He fishes out a scone. "Lemon basil?"

I tilt my head to the side. "I feel like I remembered something about a cookie . . ."

"Black-and-white cookie coming right up."

He provides me with a cookie with a piece of bakery waxed paper around it. I unfold and start working on it, one nibble from the black side, one from the white, and so forth. As I eat, I tell him about visiting New York with Talia in the good old days and eating black-and-white cookies from the bodega at four in the morning after a long night of dancing. I tell him about crashing in hotel lobbies and getting strangers to buy us breakfast in diners and coming home broke and doing it all again the next chance we got.

"Your poor parents."

"Right? I have a teenage daughter now," I tell him between bites. "I feel their pain."

"Ah, you too? Does she love you or hate you right now?"

"Hmm . . . let me check what time it is," I say, glancing at an imaginary watch on my wrist. "She's actually kind of a dream kid, roller-coaster moods aside. She isn't a great scholar, but she likes the diving team, and she seems to be that nice kind of popular at school where she doesn't make other girls give themselves eating disorders but does get asked to dances."

"That is nice," he agrees. "That's actually my daughter too. Except I think she doesn't get asked to dances; I think she tells someone he's taking her, and he obeys out of fear."

I laugh. "Seems smart to me. Just one kid?" I ask.

He nods. "You?"

"I have a son. He's twelve. He's the one I lie awake worrying about."

"A handful?" asks Daniel.

"The opposite. He's so . . . good hearted." Before I know it, I tell Daniel about how Joe reacted to his father coming back, which requires me to explain the situation with John in the first place, which I am fairly sure is bad date form. Feeling self-conscious, I steer my rambling back to how Joe guided the whole family to giving John a chance to reconnect, and what an emotional risk that was. "The world is going to be hard on him."

Daniel chews his scone for a moment and then swallows. "Or he will change the world."

I smile. "What a wonderful thing to say." I look at Daniel as he looks out toward New Jersey. Being handsome is one thing. Complimenting my child—that is a whole different ball game. And I feel something vaguely familiar when I look at the planes of his face. What is it?

Oh. Yeah. Lust. I'd forgotten all about lust, but there it is, right where I left it way too many years ago.

"What about your daughter?" I ask him, desperate to get back to small talk. "Hell-raiser? Angel? Somewhere in between?"

Daniel looks back at me. "Ah. I think she is an angel, of course, because I am her dad. But I can see that she's got sharp edges. A bit of trouble with authority and no tolerance for waiting her turn. Of course, that same sharpness is making the college-application process look very promising. She nailed her standardized testing, and her counselor says she may well have her choice of schools next year."

"Wow! Was it like that for you when you were her age?"

He frowns slightly. "Not exactly. Even then I knew I wanted to work in a school, but back then I was thinking coaching. I was so obsessed with soccer."

"Soccer?"

"Yeah," he tells me. "My parents met, married, and conceived me within two years of my mom arriving in the States. She's Korean, and he's African American, so I grew up thinking I was a special snowflake. You know which sport has dudes that look like me?"

I shrug. I have seen what seems like every possible shade of skin in pro sports. "Most of them, I would think."

He half laughs at me. "Fair enough. But back then, to my mind, some sports seemed white, some sports seemed Black, no sports seemed Korean. Except, of course, the world's sport . . ."

"Soccer," I complete.

"Soccer. I lived and breathed it. Academics felt like a second priority. Or maybe a third. Because let's not forget: girls."

"Let's absolutely not!" I agree. "Any tips on how to engage students with a similar attitude at my school?"

He shrugs. "I think your choose-your-own-reading thing sounds like a pretty good prescription. The problem is with the books, not the concept."

I frown. "But the books kind of *are* the concept," I tell him.

"What if there were new YA releases in your anthologies? Not, you know, books with zero merit, but well-written titles with relatable themes from the last twenty-five years."

I shake my head. "The budget is a deal breaker."

Daniel bites his lip. "There's got to be a workaround."

I nod. "There usually is. But not on the scale of one reference librarian at one small private school in one small town."

Daniel nods, too, and then we are both quiet. I am thinking about the anthologies, the sunny day, the cookie. The strangeness of being at a park in New York City on a date, or something like a date, with the soccer-mad jock turned librarian with skin the color of . . . well, the color of *his* skin. And I find that I want to somehow close the space that's between us. It's a blurry, confusing, heady mix.

I can't even imagine what he might be thinking. But after a long silence, Daniel hops up off the bench. "Let's go to Barnes & Noble," he says.

I look up at him. "What? Right now?"

"Yes, right now. Let's go to Barnes & Noble in Union Square and make a monster list of all the dream titles we'd want in your Flexthology. Try to come up with a few units that would work in my school and a few that would work in yours. See if there's overlap. Test our ideas out a little. Figure out what such a proposition would actually cost."

I look at him askance. "This is just a little idea I had back at my school. It's a craft project, not a proposition. I'm not looking for global revolution."

"But why not? A lot of people in your class this morning thought it was much more than a craft project. I thought it was downright brilliant. And when you have a great idea, that idea should be tested out on a larger sample. Plus, it's a bookstore. Bookstores are always good. Come with me." Daniel reaches out his hand to help me up from the bench. I look down at my half-nibbled cookie. It is still exactly half-black and half-white.

"You can bring your cookie on the subway," he tells me. "I realize it could take you another half an hour to eat the rest."

I start. I've been nibbling for a half hour? "What time is it?"

He pulls out his phone. "Quarter after three. Do you have somewhere to be this afternoon?"

I blink. I thought the date had just started, but it's been more than an hour since we met up. This guy melts time. And my brain.

"Let's do it," I say suddenly. "Let's make a list of dream books and then go plot global revolution over cocktails at this place I remember nearby."

Daniel grins. "I cannot think of anything more fun."

And the thing is neither can I.

CHAPTER SEVEN

Dear Mom,

Really, Dickens? I think you're trying to make a point to me about my sudden life as the Daughter of Privilege. I will ignore it.

Instead, I downloaded a dating book from this girl who won America's Next Top Model. So far it's pretty dumb, and pretty funny. Unlike Brian, who is just dumb. Mom, I totally backed the wrong horse with that guy. He is so blind to the way I feel—or don't feel—about him. Today in the maybe six minutes Dad actually left us alone, Brian was, like, trying to get me to take my shirt off. I'm thinking, "Kid, can't you tell you are irritating the crap out of me?" What makes him think I want to do feelies above the waist? And if that's not enough, I think he is honestly hoping I'm going to have sex with him before the summer is over. He keeps suggesting places we can be alone that have mattresses. Idiot. I am not going to have sex for the first time with anyone who is capable of playing ten straight hours of Call of Duty and then declaring himself "exhausted from a long day." Frankly, I'm not going to have sex with anyone period until I get my full ride on a diving scholarship. But even then, never Brian.

I hope you will have better luck in New York. I know you're only there for a week, but I keep thinking maybe you'll go out on a date like we talked about. Maybe you'll even meet someone cool. I think you deserve it, after all this time. Dad was asking me if you're dating, only instead of asking straight up, he was using all these dumb ways that make it clear he doesn't have the first clue how to get information out of anyone under forty. Like, he said,

"So does Mom take a lot of time to herself?" when I told him I wanted to be alone. And when I got ready to go out with everybody from dive, he asked if I got the lipstick from you, and if you wore a lot of makeup. I was like, "Sometimes." Which you know is a bald-faced lie. You never wear makeup, and you really should.

I told Dad you went out to dinner once a week or so, and no, I didn't know with whom, and then because he got so flustered about that, I said, like I was all confused, "I think she goes swimming sometimes at night because she has always showered before she comes home." His head started spinning like the Tilt-A-Whirl. It was so funny. Joe wasn't in on it, so he was like, "What are you talking about, Cori," and then I said, "I could be wrong," so now he's totally mystified about your love life. In the dating book it tells you there are three rules to maintaining a man's interest, and rule number two is always keep him guessing. Rule one is to floss, and rule three is to withhold sex, so I guess this is a pretty popular guide with parents of teen girls.

Assuming that you are still treating flossing like it's your patriotic duty and not somehow sleeping with Dad from three hours away, congrats on mastering the art of maintaining your ex-husband's interest. It seems to really be working.

Which leads me to kind of a weird question that I probably wouldn't ask in real life, but a journal isn't exactly real life, so here it is: If Dad is this interested in your sex activities, does that mean he wants to be with you again?

If he does, do you?

If you do, will you get back together?

That would be weird.

I don't think there's a celebrity dating book for that.

Anyway, just in case, I hope you're living it up in New York while you can. There. That's good advice. Maybe I should write a dating book.

Love,

Your love and sex guru, Cori

The disorientation you feel when you wake up somewhere different from where you expected to wake up is really a sensation unlike any other.

I feel that way when I wake up in the beautiful Manhattan boutique hotel with a thin line of city sun making its way through the heavy-duty curtains. The "Hey, this isn't my bedroom" feeling. Then I come to and remember I'm in New York, and my kids are with John, and everything is different today than it was two days ago, and that's really ok. Yesterday I gave a presentation, and I had a coffee date with a hot librarian, and I went to Barnes & Noble, and I . . .

Oh.

The hot librarian is in bed with me. He is snoring. I seem to have brought home a hot librarian last night. Huh.

Huh?

I pop up like a jack-in-the-box. No, like a skank-in-the-bed. I'm wearing underpants but nothing else. My breasts are just . . . bare. Where is my shirt? Or my bra? My mouth tastes like I bit off a squirrel's tail. A city squirrel. The hotel TV is on, quietly playing ESPN, which I believe we put on last night because Daniel wanted to see the Mets highlights. That's right. Daniel is a baseball fan. He sheepishly asked if we could watch SportsCenter about four minutes after the first time we had sex.

We had sex!

More than once.

Slowly, like I'm in a Mission: Impossible movie, I slink out of the bed sideways. My eyes are on Daniel the entire time, but he doesn't move a muscle or break his snore. When my feet find the hotel carpet, I dart around looking for the bathrobe, then remember it is on the back of the bathroom door from yesterday's shower. Ok. To the bathroom. Which has a loud pocket door, but I manage to slide it shut smoothly before turning on the light. In the huge, brightly lit hotel mirror, I see the startling evidence of my misdeeds: tangled bedhead . . . mascara on my cheeks . . . is that a bite mark? I see what might possibly be a small bite mark. I see, to my combined shock and relief, a condom wrapper on the counter. I see the bathrobe and grab it. I see my phone.

It's 6:30 a.m. I have a new text from Lena. It says: "Call me in the morning, you wild child."

I think I must have drunk texted her last night. I open my messages. Yep. I pretty much live texted my fall from grace. It's all there in the transcript.

Amy:
I'm on a date!!!

Lena:
No. Really?

Amy:
Really! With a hot librarian. We are at a sushi restaurant. I'm in the bathroom!

Lena:
Well, get out of there and go flirt with the hot librarian!

Amy:
You're right! K bye

And then an hour and a half later,

Amy:
I'm in the bathroom again!

Lena:
Um . . .

Amy:

With the hot librarian!

Lena:

He's in the bathroom with you?

Amy:

No! We're having after-dinner drinks. I think he wants to have sex with me. He makes terrible Latin puns.

Lena:

That's great! I mean, not the puns. That's awful.

Amy:

I'm horrified!

Lena:

You're being silly. Go get some!

Amy:

Is that allowed?

Lena:

It's encouraged.

Amy:

K bye!

That's all there is. Apparently after three high-end cocktails, I didn't need much encouraging to get naked with a stranger. I set down my phone for a second, wishing I could call Lena, and then I realize maybe

I can. I don't hear anything in here. Not the snoring, not the TV. This bathroom is pretty soundproof.

"Daniel?" I call out softly. There's nothing.

"Daniel?" I say a little more loudly. I wait for a long time. No response.

"Daniel, the hotel is on fire!" I say louder still.

When he fails to dash out of bed, I call Lena.

"I didn't mean six thirty in the morning," she says instead of hello.

"I had sex with a stranger last night!" I stage-whisper.

"Hey, hey!" The grogginess and enthusiasm mingle in her voice. "That's great."

"What? No. It's not great. He's in my hotel room right now, sleeping in my bed!"

"Where are you?"

"Locked in the bathroom."

"Well. That explains the incredibly loud whispering."

"Lena! I'm trapped in a hotel bathroom with no coffee and a stranger in my bed."

"Isn't that the name of a Lifetime movie?" she asks.

"I could kill you."

"Ok, slow down and tell me what you need."

"I don't know. What do I need? I haven't had sex in three years. Do I need a rabies shot?"

"Is he part raccoon?" Lena asks. "If not, you don't. Did you use a condom?"

I look around the bathroom and take a quick inventory. "Apparently we used three condoms. Successively."

"Well, well, well!" she says. "Nice work, Amy! I call that a hell of a comeback."

"Lena, I don't even know his last name." This isn't true. It's something hyphenated with *Seong*. He goes by Mr. Seong. His mother is a first-generation Korean immigrant. His father is . . . I can't remember. I know he told me, but it was probably while I was busy being stunned about how handsome he is. And besides, the conversation was so rapid fire we hardly stayed on one subject for long without getting sidetracked.

"Did you pick him up in a bar?" she asks.

"No!" I practically shout. "Jeez. How slutty do you think I am?"

"Not slutty at all," she says blithely. "There is nothing slutty about safe sex between two consenting single adults." She pauses a second and then adds, "He is single, right?"

"Yes! Or . . . I mean, he said he was. I guess he could be lying. Maybe I should google him. Are you near your computer? Can you internet stalk him for me right now?"

"Aha! So you do know his last name. I knew it."

"I just remembered it. It's Seong."

"S-o-n-g?"

"S-e-o-n-g. First name Daniel. Resource librarian in the New York Public Schools."

"Please hold."

I sit quietly on the closed toilet for a few moments. Then I blurt, "He took me to a bookstore and got me drunk."

Lena snorts through the phone. "Well played, hot librarian. Oooh! I think this must be him. Daniel Seong-Eason. My, he *is* a hot librarian."

"Is there a wife in the pictures?"

"No wife. This could be a daughter, though. Teenage girl? Looks like him, only girlier."

"That's the one. He has a daughter who is a rising senior. Apparently she's brilliant. Acing it at Bronx Science."

"Very nice. I can't think of a better streak breaker than this guy," says Lena. "Is it true that you haven't had sex in three years? I had more sex than that when I was a nun."

"I'm not sure that's something to brag about," I say. "Anyway, I feel pretty weird."

"Was the sex bad, then?"

"No. I mean, I'm out of practice, so it all felt weird. And now I feel even weirder after the fact. I mean, is it ok that I did this while my kids' father is taking care of them day in and day out for an entire week? Are my priorities all out of whack?"

Lena scoffs. "Wait, you're asking if it's ok if you cheated on your ex-husband?"

"Not ex. Remember, no actual divorce?" I sigh. "Mostly, I've been too busy to think about sex or dating much over this time, so it's not like I've been holding out. But yeah, somewhere in the back of my mind, I guess I might have thought of myself as being faithful to him." Even as I say it, I think of the charges on the credit card. Lingerie. Waxing. Heat rises in my face.

"Please, Amy. Don't be a dummy. We're talking about a man who left his family to live on the other side of the world with a college coed. There's no one to be faithful to."

I frown. "What about my kids?"

"You think your kids care if you're celibate? You think they want to know either way?"

I say nothing because she's so obviously right.

"But," I say, "I mean, if I was going to sleep with someone after all this time, it should have been with someone I'd been on a couple of dates with, right? Someone where there's a good chance of us having a future together. Not some random stranger from a vacation."

"Where on earth are you getting those rules from? As I understand it, single adult women are supposed to do exactly what gets their rocks off, without guilt or shame. If for you, that means sex on vacation, where is the harm in that?"

"I'm not like that."

"Apparently you are! Which is good news, because being like 'that' is way more fun than the alternative."

I am silent for a moment. Finally, I hear myself say, "It really was fun."

"Aha!" says Lena victoriously. "Of course it was! That's awesome!"

"He is cute, and he has this nice, easy way about him, and he really cares about his kid and his classrooms and teaching. And he did this thing with his mouth on my neck when we were . . . you know."

"Wow. Wow! I love it," says Lena supportively. "So now what?"

"What do you mean?"

"Are you going to, like, have a vacation affair with him until you come home?"

"What? Oh no. No, no, no. I'm just wondering how I can get out of this hotel room without waking him up so I never have to see him again. I'm going to stay with Talia tonight. It was just a onetime thing."

"A streak breaker."

"Exactly. Now I can go another three years without sex if I want to."

Lena laughs. "The question is, now that the streak has been broken, *will* you want to?"

And in the farthest recesses of my heart comes an answer so unequivocal I almost shout it out. But before I can, the pocket door slides open, and the streak breaker himself is standing in front of me.

Needless to say, he's completely naked.

———

"Good morning."

Daniel is very fit. I remember noticing and commenting on it last night. I was delighted by it then. This morning his lean, broad body isn't sexy; it's intimidating. My body is not fit or lean. I clutch my bathrobe around my midsection tightly. That is where I gestated two healthy babies, and you can tell.

"Um, Lena? Gotta go. Talk later."

"Wait, I wanna listen in!" I hear her say as I click off. I turn to Daniel, trying not to look at his flat stomach.

"Good morning?" I hear myself ask, not exactly sure why it's a question.

He grins at me. I imagine he must be taking me in, cowering on the closed lid of a hotel toilet, clutching my phone, a garble of smeared eye makeup and tangled hair and shame.

"Will you come over here?"

I stand up hesitantly and take a few slow steps toward him.

Daniel meets me halfway, puts his too-strong arms around me, and gives me a kiss that is equal parts desire and morning breath. I find it incredibly human and reassuring, and when we break off, I look up at him and smile. "I'm feeling shy," I tell him. "This is not my usual MO."

"Same here," he says, moving some of my tangled hair away from my jawline. "Well, I'm not shy. But the MO part. Using gratuitous Latin phrases is my modus operandi. It was fun, though, right?"

I nod. "Really fun."

"One thing led to another," he says.

"It did."

"I wish it could lead to another," he says, slowly slinking a hand under the edge of my bathrobe. Instead of enjoying the sensation, I wonder if my breasts are droopier than those of other women he's been with. I remove his hand and pull the robe up higher around my neck.

He looks disappointed but says, "You're right. I'd better go," and turns to find his pants where they dropped the night before. "I want to grab something for my daughter on the way up. Something from Barney Greengrass. She's in love with the whitefish salad, and I pick some up whenever I'm in the neighborhood." He pulls on his shorts and pants and starts doing up the fly. "Want to come along and have the best smoked fish of your life?"

My stomach turns a little. "I think . . . I'd better . . ."

Daniel kisses me again. "Come with me," he says. "I know this was a onetime thing, but I don't want to say goodbye just yet."

I blink. A onetime thing. Ok, I think. He gets it. Good, right? It feels not so good.

"I'm sorry, Daniel. I just can't. I didn't sleep enough, and I've got to make it to at least three more presentations today to get my hours before the conference ends."

He nods. "Of course, I get it. And then back to Pennsylvania?"

I quirk my mouth. I'm here for a few more days. Would I want to see him again during that time? Absolutely I would. But look at him. Look at me. I don't want to be around when his gin goggles finally wear off. "Back to Pennsylvania, yeah."

He smiles without teeth. "Too bad."

I sigh and look away. Is this what I wanted out of this trip? One-night stands in hotels, awkward partings, some strange cocktail of pleasure and guilt, longing and shame, all combined together?

The hell with that. I look down and touch the knot of my robe. He's already seen me naked, and he still wanted to have sex with me. He saw me this morning and didn't run screaming. What am I hiding? What am I so afraid of?

"Daniel?" I say, looking up. He's already tying up the laces of his Sperrys.

I should just let him go. I should just be happy for this little adventure and keep in mind that real life is just five days away.

"Mmm?" he says when he straightens up.

"Last night was incredible," I say. Then I stand on my tiptoes and plant the hottest, most confident, most adult kiss I can summon on his lips.

"Mmm," he says again, with a very different tone this time.

"If you're in my neck of the woods, you'll drop me a line, right?" I ask as I pull away.

He looks at me, trying to read my face, probably wondering what the hell I want. Since I don't know, either, I say good luck to him. After a moment, he starts buttoning his shirt. "Absolutely. And the same goes for you." He is fully dressed now. This is almost over. I am almost in the clear.

I nod. "Have fun with the smoked fish."

He raises his eyebrows and gives me a little half smile. "I always do," he says lightly. And then with slightly more weight, he says, "Goodbye, Amy. Thanks for an amazing night." And he kisses me and walks out the heavy hotel door, and just like that, he is gone.

———

"Welly, well, well," says Talia when she opens the door of her condo to me that night. "You're finally here."

The conference is over. I checked out of my hotel, a little sadly, went back up to Columbia for a few more workshops, and then spent a couple of hours wandering around Talia's neighborhood, suitcase in tow. Ten minutes before we were supposed to meet, she texted me to tell me her appointment had gone late and she'd meet me at her place an hour later. I wheeled my bag into an Irish pub and had a beer.

Finally, at long last, she texted and told me she was almost home, and I beelined for her place. Which, I quickly learned, was not the building I'd been trying to get into the last time I'd been on this street. Someone, I will not say who, had inverted the street number of her own apartment building in her previous text.

"*You're* finally here," I say back to her. "Look at you!"

She takes my handbag out of my hands and puts it on a table by the door, then does a little twirl. White pressed shirt, cream trousers, brown leather belt, orange scarf in her hair. "Not bad for a Sunday, right? Come give me a hug."

I oblige. Talia is skin and bones, as usual. I often wonder if she's this thin because she works in fashion or if she works in fashion because she is this thin. Either way, she's got a dress hanger of a body with a pretty but commanding face. Not actress good looks, but something more powerful than that.

"Your hair is so curly. It's gorgeous."

"Thanks. This fall will be all about the natural look for women of color, you know. You have no idea how many hours a week this trend is saving me. I'll have to quit watching TV when it goes back to straight again."

"Have you ever thought of just doing your hair the way you like it, regardless of fashion's whims?"

She looks at me and rolls her eyes. "Have you ever thought about a bra fitting?"

I look down. "That bad, huh?"

"How old is that bra?"

I think for a second. "Same age as my teenager, I guess."

"Bras are not supposed to reach their teen years. Let's put that on the schedule."

"There's a schedule?"

"Hey, Alexa," Talia suddenly calls to no one. "Text Matt."

"What do you want me to tell Matt?" asks a disembodied male voice with a thick Australian accent.

"Make a bra-fitting appointment for tomorrow with Iris."

"Done," says the voice.

"Your Alexa is Australian?"

"Like Crocodile Dundee doing my bidding," she says. "G'day, mistress!"

I laugh and then stop myself. "What's this about a schedule?" I ask sternly.

"Am I right that you've got nothing to do this week?" she asks. "You said your nerdfest was over today."

"You mean my librarians' conference? Yes, it's done now."

"So I thought of a few fun things for you to do while I'm working. Actually, Lena and I both did."

"Lena? My Lena from PA?"

"Yep, she Facebooked me out of the blue. She's pretty delightful, for a nun. She told me to expect that you'd try to spend every moment reading and watching Bravo in my apartment for the next five days. We both agreed we couldn't have that."

My heart falls as I think of six new books on my e-reader, carefully chosen for the next few days. "We can't?"

"This is your momcation."

"That's not a word."

"You're right. Ok. Your . . ." She fishes around for the perfect word. "Your momspringa."

"My what now?" I ask.

"Momspringa. Like rumspringa? Where the kids go wild before they settle back down to buggies and monochrome dressing? You're the Amish one; you know what that is."

I narrow my eyes at Talia. "I'm not Amish," I tell her. "I'm from Amish country. And this isn't a momspringa. It's a trip to New York by myself for a few days, not an extensive exploration of the outside world that exists far from my insulated, isolated existence among my family."

Talia puts her hands up and shrugs. "You say tomato . . ."

I snort and shake my head in dismissal.

"Either way. You're not reading books. You're living life. You're doing all the things you haven't been able to do since your jerk asshole douche-bag left you with nothing but two kids and a closet full of mom jeans."

I look down again. I am indeed wearing mom jeans.

When I look up, Talia is frowning at me. "Are those clogs?" she asks me needlessly.

"They're very comfortable."

It's like I just blasphemed the pope. She exhales fully and closes her eyes, seemingly searching for forbearance. "Never mind. The point is you can sit around and read anytime. This week, you grab life by the balls."

"I always thought that was kind of a violent metaphor."

She tilts her head. "Ok, let's say you stroke life by the balls, then."

There is no way I can keep a straight face to that. "Oh, Talia. I've missed you terribly, and the worst part is I didn't even know it. I'm so sorry I've been out of touch."

Talia takes my hand. "I can hardly blame you. I tried to be there for you after John left, but I never knew what to say, and I didn't feel like I was much help from here. Husbands, kids . . . it's all beyond me, you know."

I smile. "You did send me a ham."

Talia laughs. "Not the right thing?"

"It takes a long time for three people to eat a ham. Next time send a housekeeper."

She grins at me and wraps me in a hug. "You got it." She pulls back and takes me in. "We are going to have such fun, you know that? I've been doing nothing but work, work, work for weeks. Nay, months. Now I have a playmate! One of my favorite people in the world, and I haven't seen her in years, and she's here under my thumb in my spare bedroom slash walk-in closet! What could be better?"

"I can't think of anything," I say. Well, except for all that plus a few good books. "Maybe I could read just a little? Just in the mornings?" I beseech. "I get so little time completely to myself back home."

She sighs. "Hey, Alexa, tell Matt to push all start times back to eleven a.m. through Friday."

I beam at her.

She rolls her eyes again. "But promise to at least consider reading in a chic café or something? Maybe while sipping a perfect coffee or a Bellini with a crepe?"

"Ooh, that sounds amazing. I absolutely promise that will go on my schedule. Now sit down and tell me all about your life since I last saw you. Don't leave out a single thing. We need to get totally up to speed."

CHAPTER EIGHT

Dear Mom,

Talia sounds incredibly cool. No offense, but when you and she video called us last night, I was sort of astounded that you knew anyone that chic. I cannot believe what you guys got up to in college, how much fun you had, how you visited the city all the time and hung out at museums and went dancing. I am going to do all that stuff and more when my time comes.

Don't worry—you did have one responsible kid. Joe is such a weirdo. Today he went to the library for like four hours to do activities that I can only describe as mathletic. At the rate he is going he'll be getting his doctorate at Columbia before I even turn sixteen. I hope he becomes a doctor and buys me a car.

As for me, after I win the Olympics, I'm going to go be a magazine editor like Talia. Ask Talia if I actually have to write journals for that job, because let me tell you, after this summer is over, I'm never writing anything by hand again.

Other questions to ask Talia (or yourself):

1. Why didn't you visit her sooner?

2. Why aren't you as cool as you used to be?

Wait, don't tell me. I know the answer to both questions: you're going to blame it on your kids.

So help me god, that will never happen to me. I could never love any baby more than I love being cool.

Love,

The daughter you wrecked your life for, Cori

———

It is 10:30 a.m. on Monday morning, and I am standing in the offices of *Pure Beautiful*, the print and online fashion guide for, as Talia affectionately refers to her readers, "women who aren't quite ready to give up."

I am one of those women. I read *Pure Beautiful* the moment it arrives in my inbox. It always has one of those ten-items-ten-ways capsule wardrobes, and those are like porn to me. Is there anything more appealing in my world of homework and swim practice than wearing some variation on the same thing every day? A grown-up uniform? And that feeling of completeness I imagine you'd have if you owned every single one of the items in the spread, even though they average out at roughly $475 apiece. It would be almost transcendent. *Hmm,* I imagine thinking as I stare into my all-black-and-white-with-teal-accents closet, *I think I'll combine the classic black one-button crepe blazer with the crisp tailored white shirt and the . . . yes, the linen palazzo pants today. Yesterday I wore the white shirt under the teal sheath dress with the scarf, but the shirt is still clean enough. Tomorrow I can wear the blazer over the sheath dress with the scarf in my hair and the palazzo pants fashioned into a belt. Maybe I can wear the blazer as a kind of cape for day four.*

Anyway, I love that crap. And I love the pages where they show a famous person wearing whatever they wear to get Starbucks, which to said famous person probably feels like pajamas and to me looks like a ball gown, and then the magazine shows me how to make that same outfit for $75 from Zappos or Kohl's or the like. And my favorite column, where they have a financial expert who lovingly yells at people for their failure to save up for retirement and then tells them not to buy a boat. And the excellent pages upon pages of book excerpts that make it so I don't have to read all of the depressing-yet-important new books they pick but can still talk about them competently around other librarians. And best of all, *Pure Beautiful* uses a mix of model sizes. Whether size 2 or size 16, they are impossibly attractive and well proportioned, so they still make me feel plenty insecure, but at least there's some stinking variety. *Pure Beautiful* is, to my mind, the greatest magazine of all time.

And then there is the fact that Talia runs it. I imagine her as the *Devil Wears Prada*–style boss, all shine and hard surfaces and double macchiato extra hot, or else, but when I get past the very New Yorky reception with the impossibly effete man on the phones, I find what looks like a Silicon Valley office. It's a big open loft except for glass-walled, triangle-shaped offices in the corners. The art department takes up the bulk of the space, and the rest is monster printers and little tables with staff members working on laptops scattered throughout. If Talia wants a double macchiato extra hot, she can just make it herself on the enormous Italian espresso machine on a floating bar island near one side. Or I suppose one of her assistants can. There are clear glass dry-erase boards, fresh-fruit bowls, basketball hoops, and yes, a small dog. The only thing that distinguishes *Pure Beautiful* as a magazine and not, say, a Groupon office is the long glass room that stretches the length of the solid wall, filled to bursting with clothes. The fashion closet of legend. In bold Helvetica font on the double glass doors is a sign that reads, WELCOME TO PARADISE.

Talia has explained to me that only the creative departments work in this office in New York, where rent is expensive and salaries are too. The rest of the magazine's staff are in farthest North Carolina. She goes there four times a year. As a result, there are no normal people in the entire office. Just the highly fabulous. And me. About seven people look up at me and my clogs in confusion when I walk in. Several people on cell phones stop talking. I suddenly feel like I am standing there naked. Or that perhaps naked would be preferable to what I'm wearing. If I were naked, I would spread my arms wide and say in a big, bold Joan d'Arc voice, *Look upon me, builders of a magazine, writers of stories, takers of pictures! I am your reader! Kneel and quake before me!*

Luckily Talia's assistant, Matt, appears before my pronouncement. He has the look of a marine but is wearing slim jeans and great wingtips and a perfect french-blue shirt. He has the sweetest smile and looks to be about twenty. There is no question in my mind that in a room full of Ashleighs and Arandiahs and, yes, Talias, Matt had to fight to be called Matt instead of Mateo or Mathias or Mathieu.

"You must be Matt," I say as he beelines to me from the executive office on the far corner.

"That's right. Matt Clarke. Are you here to see Talia?"

"I am," I say. It is nice of him to pretend she didn't tell him to watch for the Pennsylvania rube in the bad shoes. "My name is Amy Byler."

"We're expecting you," is all he says. "I had a lot of fun getting a nice schedule together for you."

I crook my head at him. "Did you?"

"Sure. It was sort of the 'What I'd do for my mom if she came to New York City' list. You know, museums, galleries, concerts, spa."

Fair enough. "Would you book your mom a bra fitting?" I ask him archly.

Matt shrugs. "That I might leave to her."

"Well . . ." I smile cautiously, hoping Talia has honored my request to keep the bill for all this to a reasonable level. "It all sounds wonderful. Even the fitting. I'm lucky to have a friend with such a great team."

At that moment Matt starts buzzing. He looks down at his iPhone and says, "I'm so sorry—I have to take this. Should only take a second.

"Matt Clarke," he says into the phone. "Mm-hmm. Yes. Right. I hear you. Very good. Ok." And then he hangs up.

"That was Talia," he tells me.

"Where is she?" I ask. "I thought she was meeting me here this morning."

"She's in there," he says and points to a glass-walled boardroom to our left. I look over, and she is sitting in the chair facing me and looking stern. "She says we need to rearrange your schedule because . . . um . . ."

I look at her. She shakes her head slowly, despairingly, and then puts her head in her hands. "Because of my outfit?" I ask. I am wearing navy pants and a yellow twinset, all from the L.L.Bean factory store. I thought I looked preppy smart. And I have the special handbag. I adjust my position so Talia can see it better. She continues to look at me despairingly.

"Well," says Matt.

"It's ok, Matt," I tell him. "I've known Talia for a long time. That said, I didn't think I needed to be dressed up to go to a place whose express purpose is to make you over."

"Anyone could make that mistake," he says charitably. "So listen . . ." He leans in and lowers his voice. "My boss, your friend, doesn't quite realize how impossible rescheduling your haircut would be. I think the next available appointment would be sometime after the second coming of our Lord and Savior. Let's grab something from the closet and just get you there on time and never breathe a word of it to her. Sound ok?"

"But won't she notice me fishing around in the closet?"

"Oh, you can't go in there," he says like it's the most obvious thing in the world. "You go back to Jean-Peter, in reception, and tell him I'm bringing you a couple looks and we need his opinion, ok? And I'll be there in ten minutes. Dress size?"

I look at him like he's crazy. "Can you just grab stuff in a medium?"

"Medium means nothing outside of Pennsylvania," he tells me with a smirk. I can tell he's parroting his boss.

"Ok. Fine." I lower my voice. "It's just that . . ." I pause. I think about saying size 8. I've always guessed the plus-size models they use are actually 8s who lie and say they are 16s. "I don't know if you have my size in there? So pick something stretchy, maybe, that I can wear with these pants?"

Matt levels me with a stare. "We have your size. Which is . . . ?"

I hem and haw.

"I can just look in your pants, you know. I have assaulted people's clothing tags before on Talia's orders. I'm not above it."

I laugh. "Ok, ok. Hands off the pants. They are twelves."

"We have twelves. Shoe?"

"Size seven. But I cannot walk in heels."

"Talia would say you can."

"Thank god she's out of shouting range, then."

Matt chuckles. "Ok, I'll look for flattish. Off to Jean-Peter. If he makes you throw away that sweater, just do as he says."

———

Twenty minutes later I am wearing

- my own yellow sleeveless sweater,
- a killer one-button white blazer with the sleeves pushed up,
- a just-above-the-knee pencil skirt in a floral print so large that only two flowers fit on the front of the skirt, in a colorway so bold I can't look directly at it, and
- three-inch pink stiletto heels.

I stagger out of the bathroom, making tiny mincing steps, and find Matt and Jean-Peter examining me carefully.

"It seems," says Jean-Peter very carefully, "that she does not know how to walk in heels."

Matt sighs. "They didn't look very tall in the closet."

"You will have to give her the flats. She walks like the hippos from *Fantasia*."

"But in the flats she'll look like we did an Ambush Makeover."

"We did do an Ambush Makeover," says Jean-Peter.

"Please let me wear the flats," I beg.

"Turn around," Jean-Peter commands. I do a full revolution, as though I am on a morning show showcasing frumpy women from the street. "No, turn around. Face the wall. There's something wrong with your butt."

I pinch my lips together but still do as I'm told.

He and Matt start laughing the minute I am facing the back of the reception room. "What?" I ask and then start craning around to see what is so hilarious about my rear view.

"Oh, Pennsylvania," says Jean-Peter.

"What?" I try again.

"She'll have to take them off," he adds to Matt, not to me.

I think we are talking about the shoes. "Thank god! They are killing me! And I haven't even walked anywhere yet."

They both laugh some more. I turn around and try to look annoyed when actually I'm kind of having fun. "Someone tell me what is so awful about my butt."

"You have a lovely butt," says Jean-Peter. "Clearly you spend your days running around a lot. Not too much sitting. I cannot wait to get you into some good jeans."

"Then why are we laughing? And when can I take off these shoes?"

"You can have the flats on one condition," says Jean-Peter. "Remove the Depends."

"Excuse me?"

Matt jabs Jean-Peter and clears his throat. "Your, ah, briefs, Ms. Byler. There's an unsightly line."

My eyes bulge. "These aren't Depends! Not that there's anything wrong with that. I had two kids! Some women need Depends. These are not Depends. Why am I still discussing this with you? I am wearing my underpants."

"No flats, then," says Jean-Peter, and he turns back to his phone bank as though the matter is settled.

"I can't walk in these things . . . these stilts," I say to Matt, and to prove it, I sort of stumble toward him to reach for the flats. "Have some mercy."

He starts to hand them to me, but in a flash Jean-Peter has them and is holding them in the air like a schoolyard bully. "The undies, Amy. Give up the bulky undies."

"You want me to walk around New York City with no panties on?" I ask him incredulously.

"Why not? The skirt is long enough. Just get out of cabs two feet at a time. Swing on your butt and then push off with your abs and lean against the doorframe with one hand." He demonstrates an exaggerated two-legged exit on his desk chair. "See? That's just a life skill."

"It seems like it would just be a lot easier and safer to keep my underpants on."

"Well. If you want easy and safe, put that horrible pair of stretch pants back on."

There are three mirrors in this reception area, so I've seen the drastic improvement made by these guys in about fourteen minutes. Even I can see that the old pants are headed for the trash. Maybe I should just do as they say.

"Can you get me, like, a skirt that flares away from the panty line?" Jean-Peter just dangles the flats in response.

"I'll die in these shoes out there. Forget getting out of a cab. I'll be hit by one when I fall down in the street. Do you want that on your conscience?"

Jean-Peter looks at me with a completely straight face. "That would not be on *my* conscience. That would be on the conscience of whichever vile corporation made those underpants. And the person who bought the underpants. Do you want your children to be orphaned because you have terrible taste in intimates?"

I cannot stop myself from laughing at this. "Fine. You can have the underpants."

"Thank you, but no. No one wants that. Please dispose of them in the ladies' room," Jean-Peter says. Matt, who has been politely holding his laughter all this time, gives in to a howl.

Smiling, I look at him and shake my head. "You people. You . . . you . . . *New Yorkers* . . ."

But I march off to the bathroom anyway. When I come back, I feel the air-conditioning on my nethers and the sweet relief of ballerina flats on my feet. "Am I ready, folks?" I ask my peanut gallery.

"You're ready," says Jean-Peter. "Good luck with this one, Matt. Have fun at the salon."

"Thanks for all your help," I say dryly.

"You're most welcome," he says without a drop of irony. "Matt, tell them to do the brows. Don't let them forget the brows."

"Let's get out of here while I still have some dignity left," I tell Matt and bolt for the elevator.

He jogs behind me and says, "You do look just great, Ms. Byler," as the doors close. "I think Talia is going to be very pleased."

"She'd better be pleased," I say back. "She's the one who has to buy me new underwear."

—

Matt and I arrive at the salon, a surprisingly shabby-looking place in the East Village, exactly on time. A waif in a distressed denim belted jumper hands us little sake glasses full of some kind of green drink and tells us that Maeve is running a smidgen behind and we should sit tight for half an hour or so.

"Half an hour?" I ask Matt when we settle onto the grubby velvet chaise in the waiting area.

Matt shrugs. "I think she's that good," he says. "Talia said it had to be her."

"Well, you certainly don't have to wait with me," I tell him. "I brought my e-reader."

"Actually, I'm supposed to stick close today. Keep you moving through your itinerary smoothly."

I roll my eyes. "I don't need a babysitter, Matt. I'm happy to tell Talia I sent you away."

"I really don't mind. It's a nice change from the regular office grind."

"Are you sure?" I ask him.

"Very sure. My job can be very . . . intense. One day of helping out someone mellow won't kill me."

I smile. Talia is loyal, brilliant, brave. But not mellow. "Very sweet of you. So what exactly is on this itinerary of ours?"

Matt pulls out his enormous phone. "Hair today," he says.

"Gone tomorrow," I respond like a dork.

"Hmm?"

"Never mind. Just hair?"

"Oh no. Sushi for lunch with Talia at the office, and then nails. I think I will leave you alone on that portion. Nail salons give me hives. And then after the mani-pedi, you can choose between rooftop yoga or the turkish bath, and then I've just added in the, uh, intimates fitting at this place in Brooklyn, so we'll want to cab it there and maybe grab you something good from the Farmacy. By then it will be sevenish, so Talia will take over. At which point you're at her mercy."

"My goodness," I say. "That's quite a schedule." I am wondering how on earth I will pay for all this. Even John's card must have a limit. "Matt, do you have a guesstimate as to how much this haircut will cost?" In PA I usually go to a pretty nice place that charges thirty-five dollars per cut. But I have a feeling thirty-five dollars won't get me a shampoo with a garden hose in the back alley of this joint. The shabby chicness of it is all fake. It's just straight-up chic. The rug in the waiting room is a Turkish kilim, and the water in the glass-doored guest fridge is Voss. The green stuff seems to be some kind of spirulina kombucha.

"Oh," says Matt. "You don't have to worry about that. It's all on the magazine."

I furrow my brow. "Huh? That doesn't seem right."

"Well," says Matt reasonably. "We are getting a great story out of it. And the before and after pictures will be amazing."

"Excuse me?"

"The trend piece. The momspringa."

"You must be joking. What trend piece?"

Matt looks surprised by my question. "Talia didn't tell you? This whole week is on *Pure Beautiful*. We got all those before pictures when you first came into the office and got your ID made with Jean-Peter. Now we do the makeover, the capsule wardrobe, and the story on your vacation from motherhood. I haven't seen this anywhere else yet. I think it might be a reading line on the cover."

"You are kidding me."

Matt shrugs.

"Matt. I did not sign up to be a trend piece. I don't want the whole world reading about how I abandoned my kids for a week to get my nails done."

He laughs. "Why the hell not? Do you know how many people would trade places with you in a heartbeat? I do, because we get emails from them all the time. Furthermore, I am the child of a single mother. Based on that, I have the sense to know that a week off from single motherhood once every three years is not an indulgence—it's a necessity. The fact that you're getting time to yourself is nothing to be ashamed of."

I think this over. I don't appreciate getting this lecture from a kid young enough to be my son who I first met an hour ago. But then, he's just saying exactly what Talia or Lena would say. Like, verbatim.

And the common denominator? None of them have kids.

"Matt. Listen. I don't . . . I don't want to look a gift horse in the mouth. But I would have liked to have been consulted about this. For one thing, I would have looked cuter this morning if I'd known you were using me as a before picture. And for another, I don't think this is a real trend. I think this is an anomaly. I think I have two very bossy friends who are well meaning but don't have the visceral understanding of what it means to be a mother. The reality is that there are no breaks from that job. My real life is back home. This is all . . . just a momentary escape from reality."

"Exactly," says Matt. "A fantasy week for mothers. Men do them all the time. Weeks at spring training camp with major-league teams, NASCAR driving school, dude ranches. You're doing your version—claiming a new space for women. Momspringa."

"That's not a word."

"It soon will be," he says. "And all because of you!"

"Sheesh," I say with a frown. "You make it sound so reasonable. Like a feminist movement."

"Maybe it is."

"You should be the one writing the piece," I say jokingly.

"I am," Matt responds.

I blink at him.

"This is my big break, Amy," he tells me. "I don't have any real glossy clips yet. No bylines to speak of. Just dumb pun heads and art captions. I could get promoted over this. Or . . . hired away . . ."

"Ah . . . ," I say.

"So no pressure, but if you say no to this article, I will be making Talia's coffee for the rest of my life."

I laugh. "No pressure."

"Consider it," Matt says. But before I can answer, a tattooed youth with a ring coming out of her cheek and hair the color of a spring bouquet appears in front of me. "Oh, Amy," she says, as though we are old friends. "Oh, poor, shaggy Amy. I'm Maeve. And I'm about to change your life."

CHAPTER NINE

Dear Mom,

    Finally, Mom. A book I can get excited about. This only took you, what, like, eight tries?

    At first I wasn't so sure. The girl, Eleanor, seems really weird, and socially not a superstar. But she was totally relatable and actually totally great and I want a time machine so I can be her friend. And the guy, Park, sounds premium quality. I would totally hit that. Except that he's imaginary and also lived in the eighties. Otherwise, hot. Virginity worthy. After I get my scholarship. And build my time machine.

    Anyway it rained yesterday morning, and there was lightning right after we started, so practice was canceled, but Dad was doing a STEM thing with Joe, so I just sat in the employee lounge at the pool and read the book and drank free Diet Cokes. Just two, so calm yourself. I had no idea what the bands they were talking about sounded like, so I made an Eleanor & Park *Spotify channel to play while I was reading. Suddenly I looked up and three hours had gone by and Dad was there to pick me up. And I was reading that whole time! Are you not the proudest librarian in the world?*

    I hope you're having a good time today in New York. I know Lena and Talia had something planned together, something to help you do actual fun things and not just be boring in a fun city. I do want you to have fun, because you're going to be home soon, and we are hungry and need our laundry done.

Har har. We do miss you and not just because Dad cannot seem to get the dinner situation under control. Last night he just put out some store-bought hard-boiled eggs. No. Wrong. I put the Jimmy John's app on his phone right then and there.

But missing aside, we are doing pretty well. Dad is . . . he's ok. He's very interesting. He is trying super hard, and that makes us all feel like we should be careful with him, but sometimes I do want to shout at him because when he's nice to us or says things he likes about us, I want to scream, "Well, if you liked us so much, why did you leave us?"

But then also, I want to forgive him. Because he came back, and you can tell he really cares. When he apologizes for leaving us, he means it. I heard him crying last night after he thought we went to bed, and Joe said it was because he was stewed in regret. Isn't that such a Joe thing to say?

But, Mom, it's true. He is stewed in regret. He's like a big hot cup of feelings soup. He hugs us a lot and keeps buying us little "just because" gifts, and he likes to talk about what we were like as kids. He talks about "seizing every moment" and stuff like that. I asked him why he was crying last night, and he said it was because he knew he couldn't stay in town indefinitely because of his work.

I asked him if work was part of the reason he left us. He says he left because he was depressed and anxious and mistakenly believed he could run away from those problems. It sounds like a stock answer, Mom. Like what his media-relations person told him to say. I asked him the same question again. Because he left EVERYTHING in his world behind but work. He must really love his job, right?

He said that his identity as a man was all caught up in his work. That's what he told me this morning. I went to diving practice with that in my head. It wasn't a good headspace. I kept thinking, his identity as a man. What the hell does that mean? I know a bunch of other dads, and I would say that they all have being a dad at the top of their list of identities. Like, you're a librarian, and a teacher, and a friend, and a bad dresser, but most of all you're a mom, right?

Why did he keep his job but not keep us?

I don't know—I don't want to think about it anymore. I'm going to go read Eleanor & Park. *Sometimes a book about other people's problems is way better than your own. I guess that's what you've been onto with this reading thing all along?*

Love,

Your literary late bloomer, Cori

———

On day two of the makeover process, while I am making my way back to the *Pure Beautiful* offices from a very long stretch at the colorist's, I am whammied with the most powerful urge to call Cori. We've been texting at a quick clip, and I've called John's landline at least once every day I've been gone, but it's always Joe who claims the phone and patiently, painstakingly recounts the latest news for me. This means yesterday's call revolved around Joe's recent interest in geothermal heating systems. For reasons of equal parts self-interest and expediency, I call Cori's cell directly. She doesn't answer, and my heart tugs against the inner walls of my chest as I leave a "just thinking about you" voice mail. After a short while she texts me: "All good, Mom, Trinity says hi. Don't worry, I'm doing my reading." I sigh deeply. I assigned her that reading journal so she could process what she felt, have an outlet for her experiences with her dad, and not feel the need to censor herself or protect my feelings in the moment. But now I feel like I should have demanded to read it every day. I should have installed a webcam on her dresser that I could activate at will. I should have bugged her phone. I should have planted a spy on the dive team. I should have had a chip implanted in her brain that would alert me anytime her serotonin levels dipped below a reasonable baseline.

"Good lord!" says Matt, interrupting me from my mom panic session. "I barely recognized you!"

139

I look in one of the many office mirrors. I barely recognize myself. Here is what Matt, Talia, and *Pure Beautiful* have done to me in the last twenty-four hours:

1. Changed my hair from dishwater blonde with a side part, perfect for everyday ponytails, to choppy, wavy sex hair with thick fringe bangs swept to one side. Oh yeah, and my hair is brown now. Rich chocolate brown with some reddish-blondish thing happening as it gets to the ends. It looks good. Like I stole a very beautiful woman's wig, plopped it on my head, and announced, This is my hair now.

2. Waxed and plucked my brows into such a shape that I actually look five pounds thinner. Did I have five pounds of extra eyebrows? I wonder with horror.

3. Dyed my eyebrows to match my hair.

4. And then combed my eyebrows. And put some gel in them. Is this something they think I'm going to do every day? I tell them four or five times I will not. They ignore me.

5. Painted my fingernails with a kind of gel that changes color when it gets warm.

6. Painted my toenails with a different kind of gel that just stays the same color all the time, but that color is jade green.

7. Forced me to strip from the waist up and then wrestled me into a collection of bras best meant for the kind of prostitutes that charge $3,000 a night, in letter sizes I'm pretty sure they invented on the spot to spare my feelings.

8. Bought me three bras that defy not just gravity but also time, putting my breasts back in the exact spot they were before I had Cori.

9. Given me a stack of jeans to try on from the fashion closet that is so enormous I actually have to also borrow a wheeled YSL duffel to get them to Talia's office.

By the time Talia and I are having take-out Thai curry on the coffee table at her office that evening, I look ten years younger and a lifetime cooler. I'm wearing magic jeans with no gaping out the back and no pinching in the front. My beautiful, beautiful new hair keeps pulling me to the reflective glass window to gaze upon myself. Talia laughs at me every time I throw aside my chopsticks, pop up from the office couch, tousle my hair in the mirror, and widen my eyes.

"Look at me, Talia!" I nearly shout. "Look upon me!"

"I'm looking!" she says, laughing.

"I'm not even wearing makeup! I am the prettiest woman in *America*!"

She shakes her head. "Would you like to be wearing makeup?"

I think for a moment. "No. Do I have to do makeup tomorrow?" It's far too late now for me to be facing down any more makeover appointments tonight, and I'm pretty relieved about that.

"Well, you don't *have* to do anything," she tells me.

I tilt my head at her suspiciously. "I think I *had* to change out of my stretch pants. That look on your face when you saw them did not scream *optional*."

"Ok, fair enough. The makeup is more optional than the pants. I think Matt will want to do a bunch of camera-ready makeup for your 'after' photo shoot, but you can go barefaced the rest of the time and still look great, you lucky dog."

I smile. "Awww, thank you!" This may be the first beauty-related compliment I've ever received from Talia.

"By barefaced," she elaborates, "I mean with mascara, crème blush, and lipstick. You understand that, right? You are a white woman from Pennsylvania. That means you look like you were embalmed during the winter solstice and only now have been unearthed by archeologists. You're so pale that Han Solo had more color when Leia first defrosted him. You could tell me you just got off the International Space Station, and I would believe you. You look like an animated character from *The Polar Express*. You could—"

"Ok," I interrupt. "Message received. I am pasty."

"You are pastier than the fondant frosting on a Hamptons wedding cake. You look like—"

"I will wear mascara," I interrupt, to stop the tirade.

"And blush."

"And lipstick," I capitulate. "However, I will not comb and style my eyebrows every morning. That's a bridge too far."

We shake on it.

"So what's next for me, then?" I ask her. "Modeling classes? Botox? Lessons in deportment?"

Talia smiles and shakes her head. "Nah, you're pretty enough. Now we work on what's on the inside."

I furrow my brow. "I can totally see how this makeover was called for. But on the inside, I'm totally fine. Happy, busy, great kids, great job, great house, great life . . ."

"Mmmmmm," says Talia.

"No 'mmmmm,'" I scold her. "Just yes."

"Mmmmmm," she adds.

I give her some side-eye. "I let you paint my fingernails taupe," I say with a warning tone.

"What color do they get when you get hot? Oh, wait, we'll never know, because you've apparently sworn off sex."

My mouth drops. "I did not swear off sex! I just had sex! It was great!"

Talia's face cracks open. "You didn't tell me it was great."

I blush. "Well, I mean. I don't have much to compare it to. But he was great looking, and we both . . . you know."

"I do."

I shrug. "So I was happy with the experience. I give it three and a half stars."

"You should try doing it again. Go for five stars."

"With Daniel?" I ask. *Did I just ask that excitedly?*

"Sure. Or with anyone." She taps one chopstick on her lips in thought. "How about Matt?"

I gasp. "Your assistant Matt? That's like . . . like suggesting I sleep with your son!"

Talia makes a sour face. "Yeah, that is gross somehow. Sorry. I guess I just figured it would be a good way to nail down whether he was straight or not once and for all."

"He's straight. Isn't he?"

"Maybe bi?" says Talia.

I think for a moment. "We're all a little bit bi," I say. "Or so Lena tells me."

"I love that nun," Talia says. "You could sleep with her."

"Talia! Stop. I don't need to sleep with anyone. That's not the be-all and end-all of life, you know."

"Spoken like someone who has never had five-star sex."

Privately I contemplate Talia's life, not for the first time. No kids. Very few friends. Little by way of family. Work is her life. No wonder sex is such a focus for her. For me, I have other fish to fry.

"Wrong," she says out of the blue.

"What's wrong?" I ask.

"Whatever you're thinking that makes you dismiss any hope of having a satisfying love life. The idea that you're not good enough, or you don't have time, or it's not important, or you should wait around for John to come back . . ."

I twist my lips. "He's not coming back. I mean, he came back, but not for me," I tell her sadly. "He came back for the kids."

Talia sighs. "I wish I was as sure about that as you are."

I shake my head. "You know about Marika. The credit card. The waxing, the lingerie."

She nods. "Yes, but still. I'm worried, Ames. I'm worried that after all the good times with the great kids you made for him, he'll start sniffing around for you too. I think he wants his old life back, even if he doesn't yet know it himself."

Completely out of nowhere, tears prick at my eyes. I sniffle. My eyes prickle. I hold my breath.

"Are you crying?" she asks.

"No! I'm not crying," I exclaim. Then I start crying.

What starts small and sniffly begins to build on itself. "I'm sorry," I whimper. "I don't know why I'm crying." But the minute I say that, I know it's not true. I am crying at the very thought of John wanting me back. I am thinking about how much I've been through since he left us. I start thinking about how his coming home could make that all better. Then I think of how I shouldn't want that. I think of the credit card charges from Hong Kong. I think, *I'm a doormat. I'm an idiot. I'm stuck.* And I cry more.

Talia looks at me out of the corner of her eye like I'm a solar eclipse. Then she starts typing on her computer.

"Hi," she says, and I look up. She's staring into her screen. She's taking a call while I sit here weeping in her office?

"Hey, how's it going? What's up?" says a familiar voice. I lower the volume of my sobs to listen in.

"She's crying. What do I do?"

"She's what now? She doesn't cry. What did you do? Amy? Amy, are you there?"

It's Lena. Talia tells her to hang on and then moves to sit next to me on the sofa, laptop positioned where we both can see.

"Hi, Lena," I wail when she gets into the sight line.

"Whoa. You look amazing," she says. "Close your mouth and look up. Ew, blow your nose too. Yes, that's better. Amazing! I love your hair. You look so much like yourself, like the self I know. Beautiful, clear hearted, loyal, determined. I'm dazzled how I'm getting all that from a haircut."

I am about to thank her when she adds, "Where did all the rest of your eyebrows go?"

I shake my head because I don't know. "They were there one second, gone the next."

"Is that why you're crying? Because really, you look terrific. And your eyebrows will grow back, if you're missing the shade from the sun they were doubtless providing. Talia, you did good."

I stop crying. "So you two are in cahoots. I guess you knew about the magazine article?"

Lena's eyes dart over to Talia, giving them both away.

"I feel a little used," I tell them. "I thought I was coming here to reconnect with an old friend. Instead I'm being tarted up to sell magazines."

"You feel used because you got a free haircut and color?" Talia asks.

"Without warning."

Talia shrugs. "In the future I will give you due warning before giving you anything nice."

"I would appreciate it," I sniffle out.

"Are you ok, Amy?" asks Lena. "I've never seen you cry before. Maybe when John first left. But not since then."

I tell Lena about what Talia said about John. Then I fill her in on the credit card charges. Then I snivel and tell her I think I'm not over John.

Talia does not hide her disgust. "Ew," she says. "He's gross."

Lena just tilts her head at me. "Why do you think that?"

"Guilt. I feel terrible for sleeping with the hot librarian. I feel like I broke my wedding vows."

Lena looks at me with obvious pity. "Hon, your wedding vows have been broken for a long time."

I nod my head and flop back into the sofa. "So why am I crying about this now?" I ask the room.

Talia shrugs, her hands outstretched in frustration. "I have no idea! You and your new hair should be having sex with that hot librarian. You're doing this wrong."

Lena chimes in. "She says he was a one-night stand."

"Well, then, they can lie down the next time," quips Talia, without missing a beat. Despite myself, I choke out a laugh.

I take a drink of my wine and clear my throat. "You guys, I thought . . . I guess deep down I hoped . . . with John coming back like this, trying to make amends . . ." I shrug. "What can I say? We had half a lifetime together. He was there when I got my master's. When we first found out we were pregnant. When Cori tried to pierce her own ears. When Joe lost his first baby tooth in the midway of that disgusting carnival. John took me to Paris for the first time and cried with me when our kids were born and saved the wedding album when the basement flooded. That kind of love doesn't turn off like a light switch."

Lena sighs deeply, and Talia puts her arm around me. "Oh, Amy. You gorgeous idiot."

I shake my head woefully. "I know."

"Thank god for that credit card," says Lena.

"What do you mean?" I ask.

"I think it's the wake-up call you need. You've been disabused of the notion that you and John could get your old life back. Those charges show who he really is and what he really wants. It's better to find this out now and not at the end of the summer, when he's heading home to the naked labia of a woman fifteen years younger than you."

Talia winces. "That is an amazing visual, Lena. Please never say that phrase again."

I bury my face in my hands. "I can't believe I have to face him in three days."

"What do we need to do to get you ready for that?" asks Lena. "What would make you feel strong and confident around John, instead of hurt and vulnerable?"

I shake my head, because it all sounds so impossible.

Lena and Talia look at each other across the computer screen. As one they say, "Momspringa."

"Momspringa," Talia says again, this time solo. "For real. Not just for the article. Maybe the whole summer off. A summer class, a second language, a new passion, a fresh outlook . . ."

I shake my head in dismissal. "That's not happening, and anyway, I don't know if there's anything that's going to really make me feel better except good old-fashioned time and tears."

Talia says, "You've tried time and tears already," but Lena waves her away.

"Leave it all to your friends," Lena says. "I bet we can help you get your groove back."

I shake my head. "I never had a groove. I had a boyfriend, and then I had a husband, and then I had a pair of kids, a job, no husband, and a huge mortgage. No groove in there anywhere."

Lena turns her face toward Talia's side of the room. "We can do this, but it is not going to be easy. She is groove resistant."

"Tell me about it," says Talia. "She wanted to spend this week watching movies and eating pizza in yoga pants."

"I love yoga pants!" I cry.

"Can this mom be saved?" asks Talia.

"This mom is right here," I remind them.

"We have to try," says Lena. "She's too young to be put out to pasture."

"To graze on pizza . . ."

"To low in the fields of cable television . . ."

I groan loud enough to break up their little chat. "I'm sorry, guys. I know you're trying to help, but I don't want a momspringa. I want to go home. I like pizza. I like movies and yoga pants. If I'm going to feel miserable over my ex-husband, I want to do it as God intended, on the couch with a box of tissues and another box of wine and nonstop Hugh Grant movies. I don't want to be miles from my family in slimming jeans having sex with strangers."

The two of them sigh.

"It's up to her," says Talia. "We tried."

Lena nods. "We just want you to be happy, Amy."

I smile. "I know. And it's been fun here. But my life is back home. That's where I need to be."

"Then come on home," Lena says. "I'll have the wine box ready for you."

Talia reaches over and puts her arms around me. "Grooving isn't for everyone," she says sadly. "But just for tonight, since you're here anyway, how about *A Little Night Music*?"

———

Before Marie's Crisis was a Broadway showtunes singalong bar, it used to be a brothel. So we know, at some point in history, there were straight men inside these walls. On a Tuesday night, though, when it's not too full of tourists and the pianist is one of the best Broadway hacks in town, we can be fairly certain not to run into one. It's the perfect place for a moody postmakeover me, as well as my hostess, who never needs a makeover to attract attention from the opposite of the species. We can be sure to be ignored at Marie's.

Talia puts me near the left side of the piano, where we can see what's next with a subtle crane of the neck. "*Fantasticks*," she says quietly to me.

"Good time to hit the bar, then. No one can resist 'Try to Remember.'"

The pianist finishes the last bars of "Kiss of the Spider Woman," and Talia disappears. I look around me at the basement room we're in. Dim lighting, dirty walls, a slow bar, terrible acoustics. Everything is exactly as I left it. The patrons look better, younger, than I remember. And we aren't the only women, like we used to be when we came here decades earlier. That means Talia may not get to do her killer "Defying Gravity" solo, which somehow gets requested every time we come in (I suspect a plant).

After "Try to Remember," it's a William Finn medley. I don't know any of the words. I step back from the piano, find an old worn velvet bench, and drape myself across it to listen to the beautiful voices. Talia finds me there, slips a martini into my waiting hand, and slides into the crowd of singers again. I watch them laugh and sing and bumble the words. I think of everything I've lived since I've been here last. The person I was before was a shapeless shell, waiting for my life to start. Biding my time. I had nothing but time.

I drink my martini. I miss my kids.

After a half hour, I finally hear chords I know. I pull my face up just as Talia turns around and faces me. "*Dreamgirls*," she mouths and waves me over.

I climb to my feet. Talia and I sang this score endlessly in college, and we both know it front to back. By the time we come to "One Night Only," I have forgotten all my woes entirely. I've forgotten I'm not twenty-one. We sing for an hour, then two, then climb to the stairs to street level and find it brighter in the nighttime lights of the Village than it was inside the bar. Talia opens her Lyft app. I am so tired it hurts.

"See, that was fun," she tells me. She is a little hoarse.

"I haven't stayed up this late in fifteen years," I respond, and my voice is creaking too.

"Look at all you've been missing living under a rock in the sticks."

I shake my head. "Yes. But it's not the same now."

"What are you talking about?" asks Talia. "Marie's is frozen in time."

I nod. "But we're not."

Talia sighs, and it is the first time I have seen her face fall since I've been back. She shakes her head. "Sometimes I think I am," she says mysteriously. I quirk my brow at her.

"Do you ever wish . . . ," I ask her. "You know. When Simon proposed way back when . . ."

"Never once," she says. "Kids, houses, that whole thing—they never had the same appeal for me as they did for you. You wanted all that from the start. More than anything. I wanted a corner office." Talia sighs. "And as for 'having it all . . .'" She shrugs, and her voice trails away. "It looks like a huge pain in the butt."

"It is."

"But I like knowing you have those things. The great kids and the cozy house. I feel proud seeing you handle all these things I could never do."

"Me too," I tell her. "I'm proud of you."

"I just write about clothes. You've made humans," she says.

I take her by the hands. "Do you have any idea how many people you touch? How good it feels to get your magazine in the mail? How many times an empowering article, or a couple plus-size models looking great in swimwear, and a glass of wine have propped me up at the end of a long, hard day?"

Talia looks at me, and her expression is a little sad. "Oh, Amy. I've missed you so much. Stay for the week, at least. Just the rest of the week."

A cab goes by, lights on, but neither of us flag it down. "Is everything ok with you?" I ask.

Talia shakes her head, pressing her lips together tightly. "I love that magazine, but I don't know how much longer it can last."

"What do you mean?" I ask.

"Never mind," she replies. I look at her hard. She shrugs her shoulders. "It's just that I've got so many more empowering articles to publish before it's all said and done," she says, and when she looks back at me again, her normal light, carefree expression is back. "Like maybe . . . one about your momspringa," she adds with a tilt of the head.

I roll my eyes. "I'll stay a few more days," I tell her. "Just let me do it my way."

"Yoga pants and a book?" she asks.

I shrug. "I yam what I yam," I tell her.

Talia pulls me into a half hug. "I yam too," she says. We stand there on the sidewalk in a neighborhood we have navigated together since we were teenagers, and yet I'm sure both of us feel a little lost.

"Let's go get Mamoun's. Two a.m. falafel fixes everything."

She's not entirely wrong.

—

The next morning Talia and I both sleep in. She straggles out the door around nine, which for her is wildly late, and I pity her poor staff after she announces to me that they should be grateful to get "almost the entire morning off." I go out and get a real New York bagel with a thick slab of cream cheese, a fresh-squeezed OJ, and a giant cup of coffee and return to Talia's to sit around nursing my sore throat and feeling sorry for myself. I am at sea without my kids and my work. I know going home has to be the right move—being here just feels so awkward and strange. But going home while John is there feels treacherous. I can survive him not wanting me back. But I'm not sure how to get over wanting what he represents—my old life—back.

The phone rings, and I see it's the *Pure Beautiful* offices, so I don't pick up. It's either Talia calling to check on me or Matt calling to beg for his momspringa article. I don't have it in me to argue with either bulldog at the moment, so I sink into a new book from one of my favorite thriller authors and let the real world fall away.

But at some point after the first body drops, my phone rings the different ring, the one I set for John. My heart automatically surges. The kids. "What is it?" I answer, instead of just saying hello like a normal person. "Are the kids ok?"

"Good morning to you too," he says. "The kids are just fine." My cardiac rhythm restarts. "Better than fine, actually. As I'm sure you know, Cori's got this boy dangling from her line, and she's trying to decide if she should reel him in or cut bait, so I'm getting a daily lesson on the workings of the feminine mind. And then there's Joe. He's, like, the best person I've ever known. He's such a good little dude. Did you know how good he is with a UAS?"

"A what now?"

"A drone, basically. I got us each one and put a waterproof GoPro on his, and we've been charting weather patterns and cloud consistency, and we're talking about how to attach spectrometers so that he can . . . well, anyway, we're geeking out big-time."

"That's amazing." I am immediately jealous. I know nothing about geeking out or drones or . . . spectrometers? Whoa. Joe and his dad have so much natural engineer in them. I could never compete with that. Every time I try to science around with Joe, he ends up giving me a lesson in physics and sending me on my way. "What do you think of Brian?"

"Cori's dude? He's dumb as a box of rocks. I keep them in eyesight at all times. I am doing that 'Who wants a platter of Ritz Crackers' interrupting thing whenever they so much as sit on the same sofa."

"Oh, good," I say. "She can handle herself, but her frontal lobe is still fifteen-year-old goo."

"Right? And so is his. So how are you? Enjoying New York?"

I grimace. I guess now we have to make small talk. "New York is great. How is PA? Ready for me on Sunday?"

"Well, actually, that's why I'm calling."

I frown into the phone. "Oh?"

"This week is just going by so fast, Amy. I know I have no right to ask, but I need more time with these kids."

"No," I say flat out. "You have no right to ask."

"I just said that," he says.

"And I'm agreeing with you."

"But I'm asking anyway. You've had them to yourself for three years. I'm just starting to get to know them again. I can't—I mean, I'm not ready . . ."

"You could have had them for three years too," I tell him.

There is silence for a moment, and I feel mean and righteous at once. "Right," he says eventually. "I know. Yes, this is all my fault, and I owe you endless contrition and unceasing flagellation and all that. Groveling. I've done all that. I will never stop apologizing. I screwed up, and I'm sorry. But I can't undo it."

"I don't think you would even if you could," I snap. I think of Marika Shew.

He is quiet. Is he thinking of her too? "You're wrong," he says at last, and my chest contracts, too vulnerable to inhale, too hopeful to exhale. "You don't know how wrong you are."

I shake my head and think of what Talia said last night. How he might "come after me." It's nothing but muscle memory, I remind myself. "Never mind. Just tell me what you're asking for."

"The rest of the summer."

I cough. "You've got to be kidding."

"Think of how good it could be for everyone. Lena told me about your reading thing you're trying at Country Day; you could work on that. Maybe write some grant requests? Do some work on the house? Or maybe just have some downtime after everything you've done for the kids these last three years. You could spend a week in Philly, or take a road trip to a national park, or—"

"No," I say.

"The kids are doing great, Amy. And I think this is good for them. I read in a book about coparenting that children who have a strong relationship with their father are seventy-five percent less likely to get a divorce when they're adults. And Joe needs this nerd time. Do you have any idea how talented he is? There's a Tech Scouts group here, father-son STEAM stuff; we could build robots, go up to Boston for the Cambridge chess tournaments. And don't take this the wrong way, but the kids are having fun here at the condo."

"They have fun with me," I say.

"Of course they do. But. You know. They're overachievers, and you work hard, and they do too. They need, like, the kid sort of fun. Not grown-up fun. The pool in my building. Drone-flying time. Taking the diving team out for pizza after the meets. I can give them a lot of, you know . . ."

"Stuff? Money?" I say, feeling my temper rise.

"And time. It doesn't make up for everything," he says. "I am not pretending it does."

"Good."

"But don't they deserve a summer off? Instead of detasseling corn at the crack of dawn—the only gig kids around here can do to beat minimum wage—Cori can work at the public pool with her friends a few hours a week. I can take her to diving camp for a week and then send Joe to Space Camp—you know I have that friend Andy from college who can get us in last minute. I've thought it all through. I won't let them be couch potatoes, but these kids need . . . a break."

I bristle. "Don't tell me what my kids need."

He is obediently silent. I want to throttle him. After all, if the kids have had to work a little harder these last few years, he's the reason. I am angry and so hurt. And annoyed, too, because though I would never say such a thing to John, it's not just my kids who have been long overdue for a break all this time.

"Amy?" he says into the phone after a long silence.

"Yes. I'm here. I'm just processing. Coping, I suppose, with the strange sensation of a near stranger telling me how to raise my own kids."

He sighs. "I may feel like a stranger, but I'm not one. I'm their father."

I snort.

"We had fifteen years together."

I say nothing. I think of the ways he wasn't there when I needed him in those fifteen years. How alone I felt when I was hurting. When I felt lost. I think of the darkest moment of our marriage—when what I was going through by myself should have been our burden to share. I say nothing.

"You don't have to decide right now. Think about it. Come home Sunday, and we can regroup then."

"I will think about it," I tell him honestly. "And after I do, the answer will still be no."

"Fine, as long as you give it some real consideration. That's what I'm asking. Figure out what's right for you and the kids, and be honest. If it's to shut me out and go back to struggling ahead without any hope of a break, what can I do but bow out?"

I fight the urge to make a roaring noise into the phone. "I am having a break right now!" I say.

"Terrific," he says huffily.

"It's wonderful!" I lie.

"I'm so glad to hear it!"

"Just nonstop buying lingerie and getting waxed," I snark.

But he doesn't get the reference to his girlfriend's credit card habits, and I immediately feel like a jerk for the passive-aggressive slam.

"Uh?" he says curiously. "I'm happy for you? Look, whatever makes you happy. You don't have to prove what a great mom you are to me. These are wonderful kids, because of you. But you're quite clearly frazzled all the time, and all kids need to blow off steam. No matter how perfect their mother tries to be, another parent is a good thing for them. Just consider that this might actually be the right thing for all of us."

"Because that's always what *you've* kept at the front of your mind," I say bitterly. "What's best for everyone."

He sighs. "I'm sorry. I can say it as much as you like."

"Tattoo it on your forehead," I say angrily.

"If I honestly thought it would help," he says, "I would. But you're determined to be a martyr no matter what I do or say. So what's the point?"

"The point is you're an asshole," I say quickly, before I can think too hard about the truth of what he's saying.

"We should stop talking now," he replies.

"I agree," I say.

"Let's give each other some space. We can revisit this Sunday."

"My answer will still be no."

"Fine. Then I will learn that on Sunday."

"Sunday," I threaten.

"Goodbye, Amy," he says.

I hang up. "Goodbye, asshole," I say to the dead phone. But the anger is a front. Inside, I am not angry. I am broken up.

Because I know he is completely, exactly right. I have been a martyr, and I've come to like it that way.

CHAPTER TEN

Dear Mom,

Dad told us what he asked you.

He said you are thinking it over.

Are you really? I wish I knew.

Love,

Your daughter who actually does kind of want to work at the pool and go to diving camp but is trying not to sell you out, Cori

——

I don't answer the phone the rest of that day except for a few texts from Cori and my daily call from Joe. As subtly as I can, I try to sound them out about how they feel about the summer plans. I try desperately not to give away how opposed I am to the very idea. How threatened. I think about John staring down Cori's beau, then spending hours with Joe and his new drone. Diving camp. Space Camp. How much John has to offer my children. How little he has to offer me.

I skip Matt's schedule of aerial yoga, Chelsea Market lunch, museum tour, and oxygen therapy for no reason other than to spite myself and avoid talking to anyone. I'm hurting, but since the reason I'm hurting is because I feel at once replaced and rejected by John, I tell myself I don't know why I'm upset. Therefore I am not allowed to be upset. Therefore I hide. When Talia comes home around eight to fetch me, I tell her I'm in for the night.

Talia seems out of sorts as well. She is disappointed in me; that much is clear. I am sure in college I seemed tougher. Made of stronger stuff. Maybe I was tougher—I don't know. But something else is wrong with her too. I feel around for it over takeout but get nowhere. Around nine thirty, she gets a call and tells me she's going back to work. A car picks her up ten minutes later, and I am alone for the rest of the night. I finish the thriller. I drink a glass of red wine. I go to bed.

Thursday starts the same. Bagel, coffee, book. I'm getting the week I wanted after all, and my friends were right—it's lame. A couple of calls come in from *Pure Beautiful*, and I let them go to voice mail. Cori sends me a selfie in this year's swim cap, which is gold and has wings on it. She is sticking out her tongue, and the caption reads, "The face of a winner." So I send her a picture of a dachshund wearing a top hat and type, "The face of a wiener." Then she sends back a collection of emoji that surely means something to her, and I send back the shrugging-mom emoji, and we leave it at that. The interaction is shaping up to be the highlight of my day when Talia calls me from her cell phone. Seventeen times in a row. I pick up on call eighteen.

"You get your butt in here," is what she says to me when I do.

"I don't wanna," I tell her.

"Matt's up my ass. Get in here; do an after pic. He can do filler for the rest of the piece. It'll only be a one-pager, but he deserves a byline. Get in here."

I sigh heavily into the phone. "Talia."

"I have to go manage a stupid photo shoot full of stupid people in stupid Florida. You're going to be stuck here in New York City all alone with no one to nag you for the rest of your wasted week. Just do this one last thing for me. I bought you nice bras."

"I thought that was the magazine!"

"I bought them metaphorically," she says. "Wear the jeans we picked out and the white blazer. Matt will put you in heels, but you don't have to walk anywhere, so just suck it up. A makeup artist will meet you here in an hour."

"Talia," I start. "I don't feel like a photo shoot. I know I'm being a brat, but I feel—"

"Lena says you're facing down the painful realization that your children need other people in their lives besides you, that soon you'll be relegated to the sidelines of their adult lives and have no idea who you are anymore."

"Jesus! No, that's not—"

"And she said you're still wondering if you'd be better off with John."

"This is all crazy."

"She said you'd deny it. She said to take pity on you and let you come to it in your own time."

"I don't need your pity. I am perfectly fine."

Talia laughs. Menacingly. "That's what I told her. I said she had it all wrong and you were perfectly fine. And since you're perfectly fine, I know you'll come do what you promised me and Matt. So we'll see you in an hour."

"Talia—" I start. But she has disconnected. And now not only do I have to go smile for the camera, I have to do it while facing the fact that everything Lena said is absolutely true. I do still have feelings—albeit extremely mixed-up feelings—for my ex. After all, we were married for many years, some of them wonderful. He was my best friend. There was, once, a lot of love there.

And yes, it makes me crazy to think that my kids can go days— or maybe weeks—without me. If I'm not needed, if I'm not busy, if I'm not an overstretched, overwhelmed, underslept, underpaid single mother . . .

What exactly am I?

I guess I'm a well-dressed lump of self-pity, sitting around alone, moping over my ex-husband and feeling petulant in the greatest city in the world.

Damn that Talia and Lena. The two of them have to be the most annoying friends a girl could ever wish for.

———

I have some serious thinking to do. And as I soon learn, there is plenty of time to think when you're getting two hours of hair and makeup done on the set of a photo shoot.

First I get a blowout. A New York City blowout is a thing of beauty. A hair wash. A scalp massage. A conditioner. Another scalp massage. The gentle, plush pampering of hands drying your hair with a towel in delicate scrunching motions, wiping a drop of water off your brow, running a wide-toothed comb through your perfectly colored strands.

Then there are thirty minutes of blow-drying sections of my hair with a paddle brush. My locks get straighter and fuller and more glamorous with every chunk of hair. I start to look expensive. My head gets misted with the sweetest-smelling spray, and then the dryer starts up again, and I just let my eyes close and feel the hairbrush, the heat, the repetition lulling me into a trance.

Next, makeup. The artist barely talks to me. She gives me directions: "Look up," "Close your eyes softly," "Relax your lips," in a soft, heavily accented voice, with her pencils and wands fluttering around my face purposefully. For a long, wonderful spell I am just dusted with a giant kabuki powder brush, and I very nearly fall asleep.

Matt comes in and says "Nice!" and holds up a mirror for me. To me I look like a circus-clown version of myself. My cheeks are extra pink, my eyelids are downright ocher, and I seem to have stripes of contour paint down the sides of my nose. My hair is the size of a hot-air balloon. I shrug and say, "You're the boss." This whole process is strangely relaxing.

Then the photographer arrives. Her assistant moves toward a Bluetooth speaker, and I start to fear club music, but instead we get a supersmooth mix of Latin acoustic guitar that seems to further the dreamlike atmosphere. The photographer puts me in a chair, then on a sofa, then perched on a stool. I change outfits four times. They put a huge fan on me and adjust three different sets of lights. She takes endless photos, and after about an hour Talia comes in, walks past me to a laptop, points to the screen several times, and tells the room, "We got it. Thanks, everybody."

Then she gives me a funny little wink and saunters back out. Matt trots up to me and hands me my tote of clothes, books, and wallet I brought along today. "You are gorgeous," he tells me.

I look up from my perch and beam. "That was very fun!"

"And to think you almost skipped it."

"I know! I was being an idiot. Do I get to see?"

He shrugs. "I can show you the raw files, or you can wait until the finals are back. I promise you will be thrilled. You look like . . . like the perfect version of yourself."

"Oooh! Show me the raw files!" I cry excitedly, but just then my phone starts to ring. Chicago area code. "Hello?"

"Oh, good, I got you on the phone!" says a distinctly sharp, vaguely familiar voice.

"Kathryn? Is that you? How did the trip home go?" Matt gives me a wave and trots away.

"Both of my kids are alive, and my husband is worshipping the ground I walk on," she says. "I call that a successful trip!"

"I agree!" I tell her. "And meanwhile here in New York I just got a total makeover, and I seem to be a fashion model now. So I guess we both are killing it."

"Huh? Ok . . . ," she says, clearly thinking she got me after a couple of strong cocktails. "Listen, I have amazing news. I am doing a Flexthology trial at my school!"

"What?"

"I was so excited about your idea—it's so perfect for us because we are battling a huge achievement gap. So I went to my principal and sold her on a pilot program in our school. We've got a budget for the e-readers and four complete books per kid starting this fall! We'll repeat the reading assessments at the end of the program and get some metrics on how it works. Isn't that wonderful?"

My mouth drops open. "What?" I say again.

"We're rolling out your reading curriculum at my school," she says. "Remember? Did the fashion industry melt your brain?"

"No! I mean, maybe it did, but I understand what you're saying now. This is unbelievable, Kathryn!"

"It's totally unbelievable. I couldn't believe it myself when my principal said yes, but I think our meeting last weekend was kismet for this idea, because it's so perfect for my students. So I just couldn't let it go, and here we are! Now I will be able to get you all the information on public school performance that you would need to get a big money grant to do a rollout in dozens of schools! After the program, if it works, we can start petitioning the entire school district, or sell it to charter schools first and work from there, or—"

"This is just a pet idea I had for my little private school," I tell her in wonderment.

"Not anymore, it's not. I'm sending an email to you in ten minutes, spelling out some of the areas where I'll need your guidance on implementation. Can you work with me to get this started? I'm going to need a ton of help this summer."

"Of course! I'd be honored!"

"I have a good feeling about this," says Kathryn. "I think we could get some really good books to some really great kids."

I think of Cori and her reading project. Of how many books I try out to find just one that excites her—and how worthwhile that effort is. "I will do whatever it takes to make that happen," I tell her.

"Ok, more to come. Enjoy your fashion show!" She disconnects. I stand there stunned.

"Everything ok?" asks Matt, who has reappeared at my side somewhere along the line.

I blink at him in a daze for a few moments, but then I smile. "Everything is very ok. In fact, I am suddenly in the mood to celebrate. Remember that Chelsea Market lunch I blew off yesterday? And the rest of the things you had scheduled for the article? Do you think I could cash a rain check for those today?"

Matt's grin is infectious. "I believe you could. Let me go look up the rest of your itinerary and figure out what I can rebook."

Matt slips off, and the moment the door closes behind him, four young women sort of creep into the studio where my shoot was just held and start adjusting the lighting. Then one steps forward, walks away from the others, and then stops and turns back, looking fetchingly over her shoulder. Another takes a photo of her with an iPhone. This repeats in many different variations.

They take turns photographing each other, adjusting the lights, gussying up their hair and makeup, comparing the results. I watch them with obvious curiosity. My head is swimming with thoughts about the reading program, the last several days, my upcoming return home, the summer sprawling out before me. I lose all track of time.

When Matt comes back, the young women all scuttle away. "Ok," he says, giving them no notice. "You've got yourself a wonderful schedule for the rest of the day. We're going to make good use of all that hair."

"Matt, what was that?" I ask, gesturing to the spot where the women have just been.

"What?" he asks.

"There was just a gaggle of twentysomething women in here, taking a jillion pictures of themselves. Are they models?"

Matt laughs. "Ha! Models, no. Not at all. They are editorial assistants."

"Then why . . . ?"

"All the pictures? They were taking advantage of the unlocked art studio while the lighting was all perfect, I expect."

"But why do they need so many pictures of themselves?" I ask, feeling like I'm missing some very big piece of the puzzle. "Is this just how people behave nowadays?"

"Oh! Well, yes, probably. But the assistants were taking each other's photos for online dating, of course!" He laughs. "You've got to have some great photos if you want to have any luck on the dating apps. They can't all be dimly lit selfies in crowded bars!"

I look at him blankly. "All those gorgeous, young, employable women are . . . online dating?" I ask. "Why can't they just meet men the regular way?"

"What do you mean, the regular way?" he asks, perplexed. "All single women of any kind are online dating," he says to me as though I am a little slow. "All the single humans in New York are online dating. That is the only way there is to date."

"Oh," I say, though I'm still a bit mystified. "So if I wanted to date, I'd need an online dating profile?"

Matt's eyes light up dangerously. "You would. Do you want to date? Because that would make a great addition to my story."

I smile enigmatically and push all thoughts of John straight out of my mind. Instead I focus on that delicious feeling in my toes that I had when I kissed Daniel that morning in my hotel room. "I just might want to date," I tell a gleeful Matt. "You never know, Matt. You really never know."

—

When I get off the train in Allentown on Sunday, my kids don't even try to play it cool. They both hug me at the same time. Cori can't stop raving about my new look and says she's worried Brian will want to try a Mrs. Robinson, then cracks an evil grin. Same old Cori.

Joe, after just a week, is transformed. He stands taller and more poised than I've ever seen him. He tells me he missed me and I'm a way better parent than Dad, then proceeds to rave about every single minute the two of them spent together. At first the part of me that wants to be the center of their world wars with the part of me that wants them happy. But it's futile; within minutes the radiating happiness of my kids wins me over. I see what John was saying—they've relaxed around him, let themselves enjoy the ride. The pressure has diffused. The children are safe and cheerful. My worst fears about the week have been allayed.

I suggest we all go out for dinner together that evening—the two of them, John, and me—and their eyes light up so much that in the car on the way home, I feel I need to gently remind them not to try any *Parent Trap* stuff on their father and me. "We are not interested in being forced back together," I tell them. I say it once for them, once for me. "Not now. Not ever." Then we all go home to do laundry and catch up.

By dinnertime I've made my decision. Well, one look at Joe when I arrived home, and I made my decision, but by dinnertime I'm ready to talk to the kids about it. We pile in the car, and the minute I back out of our driveway, I ask them if they'd like to spend more time with their dad this summer. They sweetly try not to actually cheer at the idea. There is no missing their excitement. "Can I work at the pool too?" asks Cori, and I tell her yes, as long as she wears embarrassing amounts of sunscreen and a rash guard. "Can I go to Space Camp with Dad?" asks Joe, and I tell him the two of them should get as much nerd on as they possibly can. Then I put the car in park at a stop sign, hold one of each of their hands, look them in the eye in turn, and say, "You guys need to understand, deep in your bones, that Dad will probably have to leave at the end of the summer."

Joe drops his eyes to the ground. Cori nods somberly. "We know, Mom."

"Do you *know* know, though?"

"Yo, we *know* know," says Cori.

"You can't tell yourself you can control whether he stays either," I tell them, putting the car back in gear and driving again. "It doesn't matter how fun you are, or how good, or how little you ask of him this summer. No matter his strengths as a dad or how well you get along. You won't be the deciding factor on whether he stays."

Cori rolls her eyes—this must be old news. But Joe looks at me with hope in his eyes. "Who will be the deciding factor?" he asks. "Will it be you?"

I sigh. The question hurts. The answer is worse. "No," I tell them, trying to sound as matter-of-fact as I can. "It will be your dad. Keep in mind he works in another country. He has a life there too. He loves you—that much is clear—but it doesn't mean he can or will stay."

Joe frowns. "You always say love isn't a feeling—it's an action."

"Well, at the moment the action is that he is here, trying to give you literally everything your big hearts could desire for the summer. And just FYI: it's natural to want to jump on that opportunity, and you don't need to feel guilty about doing it."

"Oh, we're doing it," says Cori.

I smile wanly. "That's my little opportunist. You get to be the one to inform your dad that he can buy your school clothes and supplies this year."

"Are you kidding? I already told him he's paying you back for three years of private school tuition. A few notebooks are only the beginning of what I'm extorting him for."

I shake my head. "Cori . . ."

"We're worth it, Mom," says Joe. "Besides, you can use the tuition money to take us to Harry Potter world!"

"Ooh!" cries Cori. "Universal! Can I bring Trinity?" She grabs her phone, and I hope to high heaven she's not actually texting Trinity right this second, even knowing that she is. "And maybe—wait." Cori goes strangely quiet.

"What is it?"

"Mom. Look at this." She tries to block my view of the road with her phone.

"Stop it, Corinne! I'm trying to drive here."

"It's you!" she exclaims. "Joe. Look at this."

He reaches forward from the back seat and takes Cori's phone and starts swiping. "Oh my god. This is pretty embarrassing," he says. "I mean, I'm well adjusted and everything, but ick."

"What? What's embarrassing?" I say, feeling panicky.

"Shut up, Joe; it's not like it's a sex tape."

"Ok, I'm pulling over." I signal and pull off into street parking.

"Give me the phone, Joe," barks Cori.

"Hold on—I'm looking at these retweets. *Ugh*, Mom, you're, like, a sex object. I'm gonna barf."

"Give me the phone!" I shout.

"Mom, don't you have your own phone?" asks Cori. "It's from your friend Talia's Twitter account."

I take my phone out and start fumbling around with it, trying to open Twitter on the Safari browser and then find Talia's account, all while listening to Cori's and Joe's incomprehensible but excited reactions. Finally, finally, Cori takes the phone out of my hand, navigates me to some app I didn't know I had, and shows me the screen.

@PureBeauTalia retweeted:

PureBeautyMag:

Get a load of these crazy hot after shots for single mom and superwoman Amy B—see more in our Aug issue 7/26 when we introduce the #momspringa

"What's a hashtag momspringa?" asks Joe. "Whoa, there's a ton of tweets about it all of a sudden. Ew, Mom, some of these guys want to, like, meet you."

I click the hashtag. Sure enough, a small flurry of Twitterers has started peeping about where they'd take their momspringa and how badly they need one. And yes, two men have offered to, ah, entertain me.

But the photos.

Oh, those photos.

"Mom, you look so, so hot," says Cori. She is arching over the steering column so she can look at my phone. The photos are . . . they're beautiful. In them, a long-haired brunette looks at the camera with a look of quiet strength and confidence. Her lips turn up as though she's thinking about the mischief she can get up to while her family is away. Her eyes are sparkling, and her lips are parted just a bit, like she is seriously considering asking you to come sit by her. I cannot believe she is me.

And as I am gazing upon myself in awe, my phone chirps. Facebook. A friend request. The picture is tiny, but the name looms large. Daniel Seong. The hot librarian of the year. Wants to be friends with me. The message attached reads, "You kick me out of bed at the crack of dawn and the only way to track you down is to follow the clues from a trending topic on Twitter? Now I know how Prince Charming felt. #glasstwitter"

Well.

This is unexpected.

But not, I find to my own surprise, at all unwelcome.

"Kids?" I ask, so quietly that their bickering over Cori's phone stops, and they both look up at me. I crane around in the driver's seat so I can look at both of these incredible kids and they can see in my eyes that what I'm about to ask is no joke. "How would you feel if while you were at Dad's this summer, your mom spent just a little bit more time in New York?"

CHAPTER ELEVEN

Amy,

Here are those camp forms I told you about. I think the kids will have amazing trips.

I hope you're going to have an amazing time in New York too. I will admit, when we first talked about me keeping the kids all summer, I imagined you a five-minute drive away in case I got in over my head. But that's not fair to you. Believe it or not, I do really want you to be happy.

Also. This is very awkward to talk about over email, but I don't think you'd appreciate it as a phone call, either, so . . . I want you to know that things have ended between me and Marika. They've been ended for a long time. I just got the credit card statement and put two and two together, and I'm sorry for the stress I probably caused by not taking her card off the account. I took care of it yesterday.

Anyway, that relationship was . . . an aberration.
I've been single otherwise. I intend to spend that
extra energy where it belongs from here on out,
on my family.

Ok! Have fun in New York! Give my love to Talia!

-John

—

When I tell Talia I want to come back to New York, she tells me it's
a damn good thing, because she needs a house sitter ASAP. Then she
says something about how when you take positive steps in your life,
the universe rewards you by making your path forward easier. I ask her
what positive steps she's taking, and she says, "I'm talking about you,
dummy." I think of John's email. Was his ending his relationship with
Marika a gift from the universe? If so, I don't feel terribly grateful. Just
more confused.

"The universe has provided you with a one-and-a-half-bedroom
apartment all to yourself for the summer. The universe seems to have
different things in mind for me," Talia adds. "Hot, sweaty things."

Apparently, she tells me, the *Pure Beautiful* demographics are terrible in the South. "The ad sales guys say we're too Yankee. We need a
better handle on 'real America.'"

"What fashion magazine has a handle on real America?" I ask her,
and she says, "That's what I told them. And they told me to take a skel-
eton crew to Miami—as if that's any more real—to work up three winter
issues and run magazine events." I can see she isn't a fan of this idea. She
loves New York and maybe, just maybe, thinks that civilization ends at
the Hudson.

"You might," I tease, "actually like it there."

"Maybe," she replies. "But while I am gone, consultants will be climbing all over the office, trying to figure out how to get this magazine to make money, and the solution might not involve the actual magazine itself," she explains. "Paper and ink only have so much time left. This assignment out of town means that whatever is next for *Pure Beautiful*, my pretty little print edition might not be a part of it."

My face falls. "But then what will you do?" I ask her, worried.

Talia winks at me. "Don't you worry, Ames. I can always call Simon."

I blanch at the mention of her filthy rich but otherwise unexciting ex. She smirks.

"I have a contract. I will come out ok, move over to online eventually. It's inevitable. I'm just enjoying the last days of disco while I can."

I shake my head. "Don't go. Stay and fight for the magazine."

But she packs up and leaves, promising to come back for a weekend, and tells herself soothingly, "No one spends August in New York anyway." And then she laughs and adds, "Well, Amy Byler does," and like that she is gone.

It sets me back on my heels to know Talia's job isn't carved in stone. It was easy to tell myself that Talia's life was simply perfect in every way. And honestly, she did make a single, child-free life seem pretty wonderful. But of course, she isn't the master of her own destiny any more than I am. She answers to people. She takes her lumps. She just looks much better while doing it.

So suddenly I am on my own in New York. The beauty, and maybe just the tiniest curse, too, of single parenting is that you are never, ever alone for more than three consecutive hours. On the rare evenings when I would go out without the kids, I'd meet up with Lena or another friend, and we'd chatter nonstop over wine. If Cori was out at night, I was with Joe at a tournament or home grading homework while he and his friends played Settlers and ate pizzas. If Joe went to a friend's on a Saturday, Cori and I were at the movies watching stuff that would make Joe fall asleep before the opening credits were over, or she was hitting me up for a ride somewhere. Cori would go out every night if not for my school-night policies, but Joe is a homebody. I always had company.

Now, for the first time, it's just me. Completely alone. All-day-talk-to-no-one alone, if I want to be. I will have time to just have uninterrupted thoughts. Time to reflect.

Or.

Time to have fun. Time to work out until I'm pumped full of endorphins, find the best bagel in Brooklyn, have white wine lunches on downtown sidewalks, and visit every gorgeous library and bookstore in this enormous city.

I can take my beautiful hair and my beautiful clothes out on big adventures. I can wander in and out of the shops in SoHo without feeling like an imposter. I can flirt with baristas. I can read in the park. I can do . . .

Whatever the hell I want for an entire summer.

Whoa.

I flop down on Talia's guest bed, stunned, and think: *Ok, Amy. What's the first thing I want to do with all this freedom? Chinatown? The Cloisters? A ride on the Staten Island Ferry?*

Nope. Nope. Nope. One thing tops my to-do list. Or rather, one person:

One very hot librarian.

———

When it comes to writing back Daniel, my first instinct is not dissimilar to my teen daughter's. I want to message Lena, Talia, Cori, and maybe even Matt, to run through the thousands of different interpretations of his Facebook message and the further thousands of different ways to write him back. But there is something else guiding me too. Something quiet and still and sure. When I sent Daniel packing the morning after our date slash one-night stand, I felt a strange mix of victory and shame, with a tinge of fear over the top.

Now things are different. I'm not in New York for a week. I'm here for almost three months. I have time to do everything I desire. And my heart desires a hot librarian. And I've decided it's totally safe to pursue that desire. Daniel has a teenager in arguably the best high school in New York and a great job here, too, and therefore is not a genuine threat to my emotional safety. There is zero chance we will have a long-term relationship. He is, if he's interested in me, the safest possible summer fling a girl could ask for.

So instead of debating and delaying and generally distracting myself from something that might make me happy, I decide to just write him back like a grown woman. I open his message: "You kick me out of bed at the crack of dawn and the only way to track you down is to follow the clues from a trending topic on Twitter? Now I know how Prince Charming felt. #glasstwitter"

And I type back, "Sorry, your charming highness, but I had a major freak-out after our little night out. Was feeling weird because of the impossibility of our situation—me going back to PA, you in NYC. Since then, my plans have changed, and now I'm spending the rest of the summer in Brooklyn. Forgive me?"

I hit enter and close my laptop. I think that I'll be waiting a day or three days or whatever the standard rules are before I hear back. But ten minutes later my phone sends me a Facebook alert. Daniel replies, "Agreed. Situation totally impossible. But I think it would still be fun to hang out while you're here. Plus, I have a ton of ideas for your Flexthology. Meet up next week at a quiet bookish pub on the Upper West Side?"

I decide if he's not going to be coy, then I won't have to be either.

"Absolutely," I write. "Send me the time and place." Then after a few minutes I add, "Can't wait!"

There. Look at me. I am the ultimate sophisticate. Just casually making plans with a man I intend to sleep with outside of the bounds of a formal relationship. I am a modern woman! I am Gloria Steinem and Helen Gurley Brown and the slutty one from *Sex and the City* all wrapped up in one.

But when we meet up, all my best-laid plans quickly go down the drain.

—

The Dead Author is a long, skinny, deep bar, a pool table in the way back that barely has clearance for a pool cue, a broken jukebox full of dusty AC/DC and Smashing Pumpkins records, and three high-top tables, one in the front, two in the back. The ceiling is made up of pages of novels torn out and affixed, well, remotely, by way of pencils and darts. I'm not sure how they stay stuck, but they do. The ceiling is so high I cannot tell which book pages are up there, mangled and stabbed through the heart. But the big dark wood bar seems to be set onto bookcases, and when I hoist myself up to it, my feet kick at a row of titles. At random I reach under the bar and pull a book out. It is a worn copy of *The Catcher in the Rye*. Ugh. I pull out another. Also *Catcher in the Rye*, different cover, different print date. Unable to resist, I climb off the stool and look at the upper shelf of books. I'd estimate they are 75 percent *Catcher in the Rye*. Another 20 percent are *Franny and Zooey*. The remaining 5 percent seem to be a completely random collection of nonsense books released roughly thirty years ago. Fishing guides and church cookbooks and gothic romances.

Huh. Well, then, I guess I'll read *Catcher in the Rye*. I open it up, read the iconic first line, inwardly groan, and then stare off into space hoping for Daniel to show himself soon. It is probably sacrilege to say it, but I don't even assign *CitR* to students anymore. It hasn't, to my mind, aged well. Now, *David Copperfield*—there's a book I could read for hours in a bar. I take out my journal and write "Perks of Being a

Wallflower vs. Catcher" and then write "David Copperfield modern rewrites?" I hope the entries make sense to me when I go to do lesson planning in August.

After a few more moments go by, the bartender visits me. "What can I get you?" she asks, and I realize I've been sitting there for ten minutes without paying any rent on my barstool. I look past her at the wall of bottles behind her. Aha. There is an entire row of different rye whiskeys. All becomes clear. "I guess I'll have a Manhattan," I tell her. "It's the only rye drink I know."

She tilts her head at me ever so slightly. "Anything you like with malt whiskey can be made with rye."

"Oh yeah? Like a whiskey sour?"

"That's pretty good, actually. The original way it was made. Which rye?" she asks.

I shrug. "Surprise me."

She pulls down a pretty bottle and a shot glass and pours me a tiny taste. "WhistlePig," she tells me.

I sip it, try not to cough, and nod at her. "Tastes good," I lie. It tastes like a cross between nail polish remover and caramel sauce. "This your bar?"

"Yep."

"Open it in 2010?"

". . . Yep. How'd you know."

"It's called the Dead Author. Salinger wasn't dead until 2010."

She points to a sign. "Just saved yourself four bucks," she tells me. HAPPY HOUR: 50% OFF FOR NERDS UNTIL 7 P.M., reads the sign. I laugh. "How do you know if someone's a nerd?" I ask her.

She puts a drink in front of me. "They always make themselves known. Want to start a tab?"

Daniel walks into the bar just that moment. My heart stumbles. "Yes, I do. And make another one of these for that good-looking dork," I tell her.

She winks at me. "My, but that's a sexy nerd," she says. "Have fun."

Daniel pulls up a barstool next to me. He's wearing a pair of jeans and a plain brick-red T-shirt and carrying a large messenger bag across his chest. His shirt pulls just a bit across the shoulders but is loose around the waist. He looks like the dad from a diversely cast CW show. In short: dreamy.

"Sorry I'm late," he says, as I try to figure out if we're going to hug or kiss or something in greeting. Maybe not kiss. I reach an arm toward him, but the barstools are too far away. In the end we share an awkward high five. I laugh nervously. He is awfully good looking.

"Your timing is perfect," I tell him when I recover. "I was earning us the fifty percent off." I wave to the happy hour signage.

He smiles and nods his head. "Good work. As I was walking up here, I thought maybe I should have told you about that in advance so you wouldn't go incognito nerd, but then I realized there was little danger of that."

"Ha! Thanks a lot."

"You're the one who was seduced by a day at the bookstore."

"I wasn't seduced," I say. Then I think it over. "Ok, maybe I was seduced a little."

Daniel smiles at me with the corner of his mouth. "Amy," he says.

"Yes?"

"It's great to see you again. I'm glad I tracked you down."

"Me too."

"And I'm glad you said what you did, about our situation being impossible. It's good to just have that out there. You have a life in one place, and I have a life in another. Romance isn't in the cards."

"Well," I say. "Yeah. Wait, it isn't?"

Daniel looks at me strangely. "You are going back to PA at the end of the summer, right?"

I nod. "Right. Yes. But that's a couple months away." I suddenly feel foolish. "So I was just sort of thinking . . ." What was I thinking? That we'd have a summer fling and then shake hands goodbye when I went back to my real life? That doesn't sound very flattering to him.

"I mean, I don't want to just be a summer fling," he says, eerily reading my mind. "That would be hard on me."

"It would? I mean, yes. Right." I am pretty lost in this conversation. "Except, you know, I think you're the one who initiated our very fling-like one-night stand. If we're going to be historically accurate."

"Obviously, historical accuracy is of the utmost importance," he says playfully. He doesn't seem to be the slightest bit uncomfortable in this labyrinthine discussion. "The difference then, though, was I didn't know you were on momspringa."

"Oh. For that matter, neither did I."

He smiles, and even in the midst of all this forthright conversation, it is so overwhelmingly charming when he smiles. "And, if you'll forgive me for being indelicate, I also didn't know we'd have such good chemistry . . ." He makes a weird little slow-motion coming-together gesture with his hands. "You know, horizontally speaking."

I feel my face get hot. "That was above average, right?" I don't have much to compare it to lately.

He tips his head back. "That was way above average. That was some Exceeds Expectations–level sex."

"E sex?" I ask, catching his Hogwarts grading-rubric reference.

"E. Possibly O," he volleys back. "Anyway, if you ask me, there's no use in trying to 'casually date' someone you have Outstanding sex with. It has to be all or nothing."

I sigh. I guess that means it will be nothing. "But then why did you message me on Facebook?" I ask.

He frowns. "To keep in touch, of course."

"As friends?" I ask.

"Right. Exactly. Hang out with a cocktail." He raises his glass to me. "Talk books. Enjoy each other's company."

"But that's what we did last time," I say. "And look what happened."

He nods emphatically. "Good point. We will have to make an effort to keep our clothes on in the future."

"Or . . . ," I say, already surprised at what's about to come out of my mouth, "we could just see what happens . . ."

Daniel sobers a bit. "No, really. I don't meet a lot of women I have so much in common with who also are so . . ." His voice drifts off. "When you went home, back to your family, I'd be left in the lurch. I think I'd get hurt in that scenario."

I can tell he means it, so I back off, disappointed as I am. "Ok. Then it's clothes on. For sure."

"Can't have me slinking out of every hotel in New York City this summer," he jokes.

Can't we? I think. "That wouldn't be good," I lie. "Besides, I still want your ideas for my reading program."

He grins. "You do? I am so, so glad, because I have so many ideas. I brought my laptop, and it's bursting with suggestions. Should we go snag a table and dig in?"

I think about the pretty, lacy underthings hiding beneath my casual knit dress and sigh inwardly. "Sure. Let's dig in," I say in as "just friendly" a voice as possible. "Let's . . . talk about literacy."

We take our drinks and move to a bar-height two-top between the bar and the pool table. Daniel pulls out his laptop to display an impressive spreadsheet of titles, copyright situations, grade levels, and central themes. For an hour we talk about teaching and reading levels and book canons. And the entire time, two of my brain cells are having a little private argument in the back of my brain. Brain Cell One is definitely the devil. *What the hell? She's supposed to be having sex with this one!* it keeps shouting.

And Brain Cell Two says, *Shhhh. This is perfect. A romantic relationship would be dead in the water in months. He might not be the only person getting hurt.*

And then Brain Cell One says, in a huff, *What a waste. Look at him. He's like a high eight. Maybe a nine. A New York eight and a half. That's a PA four thousand.*

Brain Cell Two remains firm. *He's too attractive. And too smart. And too thoughtful. She can have a fling with anyone. This one it's better to enjoy as a friend.*

A friend! I believe it was Shakespeare who wrote, "'Tis better to have sexed and lost than never to have sexed at all," says Brain Cell One.

And you call yourself a librarian, says Brain Cell Two. *You need to get your butt to the eight twenty shelves stat.*

"What I need," I hear myself say out loud out of absolutely nowhere, "is a book on neurology."

My two guilty brain cells shut up. Daniel looks at me quizzically. "Sorry," I say. "I think I've hit a wall in my contemplations."

He nods knowingly, though, thankfully, he has no idea what I'm talking about. "I hear you. I've been absolutely piling it on. But believe it or not, I think we have a starting place here. Look at this: five different graduated-level Flexthologies, covering all of your theme areas. If we can somehow get free permissions for these or find money to buy them from the publishers, we'd have enough to run a larger-scale pilot program. We put out the word, and charters and privates will line up to be in that pilot."

"The problem is," I say, challenged but not defeated, "we'd be asking schools to pay for e-copies of books of which seventy-five percent or more of the students would read only a chapter. It'll never fly. To say nothing of the fact that very few schools have enough e-readers to institute this. That pigeonholes us with the wealthiest schools. If we don't run the pilot program at less affluent schools, how will we know if it can really reach kids in need?"

Daniel frowns. "Maybe . . ." But then he falters. "You're right. Urban schools are poor, and we already own a hundred copies of *The Scarlet Letter.*"

"Fat lot of good that does anyone," I say. "I hate *The Scarlet Letter.*"

Daniel smiles. "Careful who hears you say that. In some pedagogical circles you would be forced to wear a red *H* for *heretic* on your dress."

I smirk. "Daniel, you may look cool, but deep down you're a book dork like the rest of us."

He perks up. "You think I look cool?"

"I do," I tell him.

"Would you like to do something cool with me?"

Like sex? asks my brain. "Like what?" asks my mouth.

"It's summer in New York City," he tells me. "The options are endless. But I was thinking . . ."

"Yeah?"

"Ta-da!" he says with a flourish, and then out of his breast pocket he presents two tickets. "How do you feel about baseball?"

My eyes go wide. Baseball was probably the last thing on my mind when I thought of tonight. And yet now that I've had time to contemplate it, I cannot think of anything more perfect for this gorgeous, sunny summer evening than sitting next to this smart, interesting, and very attractive man having a light beer and a hot dog in Citi Field. My better angel must be getting through to me, because I start to see the reason of having this thing with Daniel be just friends. I'm not divorced yet, and a tiny, stupid, useless part of me doesn't want to be, so I have a steamer trunk full of husband baggage. I could have casual sex with anyone. With a decent human being like Daniel, friendship really does make sense.

"I feel like baseball is a wonderful reason to sit outside in the sunshine with a new friend," I tell him.

"You're going to look dazzling in a Mets cap," he tells me. I beam. "Amy, I'm so glad we met."

My mouth goes a little dry. "Me too," I say.

"I know I've been needing to make new friends for a long time," he tells me. "But single parenting a teenager and working long hours with my students have left me low on social opportunities. And then here you are, on your momspringa—"

"That's not a real thing," I tell him. "It's just a word my friend's magazine coined to sell copies."

"Here you are, on your momspringa," he repeats, as if I haven't spoken. "And you love your kids and your books, and you are so freaking easy to talk to. And you like baseball!" he adds.

I shake my head. "I do not like baseball. I mean, I might like baseball, but I have no idea if I do or not, because I've never seen a game before. I like doing new things, though. And I like doing them outside on a day like today."

And I like doing them with you, I think to myself.

"Good enough for me!" he exclaims. "I'm gonna buy you some peanuts and Cracker Jacks. Well," he admits, "either peanuts *or* Cracker Jacks. I'm a public school teacher, after all. Let's not get crazy."

"We wouldn't want that," I say with a smile.

—

In the basement of a department store on Fifth Avenue, there is a teahouse where ladies go to lunch on forbidden rice-and-shrimp balls and arugula dumplings and other tasty yet unsatisfying foodstuffs. Thanks to the magazine expense account, Matt and I have come here three times since I got back to New York. It is chockablock with media people who are happy to pay a dollar for every ten calories. Sometimes on the walk back to the magazine, I eat one of those giant street pretzels with mustard to fill up.

I am munching on twenty-four dollars' worth of seven-grain porridge and seaweed when Matt tells me he's made a private Pinterest board full of dating options.

"Ooooh!" I exclaim, because I am getting to know Matt well enough to know that there is no point in wasting time discussing what an insane thing that was to do. "Can I see?"

He hands it to me. It's a sea of very nice-looking guys, but they are ranging in age from thirty-five to fifty.

"Matt," I say solemnly. "You can see that these men are all way too old for you, right?"

Matt chokes on the microscopic sea cucumber pickle he's nibbling. "Those guys?" he coughs. "For me? No. Besides, I'm seeing someone. I'm talking about for you."

"Uh . . . ," I say. In my head I am recalculating the sheer quantity of good-looking guys Matt showed me. A couple of them were downright hot. Would going on a date with one of them be that bad?

But come on, Amy. Be serious. "That's a pity, because I am not interested in going out with complete strangers who were selected for me by someone I've known for two weeks."

Matt shrugs and puts his phone away. I feel my heart sink a little when he gives in so easily. Maybe I do want to see a few of those cute guys' pictures again? Just in case? "Ok," he says. "What's the plan for the summer, then? That librarian guy you were telling me about?"

I level him a look. "The plan for the summer is house-sitting for your boss until she gets back, making some book choices for my reading program, and reaching out to authors about using selections from their books for free. And I'm going to read these." I open my Litsy app and show Matt the huge TBR shelf I have going.

"That's, like, thirty books," Matt says.

"You're right. I may need to add more," I tell him with a smile.

"You know, when you have that many books, you'll probably need someone to help you shelve them. Someone like . . . a hot librarian?"

I shrug. "If you must know, I went out with the hot librarian. We decided to be 'just friends.'"

Matt tilts his head. "Is he less hot up close?"

"Oh my stars, he just gets hotter the closer you get. He is tall, dark, and handsome; a Korean Heathcliff; a librarian sex god; a dad I'd like to . . . you know. He looks as good as a champagne truffle tastes."

"Wow. Then why on earth aren't you 'you know'-ing him?"

I sigh. "To be honest, I'd really like to 'you know' with him, like ASAP. But he suggested we have a friendship because of where I live, usually, and my momspringa and everything. And he is probably right.

Because he is much more than a pretty face. He has just the loveliest way about him, and he enjoys books almost as much as me, and we share a lot of the same passions and values . . ." I think about how easy Daniel is to be with, the quiet way he elicited so much of my history from me over the course of the ball game. How I found myself telling him about John's leaving and the hardest moments afterward, and how he turned away from the batter with a full count to look at me warmly and say, "Amy, you are one tough cookie to live through all that," and the way some combination of that little bit of praise and the tenderness in his eyes made me feel so *understood*.

It was a dangerous bit of magic that zipped between us. "The end of the summer would be a killer blow if we let things get carried away."

Matt frowns. "Hmm. So you're trying to protect yourselves?"

I nod.

"But you still plan to hang out with him socially and spend time together?"

I nod again.

Matt makes a face.

"What?" I ask him.

"I think you'd better look at that Pinterest board I made."

I shake my head. "I don't need to date. I've got a full schedule of good stuff, and now I have two new friends in town to hang out with whenever I want a buddy." I tip my head to him, new friend number one, warmly. "Plus, I loved that yoga-Pilates combo class you sent me to, so I'm definitely going back there a few times a week. And I was thinking I'd add a spin class too. Do they still have those? I used to love indoor cycling before I had Joe."

Matt reaches across the table and grabs my hand. He looks me in the eyes and pauses dramatically. "Flywheel," he tells me somberly, as though he is telling me the secret of eternal life.

"Is that what they call spinning now?"

He scoffs. "Flywheel is so much more than spinning. It's music and lights and competition and challenge . . . it's a fitness revelation that will change you on the inside and out." His voice has gotten quiet and reverent, but then he almost shouts: "There's a class tonight. Six thirty p.m.!" There is a momentary pause, and then he snaps his fingers. "We need to go buy you the shoes."

"I don't need special shoes. I can just wear sneaks."

"And padded gear."

"Is this contact stationary cycling?"

"Quick. Eat your gruel," he tells me. "I have to be back in the office by two, so we only have an hour to shop."

I wolf down the generous half teaspoon of avocado on my plate and then the wild rice. While I eat, Matt's thumbs work furiously on his phone.

"What are you up to over there?" I ask him.

"I'm live tweeting your momspringa," he tells me blithely.

I roll my eyes. "No one wants to hear about my fitness regimen."

"Oh no?" he asks and shows me his phone. "Click the hashtag." I do, and I see it: people are talking about #momspringa. Specifically, about how badly they want one.

"Huh."

"The people have spoken," he says. "And they want momspringa. You've started a conversation. And my job is to keep it going."

With that, Matt and I rush to an athletic store near his office. Inside we find miles of high-end spandex and stainless steel and many mirrored surfaces. Matt sits me down in the shoe section and barks, "Shimanos, size seven," to the attendant and then tells me, "Be right back. What's your sports-bra situation?"

I smile at him, feeling assured in my attire for once. "In that department I am well covered," I say, adding what I hope is a reassuring thumbs-up. In fact, until I came to New York, sports bras were pretty much all I owned.

Matt comes back about two minutes after I've put on a pair of rigid-soled low-profile cycling shoes. He is clutching lots of hangers with stretchy gray and black things on them. "How do they feel?" he asks me about the shoes.

"Like weird bike shoes. But they fit. Tell me again why I can't wear regular running shoes?"

"Well, for one thing, you'll slip off the pedals. For another, you look cooler in these. You don't mind that a photographer is meeting us at the cycling studio tonight, do you?"

I give him a hard look. "I do in fact mind. I haven't been on a bike seat of any kind since I pushed my son's enormous head through my tiny birth canal. I will need a few practice sessions to acclimate."

He waves a hand as if to say *no problem*. "Let's do the shoot next week when you're in the zone. Tonight, we can just tweet and snap. Now, get those off so we can check out and I can get to work before Talia's voice mail explodes. On the way, pick out a water bottle." He gestures to a display of nozzle-top sports bottles in shades of metallic.

"Am I going to be shooting water into my mouth while I pedal, like a Tour de France rider?"

Matt smiles. "Hopefully. It'll make good art."

When we get to the register, I offer to pay for the gear, thinking that this is a good use for some of the last semester's tuition money that John has, miraculously, reimbursed me for over the last week. But Matt shoves me aside. "First of all, the total is going to make your eyes bleed," he tells me as he pulls out the company credit card. "And second, I still haven't spent all the momspringa budget."

I frown at him. "But—"

"Before you go through the motions of arguing with me, only to lose, let's just say we get some great photos of you trying new fitness classes and . . . doing some other new activities." I narrow my eyes at this last bit, but he ignores me. "The momspringa hashtag is trending, as you may have noticed. This is one of those rare moments when a story might actually help sell copies of the magazine, or at least raise our profile. That is definitely worth a sweat-wicking tank or two."

"But—"

"Did I mention thank you for helping my career?" Matt says. "And shut up and be grateful for this?"

I laugh and then give up and let him pay. As he's being rung up I play back the previous conversation. "What other new activities?" I ask him. "Pole dancing?"

Matt laughs. "Please. No one does that anymore."

I shrug. "I am pretty sure strippers do."

"Fair enough. But I was thinking dating."

I sigh. "Well. I guess I could try a date, if there was someone you thought was really promising."

"Good, good." Matt nods. He takes the bag of gear, and we start for the door. "But what would you say about maybe sampling a little more widely?"

I look at him curiously. "I guess I'd say, 'What's the point?' If I hit it off with the guy you pick, then I can date him. If not, I'm not exactly in the mood to shop for a stepdad for the kids."

Matt steers me down the crowded sidewalk. "There are other reasons to date besides husband hunting."

"Oh, not you too."

"It's fun," he tells me. "And it sells magazines . . ."

I throw up my hands. And yeah, maybe I give in a little too easily. "Ok, fine. A couple of dates. But you have to do all the picking men and arranging plans, and you have to help me decide what to wear. I just show up. Understand?"

"I understand completely. A couple dates a week until the magazine goes to press. Thanks, Amy. You're a real peach."

"I did not agree to that," I tell him. "I said—"

"And I'll text you where to meet tonight for spin class. Me and my new gal pal, Amy, hanging at Flywheel," says Matt. "Your mind is going to be blown."

"Matt—"

"Momspringa!" he hollers. And then he turns and walks into the office, leaving me on the street wondering if what I've actually embarked on is a mommageddon.

CHAPTER TWELVE

Dear Mom,

You'll never believe this, but I went to the library yesterday after my first day at work and checked out A Tale of Two Cities, *and you're right. I loved it! It was totally unputdownable. I was rooting for Los Angeles the whole time, but when Chicago pulled out a win in the end, I was totally satisfied with the result.*

Just kidding. I went to see the new Fast and the Furious movie with Brian and Trinity. Brian has this friend, Mom, who is so cute. His name is a pretend rich-kid name: Dalton. He goes to Catholic school, and he's apparently very good at sports. Brian and his soccer coach are trying to get him to forfeit a year of games to come play his senior year at Country Day. Dalton took me aside when Brian was talking to the bros and asked me what I really thought about that idea, and I told him the truth: That it's a great school, and if he wants to work hard, he'll get an excellent education for two years. But you can get a great education lots of places if you're interested in working hard. I said, if he wants to play soccer, play soccer—don't sit out a year just to make some rich guys happy.

He told me the rich guys are persuasive. He told me they have been inviting him to parties and introducing him to hot private school girls. I told him we hot private school girls are actually total prudes, and all we do is study all the time. I told him if he wanted to have any kind of post–high school athletic career, he'd be wise to skip the parties and focus on school and practice. He asked me if I wanted to be study buddies. Then Brian came back.

I had the best night. I'm pretty sure Dalton is going to stick with his school, and that's probably the right decision for him. But still, it is so, so good to be reminded that there are other guys in this world than the guys I already know. Maybe one day I'll meet a man who knows not to ever take me to a Fast and the Furious movie.

Dare to dream, right?

Love,

Your daughter, who is seriously thinking about playing the field (get it—soccer field? Because Dalton plays soccer?), Cori

———

Yes, I have two new friends, and Lena and Talia are a text message away, and there's the city that never sleeps for company. But staying alone for weeks at Talia's place is still making me itchy all over. This is not my house. These are not my things. This is not my life.

For the first lonely week I texted Cori too much, called to check on Joe every night, and made Lena or Talia video chat me during dinner so I didn't constantly have to eat alone.

But Lena told me last night she'd be appearing as teacher rep for a PTA meeting this evening, Talia has dinner with some advertisers, and Joe and John are chauffeuring Cori and Brian to the movies. So tonight I come home from my third Flywheel class sweaty, exhausted, and totally amped up, and I have never, ever felt so alone.

Before class, Matt's people fancied up my ponytail into a high bun and did some sweat-resistant makeup, and then a photographer came in and took pictures of me on the stationary bike pretending to be part of a larger class. She stayed and snapped some shots while the class was actually going, and I was the subject of all kinds of interest and speculation from my fellow fliers, and I felt, ever so slightly, like a celebrity.

Flywheel may be a "fitness revelation," but it is also a very New Yorky scene. The obscenely toned instructors wear pop-star headsets and play music so cool it won't reach my hometown for another three years. In the crowded "stadium" where we spin, with the teacher telling us we are superstars and our sweat flying on the jumps, I feel gorgeous, strong, unbeatable. Now, in the empty, Talialess apartment, I feel more like an imposter.

I pour myself a bowl of cereal and then start spinning my mental wheels. I should take a shower, I think, go down to the cute little Italian restaurant on the corner and eat a big plate of gnocchi at the bar by myself. I can bring a book. If I do it with confidence, no one will think anything of it.

But instead I pour the milk on my cereal. I'm not the kind of person who can go sit alone in a restaurant on a Friday night with confidence. I'm the kind of person who will probably eat this cereal and then fall asleep on the couch in my sweat-wicking athletic clothes around nine p.m.

I could be doing that in Pennsylvania, I nag myself. Or Antarctica, for that matter. I need to live! This is my momspringa, right?

I open up my laptop. After he tweeted my first gussied-up "after" shoot, Matt fielded a small passel of probably crazy men asking for my contact information so they could date me. He asked them to send a recent photo or link to their online dating profile, and then he'd pass it along to me. He also heard from loyal magazine readers who wanted to set me up with their single guy friends. He followed the same MO with them. Now he has shared a small private Pinterest portfolio of fellows that I can either thumbs-up or thumbs-down on. Like my own personal Bumble app, he tells me.

I reply, "What's Bumble?"

Matt sighs.

I haven't looked at the Pinterest board since that quick viewing at the teahouse. I've been afraid just looking over these guys would upset me. The truth is, since John left, the idea of dating widely has been almost poisonous to me. The hot librarian aside, there hasn't been anyone—not one single man—who has made me want to get back out there again. The first time Lena brought up dating after John left, I raced to the bathroom, locked the door behind me, and had a big cry before I came back out again. At the time I blamed the reaction on PMS and fear. On reflection, I suppose the very thought of dating outside my marriage made John's and my separation all too real to bear.

Well, now things are different. Now I need to make that separation feel as real as possible if I'm ever to get on with my life. So I open Pinterest, navigate to the secret board Matt shared with me, and take a look.

What I see is amazing. At home I have gone three years without ever bumping into a tempting dating proposition. Here in New York the talent is unmissable. Here are twenty men, all vetted by Matt, all looking imminently eligible. He's provided links to Facebook stalk them, and I see doctors and lawyers, artists and poets, and several Wall Street types, in a variety of cultural backgrounds, body types, and racial makeups. In their pictures they are hiking up mountains, scuba diving, and cuddling adorable children.

The easy part is the first elimination. I rule out a man with four young kids—probably great, but contrary to the ethos of momspringa— and a man whose politics on Facebook are just way too incompatible with mine. I rule out a guy riding a Harley with no helmet—if I wanted to be a young widow, I'd just smother John in his sleep. I rule out a guy who seems to have spray-painted himself orange. Now I am left with sixteen truly good-looking employed dudes who want to take me on a date. I feel like *The Bachelorette*, Special Middle-Aged Edition.

"There are too many delicious choices," I text Matt completely out of nowhere.

He must still be at the office. He immediately writes back, "Get three dips then. Life is short!"

I laugh to myself. "I'm talking about men, not ice cream," I shoot back.

He responds, "Maybe I am too."

I send him a smiley and then ask how to choose.

Matt:
Give the guys a ranking of either 1, 2, or 3. Then try to set up dates with all the 1s. Scheduling will determine who you meet first.

Amy:
Oh wow. You had a pretty quick answer for that.

Matt:
I've done this before.

Amy:
Are you some kind of mom pimp?

Matt:

I could be. Next career.

Amy:
I'll be sure to write you a testimonial.

Then I pause for a second and text him again.

Should the 1s be the people who are the best-sounding humans or the guys who are the cutest?

Matt:

Up to you. But if it were me, I'd pick the cute ones. You can date nice guys back in PA. New York is just for fun.

Amy:

#momspringa!

Matt:

#momspringa!

I turn back to my screen. The man who is a successful pianist is a definite one. I have always wanted to date a musician. Think of his fingers . . . and the very good-looking Wall Street suit is a one because, wow, he is very good looking. And the younger guy with the gorgeous eyes who says his favorite book is *Love in the Time of Cholera*. And the silver fox who looks like what you'd get if you crossed Harry Bosch and Walt Longmire. And definitely the archeologist because Indiana Jones. And so on and so forth: I rate and rate and rate.

By the end I have seven ones. I open up a beer to pair with my cold cereal, pour it in a glass like a classy person, and start tapping out quick messages. I thank each guy for contacting Matt and tell them I am going to try some first dates as part of the #momspringa article; I think that clearly sends the message that this isn't a serious endeavor. Then I ask them if they might be free in the next couple of weeks and if they'd be comfortable going on the record for the magazine. By the bottom of the beer I have contacted all seven guys. I am genuinely excited. I am incredibly hopeful. I am downright giddy.

And when one of the guys, a financial analyst, pings me back an hour later, asking for a date tomorrow night if it's not too short of notice, I am pretty damn pleased with myself to boot.

Lena:

So . . . how was the date with the money guy?

Amy:

It was fine.

Talia:

But was he fine?

Amy:

Um. Ok, yes. Tall. Extremely good looking. Like, maybe he is an underwear model? Wearing what I imagine a thousand-dollar suit would look like, not that I would know. And he took me to this place where only good-looking people in thousand-dollar suits go. Like, I felt afraid someone was going to ask me to wear a paper bag on my head to keep the standards up.

Lena:

Ha! "Ma'am, I apologize, but would you mind hiding your hideousness from us for a few hours? We need to think of our guests' needs."

Amy:

"Our very good-looking guests." And then my date would say, "She doesn't mind. She's one of those with the 'inner beauty.'"

Talia:

You'd damn well better still have the outer beauty too. I spent a lot of my August feature budget on that outer beauty. Are you keeping up with your eyebrows? Did he like your hair?

Amy:

Yes. He said my hair is what drew him to me. Which is, like, not really the best thing to say on a first date. I didn't tell him the reason I decided to message him is because of his nice teeth, did I?

Lena:

Does he have nice teeth? Because that is not nothing.

Amy:

His teeth are like a toothpaste commercial. Little rows of mother-of-pearl shells, gleaming white for as far as the eye can see.

Lena:

So he has good oral-hygiene habits.

Amy:

I would say it's beyond good habits. It's probably closer to a life pursuit than a habit.

Lena:

Like a calling from God?

Talia:

What's his name?

Amy:

Dylan

Talia:

"DYLAN, THIS IS GOD. GO GET YOUR TEETH BLEACHED."

Amy:

That's probably exactly what happened. Anyway, it was pretty hypnotizing to look at. I think that's why I ordered that second martini.

Lena:

Talia SHE GOT THE SECOND MARTINI

Talia:

Stop shouting. Only the Voice of God gets to use all caps.

Lena:

Talia she got the second martini

Talia:

I KNOW RIGHT?

Did you get laid, Amy Byler?

Amy:

I did not. But it was hard to resist him.

Lena:

She's doing it wrong. She's trying to resist him.

Talia:

I know. Believe me, I know.

Amy:

He looked gorgeous, and the restaurant was amazing, and he was kind of fascinating in his own right with his stories about traveling all over the world giving out IMF loans. But . . .

Lena:
Yes?

Amy:
Deep down, he was a tool. Do we.still say tool?

Talia:
We do, in the privacy of text convos with other people our age.

Lena:
I never said "tool."

Amy:
That's because you never dated a tool. You were married to God.

Lena:
There were days when God felt like a real tool to me.

Talia:
Wow. You'll have to let us know how many other nuns you meet in hell, Lena.

Lena:
Oh, like you won't get there long before me.

Talia:
I'm in hell now. Hell is summer in Florida.

Amy:
Hell is realizing your gorgeous tooth-model date is a tool only after the second martini. I spent the entire period from the serving of the main course till the escaping to a cab trying

not to tell him how patronizing he was being. He acted like he invented microloans. Also, he asked me if I had read the new Malcolm Gladwell, which, yes, I have, and then even after I said yes, he described the entire book basically verbatim to me. Like, maybe I read it, but did I read it with the Dylan-level insight he could share with me?

Talia:
Uch. Malcolm Gladwell.

Amy:
Right? I'm a librarian. Dig deeper, jerk.

Lena:
You New York girls are snobs. I think she should have slept with him. I mean, I would have, assuming he'd been a woman.

Amy:
I would have rather slept with a woman.

Lena:
There's plenty of chances for that.

Talia:
No need to switch teams. There are so many more men where Dylan came from. Matt sent me the six-packs today. Amy is drowning in prospects. When's your next date, Ames?

Amy:
Sigh. Tomorrow night.

Talia:

Excellent.

Lena:

Two dates in three days? Amy, you're a tiger.

Amy:

Rar.

He's a doctor, he's taking me to a pop-up dinner with some celeb chef I've never heard of. We've texted a little, and he actually seems pretty promising. He hasn't mansplained anything to me yet, and he told me my kids sounded wonderful and that meant I was probably wonderful too. Swoon!

Talia:

Eh. Doctors.

Lena:

At the very least you'll get a good meal.

Amy:

Excellent point. Last night I had oysters to start, then a pretty delicious salad thing with melon and crisped prosciutto, then scallops, then the world's most perfect Meyer-lemon cake. To say nothing of two very strong martinis.

Lena:

And you still didn't put out? Talia, this girl.

Talia:

A true princess.

Amy:

Trust me, ladies. I did the right thing. I would have spent the entire episode worried about chipping his beautiful teeth.

Talia:

Pro tip: If teeth are getting chipped, you're doing sex wrong.

Lena:

Cut her some slack, T. It's been a long time since she got laid on the regular. Maybe back when she last had a sex life, wooden clubs were still involved.

Amy:

I'm putting my phone on silent you guys.

Talia:

That's cool. We don't need you around to make fun of you.

Amy:

Good night you monsters.

Lena:

Good night your majesty.

———

The next time I come home from Flywheel alone, I take a shower, put on a pretty gray maxi dress that's low enough cut to make me feel just a smidgen indecent, and head right back out the door. No more Ms. Cereal-for-Dinner. Tonight I'm going to be bold and treat myself to a restaurant I read about in the *New Yorker*, a place that "infuses everything meaningful about the current New York food scene into a tagine and a bowl of olives."

They don't take reservations, and I'm expecting to be cooling my heels at the bar for hours, but when I tell them I'm looking for a table for just one, the hostess positively beams at me. It turns out dining here is at communal tables, and they love to fill every single stool at their wide distressed-oak high-tops that radiate from an open kitchen. So I get wedged between a rowdy party of five investment bankers and a couple on a date. Listening in on their various conversations is so fun I end up taking twice as long with the menu as I should, and when the server comes the second time, I finally just ask her to order for me.

"Ooh!" she says. "Fun. Parameters?"

The restaurant is relaxed, homey, and the pricing is reasonable. New Moroccan is what the review called it. "I'm not afraid of anything," I tell her. "I'll take your best salad, your favorite main course, and a glass of the perfect drink to go with each of them." Look at me throwing around money like an oil heiress, and I can do it guiltlessly at least this one time, because John offered to buy the kids new school shoes that will save me twice the cost of this dinner.

The server looks at me sideways. "I've got a hundred favorites, but I'll do my best. Or . . ." She leans in closer. "Chef might cook you something special, you know, if I tell him what you just told me."

I color. Three of the bankers' heads have twisted around at the word *Chef*. "That would be amazing too. I'm sure I'll be happy either way."

"I'll make sure of it," she tells me, then gives me the sneakiest little wink when the man on the date next to me waves at her and hollers, "Miss!" as though she's ten feet away. The server takes my menu and turns her attention to the couple, and I pull out my e-reader, which is loaded with a new Ann Patchett book I've been saving for just such a sumptuous occasion. I don't waste Patchett books, but this place—and this adventure of dining alone for the first time in my life—is Patchett worthy.

Ms. Patchett's words are soon joined by a creamy, tender-finishing white wine and a salad of sweet, fresh carrots; toasted, crunchy chickpeas; mint; and a honey-and-vinegar dressing of some kind with just a bit of spicy heat. I eat and eat, and when I have polished off the very last chickpea, I wait until all my tablemates are busy with their own food and then lift the plate to my lips and lick up the last bit of sticky, spicy dressing shamelessly. I put it down and check to see no one caught me, but I am found out, by someone in the central kitchen, no less, and wearing whites. He nudges the chef and says something to him and then points at me.

I try to look away, but the chef, a big, bald, tattooed man I wouldn't want to meet in a biker bar, puts down his bar mop and steps through the little hatch in the half wall between him and us.

"So," he tells me in a thick accent that I can only place somewhere deep in the boroughs. "You like the salad."

I blush but then quickly decide to quit simpering. I'll never see any of these people again, and I look really *good* in this dress, which has been confirmed by the occasional sideways leer of an investment banker ten years my junior. "I like the salad, and I hope you'll make me something special to follow it up," I tell him.

"How do you like lamb?"

"I like it very much."

"Are you in a hurry?" he asks me, tilting his head to the people on either side of me, who are silent, watching us with interest.

"Not at all," I tell him.

"Good, then come sit over here." The man starts to walk back to the kitchen but stops and puts me at an open bar seat right in front of him. "It is boring tonight—all very timid chicken eaters who read about me in the *New Yorker*."

"I read about you in the *New Yorker*."

He smiles. "And I thought you just stumbled in here from the street. I'm getting you some gray wine."

That sounds awful, but I nod and brace myself. What I get is thankfully not gray at all but more of a pinkish pour with a dry rosé-meets-citrus sort of flavor. The bottle is cool and sweaty, and my server pours a second glass for the chef, and he pours a good taste for her, and then they leave the entire remainder of the bottle sitting by me to work on as he cooks.

I forget my book and watch him work. He's relaxed and quiet, and he often pokes his staff with an elbow by way of communication rather than sparing a word. The tickets move past him with such speed. I see about five of the same exact dish, looking indistinguishable from one another, go out over and over and over again. I crane back and see the bankers ordering more wine, see the couple get their check. I keep watching and waiting, and sometimes the chef puts a tiny spoon of food up on my bar spot for me to taste. One olive. A sliver of preserved lemon. A rich, briny tomato sauce that seems only distantly related to an Italian ragù. Finally, after who knows how long, just as I notice I am getting hungry and my glass is almost empty, a plate comes up for me.

It's a ring of alternating quartered soft-boiled eggs and tiny lamb meatballs, making a shoreline for a moat of tomato-and-fava-bean sauce with bright-green olive tapenade on top. Standing upright in a little jar next to the plate are fried, stuffed sardines.

I stare at the plate, then up at the chef. "Eat, now!" he urges me. I comply, and it's phenomenal. Everything tastes of some smoky spice I've never tasted before plus the brightest, best version of tomato, parsley, lamb, egg. I could eat the sardines like french fries. I take a bite of the second one and dip it in the sauce on my plate, and the chef nods approvingly.

He is busy—he hardly talks to me for the rest of my meal. But he constantly reaches up and pours another inch of vin gris into my never-empty wineglass, and when I've eaten every last bite of the kofta and sardines, he says something to my server, and she comes back in ten minutes with a large slice of rosewater-and-pomegranate pie.

I do my best with that, but by the time my check is paid, I am uncomfortably full and very comfortably tipsy. My thanks to the chef and my server are sloppy and gratuitous, and I make a slow, careful path out to the street. It is late for me, but not for New York. Everyone is going somewhere. People are on dates. People are kissing quickly in passing or for long, unabashed hellos. I would like, I think, to be kissing a long, unabashed hello to someone. I would like to be going somewhere. Not back to Talia's, but to see someone I could tell all about this stupendous dinner and the gray wine and the semifamous, quiet, yet whimsical chef. I don't want to waste this perfect combination of satisfied and intoxicated; I want to walk up a long, endless avenue and talk and talk and talk until the sun comes up, because this is New York, and I am on vacation, and life is so very, very good.

Needless to say, I text Daniel.

CHAPTER THIRTEEN

Dear Mom,

Ok, full disclosure, this is turning out to be an amazing summer.

First things first: I dumped Brian. He was hassling me about sex stuff. Also he's just not a great guy. I was super nice about it. I texted AND called for follow-up. I told him it was because I needed to focus on diving. He didn't believe me, so I told him it was because I didn't want to have sex with him. Then he was quiet. He asked me if I was a lesbian. I just said, "Maybe," because it seemed nicer than telling him he was revolting.

So that was huge, because now I have more time to hang with Dad, who is just turning out super cool as he starts to relax and not be quite so obvious about trying to buy our love. He's really a good listener, really nonjudgmental because he's pretty much been as big a screwup as a person can be already. It's easy to talk to him about my real feelings about some things, like guys or how I don't actually like that many of the girls from my diving team or how I sometimes feel poor at our school even though I know I'm lucky to have clean water and shoes that fit and contact lenses. When I'm talking to Lena or my friends, I want them to like me, so I don't always tell the straight truth. Dad obviously thinks Joe and I are god's gift to Bucks County, Pennsylvania, no matter what we say.

Also, Dad is super into adolescence. He says I should lean into it and label my feelings and embrace them. I told him not to worry about that. He says unpleasant emotions will pass through me faster if I name them and feel them. I was like, Dad, welcome to Stuff I Learned on Sesame Street. *He said, "My generation never learned anything important like that," and he told me that's part of the reason he didn't handle his problems well. Is that true? You seem to know how to have most feelings. I guess you're a little low in the anger department—you never got very angry at Dad, and you can be kind of a martyr sometimes and then suddenly blow up at me for no reason except stupid stuff like spending Joe's bus fare on Diet Coke and then telling him to walk home. He was ten. It was only three miles. If you let me have Diet Coke in the house, that never would have happened.*

Anyway, if you had just let rip on Dad and gotten angry, it would have made me and Joe feel a lot better. We thought we might be horrible people for hating him so much at first. Lena says you were protecting us from painful truths about our father. But I think if you had told us what he told us this summer—that he was being kind of a shitty dad to us, and things were only getting worse, and he was making you unhappy all the time—then we would have understood things a bit better.

IDK. I'm not trying to pile on here. I'm just saying.

Love,

Your daughter, Cori, who read zero books this week but did look at a J. Crew catalog and gives it two stars for inventiveness of sweater color names

—

Amy:
Hey, it's late, I'm still up. You want to meet for a drink?

Daniel doesn't write back. I wander around in widening loops through Talia's neighborhood, circling her apartment like a shark. I don't want to go back there. I don't want to put on the old, soft lavender T-shirt I sleep in and climb into bed and read myself to sleep like I do every other night. I want to live! I want to taste every bite of the cookie of life! I want to—

Daniel:
Hello to you too. I'm just finishing up dinner with much-cooler-than-me friends on the Lower East Side. I need an antidote to all this ironic facial hair.

Amy:
I don't have even nonironic facial hair!

Daniel:
In that case, let's meet for a drink. Are you downtown?

Amy:
I will be in ten minutes. Does that sound desperate?

Daniel:
It just sounds thirsty. There's a Perth theme bar with outdoor seating on Pearl Street. I'll send you the map and head down there myself now.

I stare at my phone in disbelief. Did I just . . . was that a booty call? Was it a friendly version of a booty call? I have no idea what just happened, but apparently the end result is hanging out with Daniel at an Australia-themed bar with outdoor seating! Score! I jump in a cab, throwing financial caution to the wind. This is way too special for the subway, plus it's late and I'm going to be lost on the Manhattan side and the financial district is always so *dark* and I am pretty sure serial killers get excited when they see a lost, tipsy woman from Pennsylvania.

Plus, there might be cobblestone streets. It's hard to flee serial killers on cobblestone streets. This way is much safer.

Unless my cabbie is a serial killer? Wasn't there a movie like that? Oh, look! We're here!

I try to climb out without paying. The driver gently reminds me to swipe my credit card. I tip him well to make up for the embarrassment on both sides of the Plexiglas. Then I make my way carefully into the Lucky Shag and try not to read into Daniel's choice of bars too much. I order a Victoria Bitter and then think better of it and switch my order to soda with lime. I cool my heels at the bar, one eye fixed on the door. I wait.

After about ten minutes I feel a tap on my shoulder. I jump a mile and then spin around. "Holy crap! You startled me!" I tell Daniel. "Where did you come from?"

"I've been sitting on the veranda waiting for you! Come on out here. The view is kind of the whole point of this ridiculous place."

I follow Daniel up a staircase I didn't even notice before and out a side door to a long, skinny outdoor balcony with just enough room for one row of very narrow tables. From the seat Daniel waves me toward, I can see a perfect view of the first tower of the Brooklyn Bridge rising above the streets, cars, and low buildings in the foreground. One of those lower buildings—maybe three stories high—is decorated with a pastel trompe l'oeil mural of the exact bridge view it blocks, as if to make up to those at street level.

The real bridge is lit with streetlights all the way to Brooklyn, and the suspension wires are dotted with pretty white lights, and clouds of dark purple hang in the night sky.

"Well," I tell him. "This is pretty wonderful!"

"And the moon is full," Daniel tells me, pointing above our heads toward the city. "That explains why you texted."

I feel embarrassed. "Actually," I say with a little edge, "I texted because I just had a spectacular meal cooked for me personally by the chef featured in this week's *New Yorker*, and I was dying to brag about it to someone."

Daniel opens his arms wide. "Amazing! Brag away."

I inhale to give him the rundown—the sardines, the wine, the little tasting spoons, the rosewater pie—but then stop myself. "Also I just wanted to hang out with you."

Now Daniel smiles warmly. "I'm flattered. And your timing was perfect. I didn't realize it until you texted, but ten p.m. is way too early to end such a perfect summer night."

"Exactly!" I say a bit too loudly. "Look at this! This is exactly what a momspringa is supposed to be."

Daniel laughs. "There's that word again."

I nod. "I'm coming around to it. Say it enough, and it starts to sound less stupid and more like a reasonable way to handle the stresses of motherhood."

"Do dads get one?"

I pause. "Maybe single dads," I say. "And widowers. But guys who come home and 'babysit' their kids once in a while so you can see your friends for the first time in weeks, or expect you to thank them when they do a load of laundry? Nope. They don't need dadspringas. They need reality checks."

"And is that what your ex-husband is getting? A reality check?"

I think that over. "Maybe. I know he is showing the kids a wonderful time, and he seems to have it all together. Joe is in hog heaven, with all their math and science adventures together, and Cori is getting her every demand met, plus getting a chance to slack off a little. If I were home, she'd be working longer hours in a harder summer job, reading something besides The Hunger Games for the fourth time, and seeing much less of her friends on weeknights. But . . . John's right; it seems to be good for her to get a summer to let her hair down. Going by what she says in our talks and hearty use of unlimited texting, she seems to be chewing over our family situation in such a healthy, open-minded way."

"And you? How do you chew over sharing your kids with your ex-husband after three years without him?"

I shake my head. "I have no idea what to think," I say honestly. "He isn't a bad guy, but oh, how he has hurt me. If I had a crystal ball right now, all I'd want to know is, Does he leave again when I get back?"

Daniel inhales. "What are you hoping for?"

I shrug. "I don't know. I guess I'm hoping he'll do whatever makes the kids happiest. After an entire summer together, I expect they'll be bonded to him, and I have told him a hundred ways that he has a responsibility to them. But they were bonded to him before, and he still split."

"What about you? Are you still bonded to him?"

I think, for a moment, about lying. Then I smile sadly at Daniel. "In some ways, yes. I guess I am."

"So you're hoping he'll stay?"

"No," I say quickly. "Well, yes. For the kids. If he keeps doing his part as a real father. If he goes back to being unreliable and selfish, then maybe the kids are better off without him. What do you think? Is a crummy dad better than no dad?"

Daniel leans back in his chair. "Is a crummy husband better than no husband?" he asks me.

"No," I answer in a heartbeat—and the clarity of my answer surprises me. "The last three years have proven that. Life may have been harder without John, but I don't miss living with someone who was growing unhappier and more anxious by the day. By the end he was one of those dads that makes you feel like you have one more child than you gave birth to."

Daniel tilts his head at this. "If it makes you feel any better, I think those kinds of dads are going the way of the dodo bird."

I laugh. "Well, they're certainly not getting laid," I announce, so loudly that the couples at the tables around us crane their heads to stare at me. I lower my voice and sink into my chair. "Oops. I think I had too much vin gris."

Daniel's eyes twinkle. "Do you know, I don't think Cori is the only one letting her hair down over the summer."

I consider this for a moment. "I am actually trying to keep my hair up, so to speak. Last time I got tipsy, we . . . you know."

"Slept together?" Daniel asks.

I cut my eyes sideways. "Right, that."

"And had sex," he adds.

I squirm. "Are you trying to make me die of embarrassment?"

Daniel's face grows serious. "No! Not at all. I'm just . . . I'm trying to get it out in the open. Clear the air."

"I prefer the air a bit hazier," I tell him. "Not as thick as a *Bleak House* fog, but more like a *Great Expectations* mist."

"That is a very Amy thing to say."

"Can I ask you a question?" I say but don't wait for a yes. "Did you think this was a booty call?"

Daniel's mouth drops open for a moment. "I . . ."

"You did!" I say. "What about us being friends?"

Daniel catches himself quickly. "We are friends. I thought for a second that maybe . . . and then I realized I was being an idiot, so I just texted you back." He laughs to himself.

"What?"

"Eight years of Latin, and I still never thought I'd decline sex."

I look at him blankly.

"Because in Latin you decline nouns. Noun declension? Get it?"

"If I laugh, I'm just going to encourage you," I say.

"You love it," he says.

"So if you'd thought it was a booty call, you wouldn't have texted back?" I ask him.

"Well, first of all, I don't like this terminology. Booty call. It sounds like something from an Ashton Kutcher comedy circa 2002."

"The last time I was single, Ashton Kutcher was too. What is it called nowadays?"

"I guess a hookup? My students call everything a hookup. As far as I can tell, if underwear comes off, but you're not going to prom together, it's a hookup."

I sigh. "This is where you tell me that you're not taking me to prom."

Daniel nods slowly. "I would love to take you to prom, but you'd be long gone by then. So I'll have to settle for sitting next to you at the next all-school assembly."

"Only nerds attend those things," I tell him.

"So I will see you there," he quickly replies.

I laugh. We sit there for a moment. I am starting to feel more even keeled. Daniel is not looking any less handsome. "You're staying in Brooklyn Heights, right?" he asks me. "Because my beer is gone. And so is your . . . whatever that was. I could walk you home."

"Over the bridge?" I ask hopefully.

"Over the bridge."

Something deep inside me thrills to this plan. I agree, and we make our way out of the bar, through the little streets, to the foot of the bridge. The sight is even more beautiful from here, the arches of the towers rising up huge before us. We step onto the pedestrian path and start to make our way over the water, and even at this hour we are joined by joggers, cyclists, lovers: the people of New York going about their lives.

"You know, I have read Hunger Games twice," Daniel says, completely out of the blue as we walk.

I raise my eyebrows. "Oh?"

"And I have a philosophy about the problem Katniss has with Peeta."

I wait, unsure of exactly what we're talking about.

"She has a preexisting condition. With Gale. The guy she came of age with. The guy she's always loved. It makes it impossible for her to see anyone else clearly."

"Also, Peeta is kind of a weenie at first."

Daniel nods. "Ok, yes. But also a good catch. He would have been much happier if he had found someone who was genuinely unattached from the start."

"Also, if he hadn't been recruited to fight other teenagers to the death."

"That as well. My point is when we are young, it's hard to choose who to love. When we are older, it becomes an imperative."

We walk some more in silence.

"Do you think I have a preexisting condition?" I ask.

"With your ex-husband?" he says. "Yes."

I look down at our feet as we walk. "I'm trying to cure it," I tell him honestly. "For one thing, I am thinking it's time to file for divorce."

"You're still married?" he asks.

"Technically," I tell him.

Daniel is quiet for a while with that news. I cannot blame him. Every time I say it aloud, it seems more suspect. Finally, he says, "It is best we are staying friends, then."

I wait awhile before I answer him. There is so much in the air, more than any mist now. The lights of the bridge, the glow of Brooklyn, the glimmer of the city coming up behind us like a moon reflecting off an ocean of glass and steel. The walk from the foot of the bridge to Talia's apartment isn't long, and we will make it in silence, and Daniel will hug me goodbye at the door, and I will be left confused and contemplative. But for now we are still on the bridge, and I am still making sense of what he's said, and of what I've told him, and of standing this close to a man who makes me thrum with longing, who can kiss tingles into my toes, who I think I could in fact, one day, come to love, if I am not very, very careful.

"You're right," I agree, after a long, long pause. "It's good we are staying friends."

———

A couple days after my bridge walk with Daniel, Matt comes to me with another prospect. "You've got to check this guy out, Ames," he tells me, and I smile to hear how quickly he's adopted the nickname Talia and Lena picked out for me. "He is witty, good looking, gainfully employed, and definitely interested in you."

"What's the catch?" I ask Matt. "Is he missing all his teeth?"

"Enough of that," Matt says. "Have you checked yourself out lately? All we did was buy you a few bras and wax your eyebrows. Two weeks in, you're standing taller, you're smiling more, and your yoga-lates classes are doing something crazy to your butt."

I immediately attempt to get a look at my butt.

"It looks the same from here," I tell him.

"Stop fishing for butt compliments," Matt says with a smile. "Just trust me on this. The momspringa is working."

This gives me pause, because though I haven't taken the time to acknowledge it, he's right. It is working. I haven't felt so much like my own person since the kids were born. Fifteen years since I last knew my own mind so well, or had so many complete thoughts, or spent ten minutes in the bathroom putting on makeup without anyone knocking on the door. Fifteen years since I had a civilized meal with table linens in a restaurant, or woke up and asked myself and only myself what I wanted to do with my day, or gave any thought to my hopes and dreams. Fifteen years, if I'm to be frank, since I took showers on a daily basis.

I have a horrifying thought. *Do I even miss my kids at all?*

Yes. That's stupid. Of course I miss my kids. I just got done pestering them on the phone to come visit me—and they promised they will, after their summer camps. I miss my real life. I cannot wait to go back to it. My kids are my world and my job is my passion and I have everything I can possibly ask for back in PA. I will be desperate to get back there when the time comes.

And go back to teenage fights and wardrobe policing and chauffeuring to chess tournaments and wearing long-sleeved polo shirts ten months a year and being so tired at the end of the day that I can hardly stand up and wondering if I will be able to pay all my bills and feeling terribly, miserably lonely.

Even I know when I'm lying to myself. I miss my kids like crazy. I just don't miss the exhausting work of parenting them.

So I tell Matt to set me up with this guy ASAP. "What does he do?" I ask Matt.

"Oh, I'll let him tell you all about it," he tells me mysteriously. "Trust me. You will not be disappointed."

Immediately my heart leaps, and I think: *Maybe he's another librarian. Or a book critic? Or an editor?* "Does he work in books?" I ask Matt.

Matt groans. "Ok, let me walk it back, Amy. A normal human woman would not be disappointed, but no, he does not work in books. Even so, I think you'll like him. He seems fun."

"Ok," I tell Matt. "Sure. Fun is good. Fun is kind of the whole point, right?"

"Correct," he says back. "I'm setting something up for tomorrow night, downtown, at eight. Dress adorable—this is definitely one I'm sending a photographer in for."

"Aye, aye," I say. "I'll wear my snazziest outfit."

Matt sighs into the phone at the merest use of the word *snazziest*. "I think if it's all the same to you, I'll come over first and dress you."

"But I was going to be snazzy!"

"That's what concerns me," says Matt.

—

Matt, as usual, is right. By the time I'm dressed, photographed, and staggering into my Lyft ride on two-inch platform sandals, I've had pretty much the perfect momspringa day. Lesson planning in the morning, reading in a café all afternoon, spin class with my best new guy pal, funny texts from Daniel throughout. Now I'm in trim cigarette pants; a cute, flouncy blouse; and clumsy but chic espadrilles, feeling the most feminine I've felt in . . . probably ever. When I hop out of the car and see a great-looking guy with trendy glasses; thick, wavy dark hair; and bright eyes grinning at me, I get one of the best feelings in the world— the feeling of a stranger looking at you and thinking, *Wow*.

"Travis!" I call out happily. He looks exactly like his picture, only maybe taller. Compared to the Wall Street guy, he looks relaxed, assured, and grown up. I like it.

"If you are Amy, then I just won the blind date lottery," he tells me. "Which, like, seems fair considering how long I've been playing."

"Ha!" I laugh and drink in the compliment. "I guess I'm not your first time around this dance floor?"

"Oh, hell no. I've been single for almost three years, and I plan to absolutely regale you with stories of bad-date hilarity."

I nod vigorously. "That would be wonderful! That way, you won't know how bad a date I am until you run out of other women to talk about."

"Perfect. If we do this right, I could be paying the check before you even tell me your star sign."

I give Travis an approving smile, and inside I'm long-distance high-fiving Matt for finding this guy for me. A funny one. I love the funny ones. Travis opens the door to the restaurant for me, and I blurt, "It's April."

"April is not a star sign," he tells me. "It's a birth month. Your star sign is Aries."

My jaw drops. "Are you . . . like, into astrology?"

"I am not. However, my dog was born in April, and no responsible dog owner would skip the vital step of doing one's pet's star chart."

"Oh," I say, nodding. "Of course. I don't know why I didn't think about that."

"How else would I know if she and I were compatible?"

I smirk. "Is she a dog? And do you feed her and give her cuddles? From what I understand, that means you're compatible."

He smiles back. "Matt told me you were rich with wisdom. He wasn't lying."

"How do you know Matt?"

"We went to the same college."

I blanch.

"Don't worry—it wasn't at the same time. We are in an alumni group together. Matt is a virtual infant compared to me. I'm old enough to be his . . . much older brother."

"Oh, thank god." I exhale. "I know I'm supposed to be living the wild life right now, but dating a twentysomething would just be gross. Like some kind of internship gone wrong."

"Agreed, though to be honest I had to find that out the hard way. Right after my divorce I had an absolutely textbook midlife crisis. New car, rebound with a twenty-nine-year-old woman, and I was this close"—he holds his fingers next to each other—"to buying a status watch."

"Oh no," I say, thinking of John, of his girlfriend, of her waxing bills. "That is textbook."

"The thing is I was miserable that whole time. Turns out you can't buy—or date—happiness."

"Who would've thunk it?" I ask with a smile. "So you're saying money can't buy you love?"

"Yep. I'm wise enough to take Beatles lyrics as gospel now. God help us if I ever find myself on a submarine."

"At least all your friends will be aboard," I say.

"And many more of them will live next door," he bounces right back. We make eye contact. I am thinking: *Boy, this guy can banter. And my, but his eyes are nice.* I'm just starting to consider skipping dinner and going straight to kissing when the server appears.

"I'm sorry to interrupt," she says with a warm smile in her voice. "But I was starting to suspect that if I waited for a quiet moment, I'd be waiting all night."

"Yikes," I say. How long have we been seated without even touching our menus? "I'm sorry; I haven't even looked at the menu yet."

Travis nods in agreement. "You know that thing where your blind date turns out to be so delightful that you totally forget what you're supposed to be doing at the restaurant?" he asks the woman.

She tilts her head at me and says, "Oooh, watch out for this one," and then adds, almost like an afterthought, "Today's market seafood features littleneck clams sautéed in a rich brown-butter garlic and tossed with window-grown herbs and house-made angel-hair pasta. On top you'll find a tumble of microgreens harvested at service from the vertical garden"—with this she gestures toward a wall of tiny lettuces growing sideways—"and fresh foraged hen-of-the-woods chiffoned with shallot compound butter."

We smile at her politely. The moment she walks away I ask Travis quietly, "How do you chiffon food? Do you think the chef means chiffonade? Or will there actually be a little cloth covering on the plate? Can we order it to find out?"

Travis smirks at me. "You can, word nerd. I'm ordering something that doesn't require running a tiny lawn mower up the wall."

I choke on my sip of water. "You're very funny," I tell him when I've caught my breath.

"I think you bring out my funny," he says. "We have very good rat-a-tat."

"Rat-a-tat?"

"I heard it on a podcast. It's when a couple bounces conversation and banter back and forth. It makes me think of those old-timey tap dance showdowns." Travis flashes me jazz hands and a corny smile. "Rat-a-tat-a-tat-tat!" And then, forming his fingers into pretend guns, he shoots me the universal "take it away" sign.

"What would you do if I got up and started dancing just now?" I ask him.

"Propose," he answers back without a beat.

I laugh. "Oh my god. That poor server. We're never going to order," I say through my giggles.

"Hang on," he says and beckons to the server as she stands nearby discreetly waiting on us. To me he asks, "Do you eat meat?" and when I nod, he tells her, "Let's just make this super simple. Beet salad to start, and then the duck confit and the pappardelle with lamb, and then to drink . . ." He turns to me again. "Pinot noir?"

I nod vigorously.

"Pinot noir. This one," he says, using his finger to underline some mysterious bottle on the wine list for the server.

She nods. "Very good," she tells him, and there's an almost imperceptible wink shared between the two of them. I narrow my eyes for a millisecond but then pretend to have missed it, filing it away under the header: *Travis (see also: too smooth?).*

"That sounds wonderful," I tell him honestly, when she's away and he does look back at me. And it is so wonderful. Every bite is perfect, the wine is definitely not in the price category I'm used to drinking, and the alchemy of rat-a-tat, alcohol, and rich dinner begins to do its work on me. Before I know it, our entrées are being cleared away, and we are talking as though we've known each other for years. I've found out he's a comedy writer on a very popular show but started his career in stand-up. So he has all kinds of great self-deprecating stories about bombing in front of famous people. I could listen all night.

When we finally leave the restaurant, we both make as though we're going to hail cabs to go home, but then we just keep walking, working our way slowly downtown. We have another drink at a bar filled with fish tanks that just is too inviting to pass up. He tells me about his very amicable-sounding divorce. I tell him about my kids. He's easy to talk to, and we sit in front of our empty highball glasses for another half hour, knowing another drink would be one too many but also not wanting to leave. Finally he leans in toward me and softly says, "Come home with me."

I blush and flounder and let myself, just for a moment, seriously consider it. But somehow, despite all the fun we've had, I am 100 percent sure I don't want to sleep with him tonight. "I'm sorry. I can't. One-night stands don't agree with me," I say. But is that a lie? I mean, what Daniel and I did, that was pretty darn great. So why don't I want to do it again?

"Who said anything about a one-night stand?" he asks me with a faux-innocent smile. "Based on this date, I would say we'd want to aim for something closer to, say, a six-night stand. Think of the fun we could have while you're on your little adventure in the city."

"I'm flattered," I say. "But I . . ." I fumble for the right way to tell him what I'm not even sure I understand myself. Here is a very handsome, very fun, very uncomplicated man wanting to give me exactly what I thought I wanted.

But . . . he's not Daniel. He reminds me of someone else. I can't put my finger on it.

"You know what?" says Travis softly. "Don't say another word. I'm just going to have to take you out again another night and do a better job of convincing you that you cannot resist my charms."

I smile. "I certainly won't stop you from trying," I say. "But in the meantime, thank you for understanding. Tonight as I lie alone in my cold bed, I'm sure I'll regret it terribly."

"I do hope so. May I ask, before I spend too much energy barking up the wrong tree, is there someone else?"

Is there? I ask myself. Every day I'm getting a bit more comfortable at the thought of finally filing for divorce. But then there's Daniel, who I cannot seem to relegate to the friendship category in my mind. And at the same time I think of the server, the knowing nod she gave when Travis rattled off his practiced date order, the wink when he picked a bottle of wine just a bit too deftly. I sigh. "Isn't there always?" I ask, looking him hard in the eyes so he knows I am not just talking about me.

Travis nods, and I have no question in my mind he knows exactly what I am saying. "New York is a smorgasbord," he tells me without a bit of sarcasm. "And like it or not, we're all of us on the menu."

CHAPTER FOURTEEN

Dear Mom,

Never come home. Just kidding about that. Mostly. But seriously, whenever we talk you sound like you're having fun with all your museums and baseball games and Flywheel stuff. And we are beyond having fun. I never want school to start up again.

Oh! And Dad suggested this AMAZING book. It's called Mountains beyond Mountains, *about this doctor who saved a gazillion lives, and I really, really like it. He told me that he wanted to join you in supporting my reading because you're right about how important it is and how a lot of life's challenges will be made easier by reading. I told him your book choices aren't always my thing, and he said that not everyone likes fiction and he was going to start giving me some true stories that pushed me to think about what I believe and who I want to be as an adult.*

Also Dad says e-readers are soulless and he's buying me all printed editions for the rest of the summer. I told him paper books are dust collectors and to give me the fifteen bucks and I'd go to the library, and he said, "Here's thirty bucks. Buy the book and then buy whatever it is you actually want, and we both get to be right."

So I've been reading for like two hours every day since I got the book, and I cannot stop thinking about it when I'm not reading it. I'm sending that extra fifteen bucks to the doctor's charity.

OMG and I almost forgot about the big news, which is weird because it is literally all I think about: So you know how Dad told me I could go to diving camp and Joe would go to Space Camp? Well, Dad didn't just mean any old college sports camp. He got a spot for me at the Team USA diving camp at Binghamton! I'm going to be coached by the Olympic diving staff! I am, like, Mom, I am exploding with excitement about this. I cannot even express. I am going to be the ONLY one my age there—the rest of the girls are rising seniors, and they are coming from crazy elite programs and getting ready to dive for the best colleges. I don't know what kind of strings Dad pulled, but he swears they saw my tapes before they agreed to let me in and said I was good enough to hang. He said the coach who processed my application said I would be right in the middle of the pack. The way Dad told me is he sent flowers to my diving practice to arrive right as we were coming out of the weight room, and then he told me to FaceTime him on the card that came with the flowers, and then on FaceTime, he and Joe were holding a banner that said "Congratulations" and they said the news super loud and my entire team heard and everyone started cheering like crazy. I didn't even know I was being considered—Dad did it all in secret!

I am. Freaking. Out. Mom. I'm going to email you right now even though it's like five a.m. I hope you're coming home before I go. I need you to help me pack.

Love,

The happiest diver in America, Cori

—

The next morning I get up early, see a flurry of over-the-top excited texts from Cori about Team USA dive camp, and text her a quick congratulations, then text a high-five emoji to John. I had an inkling that if we tried for that camp she might get in, and I told him so, but it's him who did the work of sending the application and the videos, and him who will foot the bill.

Then I put my phone on silent and head out for a long walk through Talia's neighborhood. It's a perfect summer morning—the cafés are spilling out into the streets, and the sun is finding its way through the buildings, but it's not yet hot enough to turn the trash cans into Glade odor diffusers gone terribly wrong. This is Nora Ephron's New York, and I think of her perfectly suited couples and happily ever afters and of Travis, Daniel, Dylan of the perfect teeth, and yes, John. The man who hurt us all so much. The man who is suddenly making my kids so happy.

When we were struggling near the end, after he'd let me down, after I'd stopped looking to him for emotional support, I was utterly in the thick of American Motherhood. John was only a dabbler in the harder parts of parenting at the best of times, but we had the illusion of marital equality because of his success at work. With the mistaken premise that my stay-at-home work and his accomplished career required equal emotional energy, I couldn't understand where he got the vigor to worry about his ego being rejected or his sex drive being ignored. For me, it was all hands on deck, between our kids and our house and our work. Sex, passion, romance, I thought, could certainly wait. And maybe some part of me reasoned that when I had suffered a loss, he had been too busy to support me. So what could he possibly ask of me now?

But now, in the fresh mental air of my momspringa, I start to understand the kind of neglect John must have felt when I fell asleep in one of the kids' beds every night or stopped kissing him hello and instead threw a preschooler into his arms the minute he walked in the door. At the moment I'm walking in his shoes: my children are cared for by someone else, my days are spent in rich mental exercise, I get plenty of sleep, and I go to the gym every day. In other words, I have the emotional energy to think about desire and how good it feels to be wanted.

Yes, John had clean pressed shirts without having to ask, and yes, we had family dinners together that looked perfect and tasted as good, and yes, he never had to be on call when Joe started getting bullied for the first time or when Cori's tampon leaked at a diving tournament. Yet while I was bending over backward to meet his children's every need, his own were going ignored. And was it the chicken or the egg that started that ball rolling? If he had, only once, driven the carpool in my place, would I have suddenly wanted to greet him at the door in Saran Wrap? Or was I so incredibly consumed with the worry-work of motherhood that no contribution from him would have made me look up from my kids?

I don't know. I only know that in this month, when I have gotten time with friends, time for myself, positive attention from men, and yep, a couple of nice new bras, parts of me that were asleep for far too long are starting to wake up. I am seeing my children with a new, longer lens and seeing how grown up they are, how capable. I am seeing John as the lonely, troubled man he was when he walked out on us and understanding, for the first time, what part I played in that. I am seeing Talia's lifestyle choices—singlehood, careerism, passionate pursuits—as less outrageous and more reasonable than ever before.

And most startling of all, I am seeing myself looking down the barrel of another six years of single parenting, martyrdom, and self-neglect and feeling very, very conflicted.

—

Amy:
Guys. I'm worried

Talia:
. . .

Lena:
What's the score, Petit Four?

Amy:

I'm starting to worry that I'll never want to go back to my real life after this.

Lena:

Oh Amy. Don't be silly. You got a new haircut, not a lobotomy.

Talia:

. . .

Amy:

Are we sure about that? It was an awfully long time at the salon. And I've started to have all these weird feelings about my old life. I've even started having empathy for John.

Lena:

!!! John? Ruh-roh! Where is Talia? We need her right now.

Amy:

Her three dots keep appearing and disappearing. She must be carefully considering what to say.

Lena:

That doesn't sound like Talia. It's two p.m. Three-martini lunch maybe?

Amy:

Passed out in her Miami art deco hotel room that looks like a set from Scarface?

Lena:
Or Dexter.

Amy:
Egad.

Lena:
Talia! Are you there Talia? Are you partying with serial killers?

Talia:
DAMMIT GUYS I'M TRYING TO WORK

Amy:
It's Sunday!

Lena:
Send us proof of life so we know you're not tied up in Dexter's basement.

Talia:
I'm turning off my phone now.

Amy:
But what about my existential crisis?

Talia:
I doubt you'll have it solved before I get this photo shoot bagged and stop paying these idiot people $500 an hour.

Lena:

She's right, you know. These are some complicated things. Freedom and family responsibilities. Past loves and new lovers. Forgiveness and compassion for John—that's not so bad. In fact, it's really healthy.

Amy:

No. You're friending wrong. You're supposed to say that there's nothing to worry about, John's a disgusting slime just as always, and my kids can't live without me.

Lena:

Well . . . they can.

Amy:

How dare you.

Lena:

I'm not saying they'd like it. But, well, let me think of how to say this to you. Is it possible that a lot of your sense of self comes from being needed by your kids? And maybe you secretly always thought they would fall to pieces without you? And the fact that they're fine with John is making you feel threatened?

Amy:

I repeat: how dare you.

Lena:

Ok, take some time to process it.

Amy:

I will not.

Lena:
Maybe Talia will have a different perspective.

Talia:
I don't.

Amy:
I need new friends. Dumber friends.

Lena:
Just remember you chose us for a reason.

Amy:
Forgive me if I'm having trouble remembering what that reason was.

Lena:
Looks. It was definitely looks. TTYL girl. Your kids are here.

Amy:
What the—

———

It turns out that John has started dropping the kids at Lena's house for two dinners a week. Just knowing that actually makes me feel a lot better. Things may seem to be going smoothly back home, but he's not running the entire show alone. My neighbor Jackie has been driving them to the pool every Wednesday, and then they're eating with Lena on Monday and Thursday so that John can do international conference calls in a quiet house. For a moment I feel smug—he can't do this solo like I can. What a wimp. Then soon after that, I feel silly. Jackie is retired, and her husband is still at work all day. Her kids are off in grad school. It never occurred to me to ask her for help despite the fact that she's offered it more than once. It never occurred to me to take the kids to dinner with their favorite adult, Lena, and then *leave* and go do my own thing for a couple of hours. I've certainly heard that it takes a village to raise a child, but that doesn't apply to me, does it?

Should it?

I decide to talk all this over with Matt the next time we have lunch. I haven't let on, but the truth is Lena and Talia thrashing around in the undergrowth of my psyche can actually make me feel a little too vulnerable. I find myself getting defensive (hey, neither of them has kids; they couldn't possibly understand) and hurt (I don't joke about their cosmic foibles) and even a little bit abandoned (if I'm such a mess, why haven't they stepped in before now?).

Either way, I want to avoid the subject with my girlfriends, but it hasn't stopped plaguing me. So I ask someone who can't possibly give me a helpful answer: a twentysomething man.

Matt just shrugs. "I'm so far out of my pay grade with this stuff, you know," he admits easily.

"Just try," I tell him. "Make uh-huh noises when I talk."

"Ok," he says gamely. "Talk."

I inhale. "Basically, you've ruined my life. I liked my life before I came here, and I didn't notice that it was kind of . . . sad and lonely. Now I've been on a few dates and taken a little better care of myself, and I guess I am not exactly looking forward to going back to sad-and-lonely town in a few weeks."

Matt scratches his chin and tilts his head in thought. "I think you should probably date more."

I guffaw. "I tell you I'm abandoning my children and responsibilities and having too much fun doing it. You tell me to . . . have more fun?"

Matt nods. "Actually, yes. I'm willing to bet you have some wild oats to sow. Get them out there in the dirt, so to speak, and you might find going home to be much easier."

"But what if by then I'm not needed at home anymore?"

Matt shakes his head. "I'm sorry; I can't answer that right now. I have to call my mom to ask her how to boil water."

"Ha. Point taken."

"They're going to need you, if they're anything like me," he says. "For, like, ever, or at least until it's kind of annoying. You gotta get the fun in now while the getting's good."

"And fun is dating?"

"Well, you seem to like it."

I think for a second. He's right. I do kind of like it. Especially if you count the "friend dates" I'm having with Daniel. He and I have seen each other twice since the bridge walk. Once we just did iced coffees and a walk through Central Park. Another night we went to hear a reading of a favorite author of his and had a late dinner after. Both times it was easy conversation, goofy jokes, and the constant underlying nagging in my mind that I have seen Daniel naked and would enjoy seeing that again.

"You're right," I tell Matt. "I do need to date more. Maybe even more than date."

"Hey, hey! Look at you! Got anyone in mind?"

I pretend my brain doesn't flash the word *DANIEL* in my head like a theater marquee. "Nope. The first guy was too arrogant for me. The second one wasn't feeling me. The third was charming but seemed like a player. I'd love to meet someone that wasn't so smooth I felt I was on a conveyor belt, you know?"

Matt nods. "So someone down to earth, knows he's not perfect, and also a bit more genuine around women?"

"Exactly," I tell him. "I think those are hard qualifications to judge based on photos and Twitter feeds."

He shakes his head. "But not impossible. Let's take a look at who we have." He opens up his Pinterest board. "Who were your vetoes again?"

"Him," I say, pointing to his phone. "Him and him. And him too. And he's one I went out with. Look at those amazing chompers."

"Wow!" says Matt. "Those look costly."

"And distracting," I tell him. "I had to practice looking away."

"Ok, so let's add 'reasonable teeth' to the wish list. How about this guy?"

He points to a handsome man with dark-brown skin and gorgeous eyes named Randall. His Twitter feed is earnest and often political, and based on a picture of his apartment bookshelf, we share a lot of the same favorite authors. It's not a lot to go on.

"Sure," I say. I'm very not sure.

"Great. I'll set it up. Ok, who else?"

"One isn't enough?"

"No. One isn't enough. We gotta get those oats sowed, girl."

"Ok. Sowing oats. Got it. Then what about him?" I indicate a sexy-yet-rumpled-looking guy with a crooked smile and jet-black hair. He's got the cutest pair of glasses.

"Mario," says Matt. "Thirty-one. Is that too young?"

"Yes," I say quickly. Then add, "No. Is it?"

"I think it's totally fine. But you have to remember he won't have grown kids or, like, a retirement plan."

"I had a retirement plan at thirty-one."

Matt puts his hands up. "I'm just preparing you for reality," he tells me.

"Fair enough. But it's wild oats time. So let's do it."

"Momspringa!" says Matt by way of agreement.

"And maybe one more?" I say.

"At least," Matt says. "I like this one." He points out a white guy with a silver-fox look. Salt-and-pepper hair, a slight tan, sexy crow's-feet when he smiles.

"Ooh," I say. "That's a new one."

Matt nods. "We did a few more tweets about hashtag momspringa, and you got another round of interested parties. This guy is a partner at a law firm. Hardworking, well traveled, sounds like a fascinating guy."

"Ok, then. One too young, one my age, one too old. I like the symmetry."

"I'll get them booked. I take it most of your nights are free?" asks Matt.

I quirk my lips. "Well . . ." I have plans with Daniel for next Friday night. And not just any plans. Tickets to see Shakespeare in the Park. "I'm booked next Friday, but otherwise any time after Flywheel is fine."

"Great. Keep your evenings clear, then. We're about to turn up this hashtag momspringa to eleven."

CHAPTER FIFTEEN

Dear Mom,

I know I'm supposed to be hand journaling this right now for future discussion, but screw it, this one is email worthy because it's basically all about you. Basically, and I'm not sure if this is going to make you happy or unhappy, my friends' parents are talking about you. Actually, they're not talking about you so much as talking about momspringas. Because do you know what? Momspringas are kind of becoming a thing.

It started with Trinity. She asked me how your momspringa was going in front of her mom. And her mom wanted to know what we were talking about, so she explained it. And then Trinity's mom looked it up on social and saw all these people talking about it, like where they'd go if they had one, and how much they'd sleep (what is it with old people and sleep? If you're tired, just don't schedule everything at eight a.m. like adults love to do so much, right? Is that rocket science?), and whether the vows of their marriage would still count or if they'd have a hall pass. Some people are saying that only a bad mother would go on momspringa, which is kind of insane when you think about it. A bad mother wouldn't NEED a momspringa.

That last part is ugh, but the rest of it, the thought that you're out creating a movement and getting some of the Country Day moms thinking about something besides how many times their kids should retake the SAT test—that makes me pretty proud of you, Mom. Haters gonna hate, but me and Joe are holding our heads high whenever the subject comes up. When the article actually does come out in Talia's magazine, I'm going to buy a zillion copies and tell everyone I know you. Unless the article talks about you having a sex life. Then I'm going to die of shame.

Love,
Your squeamish daughter, Cori.

—

I have always tried to make it a practice to keep what my kids tell me to myself, but I am so proud of Cori's take on the momspringa that I ask her if I can forward her email to Talia. She texts me an *ok* emoji, and ten minutes after I hit send, Talia texts me:

Cool kid you got there.

Amy:

Don't I know it. Believe me when I tell you they are not all like
this.

Talia:

I certainly wasn't. Every time some friend's child makes me
wonder if I should have kids, I remind myself what genetics
would actually have in store for me: moody, weepy, rebellious.

Amy:

Cori is all those things too. And when she is around her diving
friends, her desire to fit in is painful to watch. If you ever need
birth control, watch a librarian's kid try to negotiate queen
bees on a sports team. Otherwise, though, she's hard to beat.

Talia:

You feeling ok about all this buzz?

Amy:

I haven't really been following it. I always forget Twitter exists.

Talia:

Go take a look, while I'm here. Search the hashtag.

Amy:

Ok.

. . .

Wow. That's a lot of tweeting.

Talia:

You and Matt have touched a nerve.

Amy:

I see that. A LOT of people seem to want a momspringa. I'm kind of shocked.

Talia:

If you really want to be shocked, google "momspringa + porn"

Amy:

I don't think I could handle that.

Talia:

You definitely could not handle that.

Amy:

Is this going to sell magazines? That's the whole point, right? I mean, will it help you with the bigwigs?

Talia:

Honestly? Probably not. In two months when the actual article comes out, will people seek it out on newsstands? Will it even still be a trend? If anything comes of this, it'll be online ad sales. Clicks.

Amy:

Clicks. Huh.

Talia:

Exactly. Underwhelming. So keep it all in perspective. All the hashtags, all the tweets, the posts and the rants, they're just clicks. They come, and then they'll go.

Amy:

So what you're saying is, continue ignoring the hashtag mom-springa and enjoy my actual momspringa?

Talia:

That's exactly what I'm saying. Speaking of, don't you have a date tonight?

Amy:

I have three dates in the next two weeks! Plus a friend date with the hot librarian.

Talia:

Oh wow. You're amazing! That's, like, ninja-level casual dating. Have fun.

Amy:

I will! Or at least, I have been so far. I'll keep you posted.

Talia:

Perfect.

Oh, and Amy? How are your eyebrows?

Amy:

They are still attached to my face. Isn't that good enough?

Talia:

Have Matt send me a picture. If they're holding hands again, you're going to hear it from me.

———

Mario

Mario is lean and tall. He has the same rumpled look from his pictures in real life, and it's delicious. When I first walk into the bar we're meeting at, my brain screams, *WAY TOO YOUNG*. But when I sit down with him and start talking, I find that I actually start to feel younger too. *So this is what John felt with Marika*, I think, when Mario not-very-accidentally brushes his hand against my leg. It's a thrill. We talk about music—something that hasn't been a big part of my life since the kids were born but that seems to define who Mario is. He names bands as their tracks come up on the bar playlist, and I nod to one I like and say, "Sounds like Talking Heads meets the Pixies," and it seems to have been the exact right thing to say. We sit closer and closer at the bar. We go to dinner and talk more, loosened up by the premeal beer. He is haughty and bold and unafraid of the world—but also has some sweet idealism and is definitely looking for true love.

At the end of the night we order Calvados—an affected move from his recent trip to Cannes. The manager sends out quenelles of apple crème fraîche ice cream set into meringue shells that pair perfectly. Mario tells me about his work.

He's a chemist working for a nonprofit, and the ink on his PhD is still wet, yet he insists with great authority that he will never go work for Big Pharma no matter what. I think of him in some not-too-distant future, falling in love, finding out she's pregnant with twins, being all too grateful for a six-figure salary working for the man.

But I can also see an alternate future where he develops a game-changing new water purifier, opens up the patent, and spends his sabbaticals hiking mountains whose names start with K. Either way, there is no question: Mario is looking for a real girlfriend, and I will not be that woman in any possible future. He invites me back to his place, and I give him a long, passionate kiss, say, "Thank you so much for asking," and then take myself home alone posthaste.

Randall

Randall takes me to a place called Ambrosia, a square Midtown wine bar that seems to be *the* place for men and women to meet, dislike each other, and then return to their law firms and get back to work.

He orders us a flight of five glasses of wine the minute we sit down. I cough nervously and warn him that I like all wines that cost more than six dollars a bottle, so the tasting might be wasted on me. He proceeds to walk me through each glass and blow my mind at how different five wines made the same year from the same grape can be. It's like getting a private master class in wine tasting, and when the bill arrives, he falls on it, saying it's a business expense. It's only then that he explains: he is a sommelier at another wine bar, which he tells me is "much cooler."

When the lesson is over, I am not sure what's next. Randall has dazzled me with his breadth of wine knowledge, passion for sharing it, and just plain good looks. However, he hasn't asked me a single question about myself. Instead, he's monopolized the conversation completely. If he likes me, it is entirely based on my appearance, which, makeover or no, is not, let's just say, a New York nine. So I presume he doesn't like me.

But then he asks me if I want to come see the bar where he works, because he "doesn't want this date to be over." And I look at him, and shallow though it may be, I don't want it to end myself. So I agree.

I only took tiny tastes of the five wines, but still, I am thinking about the high likelihood of his ordering five more, and it makes me feel a bit swampy. I tell him I'd better grab a slice of pizza on the way. We buy big greasy slices of New York pepperoni and walk up Broadway in the lowering sun. We pass Lincoln Center in the golden hour, and the glass of the Met shimmers. The fountain seems higher than I ever saw it. The plaza is empty, so we sit down at the side of the fountain and finish our slices, and I say, "Wine and pepperoni are strange bedfellows."

He says, "Let me have a taste," and I find myself kissing him softly in the square and lingering until the sun finally moves on to light another stage.

William

The name of the silver-fox partner at the law firm is William. He skips the meet-at-the-bar step and takes me straight to a hidden-away restaurant tucked just off Central Park West in the high sixties. The place is, by a mile, the fanciest restaurant I've ever set foot inside. Gorgeous, elaborate oil paintings are everywhere you look, the white linens and glassware shine for days, a beautiful fiftysomething woman in black seems to hover weightlessly near an ornate podium, and she doesn't even ask my name—she tells it to me.

"You must be Amy," she coaxes, and I nod. "William let us know you were coming. He'll be along any minute. May I bring you a glass of prosecco?"

I agree to the prosecco, and my head is already full of tiny bubbles when my date walks in ten minutes later. I start to stand as if he's a prince, but he instead leans down and puts a kiss on my cheek and sort of herds me back into my chair. He tells me there is nothing so nice as realizing your blind date is even prettier in person than you hoped. He suggests we get the tasting menu and tells me to expect him to spill at least a little soup on his tie. I tell him I'll spill, too, just to make him feel better, and the ice is broken. By the second course I know that he is still working on his own divorce, that it has him quite shaken up, and that it is his wife who did the leaving. By the second glass of wine, I know he wishes he could get her back. When the server brings our limoncello at the very end of the meal, I find myself confessing that I went through confused feelings about my own marriage earlier this summer and admit that I've now got an impossible crush on a friend of mine, Daniel, and then William and I spend a pleasant walk through Central Park's bridle path talking through the pros and cons of reconciliation with his ex and new relationships going forward. At the Fifty-Ninth Street subway stop, we part with a hug and wish each other the best of luck.

———

By the time my night with Daniel comes around, I feel something new built up inside me. Something like confidence. Six blind dates in three weeks will do that to a woman when those blind dates are flattering and fun and utterly harmless.

Daniel picks me up at the spot where the Museum of Natural History meets Central Park, and we walk from there to a nuevo Latino restaurant across the street chosen for its pink awning and proximity. The place is packed, but there are two seats at the bar opening up, and we slide into them and sit close together and talk about what we are about to see. It's *Julius Caesar*. Like most everyone in the world, I have never seen it performed live, but Daniel knows the play inside and out and tells me what to watch for and explains that the man playing Brutus is an EGOT winner. I pretend for a long time to know what that means and then finally admit I don't. Daniel explains—Emmy, Grammy, Oscars, and Tony award winner—and I tell him I have every intention of winning a Best Audiobook Grammy one day for my poetic rendition of *Everybody Poops*. He and I talk over the logistics of turning that book into a musical for a while—how else will we get the Tony?— and our passion-fruit-and-rosewater mojitos arrive, and we can't stop talking long enough to order food. Finally I suggest we order before we miss the show, and he tells me to get whatever I like and share it with him, so I order ceviche and *gallitos* and a *michelada* with hot sauce that is so spicy I immediately hand it over to Daniel and replace it with a nice, drinkable sangria blanca.

Every time we go out, Daniel eats like he's never seen food before. Tonight I take a unique kind of pleasure in watching him enjoy the hell out of the food I picked out. It makes me think back to the date who ordered my dinner for me—perhaps he got more out of it than I did. Perhaps there is something to be said for bossing people around when you are very good at it.

But when the bill comes, the tide turns; my dominance is over. Daniel grabs the check and is unwilling to even go dutch. He hands over a credit card and then says something off putting and prehistoric like "Don't insult me."

"Where's the insult?" I ask him. "We're friends, right?"

A little something moves across his face, and I cannot pretend I didn't see it. "Yes," he says. "Of course. I'd just like to treat you; that's all."

When the bill is settled, he takes me by the hand, and for a split second I worry—or hope—he might kiss me. Instead he jumps off his barstool and drags me out of the restaurant so we can make it to the Delacorte Theater in time. When we arrive, we have three minutes to spare and are that silly couple that noses in after everyone else has already arrived in a timely fashion and settled in like adults. I gawk at the set, which is a perfect replica of the Belvedere Castle that rises up just behind the theater in Central Park. "Rome looks different than I remembered," I tell Daniel in a stage whisper, and then the lights go dark and the play begins.

John and I went to see Shakespeare together from time to time. It was always a very special occasion. We needed babysitters and advance planning and usually coffee at intermission to stay awake for the third act. He'd buy the tickets for my birthday or for our anniversary, a treat for me, a gift, and he would remain quiet throughout the play and seem to enjoy it in the main, and on the drive home he would say, "That was great; we should do that more often," and then we would never speak of it again. We saw *A Midsummer Night's Dream* and *Romeo and Juliet* and *The Taming of the Shrew*, and I was always made very happy by these nights out. It is a generous gift to do something you don't necessarily want to do, at great expense of time and money, because you know it will make someone else very happy. John never once complained about it or even sighed heavily when the Apothecary spoke his already tedious lines too quietly to be understood and too slowly to be merciful.

So let it be said: this is not my first Shakespeare. And yet, seeing Shakespeare with Daniel is nothing like anything that has come before.

Dinner may have been on him, but we are clearly not at the theater solely for my benefit. He is here for his own pleasure, and I sense that if I were not here with him, he could have brought a smelly old homeless man along and enjoyed the play just as much. He sits up in his chair, sometimes even forward. He pokes me with his elbow before a good line, and then afterward too. At one point, like Julia Roberts at the opera in *Pretty Woman*, he actually clutches his heart.

When the lights come up at intermission, he seems to notice me sitting there for the first time, as though I just rematerialized after a long absence. "Well! What do you think?" he asks. And then says, before I can answer, "Crazy how much Brutus and Hamlet have in common, right? You'd think Shakespeare was trying to exorcize his own indecisive demons, but then look at his personal life and the theory loses steam."

His enthusiasm is contagious. The play isn't particularly fast paced; I have been taken in by the quality of performance but also couldn't help noticing as people around us shifted and flipped through their programs and surreptitiously checked their Apple Watches over the last hour. Daniel is oblivious—the theater and actors are here for his benefit and his alone.

I say, "I guess that's more evidence that it was Anne doing the writing, not Will."

Daniel laughs and says, "What do you call it when Caesar drops a call in the Holland Tunnel? *Motorolus interruptus!*"

We go looking for champagne. We wind around the theater talking nonstop about the acting, the set, and what did it mean when Brutus said the serpent "which hatch-ed, would as his kind grow mischievous and kill *him* in the shell."

"First of all, it's *hatch'd*," says Daniel. He rattles the line back to me in exaggerated iambic pentameter.

"Fine. *Hatcht*. Who's the second 'him,' though? I mean, I presume the serpent isn't killing himself, right?" I ask.

Daniel laughs at me and then a moment later admits he never thought about it that way.

"Who is in the shell still, after the serpent hatches?" I ask. "Is Rome in the shell? Rome was pretty well hatch-ed by then."

Daniel finds the line online and reads it to me with different emphasis, and we both realize at once that there's an ideological parenthesis missing in our understanding—Brutus is saying *we* are the ones who should kill the *serpent* in his shell, and then we both laugh and say we should probably lose our librarian licenses over this misunderstanding, and we waste so much time over this that the bells ding and we have to turn right around and go back to our seats.

Then, right away, Caesar is the guest of honor at his own stabbing party, and things get much more interesting. Daniel actually has to stop himself from clapping his hands at the portrayal of Antony as a hard-line American populist, and I am absorbed in the mashed-up world of Central Park/Ancient Rome, and the next three acts fly by in a flash. When the lights on the stage go dark, I blink and turn to Daniel, stunned.

He looks back at me. He says, "Wow. I forgot you were there," and my feelings aren't hurt at all, because I know exactly what he means, and I say, "I forgot I was here too," and he nods and says, "That's exactly it."

We go out for drinks afterward and talk nonstop at a low table in a dark corner. It's just a glass of wine each, consumed over two hours of talking, but something about my stomach is tight and high, like the wine has been pushed straight into my bloodstream, like I am at once drinking on an empty stomach and couldn't eat another bite. People clear out and the bar sits empty, but the bartender reassures us twice that they are open for three more hours. We are talking about *Antony and Cleopatra*, the sequel of sorts to what we just saw, and I say something about Liz Taylor's Cleopatra being a strange kind of style icon and how a bright student once pointed out the perversity of a white woman shellacked orange to play a brown-skinned ideal of beauty. I muse aloud about how her movie made box office records in a time when people still called some grown men *boy* in many corners of this country. And then I talk about how *The Help* could have been a YA novel if it had had slightly different marketing and how I got a disciplinary warning for assigning *Coffee Will Make You Black* to my seventh graders. And now I'm basically free-associating about books set in the 1960s, and then he takes me by the hand and says, "This is exactly how it happened."

His tone is so different from just a moment ago that I sit back and pull my hand away. "How what happened?" I ask. Are we talking about serpents' eggs or Cleopatra's milk baths or how he wouldn't let me pay for my own dinner?

He shakes his head. "You must know what I mean," he says. "How you seduced me. When we first met." He locks eyes with me, and I swear there's something desperate in them. Something just a bit . . . hungry.

I cough. I sputter. "I have never, in my entire life, seduced a single person." I am trying to keep our conversation light, but it is not feeling light at all.

Daniel inclines his head. "What do you think you're doing right now? Sitting there looking beautiful and saying all kinds of interesting things. Of course I want to kiss you all the time. It's very frustrating."

I incline my head back at him in surprise, mirroring his behavior. "Thank you?" I ask. "I mean, I'm not actually sure. Was that a compliment or a criticism?"

He sets down his long-empty wineglass with a little clunk. "It's . . . it's a little bit of both. Amy, you *are* beautiful. You're so fun to talk to. But you're making my life very difficult lately."

My eyes widen. "But! The friend thing was your idea," I tell him.

He nods. "And it was a *smart* idea. You're on your sex-spree mom-springa thing, but I'm not having a . . . a *dad*springa. I've been trying to protect myself. But you must know—must have always known—that just friends wasn't what I really wanted."

I shake my head. "If being friends was a ruse, it was your ruse. I always thought that we should just have a doomed affair."

Daniel thinks it over. "But that doesn't sound very good either."

I put my hands up, as if to say, *You didn't come up with anything better.*

He sighs and looks at me imploringly. "We've got to figure this out. I haven't felt like this about anyone in a long time, Amy. It feels intractable. You're very smart about the things I like to think about. You say the most interesting things about books. You're always going around winking at life, and great ideas come to you like you're snapping your fingers. And your kids sound amazing and your friends are devoted and you are so, so beautiful to look at and it seems like you're just getting prettier the longer we're friends, which . . . how does that seem fair to you?"

My mouth glues shut. I try not to drown in his compliments. "That's a very nice thing to say," I finally choke out.

Daniel shakes his head. "I had such a solid plan to keep you at arm's length."

I feel dizzy and confused. I've lost control of the conversation. It feels like a fever dream. Daniel reaches for my hands on the table again, but this time I don't pull away.

"I don't want to be kept at arm's length," I tell him. "I feel fidgety when you're around. You make me nervous and excited. This whole time I've been hoping that you'd change your mind and just, I don't know, grab me and kiss me?"

He checks my eyes to see if I'm serious. Then, slowly, he puts his free hand on my cheek. Traces it to my lips. Tilts up my chin.

I open my mouth to say no. To remind him that I don't want him to get hurt, that I'll be gone at the end of the summer no matter what happens between us tonight. But no words come out.

He looks at me a little helplessly. "I think I'm going to kiss you," he whispers. "And worry about it tomorrow."

I exhale. "Oh, thank god," I say. And then, because I can't resist it for even one more second, I lean forward and close the last six inches between our lips myself.

CHAPTER SIXTEEN

Dear Mom,

I bought that book you told me about. It was made into a movie, just so you know, but I clicked right past the DVD on Amazon and bought the book instead because I am a wonderful, dutiful daughter. It looks really boring. Who falls in love with a paraplegic? Wait, is the "friend" you mentioned in your last email a paraplegic? Also, is that "friend" a "boyfriend"? I know you are trying to be all stealthy, but it is the first "he" you've mentioned this summer, and if this is "his" daughter's favorite book, does that mean you've met his kids? Is it serious? Is this my new daddy? I wish you could just give me one tiny crumb of information.

Speaking of not telling Dad, Joe and I are both super nervous about our camp weeks. I don't know if you realize this, but the last time Joe was on a plane was when we all went to Arches National Park when he was seven. He doesn't remember how layovers work, and now he's flying all by himself to Alabama with a stop in Atlanta. He's freaked out. He doesn't want to seem ungrateful to Dad, but all he remembers from that last trip is how Dad lost his shit in the Chili's to-go area when me and Joe were bickering, and Dad went off by himself to have a beer, and then we missed our connection, and we all got stuck in Las Vegas overnight. I think it may have deeply affected Joe's ideas about air travel.

So I am secretly making him a map of the Atlanta airport with the gates he's most likely to have to travel between. Also, next time we talk I'm going to check with you and see if it's ok for me to slip Joe my phone when he leaves. We aren't supposed to have our phones with us at all during the day at Team USA camp, and anyway I don't have any friends there to text with, and I'm pretty sure no one will want to hang out with the youngest, worst diver there (that's me). If I want to talk to anyone from home, I can snap on my iPad from my dorm room.

If Joe has my phone, I think he'll be much less worried about worst-case scenarios. And I told him, if he gets stuck in Atlanta (or Las Vegas), all he has to do is call you, and you'll probably charter a plane to get him home.

Or . . . another option, just a spur-of-the-moment thought, just popped into my head: I could give Joe my phone to keep, and Dad could buy me the new iPhone with the 3-D camera that just came out. And since I know you are thinking it, no, twelve is not too young to own a phone. He likes to spend his free time solving math problems, Mom, so I think it's safe to say his childhood is basically over, if it ever happened at all. Besides, when I was twelve, everyone I knew already had a phone, and they made fun of me for being "almost Amish." (I may have mentioned that at the time?)

Anyway, I guess I'll check that with you too. Or . . . maybe it would be better if I just run it past Dad?

Love,

Your evil (but brilliant) daughter, Cori, who, let's face it, will probably be texting you from a new phone by tomorrow.

Talia:
Daniel AGAIN?

Amy:
Yes, Daniel again.

Talia:
Lena, are you hearing this?

Lena:
'Fraid so.

Talia:
What are we going to do with her?

Lena:
Plan their wedding.

Amy:
HUSH YOUR MOUTH
Ooh hold on I think he's awake.

I put my phone down on the nightstand in a hurry. Facedown because I know those two will be at it for a while now.

It's not fast enough.

Daniel rolls over, grabs the hand that was a moment ago holding my phone, and pulls it around him. I let him, snuggle closer, smell his chest. He yawns. "You're worse than my students with that phone," he says. "First thing in the morning, really?"

I open my mouth to defend myself but then close it again. He's right. I feel like a nineteen-year-old. I just woke up in bed with my crush. My arm is around him. His arm is around me, lower. His skin is hot. Waking up next to him makes me a strange combination of giddy and drowsy.

"I was excited," I finally confess. "You're very cute."

He smiles. "You are a knockout. And I have to admit, I am very pleased that you're still here. Last time I woke up while you were rolling my sleeping body out the door."

"Yes, but that time was a mistake. Last night wasn't a mistake. Just so you know. I wasn't drunk. I knew what I was doing."

"You knew what you were doing the other time too. I am sure of it. Consent is kind of my fetish."

I nod. Of course I knew before too. We were tipsy, but I was all for it in the moment. I just didn't know how weird it would feel in the morning. "This time I don't feel as, like, shocked by myself. This was premeditated."

"First-degree seduction?" asks Daniel.

"It was the shirt," I say. I gesture to the translucent top I had on last night, which is now flung to the farthest corner of the bedroom. "I think it was supposed to go over another shirt."

"It was not the shirt," he tells me. "It was the you being you."

I smile. Then I frown. "Are we going to do this again?"

"Do what? The sex? I certainly hope so."

I blush. "Well, yes. Or the, um, not-friendship thing."

Daniel looks down at me. "I would very much like to be not friends with you."

I sigh heavily. "I am going back to PA in five weeks. I'm worried about how we'll feel when it's time to say goodbye."

Daniel nods. "I am going back to work in five weeks. And I'm one hundred percent sure it will be awful to say goodbye."

"Phooey," I say.

"Indeed," he agrees.

We are both silent for a very long time.

Then I try, "We could accomplish a lot in five weeks. I once read the complete works of George Sands in a month."

"As worthy as that pursuit would be, I would rather try something else during the time we have left."

"Edgar Allan Poe?"

"I'm thinking more along the lines of an ancient Sanskrit text."

I shake my head at him. "The *Kama Sutra* is a surprisingly long book. We'd never make it past Marking with Nails."

"We could just skip to the illustrations."

"Good idea. That would free up time to see more plays. Hear some music, too, maybe. Go to the MoMA and the Guggenheim."

"Order in breakfast and read the new-releases section over coffee?" he suggests.

"My god, yes," I tell him. *"A thousand times yes."*

"Ok, I'll call for delivery. My treat, since I have ten thousand a year," he quips as he stands up. Some combination of his naked butt and his picking up on my Austen reference and shooting one back makes me swoony.

"Wait. Daniel—tell them to deliver it in a half hour," I tell him. He looks back at me and sees the glint in my eyes.

"Forty-five minutes," he amends and is back in my arms three minutes later.

———

I'd like to tell you what follows over the next month is a Nora Ephron montage. I'd like to say that Daniel and I tilt our heads sideways at sculpture gardens and walk over Central Park bridges a couple of times and laugh and throw popcorn at each other at the Film Forum and then suddenly we are in love and we both know it. But what transpires between us after that night is something at once less picturesque and more binding. We go to the museums but don't stop talking long enough to actually look carefully at the art. We spend too long trying to decide where to eat until we get hangry and have to go to Gray's Papaya for hot dogs. We wait on the platform for a train for thirty minutes, run out of things to talk about to pass the time, start playing *Words with Friends*, get stuck on an *X*, and then lose ourselves again in a conversation about the etymology of the word *relax* and the merits of *Zoolander* as a touchstone of generational connection. We climb onto subway cars that look blissfully empty, and then it turns out that they are being used as a toilet by homeless persons. Or the air-conditioning is broken. Or, in one truly upsetting instance, a mariachi band is practicing in that car, never moving along but just starting their set over and over and over again for timing.

It rains every day for a week, and we lie around Talia's apartment reading first chapters of YA novels we think might work for the Flexthology, and we hardly talk at all for several hours when Daniel is reading Jacqueline Woodson for the first time and I'm reading *The Girl Who Drank the Moon*. We get lost in Chinatown and end up in a restaurant we realize only after ordering has a C rating from the health department. We plan to go to the park for a walk and end up drinking martinis all day in the Plaza instead.

We don't talk about the future, at all. We talk about our lives and everything that makes them full and meaningful, but we behave as though September is never coming and we will be traipsing through hundred-degree subway tunnels for the rest of our days. The only time we even slightly bump up against future plans is when we take video calls from Kathryn, who is getting ready to roll out her Flexthology pilot in Chicago. With her, there will be a first day of school, and it will feature this project we're all so invested in. But for Daniel and me, it is forever August.

Then one day, the sanitation department goes on strike, and the garbage begins to build up on the sidewalks, and the stolen kisses on side streets in the twenties become an exercise in rat spotting. And when you are with someone so wonderful that an actual rat running across your foot on the street does not ruin your mood, you realize: *I've gone and fallen in love.* Every day we say, "We should spend tomorrow apart, because we are grown adults, not teenagers on spring break." And then every night we say, "Well, maybe tomorrow."

His daughter, Cassandra, Snapchats him a lot from her mom's house in Westchester, where she spends her summer. And by *a lot*, I mean constantly. She sends pictures of every meal, asks for movie recommendations when he hasn't been to a movie theater in a year, asks him if her mom was pretty when she was pregnant, and then tells him ten minutes later, "Don't worry Dad I'm on my ●."

I watch in amazement every time he pulls out his phone—it's always her, asking random questions about anything. This girl thinks her father knows *everything*. I am starting to think the same. He dabbles in New York architecture, can name the different kinds of clouds filling the skyline, and explains the origins of every one of those special honorary street names like Jerry Orbach Way (53rd Street) and Billie Holiday Place (139th) whenever we pass them. His favorite is called Martin Gold Avenue, after a very charitable-sounding activist for seniors who painted over graffitied mailboxes in the Bronx for his considerably long life. "He also wrote a lot of worked-up letters to his congressmen," Daniel tells me. "I'm not sure how effective he was."

I say, "Well, I have never noticed a single graffitied mailbox in the Bronx," and he says, "Have you ever been to the Bronx?" and the next thing I know we are on the 4 train uptown to meet his daughter for lunch.

—

Daniel's daughter is very beautiful. Intimidatingly so. I say this as the mother of a girl whose beauty is so deep and wide that people often notice little else. "She's so pretty," they tell me the moment she is out of earshot, and they sound surprised. Cori is quite pretty, but most of the time I see her as a girl in an unflattering swim cap, with strong shoulders and thighs from diving, taking earbuds out of her ears and striding up a ladder with purpose set into every feature on her face. Or I see her wrapping her hair in dechlorinator, wearing fuzzy pajamas, flopping on my bed and telling me what to wear and making fun of my shoes. She is not an object of beauty, like a vase or a fine tapestry, but more of an object in motion. I'm sure the same can be said of Cassandra, but what I see are Daniel's gorgeous cheekbones, plus jet-black hair and the body of a ballerina. She is sitting in the little Vietnamese restaurant waiting at a four-top when we arrive, and she looks up from her phone and then back again and then takes a picture of us just like that. I am startled and unnerved.

"This is her, eh?" she says to Daniel as he slides around and gives her a hug. I am not sure if I should pretend not to be there or what.

Daniel laughs and says, "In the flesh: Amy Byler." He gestures to me sideways, like I am the prize on a game show. "Sexy librarian, mother of two, bringer of your father out of a very long dry spell."

"She's cute enough. She lives in the country?" she asks her dad. Not once has she looked directly at me, and even so, I can feel a bit of animosity heading my way. Well. Daniel did mention she had sharp edges.

"Yes. And she's going back there in less than a month, so don't get attached." All this time I am standing there feeling like my limbs are growing longer and longer and my knuckles will soon hit the ground and I will eventually turn into a boneless puddle and wash away on the floor.

"So I shouldn't call her Mom?" asks Cassandra.

"At this rate she may ask you to call her a cab," quips Daniel.

I cannot bear it any longer, so I clear my throat. They both turn to me as though I just walked in. "I'm going to go ahead and take off my invisibility cloak now!" I announce. "I'm sorry to have eavesdropped on you for so long—honestly I forgot I had the damn thing on." I pantomime taking off a big cape and draping it on my chair and then sit down opposite Cassandra. I stick out my hand to shake.

She smiles, not particularly warmly. "Nice to meet you. I have heard some very complimentary things about you, and you have greatly reduced the rate of unnecessary 'just to check in' communications from my father this summer. It's a good start."

"Well!" I say anxiously. "I'll take it."

"Also, this lunch means free pho for me. So you are approved, and we can move on to the next stage."

"Wow, she's very decisive," I say to Daniel. "Is she like this with all your ladies?"

Cassandra snorts. "All his ladies. What a stitch. Do you also laugh at his Latin jokes?"

Daniel clears his throat. "What did Mark Antony say to his dog walker?" He doesn't wait. "Shar-pei diem!"

We both groan.

Cassandra says, "You're the first one, you know. That he's brought around."

Daniel shakes his head almost imperceptibly at Cassandra. "I've dated other women," he says. "I just haven't felt the need to take them to this restaurant, where my daughter lies in wait five days a week."

"The pho is very good," she tells me. Her eyes have a sparkle to them, just like Daniel's, but she seems more sophisticated than her father, tougher somehow. And there's no missing that she, like Cori, is lippy and quick. The two would probably get along, so long as there were no areas of competition. Cori is very competitive.

"It looks delicious. Would you order me some?" I ask her. "I can't pronounce the word properly. When I say *pho*, I sound faux."

"Oh, Dad," she says to Daniel after a polite laugh at my pun. "You're dating a female version of yourself?"

"She doesn't know Latin," he warns her. "But she loves the same books as me. And she seems content to ride around on the subway reading half the day, and she is good at pretending not to know much about things I like to be the expert in."

"Never let her go!" exclaims Cassandra, but with a hint of sarcasm. Then she turns to me. "Did Dad tell you much about me?" she asks. "Did he make it clear that I am the center of his universe?"

I nod. "Yes, he told me on our first date that no matter what happened with us you would always be top banana, and one day, when you married and had kids, I would have to move into your attic and braid your children's hair."

She laughs.

"However, that knife cuts both ways. I have two kids, Corinne and Joseph. Their kids might need hair braiding too. How is your dad with french braids?"

And then she drops the information I didn't know I needed to know. "Actually, when Mom left us," she says casually, "Dad had to learn to do my hair. He got very good at it."

I turn to Daniel, confused. "I thought you had shared custody." Who has his daughter been with all the nights we're together if not her mother?

"I do now," he says. "Georgia came back. Kind of like your guy, John, except when she came back, she was married to a woman."

My jaw drops. "How long was she gone?"

He exhales. "Let's see. Cassie?"

She thinks for a moment. "I was in first grade when she left and fourth when she came back."

Three years. Just like John, and yet it never came up with Daniel once before now. I wonder if that means it's a sore spot. "Was it hard?" I find myself asking. "To let her come back into your life?"

The question is aimed at Daniel. But Cassie says breezily, "Oh, I didn't just let her. She had to grovel for like a year straight. I was too mad."

I consider this, comparing it to Cori's iPhone shakedown—which I was pleased to hear John put the quick kibosh on—and other mild antics she's tested her father with in the last couple months. "What turned your mind in the end?" I ask.

She shrugs. "Just time, I guess. I felt like I had hazed her long enough. And also, I needed a ride to chess club while my dad was at work."

I smile. "My son, Joe, plays chess too. He's actually with his dad right now. Not exactly hazing him, but I can't say I'd blame him if he was. John did a disappearing act similar to your mother's."

She nods, and I realize this is not news to her. "Dad says people walk away from their families when they are trying to escape themselves," she tells me. "He says we have to have compassion, because they may lose their loved ones, but they'll never outrun themselves."

I nod. "My friend Lena says the same thing," I tell her. "She would add that those with the humility to come back and try to fix things deserve a chance to do so."

"Yeah," says Cassie with a one-shoulder shrug. "I know it was the right thing. Mom's, like, my best friend now. And now that I'm older"—Daniel raises his eyebrows at this—"I get what the whole thing was about. How trapped you can feel as an American woman in early motherhood. The cultural systems of maternal support have all been eroded. You're all alone. I've read, like, two books about it, and I see how my friends' moms seem pissed all the time, like they wish things were different." She fidgets, perhaps realizing now how far she's stepped out. "And also, like, you. The hashtag-momspringa thing. Like, the feeling that the only way to get your true identity back is to run away from your family."

I choke on a spoonful of soup. "Well, that's not what happened with me," I say. "I didn't feel trapped, exactly. I was tired from single parenting. That's true. And you're dead on about cultural systems, maternity leave, multigenerational support, the new expectations of superparenting," I tell her, stalling as I collect my thoughts. "And my job . . . well, it's the same as your dad's, and educators work hard. But as for the 'momspringa,' so to speak, mostly I got shoved out to sea by my friends and family. I didn't *want* to leave it all. I had no choice."

Cassandra shrugs, dismissing me in the way only a teenager can. "I'm just saying I could understand if you did want to run away. After all, you seem to be having a pretty good time now that you're here."

I look at her. She is sixteen, I remind myself. Just a bit older than Cori. She talks like an adult because she's a city kid and well read, but she's not actually mature. She doesn't really understand my situation.

But still. Is she right?

After a moment the quiet gets thick. I look to Daniel and say, in the hopes of ending this line of conversation, "Your daughter has a good point. I'm having a very good time. But this hashtag-momspringa thing has an end date."

Daniel sets his mouth in a line, but he nods. "Yeah," he says, unusually quiet.

Cassie shrugs, this time the left shoulder a bit higher than the right. "I'm just saying," she says again, and Cori has taught me that any sentence that comes after *I'm just saying* will rub me the wrong way. "Amish rumspringa ends with a big decision. Go home or never turn back. I'm not sure how your momspringa is any different."

I look at Daniel and see a question in his eyes. Is he wondering if I'm facing a big decision too? Does he think there might be a chance of my staying? His expression is a little sad, and I know mine must be too. I've gone and done it—fallen in love with him over the summer, as unlikely as I might have thought such a possibility before we met. And sometimes, when I first open my eyes in the morning and see him in bed next to me, I think leaving here will be impossible.

"It's different," I say. But as I do, I realize it's not *that* different. I am going to hit a crossroads soon. Very soon. Daniel, New York, the plays, the meals, the museums, the long, lazy days—it's all on a ticking clock. My real life is waiting for me. A choice is nigh.

And I wonder: Was I, like John, like Cassie's mom, too, trying to escape myself by coming here?

And if so, why does it feel like I found myself only after I arrived?

CHAPTER SEVENTEEN

Dear Mom,

I finished Me before You, *and it was really sad. Really, really sad.*

And it made me think, when this summer ends, things are going to be kind of weird for us, aren't they?

I know I should have thought about this earlier. But Dad and you aren't getting back together after this, are you? You told me you were dating in New York, and I know you say you're not going to give me any details, but if you met someone, that must mean you're not open to giving Dad another chance. Were you ever open to that?

If you come home at the end of the month and Dad doesn't, like, have a chance of getting you back, will he leave?

I know before all this started we talked about him leaving. But that seems long ago. It seems like things have changed so much. He's not what I thought he'd be. He is fun, and he definitely cares, and he knows he made a mistake, and he's fixing things. But he talks about you all the time, and he has a picture of you on his desk, and I can tell he thinks about what it would be like if things could go back to the way they were.

I googled rumspringas and read about this guy who left his family after one. He fell in love with the regular world. Some of his Amish friends were cautious and afraid, but he was excited and energized. He said that he knew his responsibilities to his family and the church were important, and he wrestled with them for a long time, but in the end, the love he felt for stuff like modern technology and free expression and disposable cleaning wipes transcended his old responsibilities.

Is that what's going to happen with you on your momspringa?

Whatever. Joe and I have talked, and we agree we will live with whatever Dad decides. But if he decides he wants his family back, can you please, please consider just thinking it over?

Love,

Cori

———

After lunch with Cassandra, I make up an excuse and come home alone. I check my emails and pace in circles, thinking again and again of what Cassandra said. I eat takeout and drink a very medium-size glass of Talia's scotch and watch *Notting Hill* on Netflix and cry myself a little river. It is the first night in weeks I've been without Daniel. It is miserable.

The next morning, first thing, I call Lena. I can't possibly call Talia—she knows phones have an audio-transmission function of some sort, but she's not much interested in experiencing it for herself. And besides, she is not a disinterested party. She is childless and ex-husbandless, and she unapologetically wants me to move to New York and entertain her like in the good old days. She doesn't know my family. She knows the old me. Not the real me.

But the real me has fallen in love with Daniel. I want to spend every waking second with him. I don't want to go out with any other men who order my dinner for me or try to communicate how much money they make or have long, sordid romantic backstories. I just want to lie around with Daniel and read with him and sleep with him and eat egg and cheese on a roll with him. I haven't felt this way about anyone since

John. Maybe not even John. I don't want to leave in a couple of weeks. I don't want to go back to my high-maintenance house and carpool and thankless job.

This is not momspringa anymore. This is something else entirely.

"It sounds like you are really into him," says Lena.

"I am," I tell her. "He likes me too. He's nice to me. He's his own man. He doesn't make me feel dependent or in danger. He's good at listening to me talk about my work and my kids."

"That all sounds like good news."

"It's terrible news." I am in Talia's apartment, and I open the big sliding door onto her Juliet balcony. There's an adirondack chair out there with a matching footstool. Because the balcony is so narrow, Talia has at some point removed one of the arms of the chair, the side facing the sliding glass door. You open the door, climb into the chair, and then close the door after you and take in the Brooklyn sky, locked into place.

"Why is it terrible news?" asks Lena. "Because he's there?"

"And I'm going back to the *other* there."

"Well, right now you're at *that* there. The there where he is."

I think of my surroundings. A minuscule patio, several stories up, in a one-armed chair, with the glass door so close to my face I could turn and kiss it, the railing against my shoulder on the other side. So often I think it: Talia's New York is my Wonderland.

"But I will be going back *there* soon." The sky is so bright. The noises that make it up this high—sirens, honking horns, a drill—are so muted. "You know what I mean. Your Here. His There."

"And Everywhere. Maybe if you guys really have something good, he could move to you."

"He cannot come to me." I sigh. "He shares custody of a strong-willed teenage daughter. She goes to Bronx Science. You know, the best public high school in basically anywhere. She's not going anywhere.

Daniel moving would be the same thing to him as forfeiting his custody."

Lena is quiet, and I know she is choosing her words. "There are men," she says carefully, "who uproot their lives over love."

My lips tighten. "That was not love," I say brusquely. "Think what you like, but I know John wasn't running toward that girl. He was running away from us."

"I wasn't necessarily talking about John."

I breathe in slowly, sending much-needed oxygen to my brain. There are fragrant spices in the air. Cinnamon. Turmeric. Someone in another apartment is cooking with their windows open. "I suppose that could be true for other men." Unbidden, I think of Daniel, packing up, leaving his daughter behind, and my stomach turns. "But if he moved away from his own kid, I wouldn't want him anyway."

Lena pauses. "I am loath to ask. But would you move to him?"

"Absolutely not," I say. "No way. Never."

"You seem to be enjoying New York. Beyond just the dating, I mean. You are sending such happy text messages now. You use exclamation points for everything. Two days ago you sent me a selfie of you eating a pastrami sandwich."

"Did you see the size of that sandwich?" I ask.

"Yes," Lena says. "It was a nice-size sandwich. I'm saying the city life agrees with you."

I drum my lips with my fingers and think this over. Is that true? Do I like it better here than at home with my children?

Oh god, here comes another burst of guilt, hot and dry like an August wind.

Because something tiny inside me, tiny and selfish and bad, is shouting, *YES!*

"Lena," I say. "I'm going to end this thing with Daniel. Right away."

"What?" she asks. "Wait, how did we end up with that conclusion? I was about to tell you to enjoy yourself in the time you have and then figure it out later. I was going to give you my great 'life is short' talk. I had a Rumi quote all lined up ready to go."

"I'm ending it today. I have to hang up and call him." I try to stand up between the chair and the ottoman, but when I do, there's nowhere to go. I end up flopping down again, like a fish trying to flap itself off a dock.

"No, no, no. Amy, you do not need to end it," she says. "That's ridiculous."

"I need to come back home," I say.

"Hang on," says Lena. "Where did this come from? I feel like you and I are having two different conversations."

"New York is getting to me—that's all," I tell her. I feel panicky. I want to get inside the apartment. Get out of this city air. Off this ridiculous balcony. I fold up my legs and pivot myself toward the door, open it, and slide myself off the chair and into the apartment again, nearly tumbling to my knees. Pull closed the door and lean my back against it. Breathe in the silence, the air-conditioning, the complete lack of aroma.

I look around the apartment. With Talia gone for so long, it feels as much my apartment now as it did hers when I first arrived. There are stacks of my books everywhere, my laptop set up next to sheaves of notepaper filled with lesson-plan brainstorming. On the kitchen counter are the soy sauce–packet collection I've amassed, four take-out menus, a bag of my favorite kind of granola, a paperboard box of strawberries from the market. By the door are all four of my pairs of shoes and my bag of stuff I take to spin class. It feels like . . . like I live here now. Like my kids are grown, on their own, somewhere far away, and I live in New York and work on reading-instruction advancement and go to the theater and museums and eat dinner at eight p.m. and pay someone else to do my laundry.

This is not me. This is not my real life. I have to get home before I forget that again.

I call Daniel. I get his voice mail. "Daniel, I have to talk to you," I say, and then, because I know that is going to put a knot in his chest, I just tell him. "I need to get home, to my real home. I am . . . I'm missing my kids too much and . . ." I fade away, thinking what to say. "I think it will get harder for us the longer we go," I admit. "I think, you know . . . we joke. But we were doomed from the start." I am quiet for a while, wondering if I should hang up, start again, rerecord, erase the whole message, change my mind, stick to my guns, stop being silly, stop ignoring danger. In the end I simply add, "Will you keep me posted if anything ever comes of the Flexthology?" and then hang up. He'll hear it and be mad. I know I would be mad in his shoes. He'll hear it and be mad and say, "Better off without her," and he will be. And I'll be too. There's no sense imagining a future with this guy. Joe is twelve. I have just six years left with him at home. Only three more with Cori. I'm not going to waste that precious time with doomed love affairs and dawdling in museums and, what—sex and pillow talk and bagels? *No.*

I feel like an idiot. Momspringa. What a ridiculous idea! I have been neglecting my children. I should be ashamed. Kids need their mother. I am needed at home. I can't just up and leave my life for a good-looking librarian and a wide selection of sushi restaurants. Even considering such a move calls my character into question. Even thinking it would be nice makes me a bad mom.

This charade is over. It's time to pack it up. It's time to get back to life.

—

I don't check my emails. I don't pass go. I just pick up my ephemera littered around Talia's place, try to stuff it in my suitcase, and fail. The magazine has bought me so much stuff—so much nice stuff. My cycling shoes and my capsule wardrobe and a special boar-bristle hairbrush.

And there are books everywhere that belong to me or the New York Public Library or Daniel. In the end I divide things into three repurposed FreshDirect boxes—library books, things to mail to myself, and things that belong to Daniel—and pack them up as neatly as I can in the rush I feel.

Then I realize: I'm going home empty handed. I can't go home empty handed. I need to buy some good New York stuff for the kids. Why haven't I been shopping for them all this time? I have been acting as if I didn't even *have* kids over these last two months. Dating old men and virtual children and everything in between, shopping for myself, and working out every day like a supermodel or something. Reading and the theater and art? A vacation love affair?

Am I any better than John?

John. I text him a heads-up as I whirl down to the street to find that cool Brooklyny clothing store. Cori's size won't have changed in a few months, but Joe . . . well, he could be huge by now. His dad's not very tall, but my father is kind of a towering man. I should buy a shirt in Joe's June size and one in the next size up, just in case. God, what if he needs new gym shoes? It's good I'm going home early. We need time to outfit these kids before September. And Cori needs to be getting a lot of sleep as we head into diving season. What is Joe reading right now? I turn back to my phone to pepper John with all this and see that he has already texted me back.

> Why are you coming home now? The kids leave for their camps in the morning.

My heart thuds. Camps? That can't be right. There is no way I would have completely forgotten about camps. Did I sign them up for any camps?

But of course, now I remember. Diving camp for Cori—more than a hundred dollars a day, but they've trained Olympians and all-Americans up the wazoo, and I know the price is fair. Fair, but impossible for me without John's help. And for Joe, Space Camp. Space Camp! Like we are Silicon Valley millionaires or something. The regular, full-price kids at Country Day go to these sorts of camps. Not the scholarship kids. And I nearly forgot the whole thing?

I feel so ashamed. My ex, their formerly deadbeat dad, giving them more in two months than I managed in three years. Will they even *want* to come back to me when I get there? Will he have already bought them their school clothes and Uni-Ball pens and the thirty boxes of lotion-free tissues from their class shopping lists? Did he take them to the doctor to get their school sports forms signed? Start Cori's diving curfew early? Probably he has done all these things. Probably I am no longer needed.

I let my phone slide into my handbag. Not my handbag—rather, *Pure Beautiful*'s. I am only now realizing that it came out of the fashion closet there. Look at me, standing in a teen store in my on-trend pants and borrowed designer bag trying to buy my kids' love and forgetting their schedules and their shirt sizes and what next? Their middle names? This isn't me! How did I get here? How do I get back?

I think of the moment I saw John after that farmers' market this spring. I didn't have to talk to him. I didn't have to give him a chance or let the kids visit him or extend the trip to the summer. I pretend I was coerced, but I went willingly, walking away from my responsibilities as easily as John did three years ago. I said I just wanted a short break, but I loved my momspringa from the moment I got on that train. I loved sleeping in and eating out and avoiding fights about skirt lengths and slammed doors and stifled tween-boy tears. I loved making love with Daniel and hanging out with Matt, and I even loved those first dates with all those various men and their various foibles. I haven't really wanted to go back home this entire time, not once, not for real. And now I wish I could undo the whole thing. I should never have given up everything I had. Because now I'm afraid I won't be able to get it back, and if I do, I'm afraid I won't remember how to be happy with it.

A sales guy comes over and asks me if I need help finding anything. I think about telling him I seem to have lost track of my life. Instead, I ask him for a "cool" shirt for a fifteen-year-old girl and another for a twelve-year-old boy, and he offers to give me some choices. He brings some shirts to me but also a canteen-case-style handbag with a water tower motif etched into the leather that even I can see is impossibly chic. "Yes," I say. "That one. And can you get something as cool for my son?" and the thin mustachioed man brings me a square nylon satchel in orange and gray. I look at him. "Orange nylon? Are you sure? Does it really say, 'I'm sorry I'm such a terrible mother'?" I ask him.

"They all say that, ma'am," he tells me, not unkindly. "Here, how about this." He hands me a much sharper-looking backpack made of recycled sailcloth, insignias and all. It looks like something my rich students would have.

"Yeah. That one. He's going to Space Camp," I tell the guy. I hand him my own credit card, think of how rarely I've used it these last months, with Daniel and the magazine and John paying my way. Another way I haven't been myself. Letting other people pay my bills. Forgetting all my hard-won independence.

"Space Camp. Right on," says the guy. "We should get one of these satchels made out of old space suits. That would be tight."

Joe told me once that they use lasers to cut some of the layers of fabric for space suits. They're not meant to be easily pierced or punctured. And only the arms and the joints are very flexible. The rest is rigid and heavy. Joe would laugh at the idea of a space suit backpack. I wish he were here right now. I wish instead of having a momspringa, I had brought the kids here with me for the summer and left John out of the whole arrangement. Why on earth did I think I had to get away from my kids?

All these thoughts jumble around in my head as I rush back to Talia's. I feel foolish and embarrassed, and also there are a few useful parts of my head saying, *But you did like it here*, and *But you were falling for Daniel*, and *But you did need a break!*

But I am so wedded to feeling awful and guilty and bad that I ignore them. And when I turn the corner and find Daniel pacing nervously in front of Talia's building, I am still coursing in those dark, scary feelings, and instead of running to him and wrapping my arms around him, I stop and say, "No, no, Daniel. Please don't be here. Please don't be nice to me."

His whole body seems to sag, like I have just dropped a lead apron around his shoulders. "Amy," he says. "Tell me. What on earth is going on?"

I open my mouth to try to explain, but nothing comes out. I have started loving this person, though there is still so much more to know about him, and I have to leave him now, and it hurts. I walk up to him and put my arms on his arms and lean my forehead in, in, in, until it rests softly against his. This close I can let a tear fall, because he cannot see.

We stand this way a long time. Finally, a woman comes by with a small dog, and the dog starts to sniff around Daniel's shoe with intent, and I say, "We'd better go inside before you're mistaken for a fire hydrant." We separate. I take his hand.

"Are we . . . ?" he asks, and when his voice trails off, I jump in.

"Daniel, listen, I have to go home. I'll try to explain, but it may not make sense. It's not about you at all. It's just that I have to. I have to go home."

He nods but frowns. We go inside, ride the elevator in silence. He walks in, looks around Talia's upturned apartment, starts righting the mess I've made. When he takes in the box with the smattering of his things inside it, he rubs the back of his neck, disappears into the bathroom, and returns with his razor and deodorant. It is a tacit agreement to my decision.

"I do understand," he tells me, when he has closed up his box and set it by the door. "Your kids need you."

And I shake my head and start to cry in earnest. He is kind when he sees me cry. He puts his arms around me and holds me there, sits me down on the edge of the bed, rubs my back, and asks nothing of me for a good long time.

"That's the thing," I whimper when I finally catch my breath. "That's what you don't understand. I'm not going back home because my kids need me. I am going back because they don't."

———

Daniel kisses me goodbye at Penn Station. I get home at seven p.m. that night, and the kids are waiting for me, their last night home before their own big adventures. We have Chinese takeout that I have to privately acknowledge tastes awful compared to what I was eating in New York, and then we sit around the dinner table catching up, laughing a lot, dealing cards for chocolate chip poker from time to time, and then forgetting to play while we talk. I make the kids go to bed at midnight, back in their own beds for the first time in two months; we will be up at six tomorrow to meet John at the airport. There Joe will get on a plane to Huntsville, and then we'll have a three-hour drive north to install Cori into a Team USA dorm for the week. Unbeknownst to me, John paid extra to get Cori a single. "So she can get a break from earplugs at night," he explains, and I know he is talking about the way she is such a light sleeper she wakes even when we flush the toilet in the night, or if Joe is congested and snoring two rooms away. It's a very thoughtful gesture, one that speaks of his attention to her needs over the last two months. All these things, these gifts of time and money and consideration for my kids, are like the long-overdue books we have to write off at school sometimes. If they somehow reappear after that, it is a cause for celebration.

But because it is John and I am feeling so insecure, I ask, "How will she make friends if she doesn't have a roommate?"

He laughs. "How will she not? I am just hoping she gets some diving in there between all the new besties." I am chastened, knowing just how right he is. That girl could make friends in a mannequin factory.

Sure enough, we have barely dropped her sleeping bag and duffel in the dorm room when she's off mingling with a gaggle of other divers in the TV room. "The single was a good idea," I tell John. "You've been doing a very good job."

John looks at me carefully. "It is incredibly hard work. I don't know how you did it yourself for so long."

I want to tell him that someone had to, to guilt him one more time, but why? I'm running out of the antagonistic energy that has powered my relationship with John since he left, as well as the wishful thinking that made for a heady cocktail when he first returned. I put the knife away, and the net, too, and fish around clumsily for an olive branch. "It has been nice to share the load this summer," I admit, even though I feel that nagging sense of failure when I say it. "Thank you for coming back, and for talking me into taking a break."

John looks like he could be knocked over with a feather, but he recovers quickly. "Thank you, too, for coming back early. I don't know how you knew you were needed, but you were. I'm not sure Joe would have gotten on that plane this morning without assurances from his mother."

"And Cori's iPhone," I add. "Speaking of, he texted twenty minutes ago. On the plane for Huntsville waiting to take off. The connection was a success. Now he can relax and enjoy his week."

"Is *that* what he was worried about?" asks John, clearly forgetting his long-ago tantrum in the airport, how he left me alone to manage with four suitcases and two kids on a six-hour flight because he couldn't wait a half hour for a beer. "Weird."

That night John has conference calls, so we stay over in two separate rooms in the nearest Marriott. He invites me to dinner; with no deliberation I choose room service instead, and in that moment I realize something powerful: any last shreds of longing for my ex are gone.

The next morning we hit the road early, aiming to get John back to his desk before the London office closes.

On the ride home, we talk about the kids for a long time. He tells me about all the wonderful things they did all summer, about the long weekends they took and how he forced Cori out for camping and how she ended up liking it in spite of herself. He praises my parenting a lot, which I appreciate, truly. But any kind words land on me with an asterisk: I have neglected these same kids for the last two months.

Still, he presses on. He tells me I was right to make Cori stick out her first year of dive team five years ago, because she's gotten so much happiness and growth out of it since. And he's impressed with what a capable outdoorsman Joe is despite the fatherless years. "I was a fool to assume that only a man could teach him how to start a fire," he tells me.

John keeps chattering away. I like hearing the stories about my kids yet hate knowing how much I've missed. So I say nothing meaningful for an hour straight. Silence seems to be the only way I can avoid grabbing him by the collar and asking, "What happens now?"

After all, my future seems to be held in the hands of this man once again. Will John stay in the States? Or will he go back to Hong Kong, to his old life, when this is all said and done? What will happen when I ask him for a divorce? Will he ask for shared custody?

Will he ask for something more?

The possibilities turn over and over in my head. I try not to compare his every move to Daniel's. But wouldn't I rather be in this car with someone else? With the kind of man who *stays*?

The silence gets thicker as we drive. John runs out of funny kid stories. The puddle in my gut, the emptiness and uncertainty of what comes next, feels the same as a stomach bug. Every curve and bump and jostle on the highway feels like the thing that will finally make me vomit, and yet I never do. Even John finally notices.

"Amy," he says. "Amy, what is wrong with you?"

I take a gulp of air. "I'm not feeling well. I think I might be carsick."

John sighs, and I know he's a little put out by this frailty of mine. But he rolls down my window two inches, and the cool air makes me feel instantly better. "Thank you," I say.

"Do you need peanuts?" he asks me. He is referring to the way even the shortest drive made me carsick when I was carrying Cori and Joe, and the passionate love affair with mixed nuts and peanut butter that I had with every pregnancy.

"Ha," I say. Then I think carefully of the last time Daniel and I were together and say a silent thank-you prayer to my IUD. "I sincerely doubt it. But would it be so crazy if I did?" I suddenly want him to know, without a shadow of a doubt, that I have been with another man.

John doesn't bite. Instead he says, "Do you remember when we took them to Disney?"

Disney World. John and I had always planned to take them someday in the future, but Cori was a mature ten-year-old when we suddenly realized we were running out of the magic years. Neither of the kids was much into Disney movies, but I had been to Disney as a child, and it was such a special memory of my heart. And John had never been but dreamed of going.

So we booked a park hotel and pointed our car south and drove. It was our first real car trip as a family, and unexpectedly I was carsick. We pulled over twice so I could vomit into the ditch. I chewed ginger candy and drank 7UP and finally persuaded John to let me drive for a few hours, convinced that his aggressive style of driving, or what I jokingly called "The Revenge of the Tractor Driver," was what was making me ill. But even while driving I was queasy, and we still had another full day's drive ahead. I couldn't bear it.

So when we reached a town big enough for a CVS, I went in to ask about the seasickness patch. The pharmacist grabbed it for me, saying it seemed to work great for most people, but then he hesitated for a moment. "If you're pregnant or might be pregnant," he said casually, "you need to check with your doctor first before using any of these."

And of course, I realized then. John and the kids were waiting outside the drugstore with the AC on, and we'd all been in that car for hours, with only vomit stops and a quick pee at McDonald's breaking up the trip. I went out and told them to park and go into the Dairy Queen across the street, and I'd meet them there. Then I went back into the store and bought a pregnancy test and took myself off to the CVS bathroom.

I was pregnant.

The pharmacist sold me Unisom and vitamin B6 and some Sea-Bands to use during the drive. I added in a six-pack of ginger ale and a huge bag of salt-and-vinegar potato chips. And a Snickers. I ate the Snickers standing up in the vestibule of the drugstore and then walked across the street to the Dairy Queen and ordered a Peanut Buster Parfait.

"Your appetite's back!" John cheered when I brought the ice cream to the table. Oh, how high spirited he was that day. Things weren't perfect between us, but that was one of our happiest times.

"Yep," I said and felt my heart lift to see his smile. "I think the medicine is working already. But I'm not supposed to operate a moving vehicle, so you get your keys back."

My ice cream tasted delicious. My stomach was already evening out. I was making my kids happy with this trip, and I was about to make my husband even happier. I didn't want a baby, but I didn't not want a baby either. I was surprised but not horrified. I thought John, however, would be tickled. He was from a huge family and would have liked twice as many kids, but I needed time between Cori and Joe to get my feet underneath me, and after Joe I felt too old. But apparently I was not too old.

I was excited to tell him. I gave the kids quarters for a claw machine and took John by both hands, and my face cracked into a grin and I could feel the wide wetness of my eyes and the words bubbling up the moment the children were out of earshot. "We're pregnant!" I told him. "We're having a baby!"

Now, in the car with John only an hour from home, I say, "I ate so many peanuts on that trip. And potato chips."

"God, so many potato chips. I was afraid for the global supply."

"And remember, you asked me how much weight I wanted to gain with this pregnancy."

"And you almost killed me."

"I would have been acquitted," I say. And then, because there are so many questions I can't ask him about the future, I ask him about the past. "Do you ever miss that baby?"

John shakes his head. "No. I'm sorry, Amy. But that wasn't meant to be."

"That's what you always said. But you seemed so happy at first."

From my angle in the passenger seat, John looks heavier and more tired than I remember. "I wasn't."

"You were just pretending?" I ask him.

"I was . . . faking it until I made it," he says.

I consider this, trying and failing to hold his words at arm's length. "But what if we'd had that baby," I hear myself ask. "Things would have been so different. I cannot imagine you would have left me with a two-year-old in diapers. We would have stayed together."

John looks straight ahead. "I do think about that sometimes."

"So if I'd stayed pregnant, you would have kept me?" The question comes out squeaky, and I can hardly believe I've just spoken that horrible fear aloud. But then, haven't I wondered if it was true a hundred times?

John sighs. He seems so exhausted all of a sudden, and I flash back to the way he dragged himself through the house looking weary and sighing all the time, just before he left. "I didn't, you know, 'not keep you,'" he tells me. "It's not like I returned you to the store with my original receipt."

"Well, then, what did you do? I lost our baby, and then you left me." My throat feels tight. I feel the hurt rushing back. I blink hard and try to swallow back tears.

"No," John says. "I left everything. You were part of everything. You, the house, the town, my family, my friends, and yes, my kids. All of it. I thought I just needed a short break—just like you—only it took me three years to come back, not two months."

"The two things are nothing alike," I snap, though of course I have compared us in my mind time and time again.

John shakes his head. "No, they're not. You're a better parent than me. A better person. In fact, as far as I can tell, all you want to be in the world is the person opposite of me."

I can see he is wounded. But he doesn't stop talking.

"You see the sadness of that, right, Amy? Not only have you not moved on in three entire years, you've defined yourself solely and completely as the woman I martyred."

The woman he martyred.

The words make me furious. The words are true.

"Why did you come back here, John?" I ask. I should have asked him that months ago. I should have pushed him harder. Made him explain himself. Stopped tiptoeing around, terrified of . . . what did I call it? Upsetting the applecart? The hell with the goddamned applecart. "Did you come back for me?"

He lets out a long breath. "I came back for them. Joe and Cori. And I do love you, Amy. After eighteen years of marriage, I think I'll always love you." He drops the wheel with his right hand and reaches over to give my arm a familiar squeeze. "I thought maybe when I was back I'd find the best thing for the kids would be to try to recover our marriage, and the idea hardly felt like a chore. You're as beautiful as ever, and an amazing mother, and you've been more patient with this process than anyone else would have been in your place."

I shake my head. It may have been what I wanted to hear at the beginning of the summer. Now it sinks like a stone. "I don't want that, John."

He nods, and I think I see just a trace of regret in his eyes. "I know that now. And I don't think the kids need it either."

He's right. I breathe in, try hard to breathe out. "So then what?" I ask him. "What is your plan?"

He hesitates for a second. "I think when the summer's over it'll be time for me to head back overseas. I'll miss the kids terribly, but I've got to get back into the office eventually, and there's no question you guys will be totally fine after I'm gone."

His words hit me like tumbling bricks. I wanted the truth. I thought I was ready for the truth. But now that I have it I feel beaten. Not just beaten. Completely taken apart. Nothing has changed. I have left behind Daniel and Talia and New York and everything I felt I could be there, to come back to the exact same way things were before John walked back into all of our lives.

Only worse, because now Joe, Cori, and I will know firsthand exactly what we were all missing.

———

For a while after that, John and I drive in silence. A city of pain built inside my heart throbs mournfully. The buildings constructed of regret and loss, the streets paved in fear. In my mind I walk through it. Wade through the hurt of what he just said, the monuments to heartbreak I have built inside me, traveling back through time.

The day I left Daniel in New York.

The day I saw John at the drugstore.

The day I found out about Marika.

The day John called from Hong Kong, saying he was never coming back.

The day I went in for my thirteen-week appointment and there was no more heartbeat.

It is at this last monument—a secret known only to John and me—where I can go no further. They asked me at the time, did I want to run DNA tests on the fetus? Did I experience any cramping or bleeding? Did I want to know the gender? Were we planning to try for subsequent pregnancies? But I was so stunned it was all noise. I had never miscarried before. I'd had no reason to think I would now. I was taking folate, hadn't had a drink since week four, was appropriately sick, tender breasts, eight pounds of new weight. I rattled these statistics off to the doctor to try to convince her that she was wrong. I told her, as if it mattered, as if she didn't know, that I had been pregnant for almost three months. I had already started the baby's 529 plan.

"Your phone is ringing," says John, back in the car, back in the present, back in the place where the baby wasn't born and the husband didn't stay and I spent the last five years holding on to those hurts like my life depended on it.

"What?" I ask.

"Your phone. That buzzing sound, it sounds like a phone set on vibrate."

"Oh. Yes, you're right. It's my phone."

"Aren't you going to answer it?"

I don't make any move to do so. It could be Daniel. Or Talia, home from Miami and wondering where I've gone. Or Matt, upset that I've bailed without a word. Or any number of other people I've let down.

Then it stops ringing and starts again. I get the phone out in time to see the voice mail pop up. An area code I don't recognize.

The message transcribes, slowly, slowly, and at last I read it. Then I drop the phone, stunned. "John, turn the car around. Turn it around now. Cori's been hurt."

"What?"

"There, use that turnaround there. Go back to the college."

"What happened?" he demands, but he is signaling left, slowing down at a sheriff's thruway.

"We have to go to the hospital," I tell him, and there is new terror in my voice. "It's Cori." I grab him by the shoulder. "She hit her head on the diving board, and she hasn't woken up."

CHAPTER EIGHTEEN

When Cori was newly three years old, we told her the big news. Brace yourself for a brother or a sister, we said. This is going to be exciting, but disruptive too.

At the time, Cori was speech delayed. We tried not to overreact, but we were first-time parents, and everything slightly out of the ordinary could be a portent of something dire, so I wasted hours of my life fretting and reading up on delays and harassing the poor kid with tongue exercises. Cori, the rebel that she was, responded by talking even less and pointing at things and saying, "Dat," instead of using what nouns she actually had in her wheelhouse. The speech therapists told us to pretend not to know what she was indicating. By understanding her every whim without words, they told me, I was creating in Cori learned helplessness. Maybe so, I thought. Maybe this was all my fault, as the mother. Or maybe she just didn't feel like talking yet, and we could all get off my back.

But I was cowed into following the experts' rules. So when Cori pointed at my womb region and said, "Dat," I said, "Hmm?" and she said, "Baby?" and I said, "Yes, there's a baby in there," and she said, "Cori don't want dat baby." And I told myself, well, it's a nice long sentence, so that's something. But I was scared.

With Joe, John and I hadn't been going crazy trying to get pregnant, but it had taken longer than we'd expected for it to happen, and we'd gotten to that point right before you go to the doctor to see if something's wrong. We actually had the appointments made. John wanted me to go first. Then if I "checked out," he'd go. He justified this by telling me that "eggs get dusty fast," and let me tell you, this kind of talk did not make me excited about the work that goes into conception. Sex was getting bad, and I was feeling resentful, and foreplay had transformed into comments like "Let's get it over with" and "It's go time, like it or not."

Then, thank goodness, I missed my period. I took a home test, and it was positive, and we waited three months, and then we told Cori, and she told us she didn't want dat baby. Things had been strained between me and John, and I looked him in the face and wondered if I was the only one who wanted dat baby in the whole house. It felt lonely.

But of course, half a year later, Joe was born, we all fell in love, and Cori in particular felt that Joe belonged to her. They were far apart in age, but they still were good at entertaining each other. Cori did not help with diapers willingly, but she loved feeding Joe and in fact did some midnight bottles when John traveled for work and Joe was drinking more milk than I could make myself. Half-asleep, I'd hear Joe start to stir in the bassinet next to me, but before I could even think what to do next, Cori would be awake in her room and then down in the kitchen in her learning tower, washing her hands carefully, hollering at me to come check the temperature of the bottle. Then she'd feed him while I half dozed, and while he ate, she'd chat to him using words she'd never used with me or John. "Ok, baby," she'd say. "Time to gobble up some milk. Yummy milk. Formula. We need to be nice and quiet so Mommy can sleep. Do you have to fart?"

After the bottle was gone, Cori would set it on the nightstand, crawl over my body, and go right back to sleep on the other side of me, like this was her natural place all along. In his attached bassinet, Joe would fuss a bit. I just reached a semiconscious arm over to him and coaxed gas out, did that weird thing moms do where they check for poopy diapers by sticking their fingers right into where the poop might be, took care of any business, went back to sleep. We did this strange dance as a team, a little mother-daughter pas de deux, whenever John was gone for work, and he was gone most weekdays. We were a finely tuned parenting machine, my four-year-old and I. But John, grown man though he was, was not like Cori. He came back for the weekends too tired to do late-night bottles, and he shooed Cori back to bed whenever she got up in the night to help. During the days on weekends, John would take Cori for amazing adventures, park days and picnics and baseball games and swimming. Joe and I would sleep in, and I would tell myself how lucky I was for these much-needed breaks. But I missed Cori on those days. And I never missed John on the others.

That, the weird, involuntary shifting of affection from my husband to my children, was not uncommon, I knew. I also knew it was a phase. Women with older kids told me about romantic renaissances they enjoyed when the children were old enough for sleepovers and trips alone to Grandma's. I tried not to beat myself up for avoiding sex in those early years, or substituting early bedtimes for date nights, or wearing quite so many holey, stretched-out sweatpants quite so many days in a row.

But when he left, did a secret, ashamed part of me believe it had been all my fault? And maybe, was it myself I was actually so mad at all this time?

As we speed toward the hospital, I think of all this. I think of Cori hurt, and every time she fell off her bike or slipped from a swing or tumbled off a ladder she should never have been on in the first place. I think with amazing clarity: Who cares who did what or why? This man and I combined our genetics to make something greater than the sum of its parts. We made two children I love more than I have ever loved anything else, and now one of them is hurt, and it doesn't matter why, and it is no one's fault, not John's, not even my own. All that matters now is that we get there, and she wakes up, and when she does, she finds both her mother and father by her side.

—

There is a big beautiful hospital near campus. There are pretty bronze statues in the courtyard, and valets wait to grab our keys as we fly into the drive. Everything is clean and shining. The elevators have pictures to remind you of what floor you're on. I ignore all of this and abandon the car and John in it and run into the emergency room. Cori has already been moved. I get into another line and shout, "Cori Byler?" and the LPN says, "TBI? Fourth floor."

TBI. This is something that diving mothers never, ever talk about. We talk about concussions constantly. What to do, how to recognize one, where to go, what questions to ask. But the phrase *traumatic brain injury* is one we are careful not to utter. Concussion means rest. Benching. Weeks off from school. Athletic setback. TBI means brain damage. I burst into the fourth-floor waiting room like I am personally charged with saving Cori from a painful death. "Where is she?" I holler. "Corinne Byler, UP Health Member number 320378. Date of birth nine, twenty seven—"

"Slow down, slow down," says a man at the front desk. "Are you the patient's mother?"

I nod.

"We've been waiting for you. I can take you back to her respite area, page a doctor. Do you have any ID?"

I nearly grab the poor guy by his lapels.

"Yes," I say. "Take me back." I throw my license at him, and he makes me a wristband. The elevator doors open behind me, and I dimly register John getting off. I took the stairs two at a time, and I am panting. His mouth is set in a hard line. I gesture at him, telling the CNA, "That's her dad too. Let him in. John, show him your driver's license."

"Hang on, sir; I'll be right back for you. Ma'am, follow me," he says to me. He uses a key tag to get me through a set of locked doors and down a corridor of treatment rooms. He drops me off with a nurse and says, "Mother of Cori Byler, room 428," and then turns right back the way he came.

The nurse takes me by the arm and starts to walk down another hall. "Your daughter seems to have sustained a head injury from a diving board. We are watching for mild to moderate traumatic brain injury. There is some imaging we need to do, and right now she is semiconscious, ranking pretty high on a GCS." I don't know what this means, but I'm too discombobulated to ask for clarification. "I will get a doctor in to talk to you as soon as possible," he continues. "You can see her soon, but she is, as I said, pretty disoriented; think of someone who is only half-awake."

I think of myself in the bed with Cori and Joe as babies, half-awake, listening to my speech-delayed daughter hold forth. I was still very aware of what was around me. I'm going in there now.

"This is the ICU family respite center. There's coffee and juice, and—ma'am?"

I see Cori's date of birth written on a whiteboard on the very next door, room 428, followed by the letters TBI. Not that tricky to discern where she is. I open the door carefully and peek inside. It's Cori, asleep. I bust on in.

"Ok, ma'am," says the RN sternly, following me. "You need to go to the family respite center. Ma'am, you're going to upset yourself."

Cori is in bed, with an oxygen mask and an IV stand with three bags hanging from it. The room sounds like a soap opera set. Bleep bleep. Whoosh whoosh. Cori's mouth is open, and she's drooling out of the mask. Drool means alive. I start to cry.

"It's upsetting, ma'am. That's why I told you not to—"

"I'm not upset," I tell him. "Look at her—she's breathing."

Cori turns her head toward me. Her eyes flutter open and then closed. She can hear me. I choke some more tears down and take her by the hand and say with false cheer, "Well, there you are, drooling like a golden retriever. You had me scared, girl. You're supposed to bounce on the board with your feet, not your skull."

Cori's eyes open, and there's a twinkle in them, and then they close again. I turn away.

"Are you on top of pain management?" I ask the RN sharply.

"I am quite sure we are, ma'am. But now you need to go back to the respite area. Have a cup of . . . of chamomile tea. A doctor will be in to talk to you shortly."

This time I do as he says. I go in the waiting area. I'm the only one there. The TV is on to CSPAN. The room smells of gas station coffee. The chairs are standard-issue hospital waiting room. I sit down on one and let myself cry a little.

After a short time, John moves into the room and sits on the chair next to mine. I picked one of the double-wide ones, thinking I may be here for a while, and I am thankful John has the good sense not to try to sit in it with me. This way there is a pleasant gulf between us. I set my elbows on my knees, rest my face in my hands, and go back to my crying.

John reaches over and rubs my back absentmindedly. "Did you see a doctor yet?"

I shake my head. "Not yet. But I saw Cori. She is definitely alive."

John makes a little choking sound. "Well, Christ, Amy, is that all we were hoping for?"

"It's a good start," I say. "They say she has traumatic brain injury. They're looking at pictures of her brain to see if there's been . . . permanent damage." I let my voice trail off. "Is that what you want me to say?"

John is quiet.

"You know"—I suddenly feel the need to lecture him—"the kids got sick while you were gone. They got hurt. They did stupid things and had fights and got sick and needed to be rushed to urgent care and the ER and Cost Cutters."

"Cost Cutters?"

"Lice," I say. "I tried to give Joe a buzz cut to get them out, but I did a hatchet job, and we had to go in to figure something out so he could be seen in public again."

"What are you talking about? What does this have to do with lice?" John asks.

"The point is I have had emergencies with these children of ours. Lots of them. And after you ascertain that everyone is alive and no one is on fire, you go ahead from there."

"Ok. Good tip." He sounds angry, and what right does he have to be angry with me? But of course, I'm angry with him, too, and the nurse, and anyone else unlucky enough to confirm this isn't some nasty dream.

"This may be your first real kid crisis, but it's not mine."

"This is more than a kid crisis," John says. "She's not fully conscious. There could be swelling or bleeding or brain damage."

I look up at the ceiling. Doesn't he know—you should never say your worst parenting fears aloud? "You been watching reruns of *ER*? Be cool. Don't jinx her."

"Jinx her? What is wrong with you?" he asks. "This isn't a T-ball game."

"Hush!" I say. The doctor, or at least someone in a long white coat, is coming. She walks in, stands in front of us, and says, "My name is Dr. Boch. Are you the parents of Corinne Byler?"

John says nothing. I nod, show my wristband, and say, "What do you know?"

"We've had a good look at the CT scan, and unfortunately there is bleeding—a subarachnoid hemorrhage that I believe we can operate on successfully. It would have been posttraumatic—as I understand it, she hit her head while diving yesterday? So she maybe went home feeling ok, got a bad headache—symptomatic of the SAH—went to bed, and then couldn't wake up? Is that how you heard it too?"

I nod. That is what her coach told me when I called her back. She sneaked out to goof around with her new friends at the pool. Hit her head and made the others promise not to tell. Went back to her room, her single room, and missed this morning's early-bird practice . . .

"So we need to be concerned about stroke, vasospasm, hydrocephalus—"

"What are you saying?" asks John. And then to me, "Is she speaking English?"

"Hush," I say again, louder. "Listen!"

The doctor slows down. "Mr. Byler, your daughter hit her head, and there was a brain bleed—blood in a layer of the covering of the brain. This happens to a lot, maybe a quarter, of people with a big head injury like Cori's."

"No," says John. "No."

Dr. Boch presses on. "We could see it on a scan we gave her, and we are going to need to operate right away."

"Brain surgery?" says John. "Absolutely not. We need a second opinion."

The doctor is taken aback. "That's your right, but I would recommend we proceed quickly. We are very sure of what is going on, and there are some time constraints. First, we needed to make sure to take care of her vital functions, which we have done, and she is stable. Now we need to operate on her head to stop the bleeding."

"Is this absolutely necessary?" asks John.

"Yes," says the doctor without missing a beat. "It is. Now. This is a complicated surgery, and I have performed it several times. The prognosis is much better than it used to be, but it is not perfect. I have an excellent track record, and I work with one of the best possible teams, and your daughter could not be in better hands. I just need your consent, and then I need to ask you some things about your daughter to prepare."

"Go ahead," I say.

"No," says John. "Don't go ahead. I don't know what this means." He is crying, I realize. He has lost his shit. He seems to be shrinking beside me.

I grab his hand. "Take some deep breaths, John. Sit down. I can take it from here."

John looks at me, then at the doctor, then back to me. "You can handle this?" he whispers to me.

I nod. "Yes, I can, and I will. You just try to relax. Take deep breaths. Do you need to be sick?"

"No," whimpers John. But he is holding my hand with a death grip.

"Ok, then. Hang in there and let me do this. I think we need to work quickly."

"Yes, your wife is correct," says the doctor. "I will answer any questions you have as best I can, but the truth is we cannot delay this surgery."

"We don't have any questions right now," I lie, because of course all this time my mind is spasming with panic and questions and blinding, incapacitating fear that cannot be allowed to take over. "Tell me what you need to know, and then after that have someone bring me a bunch of pamphlets or whatever. Or send in an intern who can explain it to us slowly? The point is let's get moving."

"Good. Now, does Cori smoke?"

"No."

"Use cocaine, to the best of your knowledge?"

"No."

"Any chance she could be pregnant?"

"No."

"Does she take oral contraceptives?"

"Yes."

"*What?*" cries John.

"Ignore him," I say to the doctor.

"History of high blood pressure?"

"Paternal," I say.

"Any previous concussion or traumatic brain injury?"

"No."

"That's fortunate. She must be a strong diver."

"Very."

"Good. Let's get her back on that board. Someone will be coming in with paperwork and some long, detailed medical histories for you to fill out. You'll need to be very, very patient. This procedure takes as long as it takes. But usually at least eight hours. The CNA will provide you some information on family self-care, as well as directions to the cafeteria."

"Thank you," I say.

"And the chapel," she adds, "is on the fifth floor," and I know from that, more than from any of the medical talk, that things are as serious as I feared.

"Ok," I say, nodding my understanding. "You fix her, ok?" I tell her. I hope I sound threatening, not desperate.

"That's my job, and I'm very good at it. Your job is to hang in there while I work. Is anyone else coming? Maybe someone to look after your husband?" She tilts her head at him, and for the first time I notice he has let go of my hand and is retching into a wastebasket.

"He's not my husband," I tell her, though I'm not sure why that's important at the moment. "But I will try to find him a minder."

The doctor nods. "Your daughter is in very good hands," she tells me again, and I think oddly on the fact that among a doctor's many jobs is the task of getting the family to leave you alone so you can work. I'm glad I'm not her. And yet I wish I could go with her to be with Cori.

"Can I come?" I ask her.

"Why don't you come give her a nice kiss before she goes into the OR," says Dr. Boch. "Everyone knows the best medicine is a kiss from your mom."

I press my lips together tight to keep from crying. I am thinking, *Really? Even at fifteen? Even for a TBI?* The doctor puts her hand on my back gently and leads me to Cori's bed.

"Ok," says Dr. Boch to the staff when we walk into the room, now crowded with scrubs. "This is Mom; she's going to hold Cori's hand and help her get off to sleep. Is anesthesia here?"

"Present," says a tall, thin man, and he introduces himself. "I'll put this mask over Cori's mouth and nose, and the anesthesia will be delivered continuously using a carefully calibrated machine. She'll be fully unconscious and comfortable until the surgery is finished," he tells me.

"Be careful," I tell him. "She's a good one."

He nods. "I can tell." Then, as if he's in a play, he tells the room we're ready to move. "Give her a hug and a kiss if you'd like," he says to me, and I hug her and kiss her, and though her eyes are half-closed, I tell her she looks great and I can't wait to see her later today, and then I tell her I love her, and then I start telling her all the things I love about her—her strength, her bravery, her spirit—and then the anesthesiologist interrupts me and gently says, "Ok, Mom, time to go," and Cori is wheeled away.

And I am grateful, when she is gone, to find her room empty, to watch the doctors and nurses and cast of thousands trail away to the OR. Because though I would rather Cori be anywhere else but in the OR with a neurosurgeon, since that is where she is, at least she will not be able to see me cry.

CHAPTER NINETEEN

Dear Cori,

You've asked me, over the last couple of months, if I could take back Dad. You asked me if I would change on my momspringa and never be the same. You wanted to know what would come after August ended.

I didn't know the answer to any of those questions, so I didn't even try to answer them. Then you sneaked out of the dorms with the cool girls and hit your head on the diving board, and you were too embarrassed to go to the coach, so you just went to bed alone, and now you might never wake up. And I have to tell you, it feels like that is all there is in the whole world, and all your questions, and all the questions in the universe, are easily answerable, except for the only ones that matter right now: What will happen to my beautiful, perfect daughter? Are you going to be ok?

And I hate this. I hate that now that I know the answers to your questions, there's no way to tell them to you. Except in my heart. So I'm going to tell them in my heart. And I'm going to pray and pray you hear them, somehow.

So: Will I take back Dad? Honestly, I don't think it would make any of us happy. And I won't do it just to make him stay in your lives. If that's the only way to get him to stay, none of us really want to be with him, do we? We can do much, much better than that. But if you want me to be with Dad because you believe it's what this family needs, he and I will try to hear you out, because you are the smartest, bravest, most clear-hearted girl I have ever known. And I will trust you to the end.

Have I changed on my momspringa? Yes, but not in the way you think. I didn't revert to my party girl days with Talia. I didn't ever, not once, regret having you and Joe. I didn't get sold on the fancy clothes or the high-heeled shoes or even the fashion-closet purses (though I am never going back to ill-fitting bras, and I vow on my mother's grave to spend whatever it costs to get you good support when or if your breasts ever need it). I liked dressing up from time to time, and I liked having time to myself, and I liked going out on dates. So the change you'll see when we all get home is that I show you how creating an enjoyable life—not just a vacation but a life—is just another important part of being a mother, like serving vegetables once a week or lecturing your kids about slouching.

When you get better—and you're going to get better, baby—you're going to date a lot, and go to college, and meet someone wonderful, and have a kid, maybe even in that order. And you're going to remember me and never, ever sell yourself down the river to be some kind of perfect mom. Not for a second. When you feel the urge, you're going to put on the well-fitting bra I bought you fifteen years earlier and leave your kids in the care of a moderately competent person and go do something that is only for yourself, and if you don't know what that should be, then you're going to think about it until you do.

And your last question: What will come when the summer ends?

You'll come home. It's the only answer in the world that matters.

You'll come home, and together, we'll figure everything else out.

———

The first three hours that Cori is in surgery, the time goes very, very quickly. That is because I am crying and looking up medical terms and crying and looking up brain disorders and crying alternately, and this is very time consuming. It is not until almost noon that my phone battery gets low enough and I get dehydrated enough to peek my head out of Cori's empty hospital room, and when I get to the respite room, I find John asleep, sitting maybe three feet away from a TV blaring cable news directly into his face. I look at his sleeping form. He looks all tuckered out, like a child who played outside from sunup to sundown.

I know if he is sleeping during our daughter's brain surgery, he is very tired. The kids, of course, have worn him out. Just like they wore me out before I left. But also, John powers down when he's overwhelmed. He did it during my first labor and during shake-ups at work and after the third baby was lost. It has always seemed to work for him—he'd come back rejuvenated and ready to move on. But for me it was just one more way I felt lonely.

I look at his sleeping form and find myself stunned that I ever shed tears over this man. Three years ago, without realizing it, I escaped a life sentence with a partner who literally slept through the hardest moments in our lives, leaving me alone to deal with them. The worst thing that ever happened to me also happened to be the luckiest moment of my life.

If Cori is ok—please, please, she *has* to be ok—I will never waste another sad thought on my marriage again. I will celebrate what we had, our wonderful kids, our happier times. I will help John be the best father he can possibly be, wherever he chooses to live. But I will also date, live my life for real this time, and stop pining for something that wasn't that great in the first place. There's no Daniel in PA, that's for sure and certain, but maybe I'll meet someone pleasant enough. Or maybe I'll travel to New York every once in a while to see him. Maybe we'll find some way to keep close . . .

If Cori lives, I promise to the great beyond, *I'll live too*.

And if she doesn't . . . well, then whatever I do won't matter much either way.

—

After the first six hours of surgery, I start staring obsessively at the entry to the respite lounge. Every single time I hear steps or see a shadow moving outside the room, I pop up in my chair. After an hour of this I decide to take a walk. It's going to be another hour or maybe two, and this vigil will only make me crazy.

I walk out to the nurses' station to let someone know I'm on the move. But when I say I'm setting off for a walk, the nurse on duty tells me that my sister is on her way in. "Or the patient's aunt, maybe?" she clarifies when I look confused.

Lena. Thank god. "Oh, that's great. I didn't realize she was coming," I say and head to the elevators to meet her. The timing is perfect—the doors are just opening, and there is my best friend, and her arms are around me, and at last I don't feel quite so terribly alone.

"What are you doing here?" I ask when she's let me go, hugged me again, and then handed me a half-drunk chocolate milkshake. "Is this for me?"

"It was supposed to be for you, but I've been so worried I might have had a few sips. It was a long drive, you know. I kept it in a cooler for a while, but then it started shouting at me, 'Let me out; let me out!'"

In spite of everything inside me, a laugh comes out. "Lena, how did you get here? How did you know we were here?"

"You don't know?" she says curiously. "John texted me."

I look heavenward. "He did something right," I say. "See!"

"Are you talking to God?" she asks.

"That's your job," I tell her. "I'm just doing whatever it takes not to crack up while we wait for the surgery."

"How much longer?" she asks.

"An hour. Two, maybe? It takes forever. Her brain is bleeding." I start to tear up.

"Oh, Cori," says Lena. "How did this happen?"

I am about to tell her, but the elevator pings again, and the doors open.

"Talia?" I cry.

"What is going on? Why are we at the hospital?" she exclaims. She, too, wraps me in an enormous hug. It's so out of character I start crying again. "Here," she says and hands me a giant stuffed cheetah.

"What on earth?" I ask through my tears.

"Everything else in the hospital gift shop was so awful," she says. "I figure we can at least skin this and make you a nice coat."

"Oh my god, Talia, I'm so glad you're here."

"When a nun calls you swearing like a sailor and telling you to get your ass upstate, you get your ass upstate," she says.

"Former nun," corrects Lena.

"Did you fly here from Miami?" I ask Talia.

"No, no, I flew into New York yesterday, planning to surprise you and do a deep Florida detox for the weekend. Look at the sun damage to my hair." She tilts her head and gestures to her still-perfect natural curls. "But you weren't there. And your stuff was all in boxes. And I was like, 'What?' And then Lena called me, and I was like, '*Shit.*' And then I borrowed an ex-boyfriend's car and drove here, and may I remind you that I do not have a valid driver's license? So I have had a very harrowing day."

I am shaking my head and crying. "Me too," I tell her.

"So I've heard. What happened?"

And before I can even answer her, the elevator doors ping again, and this time all three of us face the doors expectantly. A hapless and confused orderly gets off the elevator while we stare. When she's out of the lobby, I say, "Cori hit her head on the diving board at camp. She didn't tell the coach because she wasn't supposed to be in the pool, I guess. She went to sleep, and then she didn't wake up when they knocked for practice, and she'd given her cell to Joe. The counselor let herself in and found her in there and called 911. The coach called me and told me to come here."

"This is awful," Talia says.

"Cori is so tough," says Lena. "You haven't seen her in ages, Talia, but she's like a cross between a bulldog and the Highlander. She is going to get through this."

"Please be right," I beg her. "She's so . . . I can't . . ."

Lena and Talia hug me together. One of them shushes me. The other says, "You won't have to."

The elevator doors ping again. This time I just keep crying, holding on to my friends for dear life. The doors open.

Daniel walks out.

"What?" I say.

Talia and Lena break away from me. "Is that . . . ?"

"Daniel?" I say.

"Is it ok that I'm here?" he asks.

By way of answer, I run to him. "My daughter is hurt," I say. I want him to know exactly what I know. I want to shove it into his brain. "She has bleeding on her brain. She is in surgery. Her dad is asleep."

"Oh, Amy," he says. He holds me for a moment, then pulls back and looks into my eyes. "Are you doing ok?" he asks me.

"Definitely not," I tell him. "But it's better with you all here." Lena and Talia are looking at us curiously.

"Did you call him?" I ask them both.

"I don't even know who he is," says Talia.

"He's the hot librarian," says Lena, and Daniel colors. "He's the one who has been sleeping in your bed for the last month."

"Aha!" says Talia. "You left your sports watch. I'm so glad it's not yours, Amy."

I smile. "It's his. Daniel, meet Lena and Talia."

He gives them a quick glance. "Nice to meet you. Wish it was in better circumstances. When does she get out of surgery?"

I look at my phone. "Soon. Or in hours. It all depends on what they find. But we should go back to the room just in case."

"Someone has to wait here," says Daniel. "Matt will be here any minute. He's the one who told me."

"Matt?" I say. "Talia's Matt?"

"What about Matt?" asks Talia.

"He's coming here," I say.

"We drove together," says Daniel. "He's parking the car."

Talia shakes her head in wonder. "Ok, you two go inside and wait for the doctor," she commands. "Lena, you and I are going to meet up with Matt."

I go to the new CNA behind the reception desk and tell her Cori's family is here. "Two aunts, one uncle, and a . . . cousin," I say because Matt is too young to be anything else. She raises her eyebrows at us: Talia is Black, Lena white, and Daniel Asian.

"I'll sign them in," she says, though she is obviously skeptical. She takes Daniel's ID and beeps us back to the ICU. The moment the doors are shut behind us, Daniel takes my hand. "Is this ok?" he asks. "It doesn't have to be an 'us' thing. I just . . . Matt called and said your daughter was seriously hurt. And I couldn't not come here. Just because, no matter what, I really have come to care, you know."

"It's good you came. But how did Matt find you?"

"Twitter," says Daniel. "I, uh . . . when your momspringa photos first went up, back in June . . . well, I direct messaged the magazine's account. Saying we'd gone on one date and I was hoping they'd pass along my phone number."

"You did?" I say in surprise.

Daniel shrugs. "It sounds kind of desperate. But when I saw the trending hashtag and realized it was you, I was . . . too tempted to let it lie."

"Matt didn't tell me that," I say.

"Yes, and I had some words for him about that today," he says. "But it all worked out once I found you on Facebook." He falters. "I mean, worked out as far as it worked out. That's not why I came. I'm not going to pressure you or anything. I'm just here as a friend."

I nod. "I'm glad you're here. Friend or otherwise," I say. "It's just . . . my preexisting condition is here too." I tilt my head into the doorway of the respite room where we now stand.

Daniel doesn't flinch. "Good. Cori needs her family."

"He's asleep at the moment," I say. "I think his brain overloaded and then powered down."

Daniel laughs. "Ok. Well, I'm done avoiding preexisting conditions anyway. In fact, I have a new policy that if you don't have a preexisting condition by the time you're our age, you haven't been doing something right."

"Maybe, but I'm basically uninsurable at this point," I tell him. "And I'm too worried about my daughter to care."

He nods and squeezes my hand tightly. "I am here for you. How about I am in charge of feeding you, watering you, and holding your hand if you're scared."

"I'm very scared," I tell him.

"Then it's probably best that you don't let go."

I look down at his hand. Up into his eyes. *Yes*, says my heart. It's Talia and Lena and Daniel and even Matt that I want here with me now. I want Joe to be here when we know everything is going to be all right, and Cori to laugh at my soggy tears when she finally wakes up, and John to be a wonderful father and nothing else, and Lena to be arm's reach away, and Talia to be showing up with stuffed cheetahs, and Daniel to be holding tight to my hand. Wherever these people are, New York, Pennsylvania, or a hospital upstate, that is where I also need to be.

I put my head on Daniel's shoulder. "Thank you," I say to him, and then there is a shadow in the doorway of the respite room, and the shadow turns into footsteps. And then at last, finally, the footsteps turn into blue scrubs, and the unreadable face of Dr. Boch stands before me, and she inhales and begins to speak.

CHAPTER TWENTY

A week and a half later

"Amy, are you ready?"

Daniel is holding my hand again. Firmly. I shake my head.

"It's too soon," I tell him. "I can't do this yet."

His mouth forms a line. "It's time. Everyone is going to start to wonder."

I inhale. Ok. He's right. It's time. I can do this. "Is she doped up?" I ask carefully.

"No," he says. "The opiates wore off hours ago, and she hasn't asked for a new dose. I think she's really on the mend."

I whisper a silent prayer of thanks for this for the thousandth time. "Let's go tell them, then," I say, and I drop his hand like it's on fire. We separately cross over the threshold into Cori's recovery room, where she is sitting in her bed, next to Joe, watching an Animal Planet dog show in Spanish. Joe is shaking his head. "I still think I should have come home sooner," he says to me before I can even speak.

"Why? Why would you miss out on Space Camp when it turned out she was going to be ok and couldn't do anything but rest anyway?"

"I don't know. I feel guilty is all, that I wasn't with her when she needed me most."

Cori punches her brother in the upper arm. "I didn't need you; I needed a neurosurgeon. Unless you actually got your medical license in Alabama, instead of your nerd certification."

Joe frowns. "The support of your dearest sibling is sort of being taken for granted here."

"Nah," she tells him. "It's just that you got here at the exact right time. Mom was starting to drive me nuts, and Dad's in Chicago, so it's all on you from here on out."

Daniel looks at me, one eyebrow aloft. "He's gone again? Already?"

I shrug. "He just went out to take some meetings," I say, not mentioning that I suspect having Daniel around was weirding him out enough to make that sound like an extra-good idea this week. "He'll be meeting us back in PA for the rest of the summer. And the kids will see him again at Thanksgiving and winter break." I've talked to the kids about this endlessly now that Cori is in the clear, and John has too. Yes, yes, the kids keep telling us. They are ok with this plan. Yes, they want to spend Christmas vacation overseas. No, they never expected he'd stay. Yes, they had fun, but they want to go back to their real lives soon, and they'll see him again every couple months anyway. And all of next summer. Plus, Cori helpfully points out, per the quickie marital settlement agreement that a judge will be hearing just before school starts, he'll be paying me back child support, which makes this entire summer "worth it."

Daniel knows John and I filed for divorce, but he hasn't been privy to any of the family conversations, as he's been trying to be a "friend" of mine and give my family lots of space. He looks consternated, so I add, "This is just the reality of John."

Joe nods. "He's not perfect. But he's our dad, so no criticizing."

"Ok," says Daniel. "Well, your mother and I came in to tell you two that—"

"We know," says Cori. "You're dating. Everyone knows. I think one of the Kardashians just tweeted about it. Please don't say it out loud, ok? It's gross to think about your mom having sex. Unless . . . do you need us to give you the facts about safe intercourse?"

"Ew," cries Joe. He sneers at Daniel viciously—or as viciously as Joe has ever sneered. Apparently no one is good enough for his mom. I could have brought home the pope, and Joe would have found fault.

"No thanks," I say. "We can talk to our doctors if we have questions. But what about your, um, feelings about us being a couple?"

Cori shrugs. "Do we have to move to New York?" she asks.

I shake my head. "All three of us are going to be going there together from time to time," I warn. "And one weekend a month you'll be staying over with Auntie Lena."

"Can I have Diet Coke when I'm there?" asks Cori.

I ignore her. "But the point is no one is moving. We have our lives here, and Daniel and Cassie have their lives there. We'll figure things out our own way and reevaluate when Cassie graduates next spring."

"At the moment she's planning on applying to Temple and Princeton," Daniel says. "So she may make our lives that much easier by moving nearby."

"Whoa," says Cori. "Princeton." Her eyes are wide.

"It's not a competition," I say.

"Well, not a fair one," she says. "It's not my fault I'm too brain damaged to go to Princeton."

I laugh. "You cannot apply that excuse retroactively. Anyway, there's nothing wrong with you. And I know, because I have made them order every test they have in this hospital."

Joe raises his hand.

"Joe, you don't have to wait to be called on," I tell him.

"He's a teacher," says Joe, giving Daniel the side-eye.

"I'm a teacher," I say in wonderment, mostly to myself.

"Ok, Joe," says Daniel, "go ahead."

"Can I apply to Bronx Science?" he asks.

I look at Daniel. He looks at me. He is grinning.

I shake my head. "Let's just slow things down a bit here, people. We're dating—that's all. Stop moving in with my new boyfriend."

"What?" Joe says. "Cori will be graduated and working at the beauty parlor by then." Cori gives him a mild shove at this. "Country Day doesn't even have a second year of physics. Plus their chess team kills ours every year."

I dismiss him and say, "We'll see," but I can't help but imagine it. Moving to NYC in two years. Joe kicking butt at an academic magnet school, truly challenged and growing into the best he can be. Me teaching in a school library that could really use me, building out Flexthologies for truly underserved students. Daniel and I living together, in the same amazing city, reading together every night. I have to admit it sounds pretty nice.

"I'm not going to work at a beauty parlor," sneers Cori. "I'm going to dive for Penn State."

I hold my hand up firmly.

"When I am fully recovered, and the doctor says it's ok," she adds.

"And your mother masters Transcendental Meditation," I say.

She cuts an exasperated glance at Joe.

"Don't worry about Mom," says Joe. "She's going to be too busy to notice, what with her new 'boyfriend'"—he uses air quotes—"and the big NEA grant he got for her."

Cori inclines her head. "What's this? A NRA grant?"

"NEA. National Endowment for the Arts," says Daniel. "Your mom's Chicago friend, Kathryn, helped me put together a grant proposal a while back, right after the library conference. Ever since she and I heard your mom talk about the Flexthology, we just knew it had legs, whether your mom believed it or not. Finding a way to get it off the ground was a Hail Mary to get you to keep going out with me," he adds to me with a wink.

I shake my head in wonderment. "I still can't believe you two managed that on the sly."

"Wait, is this for that e-book reading-choice thing you started at Country Day?" asks Cori. "That was actually kind of fun. As far as reading goes."

"Yes, exactly," I tell her. "We couldn't think of a way to get it funded on a larger level—school boards are such slow-moving machines, and we were trying to get free rights to some really valuable novels to make the financials work and have it represent a diverse population. But then it hit us—well, it hit Daniel. Rather than try to get the rights from the authors for free, we could get *someone else* to pay the authors. Like an agency whose very purpose is to support artists on the community level . . ."

"So I put it to Kathryn, and she knew a grant writer on the PTO, and one thing led to another . . . ," Daniel says. "And now your mom has a lump sum to run a pilot program in underfunded schools."

"So you're dating this guy because he got your big dorkfest librarian thing funded?" asks Cori, incredulous.

I laugh. "Nah. I'm dating this guy for the Latin jokes."

Daniel perks up. "Why did Marcus Aurelius make his kids eat grits?" he asks the room. "Because he wouldn't accept ad hominy arguments!"

We all cringe. "Mostly because he's very attractive," I amend.

Joe looks at Cori in horror. She makes a dramatic retching sound.

"Cori," I say. "I've missed your nuanced commentary. If I haven't said it enough, thank you for doing such a good job at staying alive this week."

"Yes," adds Daniel. "I especially appreciate it because otherwise I wouldn't have gotten to meet you. And I'm pretty sure your mom wouldn't have called me ever again, grant or no grant."

Cori says, "That's kind of a selfish perspective on the value of a young woman's life."

"You and Cassandra are going to get along very well," he says. I smile and nod, though I am not so sure. The beauty is they don't have to. Daniel has given me a way to be where I need to be, to celebrate all the things I discovered in myself in New York, and still fulfill all my responsibilities in PA. For me, life after John doesn't have to mean martyrdom and loneliness, or some *Brady Bunch*–style mishmash of two already happy established families. There is a third way.

I get this now. I get now that you can love what you have, love your kids and your life and your friends, and still want more. I get that it's ok to go out and get more—more love, more friendship, more fulfillment—and still be a wonderful mom.

Because of Daniel, because of my friends, because of Cori and Joe, I finally understand that traditional math does not apply to mothers: I can be 100 percent a mother and, though it isn't easy, still be 100 percent myself as well. It means changing how I think. It means understanding that to care for my children well, I must never again forget to care for myself.

And for me to learn all that once and for all, it took more than a village. For me, it took a #momspringa.

———

Hey you,

These are going to slay you, I think. They've been coming in all month since the issue released, and some are addressed to us, but some are definitely meant for you. A few of my favorites are on top. And have you checked out our Twitter feed lately?

xx
Talia

PS: You'll be happy to know Matt got a promotion. Well, technically it's a promotion, and there's a big raise, too, though I'd sooner die than do that job. Online Marketing Trend Strategist. Ick. Better him than me. But he's thrilled, and he's going to be crazy good at it. He made up a care package from the fashion closet for you as thanks for being the face of momspringa. I tucked some things in for Cori too. Enjoy. Don't forget to wax!

———

Dear *Pure Beautiful* magazine,

I never write in to magazines, but I just want to write you and tell you how great your article "Do You Need a #Momspringa?" was. I had no idea "momspringas" even existed, but once I found out, you better believe the first person I told was my husband. I told him, if you don't give me a momspringa in the next two weeks, I am leaving you, and honestly, I think I mean it! I have three beautiful children and I have done nothing but wipe noses and change diapers for the last seven years and "for fun" I make dinners that my three-year-old would rather "die" than eat and then I make a second dinner for him and then my husband comes home from his weekly—yep, every week—happy hour with the guys too tipsy to put the kids to bed, plus he has his bowling nights and he works late and on Sundays he just sleeps and sleeps while I wrestle the kids to church so that my own mother won't disown me, and let me tell you, she has all kinds of ideas about how I *should* be parenting and keeps saying it's time for me to "lay down the law," but where is she when the healthy meal is set out and no one has touched their green beans? I will tell you where: she's standing by the freezer handing out Dove Bars! And my youngest doesn't even have all his teeth yet! And I am telling you, if I don't get a night by myself alone in a bed with no one else in it for at least eight straight hours, I am going to run away forever!

So thanks for publishing that piece. Though it was kind of crazy that the lady in the story did exercise classes while she was away from her kids. I would never make that mistake.

Yours,
Becca Aldt, Omaha, Nebraska

—

Dear Amy B.,

I asked the magazine that printed your story to pass my note along so you would know what an inspiration you've been to me and my friends. I found your article in my dentist's office, and as soon as I read it, I knew I had to talk to my girlfriends—we call ourselves the Monday Mamas, because we were all in a group-therapy class six years ago when we all had postpartum depression at the same time. Things are a lot better now thanks to lots of support and good meds, but parenting is still a ton of work, as you know.

Anyway, there are four of us Monday Mamas, and we decided right then to help support each other so we would each get one week on a momspringa. We are going in turns according to our work schedules, and while one of us is gone the other three of us are going to carpool the kids to school and look after them with sleepovers and share the work as needed. We've each been putting fifteen dollars a month together into a "spa fund" since our kids were really little, but in all this time we've never ever found a way for the four of us to get even one night off together to stay in a hotel and get a massage. Now, instead of that, we are divvying that money up four ways, and each of us will have enough to stay in a hotel and just have some quiet time to think and relax for an entire week.

I know from your article you read a lot, but when my momspringa comes, I am going to go to the movies every day, because I haven't been to a movie since my first daughter was born, and I don't even remember what movie-theater popcorn smells like. I just remember, a long time ago, how much I used to love going to the movies. My friend Calla is going to spend her time in the swimming pool. She used to be a masters swimmer, but the only gym in town with childcare doesn't have a pool. Noelle has a little boy who just weaned, so she says she just wants to sleep the whole week, but I bet once she catches up on sleep a little, she'll have enough energy at least to take a few nice long walks or read a good book. And my best friend, Anne, well, she is taking her guitar.

Amy, none of us have family nearby, and not all of us have very sympathetic partners right now, and until your article came out, it just never occurred to us that it would somehow be possible to take a few days to ourselves, much less that it would be "ok." But after we read your story, we knew it wasn't just ok for moms to take breaks—it was required. So thank you so much for being brave and giving us the push we needed.

Sincerely,
The Monday Mamas, Baraboo, Wisconsin

—

Dear *Pure Beautiful* magazine,

I would like to write to register my disappointment—nay, my outrage—at your irresponsible hero worship of that pathetic excuse for a mother you featured in your article about mothers running away from their responsibilities. I realize that you have to sell magazines, and that means your pages will be full of sex and other abominations, but to discover a seven-page (!) article about a woman who abandoned her OWN CHILDREN to a man who was virtually a complete stranger, only to jump into the beds of every man in New York City and spend her every waking moment worried about "makeovers" and "health clubs," goes well past even the worst thing I could have prepared myself for. What if your article causes other women, normally good, responsible women, to do the same? Did you ever think of that before putting this dangerous article into print? The thought is nothing short of REVOLTING. Shame, shame on you, *Pure Beautiful* magazine. Think of the children.

Please cancel my subscription immediately.

Sincerely,
Deborah Stuckey, Phoenix, Arizona

———

SEARCH: TOP TWEETS featuring #mymomspringa

@eatpraysway
I'd take #mymomspringa in New York just like that lady but I would wear way better clothes. @purebeautymag

@themommymess
#mymomspringa: just one big bed, a dark cool room, occasional room service. wine.

@lawyerrenee
I would kill for #mymomspringa. I'd go to stay with my childless friend at her lake house in the middle of nowhere. See how the other half lives. Maybe learn to sail. No, I'd just nap.

@momofmatt
Even just thinking about #mymomspringa makes me happy. Two weeks till the beach, baby! Thanks @purebeautymag for starting the convo.

@noahthefarmer
Can I have a #dadspringa? My baby isn't born yet but my wife is working constantly on her new cookbook and I need to escape kitchen duty. #mymomspringa
    @neanknowsnothing replied:
    @noahthefarmer No.

@georgieporgie3
#mymomspringa would be in Venice. No, screw Venice. Tuscany. With that guy from the movie. And Matt Damon #backupplan

@kathryninchicago
#mymomspringa is: Literally anywhere my children are not. #realtalk

ACKNOWLEDGMENTS

I'd like to thank Chris Werner, Tiffany Yates Martin, and the inspired team at Lake Union for getting this story into the world with such enthusiasm and verve. Holly Root, you are wonderful.

I'm very grateful to all my friends whose support and expertise made writing this book possible, especially Abbie Foster Chaffee, Kris Adams, Jennifer Ferreter, Mandy McGowan, Sara Naatz, Dr. Sandra Block, Lexy Spry, and Aimie K. Runyan. Thanks, too, for all the readers who were in touch between books. You are so inspiring.

To the Tall Poppy Writers, my gratitude and adoration. Thanks to Griffin Wimmer for listening to audiobooks while I edited and Sally Harms for hosting Grandma Camp while I edited. To my son's guides at Isthmus Montessori; our extended family, related and otherwise; and all the moms I've met in the last seven years who have inspired me to tell this story, my deepest appreciation. To Chris Meadow, my thanks and love are as bottomless as the beermosas at Karben4.

ABOUT THE AUTHOR

Photo © 2018 Lea Wolf

Kelly Harms is an author, a mother, and a big dreamer. She lives in Madison, Wisconsin, with her sparkling son, Griffin; her fluffy dog, Scout; and her beloved Irishman, Chris. Before this midwestern life, she lived in New York, New York, and worked with many of her author-heroes as an editor at HarperCollins and then as a literary agent. When she's not lost in a book that she's either writing or reading, you can find her on the water, in the water, or near the water. Say hello anytime at www.kellyharms.com.